First Persons

Also by Austin Wright

Fiction:
Camden's Eyes

Anthology:
The Art of the Short Story: An Introductory Anthology (co-editor)

Criticism:
The American Short Story in the Twenties

First Persons

A Novel by Austin Wright

Harper & Row, Publishers
New York, Evanston, San Francisco, London

The streets and buildings in Ralph Burr's novel have been taken from a certain city and university in the Midwest that may be real. The people come from a different world and can only be found inside this book.

FIRST EDITION

Designed by Gloria Adelson

Library of Congress Cataloging in Publication Data

Wright, Austin McGiffert, 1922–
  First persons.
  I. Title.
PZ4.W9472Fi   [PS3573.R49]   813'.5'4   73–4167
ISBN 0–06–014759–8

To my mother
and the memory of my father

Part One

Chapter 1

This morning in the midst of accelerating spring, early May, watch that man as he goes through the city park. Crossing the empty playground in the hollow to the path in the woods, he goes to the bottom of the steps and looks up. Carrying something. The bright morning, the sun, the air cool, small young leaves speckling green through the woods, not yet heavy enough to make true shade, and the sun shines on the man's head. He begins to climb the steps. Eighty or a hundred broad stone steps going up through the woods from the playground in the hollow to the top, where you come out upon a circular driveway with a small bandstand in the middle. Beyond that a grassy slope down to the avenue with the cars and buses and hospital buildings.

Watch that man as he climbs—slowly plodding. He is going to the university. The steps too far apart to be negotiated in one stride, yet not enough to accommodate two without discomfort, without narrowing your natural push and seeming to mince. The man climbed slowly, half-striding, half-mincing, one long stride then a narrow limp up, one long stride then a narrow limp, etcetera. Puffing a little, taking it easy. Looked up the flight of steps ahead of him, sky through the trees at the top.

And from the top coming down the same steps, someone else. Watch her too. Go back a little and watch her approaching. Waiting for the light, so that she could cross the avenue. When the light changed, she began, taking slow tiny steps, step step step, which brought her halfway across when the light changed again, making the cars in the first row wait, trusting that no one would release the traffic against an old lady in the middle of the street trying to get across. So they all wait and on she comes, step step step, regular, clocking her way across the street, making them wait, so that by the time she has got across the light has changed back to red and the car on the inside lane has had two reds to wait for.

Now she goes into the park, up the grass slope to the top by the straight path, while the automobile drive circles S-ways to the same destination. An old woman in a black coat, very short and small, carrying something, hair white and thinning, soft with ringlets on the top, and she walks always in this rhythm as if walking kept her heartbeat going. At the top she crosses the drive to the circle with the bandstand, passes that, and crosses the drive again to the path that takes her to the top of the steps going down through the woods—and starts down the steps without breaking her rhythm, taking two little steps and a shorter one for each step downward. Looking down and seeing the man coming up.

Does each hesitate on seeing the other approaching? The narrator cannot say, for he does not yet have access to their thoughts and can only report things externally, what they do and say. Unless we change the rules. If either hesitates, it is so momentary as to be indiscernible to an observer, who sees them only approaching each other, the man plodding upward, taking his time, puffing a little, the old woman descending with her tiny steps, two at each level and then another little one down, all in the same even rhythm with which we saw her cross the avenue in front of the angry patient waiting cars and climb the grass slope to the bandstand circle. As she descends she pretends not to look at the man climbing up. And the man pretends not to look at her. You can see their eyes looking in other directions, at the budding leaves, the branches, the bushes on both sides, making only the quickest most blinklike checks on each other, keeping track so that they know where they stand in relation to each other at each moment.

Until they meet. Two steps apart, at which point, as if faltering, she stops—as if for a moment, as if to see on which side he intends to pass

—looks at him now for the first time directly, a question in her eyes. At the same moment as if compelled he too stops and looks at her in the same way. Or is it the same way? The narrator hesitates to interpret. Only to report that as they look at each other they register recognition. Say something, a word or two. A slight bow, tilt of the man's head, hand extended, palm upturned, gestures her to pass. Or perhaps they have a more extended conversation, even a vigorous, animated one—this can be decided later. Or perhaps the opposite, perhaps we are mistaken, perhaps it wasn't even recognition that registered in their eyes when they lifted them to look at each other. In any case, after a moment long or short, he gestured her to pass and the rhythm of her steps resumed automatically, as if she had been like a little engine running in neutral while she passed, going back now into gear, and with head slightly bowed she passed the man downwards and he turned as if to continue his climb.

But note this. Just after she has passed, one step down, he turns around and looks at her again, her back, going down. And looks around elsewhere too, perhaps. Up and down, into the woods . . . It was very quick (although memory isolates it as if very slow), and it is impossible to know exactly what happened or how much. Except that the man did not actually climb any more steps just now, but only looked about, as if searching, though he could not have searched for very long because she was only two steps further down when . . . Figure two and a half of her little steps for each step down, or in her rhythm the equivalent of six step-units, amounting to some four seconds of clock time, during which we may observe the man reach down and pick up a large rock full of fossils, heavy but not too big to grasp in one hand, and we may observe him also hesitate, but it could not have been more than four seconds clock time, since she was only two steps further down at the moment when he caught up with her and struck her on the head with the rock full of fossils. It made a bang, loud and muffled, like two rocks striking each other with a muffling of hair in between, and she fell instantly and noiselessly, like a puppet whose strings have been cut. No gasp of breath, no cry. The man looked at her as if surprised, how motionless she lay, like a fallen tree branch under her coat. Her hand twitched a moment, as if someone were giving it electric shocks or short-circuiting its nerves, and then stopped, and the man wondered if she were dead or whether he ought to strike her again. But the idea of striking her a second time where he had already struck was disgusting to him. He saw the shape of the back of her head and knew that she must have died, and then he realized that he had already flung the rock with fossils off into the woods, where he could hear it still bounding and rolling down the slope until it came to rest against a boulder next to the brook.

Now watch how frantic and nervously the man flings about, trying to decide what to do and bring himself to do it. First a panic leap upwards, up the steps, but instantly checking himself as if he had just thought of something—turning about now and starting down instead, stepping gingerly around the old woman's body, and again checking himself by another thought. Then he stands over her, looking up, looking every way except at her, elongating his body as if trying to stretch himself away from her without being able to move, as if she were on fire and it was burning him to stand next to her. Stretching away from her, and then suddenly, while still looking mostly up in horrible fear (obviously) that someone would come along, he reaches down and lovingly grasps the old woman by the ankles to drag her off the path into the bushes. Avoiding the bloody head, afraid of staining his clothes with blood. Lighter than he expected—except that actually he expected her to be light as a shell, whereas she is about as heavy (he would guess) as a German shepherd or a Great Dane, which is pretty heavy for dragging, and makes him puff some more. But there is a small hollow below a boulder just beyond the bush, full of dead leaves, and after a moment he gets her there and flings her and she falls, arm flying out, and lands face up among the leaves. Cover her? Watch how quick and frantically he kicks and scrabbles some leaves over her, not very effective, and then drags a dead branch with dead leaves to shield her at least a little from the view of the path. Back to the steps where he stands and looks to see if she can be seen, realizes that she cannot, not because she is so well covered but because she is out of sight in the hollow. Now he takes a moment to glance at the ground at his feet, sees the signs of tracking, kicks the dust a little, and then suddenly, heavily breathing, darts upwards, long strides now, one for each step as fast as he can go. At the top, slows abruptly, looks about, sees a park workman driving a yellow mowing tractor at the other end of the meadow far away. He walks now toward the meadow and begins to cross it toward the university, briskly but as casually as possible. Look at his face, though: the face of a fiend, deep ravages of vicious lines creasing his cheeks, wild mad brutal eyes peering out from his brows, thin lips, jaw working, panting like a dog, foam at the mouth.

This happened and might well become the central or at least precipitating incident of a novel with as yet no title. Or a tentative title of *The Devil in Burnet Woods,* since the park where the murder took place was called by that name—until we know more clearly who the novel is about.

Chapter 2

As an alternative on the same or a similar morning, let them watch this much-more-ordinary-looking man as he walks from his house to his office at the university. Walks from the large old white wooden house, set back from the street by the width of a modest lawn. Does not require a power mower. The house, they must know, is full of animals. The man—they should also be told—is forty-five years old, moderately tall, putting on weight but not yet fat, with a gray mustache. He walks briskly, not strenuously, out to the sidewalk, where he turns right and goes down this street past budding trees springing into leaf. The day is fine, warming, sunny, the season is the accelerating of spring (earliest May), and the man himself need not yet know that he has been chosen protagonist of a novel. The tentative title of this novel can be *The Man in Burnet Woods*. The protagonist's name is Burr. Make that Ralph Hathorne Burr, forty-five years old, New England heritage, intellectual, academic. Curious, too, looking for birds as he walks.

They must watch him all the way and see all the way into his mind, clear as glass, to satisfy themselves that nothing is being concealed, and therefore this must be a novel in the first person, of course. "I." Of course the man does not know (I did not at that time realize) about *The Man in the Woods*. He was merely going to his office at the university, a routine, leaving his animals behind (yes definitely there were animals in my house, I confirm it), carrying his briefcase (papers

I should have read last night and—perhaps—did not), walking down the street to cross into the park two blocks away, to cross through the park on his way to the campus.

In the first person, I heard cardinals singing in the maple trees and the dying elms. Looking for birds, past the big and the medium-sized houses to Jefferson Avenue, across that and into the park, and through the park to the other side, to the university campus and his office. They'll need a narrator to explain that the protagonist was a professor of English at the university. Unfortunately for his readers perhaps, Mr. Ralph Burr was a professor of English and the novel about him would have to be an academic novel. Would have to deal with university life, with academic intrigue and department chairmanships and swapped faculty wives, talented students who are crazy and square fraternity boys and a great deal of intellectual namedropping to show that you are up on the historical currents of the time. Too bad, a novel for a special interest group. The narrator should make clear early that Professor Burr's most urgent desire as he walked to work this morning was (as far as I knew) to be appointed next head of the department, replacing George Elias who retires in September. The search committee is now meeting . . .

Watch him enter McMicken Hall on the ground floor, through the long corridor in artificial light past rooms below ground level, the corridor full of students changing classes. Already sweaty inside his clothes —the morning walk through the park, up and down hills on his way to work, for the sake of his health, did that to him—catching his breath, trying to relax and breathe deeply so that he would not sweat too much, he did not look at the students he passed. The narrator should introduce him to them: "Look kid, this man you are passing, this man with the little gray mustache, a man already important in the university file and destined for greater importance. You will be hearing more from him: Ralph Hathorne (pronounced Hawthorne or even Hoarthoarn) Burr (as in Aaron), A.B., M.A., Ph.D. Professor of English, Office Hours MWF 10–11, McMicken 236. Future chairman of the Department of English." He took out his privileged elevator key (Narrator: Only full-time faculty members, staff members, janitorial staff, and handicapped students have keys to the elevator) and turned it once to call the elevator.

Waited, with the little red elevator light, then went up, slowly, two flights, and along the corridor to his office. His office was in an alcove with three other offices. It had a frosted glass window in the door, and he shared it with Harvey Kessler, who was not in. He let himself in with his key and went straight to his desk, where he sat down and released a gasp of air.

Sat down in his swivel chair and got up immediately, went to his door and shut it. According to the narrator he then went back to his desk and sat down again. Passed his hand over his face, then looked at his hands, looked at his sleeves, looked at the door again, which he had shut. Looked at the door and, according to the narrator, realized then that it was not customary for him to shut himself in his office behind a closed door, as if he had secrets. So he got up—puffing—went to his door and opened it again. Then back to the desk and sat down. Puffing. Peering with squinted eyes from his desk into the hall, the alcove, as if looking for someone. No. Burr. Ralph Hathorne Burr.

First person, we agreed. Outside the window (not into the hall) I saw a tree turning into leaf, the green of new leaves translucent, radiant. Below, grass, a walk, parked cars, students with long hair, beards, mustaches, girls with long hair almost to their waists, blue jeans. I felt exhausted from my walk through the woods. Exhausted to the point of being shaky, nervous for no good reason. I got up and closed the door, as if afraid of someone coming after me. Then I realized that it was not customary for me to close my door, as if I had secrets, so I got up and opened it again and returned to my desk, wondering what was wrong with me. A phenomenon that I shall try to describe.

Timid, gentle, introspective (not knowing yet that he had become the protagonist of a novel) Burr sat at his desk and wondered what was wrong with him. They should know about his empty house, his dead wife, his gone children. His animals.

A phenomenon that I shall try to describe. Because I realized suddenly that I had arrived in old age, without warning, without planning or preparation—which was pretty ridiculous, since of course I have seen this coming, thought about it, feared it, all my life. I leaned back in my chair, daydreaming, distracted from work by this sudden sharp sense of the change that had taken place in my life—that is, I mean, this sharpened consciousness of what an old man I had become and what an irreversible process I was. I wondered how old I was and discovered that I couldn't remember, that I lost count long ago under a pileup of frosted years. Outside the window it was morning and it was ripening spring but I saw it through the deepening shade of late afternoon and the chilling dusk of late autumn. I thought now of all the things I had lost or failed to get: remembered how long ago I had wanted that department headship but had failed to get it, how even longer it was since I had had a wife and children now gone, long and far away and who knows whether even the children are still alive? And whether the students I had are still alive or the colleagues with whom I taught in the old days? And all the work I intended to do, the book I intended to write, the reputation that I hoped would reach beyond the campus, beyond the city—reputation for what? did I ever know? I asked myself full of wistful lateness. Thinking how to make this feeling clear to them by analogy: conceive how frightening the late afternoon would be if you knew that there would never be another morning, or how terrifying the onset of autumn, the dying of trees, the cold, the storms, the coming snow, the shrinking days, if you knew there would never be another spring. So it is with me, now, Ralph Burr, burr, finding myself suddenly at the age of seventy-two (how did I get to be seventy-two?) not knowing how I got here, no memory except of years and years somehow lost, and knowing full well there will never be another youth or middle age for me—will there? And indeed, how did I ever get to be seventy-two? As if in one careless moment, under some great pressure from above, I forgot for an instant to count the passing time, and in that one moment of forgetfulness, whole months and seasons and years slipped by, almost a whole life before I could grab hold and start counting once again.

Needs a narrator to warn them against the lying first person. Because Burr is not seventy-two, not yet, although he most assuredly will be someday—if he lives that long. But why should I lie about a thing like that? According to the narrator it was not age but some feeling of sneaking doom. Some feeling of shock that had slipped up on him (in him) this morning, no one knows how. Slicing around in his brain like a knife, the cause forgotten.

Something had startled him, as if he had been attacked or ambushed,

11

and he was still trembling, only the cause of the trembling was lost. But it was not age, he was not yet old enough to worry about that except in his private thoughts—it had to do with the day, the season. The recognition that another spring was shaping itself toward a summer. Something frightening in the spring. The cruel month with its sooty showers. Life uplifted in green erections the competitions all over again. Trembling, he tells them, I'm exhausted with competition, done, tired, worn out, finished, can't compete anymore. Nonsense, they say. You want to be a chairman, don't you? The battle hasn't begun yet. Then why do I feel so rotten, I ask, why am I trembling so, why such a cold and icy feeling of shock?

Student looks in door, leans in without knocking, long blond hair hanging loose around his pale girlish face: "Hey, where's Kessler?" Burr looked at him. Sweaty shiny face, hostile gray sleeveless shirt like an undershirt. *Mr. Kessler has not come in yet.* "Well where is he? We're suppose to talk to him about our papers." *He has office hours at one o'clock.* Right there on the door, that white card, right in front of your nose. "I have a class at one. You expect him this morning?" *I have no idea.* "How can we talk to him about our papers if he isn't here?" *You should make an appointment.* "Never see him. Doesn't keep his appointments anyway." The student came in and turned Harvey Kessler's swivel chair. "Think I'll wait for him. Mind if I wait here?"

This was the skock he had been feeling—yes, this was exactly the shock, that same feeling of trembling, terror even, as he prepared himself for what had to be done. *Yes,* said Burr.

Meanwhile the student had sat down in Harvey's chair.

Yes, repeated Burr. *I do. . . . No. Would you mind* (politeness at all times) *waiting out in the hall, please?*

The student apparently did not hear him. He was leaning back in Harvey's chair and already seemed to have begun reading the raggedy paperback book in his hand, leaning back in the chair, the book in one hand up in the air, directly over his head. The student's plump cheeks were a strange dull iron-gray color. His clothes were the same color. His long hair was fiery.

Try again. *I said, would you mind waiting out in the hall, please?*

"What?" said the student, surprised as if he couldn't believe what he had heard. "Oh." Raised eyebrows, looked around as he started to get up. "Okay. Sure." Got up, with an increasingly incredulous look on his face, making a big point without words of what a crazy unreasonable constipated type (anal) this guy must be who wouldn't even let you wait in his office. Out in the hall, the alcove, the student looked around. Evidently—he made it obvious—the chairs in the alcove were either all occupied or they had all been taken away. Standing next to the door the student leaned against the wall and slid down to the floor, until he was seated on the floor, legs crossed Indian-style, almost inside the door. As if he had been assigned to keep watch. Made Burr think he should get up and shut the door again—it would make the point more clear. But don't make a point of it. Keep calm: The student didn't know—how could he?—that Burr had become the protagonist of a novel.

Squatting by the door, reading, the student thought he understood the shock and trembling Burr was feeling, that showed on his face to anyone who might look in and sounded in the shake of his voice in answer to anyone who spoke to him. Professor Burr. The student had his own idea what it was, supposing that it had to do with such as himself, these hostile-looking students who think they can sit and wait in your office without regard for your privacy, much less your possession of this place. Students who deny your right to property, your right to your office, your right to your time, ultimately your right to your career. Who claim everything from you and allow you nothing of your own. Yes. According to the student, what he felt as shock and fear was really boiling indignation.

Because of the word he had heard that we are going to close down the university. That is why he felt so shocked. Such fear. Such trembling. Where did you hear that, they ask, incredulous. If you want us to believe your story, they will say, you must make it coherent with rational connections, and you must explain how you got such information, where you picked it up. Tell them it came in the night, says the student. Or early this morning—tell them it does not matter how you heard. Let it suffice that you know, that among the students—not the ordinary ones in your ordinary classes but the ones you don't see, the bitter powerful ones behind the scenes, the ones to reckon with, that you cannot argue with, that won't listen to reason or respect their professors, the ones who will lead the terror of the faculty when the time comes—but who are they? where do they live? can you find one, identify even a single one? am I one, for instance, and don't you wish you knew? —among these students last night, gathered around candles in a dark off-campus basement apartment, you know a decision was made. To close down the university. To set up a pretext and demand compliance, some demand that the officials of the university even at their most compliant could not be expected to grant. And since they fail to grant it within the deadline (will twenty-four hours do?) the troops will come out, shouting "Strike, strike! Close it down! Close it down!," raising fists, tromping through the hallways chanting and marching, invading classes that have the audacity to meet, ordering the squares out, shouting obscenities at the professor if he tries to speak, laying hands on him perhaps—yes, even that happened in China—hands on him, picking him up, carrying him out, jeering and laughing, dumping him down the stairs perhaps or (better) out the window.

A girl in a short red dress tap taps on the door frame making him look up. A very short dress, miniskirt, and long straight yellow hair, smiling because she thinks you should be glad to see her, because anyone would be glad to see her, whoever she is—asking, "Is Mr. Kessler around?" *Haven't seen him.* Again. She stands near the waiting student who is sitting on the floor, reading, and Burr wonders if she realizes that the student has put down his book and is looking up at her. Looking up her short skirt, that is, without moving his head. Notice the expression of calm curiosity in his eyes and real, genuine, interest. Probably the girl, smiling at Burr, does not realize what the student is looking at because it has not occurred to her that he would be interested. Or else she has not noticed that he is looking because she assumes he is still reading his book. Or else she knows that he is looking and stands there without moving so as to help him look, as she asks, "Do you know when he will be in?"

Couldn't say, says Burr.

"Okay," she says. "I'll come back later," whirling about and going away. The student's head turns to follow as she goes and then turns quickly to Burr and gives what can only be interpreted, says the narrator, as a knowing smile of complicity. Which I find irritating, to tell the truth, for its assumptions, as if I had been sitting there with him, seeing the same things he saw.

It doesn't matter how you found out, however, the narrator will say, and therefore it could not have been the student revolution, no matter how hard you try, for you can never show that this conspiracy was anything but your own imagination, composing a screen for more personal things. It must have been something last night, living alone in that big house that was never meant to be lived alone in, as it got late in the living room and the darkness upstairs and the darkness downstairs, and the animals, the big dogs in the pen outside, and the smaller dogs with the cats chasing each other out of the living room light into the dining room shadows and pouncing out upon each other—ambush. Another ambush as he climbed puffily up the stairs on the way to bed, ambush at the top of the stairs, the black and white cat leaping out at you and racing away into what used to be Elaine's room, claws skidding on the floor as she goes—expecting you to give chase, which you never do except in your most lighthearted moods. Which was not the case that dark and solitary night, last night. Said the narrator: Late that night the animals in his house were sportive, trying to make the professor feel less lonely. Playful animals doing their best to cheer up God.

I knew the black and white cat was waiting for me at the top of the stairs. In fact, she did not even have sense enough to hide and conceal her ambush. She stood there waiting for me as I came up, back arched, and it was I who had to lunge at her, I who had to pounce, so as to make her scurry—for these cats never had the brains to make the game right, and it was always I who had to invent the game for them, stand behind corners and ambush them—alone in the house at nights. Explained the narrator: The professor had lived alone in this house ever since his wife . . . a year and a half ago, though he kept their rooms open for his children if they should ever come home to visit. Or else the narrator might say this: The professor had decided to move, for a man alone in a big house . . . but he had not yet found a place to move into. Or else:

15

The professor had finally, after a year, sold his house, but not having found a place for his animals? . . . At any rate, the shock that was trembling him this morning must be attributed to what happened last night when he got to the head of the stairs after the cat had scurried away, and he was seized with an idea that seemed irresistible. The narrator will know this, try not to tell: How as he stood in the middle of the upstairs hall, it occurred to him, and he unbuttoned himself there in the light and revealed himself to the cat.

Either the cat didn't notice or made no distinctions and didn't care, preferring games of running and chasing and hide and seek, and Burr was on the whole glad of that, while he remained in the middle of the hall, between Elaine's and Harold's and his own bedrooms, and took off all his clothes and dropped them on the floor. Then admit to the narrator how he went downstairs again into the dark, all naked, and walked through all the dark rooms of the house, the living room, dining room, and kitchen, even out into the porch, all in darkness and all bare, and upstairs and into all of the bedrooms, while the cats and dogs watched him from their points on chairs and behind sofas and behind beds, until he went into the bathroom and became an adolescent again. Which was a pretty good proof, he figured, that time had run off its track, and no wonder he felt depressed and shaken this morning, with a feeling of desperation, a need for change, a need to run away and start a new life, maybe, even.

It must have been something on his walk to the office this morning, though, since last night was too long ago for this resonance of shock, and the morning when he got up was so bright and sunny and the flowering shrubs so full of color and erotic ecstasy. It will be necessary in any case to describe that walk precisely. I was merely walking to work as I normally do on pleasant spring mornings, for the sake of the birds and the exercise. Exercise for the sake of health (the narrator can take time out elsewhere to describe what is wrong with his health, those messages his body sends from time to time, full of warnings that the doctors ignore).

Keep your eye on the narrator to make it as clear and exact as he can. How I had to wait to cross the street into the park, wait for a line of twenty cars to pass—any one of whom might well have seen him and recognized—but I was watching only for a gap between cars, not thinking ahead of that, and I took my moment to cross. Then on the sidewalk in the park at the edge of the woods, I walked beside the park road down the hill to the pond. There was an occasional car that passed me on the drive. The sun on the new flickering leaves, vibrating in the light, the bright green of their earliest life, while the narrator remembered the darker green of late summer, the late summers of years ago, here and in New York and elsewhere, and the late summer that will come out of this brightness that is now beginning. And looking for birds as I walked, though not making any special effort, walking briskly so as to get to the office: still hearing cardinals and titmice (the small gray bird with a crest and a loud ringing song) and robins and a flicker—too early in the season for the wood thrush to sing, maybe next week, in the dark gloom of the trees below, on the other side of the hollow to my right. I came to the pond, by the small pavilion, still boarded up, and the empty benches and the flower beds between the walks still barren and brown. The pond bends along the road, silvery, some dirty white ducks, sometimes idyllic but just failing of that this morning, the water brown when you look into it, muddy bottom. I crossed the road to the little nature museum and I went down the concrete steps beside the smoothed stone slide into the playground, and there was nobody around on this bright morning of a school day: empty swings, abandoned seesaws, picnic tables under the trees. No trouble yet, nor did I have any sense of trouble or change impending. Ralph Burr crossed the playground and began to climb the steps through the woods, without awareness that anything terrible had either happened, was happening, or was about to happen. Up the steps slowly, one by one. Stone steps, a little too deep to take one step at a time, not deep enough to be comfortable taking two. Around the steps (eyes down) dirt and dust and little white flowers, and violets. Bushes on both sides with bud turning into leaves, just beginning to block vision (eyes right, eyes left) into the woods on the hillside around you. Large trees everywhere, but still not leafy enough to impede the morning sunshine on your back as you climb—step-by-step, puffing heart—the steps. Breath going, a musical rhythm, automatically you count the steps as you climb: thir-ty-seven, thir-ty-eight, thir-ty-nine, foe-are-ty.

At the top you come out upon a circular driveway where cars park, and in the middle a small bandstand with benches piled to the roof. In the summer these will be placed around the bandstand under the shade of the trees, and there will be band concerts in the twilight. I crossed in front of the bandstand and went on to the broad grassy meadow, down another slope and up to the other end of the park, where I crossed another street and climbed a slope to the edge of the university campus. Hot, sweating, out of breath after all that exercise, I took the elevator to the second floor, where my office is, and let myself into my office with my key. Students in the hallways, classes going on, it was just after ten o'clock. No sir, I didn't see anyone in the park that I remember, except —yes—a workman on a yellow mowing machine at the far end of the meadow as I crossed, yes, I remember the workman. But there might very well have been others, because I am not necessarily observant at all times, and maybe I was preoccupied. But certainly I didn't see anything worthy of notice, did I? The reason I am still puffing, feel the heavy heartbeat, the sense of shock, the anticipation of a failing heart, is that I am still not used to the simple exercise of walking through the park, the up and down of slopes across grass, and the long steps up through the woods, steps that don't quite fit your natural stride.

Chapter 3

The student sitting in the doorway with his book, in his gray jacket, his gray jeans, his gray skin—I felt him crowding me by his presence, blocking my exit, keeping watch though he did not look at me, crowding even though he was at the other end of the room, with Harvey's desk and the length of a bookcase between us. Sat there, calmly reading, thinking about revolution, and not knowing (Burr could only assume) what there was to know about me.

Tell the narrator again how I waited to cross into the park. Not counting the cars, but it was a long wait, there must have been at least twenty before there was break enough to let me through, and now I can remember none of them, not a single one of the cars that went by. Because I did not think there was any reason to notice or remember. I crossed and went down along the park road toward the pond, listening and looking for birds as I walked. Cardinals and robins and titmice and a flicker. Plus the usual starlings and sparrows. Stopped by the boarded pavilion to look at the pond, bending along the road, silvery reflecting the light, with some dirty white ducks, and then I crossed the road to the nature museum—a small two-room stone building—and descended the steps to the playground, which was deserted on this bright spring morning, all the kids in school. Then Ralph Burr crossed the playground into the woods and began to climb the steps, without any awareness. . . . Up the steps slowly, one by one, eyes down (dirt and dust and little white flowers and violets) and eyes right and left (bushes and buds turning into leaves, just beginning to block vision) and a sense of great trees around that he did not actually look at. Breath going, a musical rhythm, counting steps: thir-ty-seven, thir-ty-eight, thir-ty-nine, foe-are-ty.

Yes I did happen to see, eyes down, a spot of redbrown in the dust at my feet. And the look of scraped earth to the left, as if something had been dragged across the dust. Just happened to notice that, attracting my attention, which was what made me look up, more to the left, the signs of dragging through the bushes, through the leaves.

(Q: Did you know that this was the site of another murder several years ago, when this city was undergoing a series of stranglings? A: Yes, I remembered that. Q: How did you happen to know about it? A: I read about it in the papers. They had a sketch map in the papers to show where the murder took place. Almost the same spot as this. Q: Would you say that it was a similar case? A: Sounds very similar to me. I understand the old lady in the original case was walking her dog, and the dog was left with the body. I remember noticing the map and the location because this park was familiar to me, and I have often enjoyed walking in it.)

So that when I saw the signs of dragging, it occurred to me as a possibility, and that was why I stopped. It was only for a moment, curiosity, knowing that I had to get on to work and did not have time for diversions—just enough to pause and look into the bushes to see if I could see what it was that had been dragged here in the woods, halfway up the steps. And that was when I saw in the leaves first something black and then something—not white but skin color—and I leaned forward, pulled a branch aside a little and I saw in the leaves clearly a face, eyes open, blue eyes, looking at me. Lying on her back, looking up at me, mouth open, I thought she was about to speak, to ask me something. That was how she looked—as if she were going to ask me a question, to ask me to help her get up out of this thicket, or maybe simply directions how to go somewhere. A small face, neat featured, you might almost mistake her for a young girl. Only she kept hesitating to ask her question and she kept looking at me, and then I realized she was looking

20

not at me but above, beyond me, at the great trees, nor was there any movement, and her eyes were shiny like glass, and I realized that she was dead. It was a conclusion I drew, an inference, followed by the inference that it was she who had been dragged off the path, and then the slow and difficult further inference that someone else must also know about her death and had tried to hide her, leading to the terrifying conclusion that she had been murdered and the murder had not been discovered yet.

(*Narr:* So what did you do then?)

My instant thought of course was of lawlessness and chaos let loose upon the world and my next thought was that the murderer was probably still around, probably watching me. This would frighten you of course: immediately you would think that the watching criminal would try to get rid of you, just as he got rid of the old woman. I whirled round, expecting the rock to fall on me, and then I became aware (of course) of the depth of the silence of the woods against the farther sound of the traffic on the streets beyond the park. Under the force of fear I thought the most urgent thing was to get away as quickly as possible. I went back to the steps and looked about. I climbed rapidly to the top, looking around, turning my head back and forth, all the way. You would have seen me turning my head in that furtive way as I walked, as if I were running away from something, although actually of course what I was looking for was the murderer. Then when I got to the top, I crossed beside the bandstand and went on to the meadow. I knew that I should notify the police (*Narr:* Why didn't you notify the police?), but I wanted to get as far away from the crime as possible first. On the meadow I saw across on the other side a tractor mower, yellow, with a workman driving it. I am sure he saw me.

(*Narr:* Why didn't you tell him?)

I did not tell him, I crossed at the opposite end of the meadow from where he drove his tractor. I kept going, not thinking of telling anyone, never thinking of it because I did not think there was any reason to notice or remember. I did not think anyone would notice or remember me as I stood there waiting to cross the street, because I did not think there was any reason why I should, not expecting anything to happen.

I crossed and went down along the park road toward the pond, listening and looking for birds. I saw a flicker beside the usual robins and cardinals, and on the pond I saw a cluster of yellow ducks. I went down the steps into the playground, which was empty—the playground was empty. Swings and seesaws and picnic tables under the shade of trees, and I saw no one. I went into the woods and went to the foot of the steps and looked up and put my foot on the first step, looking up.

Looking up, I could see the sky at the top, shining under the arch of trees at the top, and I saw (*Q:* Did you know that this was the site of a murder, several years ago, the so-called strangler and an old woman out walking her dog?) two people, indistinct, in dark coats, halfway up. It was a movement, I could not tell, they seemed to be blocking the steps. I hesitated and stopped. I realized then that it was the old woman (*Q: The* old woman? You knew her? You had seen her before?) coming down the steps, and the man apparently had just stepped aside to let her pass, holding his hand out as to show that the way was clear. And then he bent down and, as I looked, he seemed to follow her with his hand up, and it was very quiet, and he made a quick gesture like cracking a whip. I thought he was behind her, and I did not know what the gesture was—I thought he was striking a mosquito or waving to someone or perhaps he had been stung on the wrist by a bee and was trying to shake it off—but I heard a crack like a branch breaking and I saw the old woman drop as if her marionette strings had been cut.

I saw the man look—quick—over his shoulder, and I darted behind a tree to be out of his sight. Still it did not occur to me that he had struck her—I thought she had tripped and fallen, and I thought that he would help her to her feet—until I saw him fling away the rock full of fossils into the woods and heard it bounding until it came to rest against some boulders, and then behind my tree I looked, and I saw him leaning over her, and after a moment he bent over and picked her up by the ankles and I watched as he dragged her into the bushes. I waited. After a moment he reappeared. He looked up and down, both ways, and then abruptly turned and continued, puffing—no, abruptly turned and raced, with broad leaping steps, up to the top. As soon as he was out of sight, I stepped out from behind my tree and—

I ran, back across the playground (no one was there, empty picnic tables), quick panic, not to go through the woods today after all but up along the road all the way? No. (*Narr:* Did the man on the yellow mower see you? What did you see on the road today? Did you notice any of the cars that were parked there?)

No of course. I knew obviously that if there was any chance of helping the old woman at this stage I should help her. Not knowing of course what I could do, doubting that I could do anything even if she were still alive, which was unlikely, nevertheless I knew that I should go to her and see and then bring her whatever help might be possible—from the hospital which is just beyond the park, of course. But of course I could not race as the man (the murderer) had done. Forty-five years old, and out of condition I had to make my way up slowly, puffing, those awkward steps that don't fit the natural stride, and I was puffing with a special agitation because of what I had seen. I used the rhythm of my steps to keep me from collapsing from shock, to regulate my breath and maybe even my heartbeat, counting almost automatically as I went—thir-ty-seven, thir-ty-eight, thir-ty-nine, foe-are-ty. This was the spot, signs of the earth stirred up, dragging in the bushes, a spot of blood in the dust. I went and looked where he had dragged her. At first I saw nothing, and then beneath a branch, just lifting it, I looked in and saw the black cloth of a coat, and after a moment I saw her face, looking up, looking at me. I said, "Are you all right, Madam? Are you hurt? Can I help you?" No answer, no change in her look, no blink, and then, and then, I knew. Knowing that flung me back on the path as if it had been me (instead of she) with panic need to rush, to race, just as I had seen the man do —before I took hold of myself the next moment. Saying now to myself, it's not a doctor she needs, it's the police. So I turned and continued up to the top of the steps, fully intending to go for a policeman. When I got to the top, I turned and went by the bandstand and over to the meadow, where there was a workman on the other side driving a yellow mowing tractor. I looked and did not see the man on the steps anywhere.

(*Narr:* Why didn't you go right down to Clifton Avenue and call the police from the hospital across the street?)

Would this be a case of abject cowardice, that by the time Burr got to the top of the steps and came out into the open it occurred to him that the murderer would be waiting for him? Hiding, very probably, in the bandstand watching to see whoever might emerge from or go into the path into the woods. Get rid of witnesses. The thing for Burr to do was to avoid attracting attention to himself, the murderer's attention—to act as if he had not noticed the body as he passed it on the way up the steps, as if he were simply on his way to work as on any other normal day. Besides, how could he identify the man in any case, not having seen his face, only his silhouette, from a long distance at the bottom of the steps? And unable to identify the man what else could he tell them that they wouldn't soon find out in any case: that there had been a murder? an old woman struck on the head in the woods? dragged into the bushes alongside the steps? Was Professor Burr afraid to tell the police for fear that it would damage his chances for appointment to the department headship he so dearly craved? Was he afraid that, unable to identify the criminal for the police, he himself would be charged with the crime? Is that the kind of novel he had become protagonist of? Passivity, impotence, fear, and indecision?

So just before I started up the steps I looked up and looking up, I could see the sky at the top, shining under the arch of trees, and then I saw her at the top of the steps just starting down, and I knew who she was *(Q:* You knew her?), I knew her and I had passed her on these same steps on at least two or three other mornings. I looked up and saw her coming slowly down, taking her short little steps, and then I started up, those awkward steps, slowly, one by one, eyes down (dust, little white flowers, violets), eyes right and left (bushes and buds turning into leaf, blocking vision), and sometimes I glanced up at her as she came down, and I saw that we would meet about in the middle. *(Q:* As you climbed, did you know that there had been a murder in this very same spot about five years ago, an old lady walking with her dog early in the morning? *A:* Yes, I knew about it, it had been in all the papers complete with a sketch map to show where it had taken place. *Q:* As you climbed, with the old woman approaching, were you thinking about that old murder that had taken place here?)

At the forty-first step I stood aside to let her pass, said Burr. As she passed she looked up at him—a very small old woman with clear blue eyes—and she looked more anxious than she ought to have, considering that we knew each other. When I got to the top, I slowed down, checked myself, reduced my pace to a slow walk. I was breathing heavily because of the climb of steps and I am out of condition. Before I came out of the woods to the circle I stopped and brushed off the front of my suit briskly (a few leaves and twigs), looked quickly as if to see if there were any bad spots. In the circle students had already begun to park their cars around the bandstand, from whence they would walk like me to the campus. As I came out, a car with a boy and girl was just pulling up to the curb on the other side of the bandstand: I could not tell whether they noticed me or not. I walked by the other side of the bandstand to the meadow, a steady controlled pace, not showing any nervousness at all, carrying my briefcase. I came out to the meadow and saw the workman on the yellow tractor mowing on the opposite slope. I crossed the meadow at the near end and never went close enough to see his face. When I was across the meadow I came out on the sidewalk along the avenue with students walking to the campus. I walked among the students, and nobody paid any attention to me.

The waiting student, guarding him in the doorway, grunts and scrambles heavily and clumsily to his feet. "Listen hey," he says. "When Kessler comes back, tell him I was here, will you?"

"If I remember, okay," I say. "What's your name?"

"Just tell him. Okay?"

"Okay, if I remember. You want to be sure, leave a note."

"Nah, just tell him. You'll remember."

"Yes, but what name? I don't know your name."

"Aw that's all right. He'll know. Just tell him I was here."

"How can I tell him, if I don't know your name?" But I guess I didn't speak loud enough, because already the student was gone. Make up a name for him, says the narrator. Call him Andreas Lynch. Or J. Edgar Hippy. Probably the brother of the girl who was here, whose name might be something like Mini Gradation.

The student did not know that Burr had become the protagonist of a novel. But Burr knew now, and he thought it would require all his courage and his strength. And integrity. The title frightened him, though, and he changed it to *The Man in His Office*.

25

Chapter 4

He was glad therefore that the student without a name had gone away, leaving him free to get up and shut his office door so that he could think over his new role in solitude. No class until eleven anyway. When he went to the door, he saw three girls sitting in chairs in the alcove, waiting probably to speak to other professors. He glanced at them questioningly. None of them paid any attention to him, and he shut his door.

From the moment he had bent down to pick up the rock full of fossils, from that moment, feeling it under his fingers, or certainly from the moment he tightened his fingers and detached it from the ground, felt its weight, or at least from the moment he held it high in his hand, standing up again and looking at the back of her head as she stepped down to the next step, he knew that the most important thing was firmness and resolve. No hesitation now, no vacillations. You pick your course, set it, and stick to it, regardless how your imagination and fear may try to sidetrack you. The rock was heavy in my hand. I knew it was full of fossils, I had a sense of age, but no time to think of that, I knew (firmness) that I must either do it now or not do it, there was no half doing it, no starting to strike and then drawing back, no diverting the blow, which might then merely scrape her head and give her a fright and leave me, leave all of us, merely embarrassed. It was strike altogether or don't strike at all. And the next moment—after that had been settled —I knew it was a matter always now of sticking firmly to the best plan, trusting to its odds, and never allowing paranoid fears or an overactive imagination or the complexity of things to shake my confidence in my clear simple intelligence. Above all, don't panic.

I knew there was a remote chance that someone might have seen us or that someone might yet see me, standing here with the rock in my hand as she lies at my feet—but only a remote chance, since I had seen no one above or below just before. I knew that this was the crucial moment, right now, if somebody should appear either above or below, and there was nothing I could do but trust the odds and use my intelligence to get her out of sight as quickly as possible. But life is full of such risks, and the man who doesn't take the well-chosen risk at some point in his life, etcetera. I considered then two alternative courses of action. The simplest would be to leave her where she had fallen and continue on my way. The danger with that plan was that someone might come along, from either above or below, before I had got completely off the steps (out of the woods, I mean), in which case I would have to face questions as to why I had left her lying there dead. And if I said that I was merely going to fetch the police, I would nevertheless have to contend with a great suspicion, since it would be obvious that she had only just died.

Better therefore to hide her and give me time to get well away before her discovery. The great risk here was that I might be discovered in the act of hiding her, and I knew there was no excuse that would get me out of that, but as I have already said, a certain amount of risk is necessary in anything you try to do. I saw the hollows filled with leaves behind the bushes and under the boulders. I saw a place where I could roughly conceal her (certainly there was no need to hide her carefully). Mainly it was a matter of not wasting time. I flung the rock away and immediately bent down and took her by the ankles to drag her into the bushes. Taking care at every point of the things one might, if careless, forget. Was she dead? I did not know but I was satisfied from the wound that if not she soon would be. Blood on my clothes? There was no great amount of blood. It was on her head. I dragged her by the feet, being careful to keep her head away from my clothes. Thistles and leaves and twigs brushing against my clothes? I saw no great problem there; I could

27

brush them off at an early opportunity. I dropped her into a pile of leaves and, since still no one had come into sight above or below, took time to cover her roughly with a dead branch with dead leaves. Then I went back to the path and continued up the steps as rapidly as I could without actually running or giving myself (out of condition) a heart attack. When I came out on top, I figured that I had safely passed the critical moment of danger. Now the important thing was to walk as casually as possible—my usual walk to the university. No, I had not seen anything on the steps. Of course I would prefer that no one be able to say they had seen me walk here at all. Therefore I avoided looking at the couple that was just then parking on the other side of the bandstand, and I satisfied myself that they had not noticed me. So too I guessed that none of those twenty cars that I had had to wait for in crossing over into the park had noticed me, any more than I had been able to remember any of them—despite the possibility that some student of mine might have been in one of them to say that I had been seen entering the park at the time of the murder. So that it would be only foolish of me to deny that I had come through the park if the evidence of this should emerge, and in such a case I should also admit climbing up the steps, but no, no sir, I saw nothing on the steps, I had no idea whether it was before or after I had passed or that there was a fresh body in the leaves not fifteen feet from where I had (puffing) walked.

And so I walked, seeing no reason to be afraid of the man on the mower, either, working at the other end of the meadow, simply being careful not to get too close where he might get a look at my face, and I took good note of the fact that he never looked at me, and quite possibly was not aware that I had passed at all. And when I came out on the sidewalk, too, among the students walking to the campus, I think no one noticed my emergence from the grassy slope at the side and, therefore, I realized by this time I was safe. And from now on the policy of firmness required only that I keep bearing steadfastly in mind how safe in fact I was—that I had done the job and got away unobserved, nor had I left anything behind to betray me. And if I simply kept this in mind, remembering that every passing moment strengthened my safety, and did not panic or give myself away, why then I would be all right, and it would be as if it had never happened at all.

Or was it rather the opposite of this, that he did not know what he was doing, as if he did not have any mind at all, as if his mind had actually stopped? Who would ever be able to recover whatever inexplicable spark of murderous rage he must have felt, sufficient to lift his hand suddenly with a rock against the old woman—yet totally and forever forgotten in the next moment as he gazed, appalled, at the lump of her as she lay there at his feet with her strings cut. Who did that? he asked in the silence. Did I do that? Why should I have done a thing like that? Not able, in fact, to believe that he had done a thing like that, though the rock was still in his hand and the memory of the crush of the blow still stirred in the nerves and muscles of his arm. And then it was without thought that he observed himself bending over her and taking hold of her by the feet (only then noticing that she wore pants instead of a dress) and dragging her into the bushes. Watching himself as he worked, not knowing what he would do next, wondering why he was doing as he did, and whether it was—given the conditions—the right thing to do. Who is doing this? he asked himself. Not I, not I. He asked himself who he was, and reminded himself that he could never do such a thing as this man was doing. Then he resumed his walk up the steps. He admired the man's calm as he walked up the steps, as if nothing had happened. When he got to the top he wondered if anything had indeed happened or was it all merely something that he had imagined?

It must have been fear. Yes, I can remember the fear if I look back hard enough, concentrate enough power of remembering on those endlessly long yet short moments on the steps in the woods. After she fell, I said, 'Why did you do that?' and 'Never mind why. Do something, quick,' he said, and I said, 'We must try to help her,' and 'Too late. She's dead,' he said, and I said, 'Maybe she's not dead,' and he said, 'Hit her again, kill her, kill her, she mustn't live,' and I said, 'I can't hit her,' and he said, 'She must be dead then, yes dead, look at the indentation in her head and the blood oozing through,' and then he moaned, 'oh, hurry, hurry, hurry!' and I said, 'We must hide her—help me hide her,' and all the time we were dragging her into the bushes he kept shouting at me, 'hurry hurry,' and 'watch out for the blood on her head, don't get it on your clothes,' and, 'can't you hurry? They're watching us, watching every move,' and then I said, 'We must cover her,' and he said,

'Every moment you delay, they're gaining on us,' and on the steps I said, 'We mustn't be seen panicked,' while he kept tugging at me, 'Run, Run. Run.'

Nothing can be worse than panic, though, at least after you have reached a certain age if not before. Burr would remember, if he tried hard enough, beyond the fear to what kept the fear in check, what I must have recognized and decided on, even before I used the rock on her. To avoid panic, to make the whole thing possible, what it required was the maintaining of my dignity at all times. And what this required was the decision in advance to surrender if need be, the willingness to accept the loss of everything including life itself—the deep suicidal gambit, which was not a commitment but a wager I must make, with my willingness to accept the loss if I lost. Of course I must have committed myself to such a wager before I ever lifted the rock against her, and I can remember it like the drawing of breath before diving into the water, even if every other motive is forgotten—otherwise I couldn't have done it. Otherwise I must have screamed instead of striking, and after striking I must have run howling into the woods like an animal.

Even as he bent to pick up the rock full of fossils, then, he must have said to himself, Are you ready for the full consequences if this should fail? He must have said, Are you ready to give up everything, to die, as of this moment, if it doesn't work? Telling himself that only by being ready could he hope to carry it out. And afterwards, he must have been saying to himself at every point: Calm, calm, keep your dignity—knowing that only in this way could he hope to get away from what he had done.

So I said to myself, Now. It is perfectly possible to get away with it —it is *easy* to get away with it, now, with good odds, unless you act like a stupid idiot. This first moment is the supreme risk, that someone should come into view before you get the body out of sight, but the obvious thing to do is to *get the body out of sight,* quickly and intelligently, and the only way to do it is to be prepared for the possibility it won't work. Which means the willingness to surrender if you are caught, the acceptance even of death if necessary. (Don't think of running and trying to hide in the woods. Once you get into that pattern you are lost, the woods too small, no way out.) Then having covered the body, returning to the steps, I said to myself, the moment of crisis is already passed, from now on it all depends only on keeping control, with dignity. By the time I got to the top of the steps and came out into the circle, already I knew that I had gotten away with it. Already there was no way they could catch me, and already I was warning myself that the only danger remaining was myself, some stupid breakdown of my nerves.

You have already gotten away with it, he admonished himself. Warning, where the only remaining danger lay, in the enormous literary tradition of retribution that threatened him: This you must avoid, he warned himself, this you must be on guard against at all times, which you do by remembering at all times that it lies all within the mind, your own mind trying to betray yourself, with power of suggestion from the literary minds of others. The tendency to be hysterical—beware of this—to lose your grasp on what is real and what is imagined; the tendency to imagine people watching you when you saw none; the tendency to imagine people noticing you where you would not notice them; the tendency to speculate on your narrow escapes, what would have happened if the narrow margin had failed, until you break down that margin yourself by the very force of your worry; the tendency to worry about what other people are thinking, what they suspect, until it forces you to challenge them on these points, thereby planting the very suspicion that you were trying to kill; the tendency to assume that something is building up against you behind the scenes that you know nothing about; the tendency to reflect and keep reflecting upon the crime, trying to remember what you did wrong, until finally your memory becomes so totally unreliable you have to go back to the scene of the crime to check it out; the tendency to let your fear of the crime dominate your thoughts, become an obsession, until you can do nothing that does not refer to the crime, paralyzing your work and the rest of your life, as if the crime were not something you had successfully got away with after all and could not safely be left behind in your past—ah yes, beware especially of the power of the almost universal literary tradition that tells you that all murderers are ultimately caught or give themselves up, the tradition that denies to all protagonists (as well as most villains) the power to carry out a crime and get away with it, for remember these traditions are the work only of minds of men thinking about crimes, their wishes and fears concerning crimes, whereas, said Burr, in real life there is such-and-such a percentage of actually unsolved murders in our society and such-and-such a probable number of live former murderers (ex-murderer—one who has committed a murder in the past but is not engaged in such an activity at present) living among us normal lives.

As he walked across the meadow, then, watching the workman on the yellow mower on the opposite side, Burr was admonishing himself to be very simple about it: This was not a situation calling for great sensitivity or delicacy and subtlety of feeling and thought. This was something he had happened to do. It was done and there was no undoing. Be prepared to take the consequences, he warned himself, in case some accident should trip you up—and the consequences will be most dire, of course, but no worse than death, and he considered himself prepared for death. For the rest, the thing to do was to avoid all the traps that the literary tradition set. Do not go back to the scene of the crime. Do not allow yourself to speculate about the authorities. Do not allow yourself to show interest in the crime (if possible, you should avoid reading the papers altogether today and tomorrow). Do not allow yourself to think about the crime any more than is necessary. A wound in the fabric of your life that only time can heal.

As he came into McMicken Hall, momentarily blinded by the darkness inside, after the sunshine outside, momentarily dizzied by a spell of forgetfulness, he asked, What am I doing *here?* (amid all these people, these students, these crowds) and immediately afterwards, Who the hell am I, anyway? And then the narrator replied, "You are Ralph Hathorne (pronounced Hawthorne or Hoarthorne) Burr, Professor of English, Office Hours, MWF 10–11. McMicken 236. Future head of the department of English. You are the protagonist of a novel called *The First One in the Department,* requiring all your courage, strength, and integrity." Yes, said Burr, I suppose I am.

Chapter 5

In his office that morning, after the student had left ("But what is your name? You didn't tell me your name?" "He'll know, just tell him I was here."), suddenly it occurred to Ralph Burr, suddenly it occurred to me, Why I really haven't done badly. Surprise and delight. I have really managed this thing pretty well, got it pretty much under control. For a man who only this morning, scarcely more than an hour ago, crunched the head of an old woman with a rock full of fossils, and now sit in my office at my desk like any other day, I really haven't managed things at all badly, not at all at all.

For he had coped. He had managed to keep his office door open, and he had dealt then with the student who wanted to see Harvey Kessler. He had managed to tell that student that he could not wait in the office. He had been polite to the girl who wanted to see Harvey, and he had had the presence of mind to ask the student to leave his name when he left, and it was not his fault if the student was unable to see the reason for that.

After the student left, he got up and shut the office door once more, but it made him uncomfortable after a few minutes because it left him wondering all the time what might be happening out in the hall, so I got up and opened it again. I saw the same three girls still waiting in the alcove for whatever professors they were waiting for. I looked at them and they looked at me. Then I said (he managed to say): "Any of you looking for me?" No response. They all looked away: one looked at her book, one at the ceiling, the third at the wall as if she had not heard. No one wanted to take responsibility for answering his question —which was a sufficient answer in itself. I wonder if any of them noticed anything peculiar about my behavior (wondered Burr) opening and shutting doors, asking questions, but they all looked too indifferent to be wondering about anyone, and then he remembered—I remembered how well, how exceptionally under control and well-managed everything was going this morning.

Managing not at all badly—repeat that. Keep insisting on it, repeating it. Harvey Kessler comes in, heavy boots thumping heavily on the floor. See how naturally and normally we respond to him, observe him, deal with him. Describe him (our powers of observation): a big man in a denim jacket, a red neckerchief loosely about his neck, a heavy black beard unshaped with streaks of white, a total beard continuous from sideburns to mustache to chin, with no shaved places, also hair to the shoulders with streaks of white, head enclosed with hair and whiskers, prophetlike. Speak (voice control): "Some student was here to see you, waited awhile, and then left."

"Who was it?" said Harvey (powers of attention, ability to listen, to grasp the words of a language, a human language, unimpaired—sign of the high human intelligence, superior to any other animal, with education beginning in the cradle and mother's voice, learning, mastering words, sentence structures, intricate complex patterns of thought, an endless and endlessly manipulable supply of communicable messages from one mind to another—all this unimpaired. Yes, I did, I understood what Harvey asked me. He asked: Who was it?).

Show memory and pass a judgment from intelligence: "He wouldn't tell me. I asked him his name and he wouldn't say. Merely said you'd know."

"Ah," said Harvey. "That was Krunik."

"Krunik? How the hell do you know that?" Display astonishment at the things that ordinary people would regard as mysterious or inexplicable. Show thereby your intelligence at work, and your feelings tied also to the workings of your intelligence, involved sufficiently to intensify your question with a mild oath, indicating also a judgment upon the irrationality of not only a Krunik but a Harvey too when the ordinary limitations of human communication seem to have been transcended without a clear explanation—show your own immersion in the ordinary operations of human life and human communication by your expression (oath-intensified) of bafflement at the phenomenon.

"Berthold Krunik. Must have been," said Harvey.

Stare at him with humorous disbelief, put all the disbelief you can muster into that stare to challenge him to an explanation, smile with it and gather all your intensity into that smile, gather *everything that is in your mind* into that disbelief, and make him see it, make him see that everything in your mind is gathered into your disbelief of him, so that he will know your incredulity (know that there is nothing on your mind but that) and offer some kind of sensible explanation.

"Okay," said Harvey, grinning. "Pale, sloppy, round gold-rimmed glasses, fiery long blond hair sweeping around?" Grin is proof how well you are managing things.

"The description fits," I said.

"Sure it was Krunik. Could only have been Krunik."

Take another step. "There was also a girl," I said. "Red miniskirt."

"You didn't get her name?"

For this one Harvey is as baffled as any ordinary citizen would be. "Sorry," I said. "Blond hair. Eager-looking."

"And you didn't get her name?"

Show normality, shake head sadly. Grin. Everybody grin and shake heads sadly. "Too bad. Too too bad. Well, she'll be back I trust." Assume so.

Settle down to work then, each at his own desk. Harvey sat at his desk, looking at papers that he took out of the file. A sign of how well Burr was doing was that he was able to sit at his desk and work, leaning back in his chair looking out the window, at the tree outside, a female cardinal hopping around among the branches. He had a class scheduled for eleven o'clock, and another sign of how well he was doing, how well he was managing in such a crisis as this, was his knowledge that he would meet his class and carry on just like any other day. ("Lost in meditation?" the voice of Harvey Kessler, sounding from somewhere deep in the distance behind him. Heard somewhere, some time ago, no one knew just how long ago, whether recently or longer than that, and by now it was too late to make any reply—especially as it didn't seem to mean anything anyway. Lost in meditation? *Who* was lost in meditation? *Where* was meditation? How could you answer the question until these points had been cleared up?)

The telephone on his desk rings and startles—made him jump. Momentary jolt—look how it made him jump, did anyone notice how he jumped? did Harvey Kessler notice? Say rather that the telephone screamed at his elbow like an electric shock of sound, so no wonder he jumped. Someone is coming. Did not signify any real loss of control or management of things in a crisis like this, as proven by the way Burr reached for and grabbed the phone (showing how perfectly, still, his faculties were functioning, his ability to infer from the sound that the telephone was ringing and to know from this that the way to stop it was to pick up the phone and the way to do that was to grab it) caught as you might catch some escaping animal, cat perhaps, pinning it down by the middle of its back until you could improve your grip, and then picked it up. Keeping perfect control despite the suspicious thoughts that inevitably must occur to one in a crisis like this: "Hello."

Control yourself, why should you be ("Hello." "Oh Ralph?" (big rich commander's voice as per uncle perhaps bygone father but dead, one who calls him by first name of course)) frightened? This was the shock that he had discovered in himself on arrival at the office, sitting in his gullet like a large undigesting stone, lodged there, asking how to be vomited, issuing forth in a sudden flooding ejaculation of ("Yes." "This is" (of course Elias chairman, word from high up? Why is the chairman calling him in his office in the middle of the morning? What can he) "George" (want? George————, last name familiarly omitted, meaning George Elias, head. Draw the inference, fill in the gaps: E-l-i-a-s). "I wonder if you would be so good") terror. They would get at him through the ("as to drop in my office for a few minutes. I want to ask you") head. Going through channels. Controlling yourself—why should he be afraid, if there wasn't anything to ("something. Can you spare the time?"

Suppose you say no? No one says no to Elias. No one says no to the po-author-detec-daddies. "Yes sir, certainly," said) fear? Summons (Ralph Burr. "I want your advice on a matter. I won't keep you") to the head always frightened him unreasonably, the old complex of the child and the authority figure provoking ("for long." (Bail? no bail for certain cases)) guilt in advance for unspecified ("Yes, I'll be right over") and unknown crimes and offenses. The question was whether it was time to run, and then he remembered how well he was managing things, and he knew that control meant to ignore the guilt until it is pinned on you. So children feel guilt when the boss calls—general guilt on general principles, never knowing what forgotten or even never-known thing they will be charged with. And bosses are smooth and oily, asking your advice on how to set the trap for you, calling you by first name, and himself also by first name, leaving his last name a blank to conceal the knife. Every detail counts, said the narrator (taking hold, steadying the protagonist, who was in danger for a moment of losing his excellent control). Who then has George Elias been talking to just now to make it urgent enough for him to call you and make you come to his office to give him advice? Someone who was looking down (dirt and dust and little white flowers and violets) or eyes right, eyes left (bushes on both sides with buds turning into leaves, just beginning to block vision, and large trees everywhere) but not up, never up, until he looked up just in time to see marionette strings cut, reporting now to the authorities, to the head, the head of heads of heads? He stopped abruptly outside the English office door. But of course, said the narrator, you fool! The English department is not the police department, it is not the head of the department who makes arrests and conducts inquiries! I looked through the glass and saw the younger secretary (Natalie Fleet) at her desk, typing, looking calm, and I held my breath and went in. For he realized just in the nick of time how narrowly he had escaped one of those traps of confusion that the literary tradition had set for him.

He passed Natalie and went in to George Elias' inner office. In perfect control again. "Come in Ralph glad to see you," the big man getting up to shut the door behind them to insure private conversation, and I knew that I would be all right now. Sat down in the chair beside his desk, facing him—the witness chair. "I just wanted to ask your very special advice, because you are Harvey Kessler's friend, you know him pretty well, wouldn't you say?"

Notice how judicial and cautious Ralph Burr manages to be, even in situations like this. "Well," I said, "We share the same office. I don't know as this means I know him very well."

"Oh?" saith the Lord. "I thought you and Harvey were pretty good friends." But it all depends, Mr. Elias, on what you mean by a "pretty good friend." A question might be raised as to whether Ralph Burr has any pretty good friends at all—which might tend to alienate the novel's readers, however, warns the narrator, rather than evoking the kind of compassionate sympathy you no doubt would prefer.

But Ralph, always concerned with managing himself well under this kind of pressure (if you want to become department head you have to be able to manage yourself under all kinds of pressure and be able to follow quick changes of subject), braced himself now for a change in the subject that had been concerning him, one way or another, all morning. Seeing now this new subject, entering areas of university or at least departmental politics, where everything is always a little sticky and obscure? And rivalries and factions and whether it is a good idea or not to be regarded as Harvey Kessler's good friend? Meanwhile there is a tree outside Elias' window and a cardinal in the tree.

"I don't mean to spy or to tattle," said Elias. Suddenly Elias began to talk in italics, and it made Burr extremely nervous, trying to listen, to pay attention, to understand what was being said, because he heard him speak (in italics) and then he heard him speak again, and it was hard to keep his voices distinct. *I don't mean to spy,* said Elias, but I mean to investigate because I already have spies, *or tattle, but as you know I have received many complaints* from witnesses in the woods, *about Harvey Kessler,* who lives in the woods. *This is no new thing of course, and it is part of my job* to make arrests, *I might almost say a routine part of my job as chairman,* said Elias. To gather witnesses like you—I want you to be a witness, said Elias.

"Complaints about Harvey?" said Burr, feigning surprise, feigning ignorance of what he was talking about. The narrator knows that Elias' remarks have a familiar sound at this point, explaining that Elias knows that Burr is a candidate to succeed him as chairman and, though he has officially resigned as of next September, he does not actually believe anyone can succeed him in the job. He likes to keep reminding us of that. However, there is static, and it is difficult to hear the narrator clearly at this point.

Oh, yes indeed, always complaints, said Elias. *Mostly from students, chiefly the conservative ones of course, and sometimes from parents.* Sometimes a policeman will complain, *sometimes one of the deans. I hear occasionally from a citizen in the town who thinks he has got wind of what goes on,* or a workman on a yellow mower who actually saw it. *Once I had to speak to a reporter about him and once a detective, and once I even had to answer for him to a member of the Board of Directors.* "His politics, I suppose," said Burr, seeking to change the subject. *Oh my yes indeed. His politics* and his violent methods. *Sometimes I hear because some student is offended by obscenity in the classroom, but I suppose that has become commonplace nowadays. Or because he criticized the American dream. Or the war.* There was a complaint that he went through Burnet Woods yesterday morning. *There was the flag incident, you remember that,* he carried the flag through Burnet Woods. *And his advice to the guys to get their chicks and get laid.* Or was it this morning? He saw the lovers in the bushes in Burnet Woods this morning, his own students getting laid with each other. *I hear quite a lot of talk about things like that, you can well imagine. Of course I always stand up for him. I protect him. It's part of my job as chairman.* Part of yours too if you ever make it. But of course there is a limit to what kind of outrage I can put up with or to what extent I am willing to shield a man for who knows what atrocious crimes.

"Of course," said Burr. "You have to."

This latest thing is more difficult, though, said Elias. (Leaning back, smoking a cigar.) He said, You walked to work this morning, I wonder if you happened to notice it? *I have students objecting because he seems to be denigrating the literature they are supposed to be learning. Attacking Mark Twain, Crane, James, Faulkner, for being establishment, for being obsolete, for being prejudiced, racist, sexist.* Attacking them for being old ladies. *Attacking the novel itself, the whole genre* with a rock *for express-ing middle class complacency, the artistic tool of the power elite* on the back of the head. *Attacking literature itself as somehow dead. The written word is dead.* The old lady is dead, *the wave of the future is sound and light and communication through assault on all the senses.* She fell noiselessly. *According to this student I saw this morning,* he saw the old lady get killed and *he criticized the students for being passive, for being bourgeois, elite snobs, for majoring in English, can you imagine that?, and for reading novels and not* reporting the crimes they had seen or *taking part in revolutionary action. Makes you wonder, doesn't it, what Harvey is doing teaching English courses.* According to the student you were there, *of course I knew the student is distorting* nevertheless you were there and saw the man strike the woman on the back of the head, *but I would be curious to know* if you could identify him, *curious to know just what actually goes on in Harvey's classes,* if you could come forth with a positive identification, saying, yes I saw Harvey Kessler kill the old woman, *wouldn't you?*

Why don't you ask him, said Burr. No, checking himself, rephrasing (self-control): "What does he say when you ask him?" The polite as-sumption that the policeman will question the suspect himself before asking others questions about him. At least I should hope they would treat me like that.

The students don't understand his subtlety and irony, I suppose, said Elias. *He's trying to shake them up, make them defend themselves, account for themselves. Very bracing.* I realize of course, said Elias, that you weren't actually there. You saw the old lady lying in the leaves afterwards. *I just wondered if you have any clearer idea of what goes on.* Because according to the student you were there. You were the only witness. *I just wondered if you have any ideas on how we might approach Harvey without offending him* or making him feel threatened, to get him to confess—*you know*—tone himself in *it down a little, to keep his classes* from murdering other classes *a little more specifically confined to literary matters* to hit the old lady just not quite so hard. *Not that I object to revolutionary ideas* including murder, said Elias, including specifically murder when necessary *but just that they should be kept—*

don't you think?—just a little more within the framework of relevance of a literature course? Besides, he said, nobody gets executed for murder anymore.

His voice sank, and I lost track of it. I was remembering how it was this morning when I came through the woods on the way to work, how I crossed the playground and began to climb the steps through the woods. I remembered climbing up the steps slowly, one by one, steps too wide to take one at a time, not wide enough for two comfortable steps, so that you climb with an irregular limping rhythm, thir-ty-seven, thir-ty-eight, thir-ty-nine, foe-are-ty. Next I remembered looking up the whole line of steps to the top, where the sky shone brightly through the trees at the top. And I remembered then the rock full of fossils. And I remembered—I looked at Elias talking, I looked at his head, the head's head—and I remembered the discoloration of the head, the deep indention, red stain with dust and twigs. And I remembered *myself.* Tell Elias it was not Harvey Kessler. Whoever it was, it was not Harvey.

"But of course the chief thing I wanted to talk to you about," said Elias suddenly. Ralph Burr was startled, pulled back from daydreams and fantasies like a child in kindergarten: so that wasn't what you wanted to talk about? Softening, paving the way for the important thing, which is now? What? "I wonder if you are aware of this letter that Harvey has sent to the members of the search committee?"

He handed the letter to me. I tried to read it. The trouble was that I couldn't read it. I saw words but they danced about. They did not form into sentences. They refused to fall together into any kind of compre-hensible pattern. But the oddest thing of all was that although I couldn't read the letter somehow I knew exactly what it was about, and I seemed to know also what it said, even though I could not tell you the order of the words in which it said what it said. It said—it was about something like—this:

Before the search committee submits its choice for the new department head to the administration, it should submit the names of its two (or perhaps three) preferred candidates to the faculty of the department and also to the English majors to be voted on, for either approval or disapproval. I do not ask for an election, but I do ask that the department, including the students, be given veto power on any candidate whose name is to be given to the administration for the job . . .

"What do you think of that?" said Elias.

I thought, *I am still a candidate.* Suddenly I felt all my powers of concentration joyfully gathering about a real issue. I said, Since I am a candidate I must be innocent, and I must consider all the possibilities before I answer Elias as to what I think about it. And it was a sign of my mastery over the situation that at this moment, when I needed them, my powers of concentration worked. I said, which way will I have a better chance? Will it be better for me to be subject to a vote or to be directly appointed without a vote? I thought, who else is likely to be recommended? and I remembered that the two other candidates were likely to be Kail and Stone. Then I understood the motive behind Harvey's letter: that Stone was likely to be favored by the administration but that he was hated, especially by the students. Quite obviously this was an attempt to stop Stone. It was unlikely to hurt me, though. This was a reasonable inference—if students felt they did not know me very well and my colleagues felt generally formal with me rather than close, this did not mean they would vote against me. This being the case it would be to my advantage to speak in favor rather than against, and I said:

"I don't see any objection to this, do you?"

Elias smiling. "The administration might object, but I don't see that it's any of their business if the search committee decides to operate in this way. Of course they are not bound by anything the search committee might recommend in any case. They can pick whoever they damn please and there's not a damn thing any of the rest of us can do about it."

"They're not likely to go against the department, though," I said.

"No. They're not likely to."

So I left the office with a sudden strong feeling of almost exultant happiness, merely to have heard myself talk about a changed subject so clearly even if so briefly, knowing I was still a candidate and could still cope with authority, even a head, without losing my head.

I returned to my office. After a while it was time to go to my eleven o'clock class. I went to the classroom and looked at the students. There they all sat, twenty-five students, boys and girls, looking at me, waiting. I wondered a moment. And then I remembered. And then there was nothing else to do, so I said, "I'm sorry." What? They still waited. "I mean," said Burr, "I'm sorry. I can't . . . I mean. Next time, I mean . . . There will be no class today. No class. Okay? Understand?" And then most of the twenty-five breaking into grins and some of them even, maybe, cheering.

Chapter 6

The narrator should make Burr explain why he dismissed his class that morning. The reason I dismissed my class—I did not know he was going to dismiss his class. At the time he went to the class, walking through the halls, carrying his notebook and the text, Burr was feeling pleased with himself for being able to do this, maintaining his calm at such a time of crisis. He thought, "I am able to meet my class today," which meant that he was able to function normally, which meant in turn that he could expect to function normally in whatever stresses should turn up during the next days or weeks. He was not likely to collapse or break down or give himself away.

He went into the classroom and looked at the students, twenty-five of them, waiting for him, looking at him, including Harold Fenner, Cora Angleburg, the pretty bright girl Teddy Baer, Ingrid Shulman, Jeff Cohen, Mark Lipowsky, George Steffinger, Dennis LaRue, Maureen Flapp, Steve Gioto, Norm Hunk, Lou Verm, and Barbyra Stickhaus. He looked at Mark Lipowsky and realized that he had forgotten what he had planned to do in this class today. Barbyra Stickhaus looked at him, opening her notebook, touching her pen to her lips, waiting, and he could not remember what book the class was supposed to have read for today. He remembered then that he couldn't remember what course this was, whether Freshman English or the advanced undergraduate course in modern American poetry, or a course in great nineteenth- and twentieth-century novels, or some more experimental course he had discussed, once, with George Elias and Harvey Kessler. Not knowing what book or what poem they were supposed to have read for today, still less could he remember whether he had planned for a discussion or a lecture. And if he had planned for a lecture, he could not remember what the lecture was, nor was he aware of having brought any lecture notes to class —nor could he remember, either, any plans for how a discussion might go, what questions he had intended to raise or what issues or problems he wanted the class to work on.

He saw Ingrid Shulman looking at him with hopeful voluptuousness (so he always interpreted that warm sleepy half-smiling look which suggested also that she was still suffering, ever so slightly, from a cold) and bright pretty Teddy Baer looking crisp and critical, challenging him to be brilliant and refusing, as always, to accept anything less, and he saw the book that they all now had waiting on their desks: Henry James, *The Ambassadors*. My God, said Burr. He tried to remember what was in *The Ambassadors*, whether in fact he had ever read it. Why, he always assumed he had read it, of course, but just now he couldn't find it in his memory. Then—well, yes—tell Elias, now he remembered he had been reading it last week, rereading it, obviously, since (he remembered now) he had written a paper on it once, long ago. Last week he had been rereading it—apparently, said Elias, in preparation for this class—but though now he could remember the *act* of reading it, he couldn't remember anything about the *experience* at all. What was *The Ambassadors* about? What kind of protagonist did it have? Was he like us, better than us, or worse than us? What kind of problem did he have to contend with?

Paris, whispered Elias, like a prompter in the wings. "Live, little Bilham, live!" Who said that? A garden of artists and civilized people at the height of civilization. "Who?" The man looked at him. "You," said the man—he had the face of a Russian workman—"you are a murderer!" St. Petersburg, whispered Elias. Another book. He saw Barbyra Stickhaus looking at him, waiting for him to do something— improvise, said Elias. Ask a student to tell you what the novel is about. Pretend you haven't read it, make them describe it to you, make good pedagogical use of your amnesia. But he heard Cynthia interrupting. Murderer! she said. Whispered, hissed. I'm going to tell the class, she said. Murderer. He saw the rock full of fossils, he felt the impact, felt it give way, yield. It seemed as if no one had ever called him a murderer before. But it wasn't they, it was himself. It seemed as if it had never occurred to him before, never in all his life, that he was a murderer. Why, he said to Elias in most profound astonishment, I am a murderer. Ralph Burr is a murderer. Professor Ralph Burr is a murderer. No wonder he couldn't remember *The Ambassadors.*

He had changed his career. No wonder he couldn't teach. He said, "I'm sorry. I can't. Next time? There will be no class today. No class. Okay?" As he left the room, the students passed by looking at him anxiously, solicitously, yet no one daring to ask the question. He felt for a moment—I felt for a moment a surge of tears, I felt like crying, wondering if I had lost my career, so swiftly, so easily, so devastatingly quick. If I had ceased to be a college professor by virtue of one brief moment in the woods that had moved off into the past just like any other moment. Why should I have ceased? I wanted to teach. I loved teaching, I loved students, I loved books and literature, and for a moment I felt like crying at the loss, the wasteful loss of all that. And then I remembered the importance of managing it well and not allowing myself to panic. Panic, said Elias—that is exactly what happened to you there. Be glad you handled it as well as you did. Take the day off, allow yourself to get a little control over the shock. Come back tomorrow, by then you'll be your natural self again.

I went back to the office—he walked back through the hall, head down, meditative, unseeing, past students, like a monk, reflecting still on how he had managed to go to class so unaware how unprepared he was. For he had been working on that class this morning in the office —that was the point—all morning at his desk, while the student waited outside and then went away and after Harvey came, all that time Burr supposed that he had been working on the discussion for his class on *The Ambassadors,* whereas actually—without even knowing it . . . Quite another discussion altogether.

Therefore he needed more time. Time to let his mind do whatever it had to do in order to manage the situation properly. He came to his office door and looked in. Harvey Kessler at his desk, the girl in the red minidress sitting in the chair by the side of Harvey's desk. Her chair was pulled up to the corner of his desk, which made them look intimate— it was a way with Harvey Kessler when he had conferences with girl students, they always seemed to sit in such a way as to look intimate, as if the conferences had to be whispered, although actually at the moment Harvey was shouting—"God damn it, I don't give a shit what your high school English teacher used to say"—and the girl was giggling, and Burr wondered how it was that Harvey managed it, whether he invited them to sit close, or they did it themselves, for Burr had never been able to determine. Now, though—as he stood in the door about to go in, and Harvey looked up quickly at him (surprised? because Burr was supposed to be in class), suddenly he realized that the office wouldn't do, he couldn't do his thinking (or whatever it was) in the office, not with Harvey there, not with people coming in and out of the alcove.

Go to the library, suggested Elias, and Burr turned, thinking to do that, but the moment he asked Elias where in the library he might go, and the picture of the library, of the reference room with its long rows of tables under a vast roof, of the stacks, close together with student carrels at the edge, of the graduate reading room and the periodical room, of all the people in all the rooms, sitting at the tables with piles of books, notebooks, cards, and the guard at the exit—and everybody looking at you, trying to decide what it was you were trying to hide— no, the library would not do, no better than the office, perhaps worse.

Go home, I am sick. Home in the middle of the day? Days of schooltime, long years gone yet alive and new as if still going on, while his mother keeps him home from school because he has a cold. And so kept home, he stays in his room, looking out the window at the houses down the street during the descending guilty childless quiet on the street, watching the woman two lots away hang out her wash, and the postman coming down the street one house at a time, and the grocery delivery truck, and the big brown United Parcel van—the pale morning accompanied by the hum of the vacuum cleaner, while the simple act of sitting where he is, by the window of his room looking, is intensified by the luxury and guilt of not belonging there, of thinking he should be somewhere else, of thinking that and deliberately negating the thought with the deliberate knowledge that he had been granted a special privilege. And if he went home now, though Mother was nowhere any longer, and spent the rest of the day alone in his house, alone with his animals, would there be the same luxury of guilt?

You'll have to go through the park, he said. What? Burnet Woods, in order to walk home from here, he said, you'll have to walk through Burnet Woods. Suddenly Burr remembered something he had seen in Burnet Woods this morning—something that wanted to catch him, like a trap set for him. I won't, said Burr. There's no other way, he said. You didn't bring the car, how else do you expect to go home? I can go around it, said Burr. I can walk down Clifton Avenue and around Burnet Woods, it won't take much longer. You dare? he asked. And then he remembered more clearly what the trap was, and he didn't even dare that. To show himself back in that area so soon? I won't do it, said Burr. If I can't go home without going by Burnet Woods, I won't go home. You need the rest, he said. The time for recovery and the healing processes of therapeutic thought. I'll go downtown, said Burr. I'll take a bus and go downtown. I'll lose myself in the downtown city for a while, I'll sit in the square and look at the fountain.

As the bus approached, I felt an impulse to throw myself under the wheels. It was not a strong impulse, though, and did not cause me any trouble. When I got on the bus, they looked at me. There was a fat man, with an enormous belly and great swine-like cheeks, a black woman with thin curly white hair very much like———, a couple of male students, a nurse, a woman in an orange print dress with orange hair, chewing gum, and others, and they all looked at me. In that instant, as he got onto the bus, he lost his professorship. Dropped off him like a loose garment, without his feeling it. (Actually, the narrator tells us, this happened whenever Ralph Burr got onto a bus or into a city crowd anywhere. It was not peculiar to this day. On this day, however, he noticed the loss.) Lost his professorship, lost his tenure, his rights and privileges (as well as his responsibilities), lost his fringe benefits—lost, so it seemed, in one exposed moment, everything.

The old man across the aisle gave him an angry look. He glanced around at the nurse, who turned sharply and looked the other way, out the window. The bus lurched as it went around the corner. He leaned his head against the cool glass, trying to hide his head. He saw people on the sidewalk. He saw a man, then another man, many men and women with deep-lined, gaunt faces, poor-clothed, undernourished, threadbare, Appalachian, he thought, poor. He did not want them to see him.

Nobody knows, said the man. You're safe, so far. We were descending the hill into the downtown part of the city, with a clear view for a minute or two over the top of the city, the roofs stretching away, broken by the lines of the streets, to the little cluster of high buildings in the distance. Overlain by a thickness of haze, grayblue. Made you think, for a moment anyway, of some teeming roasting burning suffocating center of over-population with roofs blackened by the burning of human breath, like Calcutta, and then we came down into the city itself. Shabby store-fronts, warehouses, food stores for welfare customers. "Your welfare vouchers buys more here." A man bent, shuffling his feet, tiny steps, that was all he could take. Two guys with wire-thin necks and long yellow hair, sneering at each other, a fat woman in a print dress watching, cursing them, or cursing one, or cursing both. Suddenly one reached out and jabbed the other, a blow, light, cautious, tentative, yet angry, the possible beginning of a fight (could not see the rest as the bus moved on), and just then suddenly Burr remembered again, as if he had forgotten, or even as if he had never noticed until now, the arm with the rock uplifted (his arm), and he remembered also the descent of that arm, the force of it, remembered even (as if he had not noticed before) the sudden strength poured into his muscles to make it come down as hard as it could (his strength), remembered also the eye fixed on the target, the target the head turned away, descending the steps with the silky thin white hair with little ringlets on top, remembered how he directed that heavy explosive rock-breaking force upon that delicate target until it crashed, and remembered the clench of teeth (his teeth) at the moment of crash, as if he were trying to break the world and all its history upon the fragile head of that poor old lady. And now, as he remembered it, as if for the first time, it came to him as absolutely incredible and unlimited in its horror, and he heard himself asking someone, asking him: "And did *I* do such a thing as that? Is it possible, is it conceivable that I, I, I, could have done such a terrible thing as that, I who never . . ." What did you never? asks the narrator. "I who never struck anyone in all my life," he said, trying to remember if that was true. Think, said the narrator, what claims you want to make. What indeed do you want to claim to have been before you did this? "And is it possible," meanwhile Burr kept asking the narrator, "that I could have done this? Or that it happened to me? How could anyone else believe such a thing of me, if I can't believe it myself?" The question kept repeating itself: Is it possible? As if it were not possible. As if that violent moment remembered had no connection with anything else he remembered or thought of as occupying his mind. Unable to think of any reasons why anyone should do such an act, as if to his life had been attached someone else's memory, grafted onto him by somebody else's cruel imagination.

All the while the narrator kept asking him to explain his incredulity —what it was about himself that made it so impossible for him to do the thing he definitely knew he had this morning done? But I could not attend to an answer just then. I had enough on my mind just to keep that constantly descending rock with fossils from landing on my own head and squashing me flat.

Got off the bus at the end and walked over to the square. This square is new in the middle of the downtown section of the city, and you can still feel its newness as you walk into it—the broad open plaza raised above the street level, the glassy new buildings lined in coppery steel rising on two sides and the old high buildings on the other two, and the old fountain with its green statue on one side and a flower stand with a red and white canvas top. In the late morning sunshine, shoppers crossed the square. People stood in the middle or around the edges, looking at the buildings, at the fountain, at the other people. Were there clerks and secretaries taking a late morning work break from the nearby offices? He came into the square and sat down on a bench. Felt the warmth of the sun in his back, with consciousness subsiding.

A man sat down beside him. Burr did not look at him, until he became aware that the man was looking at him—looking at him insistently, demandingly. He was a middle-aged man or more with a red high-blood-pressure face and an old shabby blue suit. His eyes were prominent and white looking at Burr, a look of familiarity, maybe cajolery, maybe a little threat. "Nice morning isn't it?" he said. Voice very rapid and slurred, as if the whole sentence were one word. *Yes yes,* said Burr. "Nice place to sit take the breeze. Take a little time off from work, watch people go by." According to Burr he looked more like a drunk than a cop, but Elias said that was probably a disguise to take you off guard. "You work around here?" asked the man. Be careful what you say, said Elias. Don't reveal anything you don't have to—better not let him know who you are, if you can help it. *Hm,* said Burr, vaguely nodding. The man grinned like a child, not satisfied, "Yeh, where do you work?" None of your business, occurred to Burr, but no point in being needlessly hostile, and he merely shrugged and said, *Around.* The man grinned again as if he had found Burr's weakness, and said, "Don't care to say? You're a wise man, mister, never too careful with strangers, like I say. I agree with you. Always steer clear of strangers, that's the best policy. All this crime in the streets today, isn't that right? You gotta be careful, that's what the man in the street wants. Who knows who might be a criminal? You, or me. Who knows?" He knows, said Burr. Not necessarily, said Hoffman. He's trying to guess, to fill it out on the basis of what information he does have. Probably not a cop, he suggested. More likely a little crook himself, aiming to put the screws on you. "I'm a law norder man, myself. You believe in law norder?" Burr said nothing, and they sat there quietly for a few minutes. Suddenly the man laughed. And pointed. "Look at that there." It was a well-dressed girl walking across the middle of the plaza, short skirt, good legs, prominent bust. "Lots of good stuff to see to sit in the sun and watch the stuff go by," said the man. Burr nodded, and the man went on, more eagerly: "Yagree with that, Mister? Yeh you bet, it's a good thing to sit and watch it, you like to sit here and watch it? You like that, mister? You think it's pretty good, ain't it?" Burr nodded but refused to smile. Revise, said Laura. The man's a homosexual. Maybe a blackmailer too but first of all homosexual, and probably doesn't have any information of the kind that you are worried about.

51

"You married, mister?" the man asked. Don't tell, warned Laura. But I couldn't totally ignore him—never was able to do that. *Was,* said Burr. "Was?" said the man. "Divorced?" *Died,* said Burr, wishing he hadn't said anything at all. "Ah!" said the man, shocked. Divorce, yes, but death he had not expected. "That's a bitch. I know what you mean— I been through it all, I know what you feel." Doubt it, said Laura. And you would think, said Burr to me, that a man could go into a public place like this square in the middle of downtown and be left to himself, lost in crowd anonymity, without running the risk of strangers, cops, black-mailers, and homosexuals, all of whom look like drunks sitting down and pressing on you. You can't stay here, that's obvious, said Elias. Go to a movie. Burr got up. *Excuse me,* he said, *I've got to be going now.*

Man looked frightened, jumped up with him. "Go already? Listen, please, forgive a harmless stranger. Be careful of strangers, but a law-abiding citizen down on his luck. Could you do me a favor before you go?" Burr stopped and looked at him. "Haven't had any work for six weeks." So we were right in the first place. Burr waited. The man waited, too, as if he expected to say something at this point, and when Burr didn't speak, he said, "Hanh? I'm a law-abiding citizen and I support law norder but I can't get no work." So Burr said, *What do you—?* Unfinished sentence. After a moment the man said, "Nothing to eat since yesterday." So Burr put his hand into his pocket, while the man watched. Felt pennies, quarters, dimes. Suddenly had a better idea, took out his wallet. The man's white eyes began to gleam. Burr handed him a dollar. "I knew you," said the man. "I knew you would. I knew by your eyes." *Eat,* said Burr. He turned and left fast, not wanting to hear any more. Knew you for a sucker, said Cynthia. Hah. Good deed, said Mother, make up for some bad deed you might also have done today? "Hey mister!" The man was right behind him, running. Heart failing, Burr turned on him. "I just want you to know—I'm sorry about your wife. My condolences." Waving the dollar bill. *Thanks,* said Burr, turning away again.

Chapter 7

He crossed the street to the movie theater. Just after he crossed he met a student, who said, "Hi Mr. Burr." He checked his impulse to run away, and after a moment also his impulse to deny the student or pretend he didn't know him. *Hello,* he said. Though he could not remember the student's name or what class he had been in. Only it was this terrible feeling of having been caught in some crime when the student spotted him. It was only a moment, he did not stop to talk, just gave a quick nod and walked on, as if to reduce the incident as nearly to nothing as he could. But they kept arguing about it afterwards, as he went on towards the theater. She said, But why don't you want him to see you? He said, Because I don't want to tell him any lies. She said, I don't understand. He said, Because he thinks he was saying hello to some professor at the university. She said, He thinks you are Professor Ralph Burr. What of it? He said, Because that's what he thinks, because I would not want him to be deceived. She said, But you *are* Professor Ralph Burr. He said, What right has the student to think that? What right has anyone to think that? She said, Well, you don't know the student's name so doesn't that leave you even? He said, That's the worst of it. He has a name for me when I don't have a name for him. She said, But you are Professor Ralph Burr.

Just now, though, it seemed very doubtful. Just now he felt as anonymous as a red-faced drunk in a crowd. It was hard to believe, indeed, that he had ever been a professor, so long ago it was, or that he had ever had tenure (like an old hose used for a lifeline that had been left out in the winter, had frozen and cracked and got encrusted and filled with dried mud). Married? Was—he had said. Wifeless, children gone, and now he couldn't even go home. No place to go except down into the center of the city and even there you couldn't sit in the square because of people who come up to accost you, either blackmailing strangers or students who think you resemble someone they know. Not knowing what he was, he went up to the box office and paid his way into a movie. He thought this way he could escape being recognized by people who might think they knew him.

The big empty dark barn of the theater, splashed with the light of the French countryside reflected from the screen. The woman reading the comic book had sold him his ticket without looking at him. The man with glasses looked at him as he took his ticket, going in. The boy at the entrance to the aisle looked at him as he passed by. In the theater, in that reflected light of French countryside, he saw all the empty seats and took one in the middle. He counted six other people in the audience, scattered around, each isolated by many seats in all directions. Asylum, said Elias. Sanctuary.

In a small French village, in the deserted square where two roads come together, with houses with buff sides and brown-red roofs, a boy is crossing with his schoolbooks—in my path as I come bearing down on the square in my high-powered car. In the way, he looms up in front of me as I swerve, but it is too late. The girl screams, the books fly up, I look back and see him lying in the dirt behind me, broken. Stop, stop, you hit the child! cries the girl. Shut your trap, I tell her, stepping on the gas and roaring out into the countryside, past the French fields in beautiful color on long straight roads lined with tall thin trees. Which crime is worse? To knock down a boy with an automobile or an old woman with a rock?

(Just then a young woman in slacks with a high-piled hairdo came slowly down the aisle. She stopped at my row and I was aware that she was looking at me. I refused to look at her—whatever you do don't give yourself away. After a moment she sat down a seat away from the aisle in the row in front of me. I wondered if I was cornered already, how could I get away now? Whoever would have expected them to send a woman after me?)

The father of the boy roars when he discovers his child's broken body and death, and gathers together his paternal love with all the impacted energy of his lifelong self-control into a lethal bomb of hate, vowing to pursue and find the killer of his son, so as to murder him in revenge. As his need for vengeance grew, I wanted to avoid him, though he remained before me, always in sight, making his plans. Timidly, I asked, wouldn't you think it was even worse to kill an old woman with a rock, because at least that was deliberate, whereas the death of the boy was an accident, and then he explained, the death of the boy was worse because the boy had a father who loved him with a love full of hatred ready to take vengeance on all his enemies, whereas who was there to avenge the death of an old woman in the woods?

(The woman in the row in front of me spent several minutes looking around at the other patrons in the theater—not just me but others too. She was chewing gum. It occurred to me she had a different aim—and I felt a thrust of excitement—but only for a moment. No, this was not the right time. I was still afraid to look at her and figured there was no point in taking unnecessary chances.)

He hunts me by trying to find in all the garages in the countryside a car with a crumpled right front fender or one whose such fender has recently been replaced. You would not expect such a hunt to succeed but there is a cinema tradition behind him that guarantees his success through a sequence of lucky accidents. He finds a girl connected to me, and through the girl he comes to me. I turn out to be the wealthy owner of a garage in western France. There he discovers the crumpled fender. He comes to the house for a visit with the girl, for I am her brother-in-law, and he makes his plans for taking vengeance upon me. I am loathsome. The girl hates me. Everyone in the family hates me. You want him to kill me. I want him to, against my will, because I am such a contemptible and vicious character. Yet when I struck the old pawn-broker woman with an axe I had rather magnificent ambitions, to prove what I was capable of. Yet that too was worse, wasn't it? I asked. Would it not be worse to go to the old woman's flat with a deliberate plan, hiding an axe under your coat, than simply to strike her on the head with a rock as you pass in the woods, without any thought in advance?

(Suddenly the woman in front got up and moved several rows down the aisle and took another seat. He could hardly see her now from where he sat. He wondered what was the matter with her.)

Everyone hates the garage owner so much that it is hard to remember who I am, the pursuer or the pursued. I know that everyone in the audience is pursuing me, and it is hard not to share their feeling and join in the chase. I live in the house now, pursuing him, making my plans, with the girl who does not know who I really am or what I really want, and I write notes in my diary and think deep about the trap that will best satisfy my need for vengeance. One day we are climbing a cliff by the sea, the others in the party some distance behind us, my victim and I close to the top. The photography from here, the color, is beautiful. Suddenly quite by accident my victim teeters, loses his balance, falls, hangs on by the fingertips dangling over the edge. All I need do is stamp on his fingers, make him let go. Yet something prevents me. I reach down and pull him to safety, postponing my revenge until another time. (So I asked him which kind of crime is worse. Is it worse to drown your mistress in a rowboat because she is pregnant and stands in the way of some deep yearning chance you have to rise in the world with the society girl . . . ? Crime of need because you can't stand the deprivation anymore. Or is it worse, I asked, to be mad with images of figure eights and loops, to seize your victim and tie her, spread out by hands and feet to four stakes in a field, and before you strangle her burn her skin with cigarette butts?)

He could not swim and I planned to take him out in a sailboat with me, to terrify him and play upon his pride and force him to take the tiller and to arrange for the boom to swing over and strike him and knock him into the sea. (Which is worse, to do it for vengeance, for some implacable hatred to make him pay for something he had done to you, or to do it to a person of total insignificance, without emotion, cool and calm and without plan, totally impulsive, for motives totally forgotten or purely literary?) Only he drew a gun on me and prevented my sailboat trick. (Which is worse, to be Hamlet pursuing Claudius, or Hamlet pursued by Laertes?) Instead I either abandoned my plans and someone else executed them or I did them and someone took the rap for them. He died of rat poison and I was seized by the police and questioned. (She asked which I would rather—to be pursued by the machine crunch of impersonal police, the computer efficiency of law, or to be the object of someone's bitter vengeance? To be hated so viciously, so bitterly? Which would you prefer, she asked?)

When the picture ended, he got up to leave. It was automatic, habit. As soon as he got into the aisle, it occurred to him—why leave now? A few more people were straggling into the theater, and no one else seemed to be leaving. Wouldn't it be safer just to remain here and see the movie again? But he was already in the aisle. He thought people would notice his indecision if he didn't go out. Besides, he did not think he could sit still that long. He thought the waste of time would make him sick, the nauseating idea of sitting through an ordinary movie two times in a row. Besides, he didn't seem to have any choice in the matter, having already got to his feet. He looked about and did not see the young woman in slacks anywhere. Was she a prostitute or a police snare? She had actually stared at him, a long stare demanding an answer that he had refused to give, and it made him tingle with a sense of either lost opportunity or narrow escape, he wasn't sure which.

He came into the lobby and saw with a shock that the game was up. He saw that the sidewalk and street outside the theater were illuminated by a great floodlight, bathing the whole scene in dazzling white light, and the crowd was there waiting for him, masses of people, curious faces, girls, old people, middle-aged, gathered against the glass looking into the lobby, looking for him to come out. He saw two policemen by the door watching him with guns drawn and handcuffs ready, and momently he recoiled, thinking to run back into the auditorium. For what? To be shot through the back like a fugitive? He remembered his dignity, and his general plan not to show anything, not to acknowledge a suspicion of guilt until forced. Pretend you don't know it is you they are after; if you are going to be caught, you are going to be caught. And then oddly enough, the two policemen, as soon as they saw him, turned away as if they did not want him to know they had been looking at him, and they hid their guns and handcuffs somewhere, for when he looked at them he could no longer see them. And as if by the same signal, the crowd too seemed to turn away, the masses that had been crowded by the window turned and started to walk away and then there were just a lot of people walking by with shopping bags pretending not to see what was coming through the lobby of the theater, or as if they did not even know there was a theater there. And by the time he got to the door and saw that the floodlight was only his error for the sunlight of midday, for he had forgotten that it was still only morning when he went into the theater, the two policemen seemed to have disappeared altogether, and he was allowed to go through the door onto the street without being stopped, and to mingle in the crowd, and no one paid any attention to him, and he realized that he had not been recognized yet. Then I told him, almost angry—I said, Damn fool, you got to watch that kind of thing, the literary tradition is making you hallucinate and behave irrationally, exactly what I warned you against. You have got to keep your mind on the facts and trust to the facts as you understand them.

Facts: The only known witness was the old woman herself and she is gone. No one else saw Ralph Burr as he climbed the steps or emerged from them, as far as is known. There is no other way in which he might be tracked down, for he has said nothing to anyone to connect him to the crime nor would anyone think of any reason for connecting him with either the crime or the victim. In this downtown crowd furthermore he is unlikely to be recognized even as Professor Burr, much less as a man who was walking in Burnet Woods this morning. The important thing is to remember such facts and keep your head.

Since it was two o'clock in the afternoon he went into a counter restaurant and had a hamburger and a piece of pie. The plump waitress in a dirty white uniform gave him his plate without looking at him and went back to talk to the other waitress at the other end. A workman with glasses was eating, a few seats away. No one paid any attention to anybody else. As I ate I decided to go home, go to the house and stay there for the rest of the day. It was as if I had to go through a probationary period before I could resume a normal life, and while I was in it everything was a crisis.

I went to the bus stop. I saw the afternoon paper for sale at a stand next to the bus stop. I glanced at the headlines without appearing to look at them—they had something to do with school taxes. I wanted to see the paper but I did not dare buy one, as if that would betray to the onlookers too great an interest in the murder. I told him that was ridiculous, but I still did not buy a paper—this time because I knew that a paper would be delivered to the house later this afternoon anyway.

The bus left the downtown section and climbed the hill and passed the university. I looked out the window as we went by Burnet Woods. I could see the students' cars parked at the top of the hill where the circle was, but the woods and the steps were on the other side of the hill. I saw two kids playing frisbie on the grass, but I saw no signs of police or other evidence of crime. I asked him if he thought a crime in the park might not even have been discovered yet, and he said it certainly ought to have been discovered by now, for there would have been a lot of people in the park on a day like this and a lot of people would have used those steps.

Lots of people on those steps shocked him with a sudden horror at the risk he had taken, to strike with that rock outdoors in full view of anyone who might easily have appeared at the top of the steps at just that minute or at any time within the next three minutes or however long it was to drag her off the steps and into the bushes. That terrible moment of exposure, which never even seemed to have occurred to him at the time, as if he had supposed he were acting under a charm and nothing could possibly happen to him.

Retrospective fear that almost shocked his breath away. When he got off the bus, it seemed to turn into another kind of fear, a future fear that seemed to be waiting for him ahead at his house. Not so strong as the shock he had been experiencing earlier, but it was there just the same, too strong simply to be talked away by reference to the facts. I turned into my street, saw my big white empty house up ahead, halfway up the block. Still there, waiting for me, animals inside. As long as there wasn't anybody else inside. That's what he was afraid of—the police at the movie theater had decided it would be more discreet to arrest him at his house. Again it was a question of dignity and doing nothing to invite suspicion before suspicion had been actually displayed. I walked on toward the house. Fingers trembling as I looked in the mailbox. Three routine bills, nothing else. Found key, unlocked door. Came into the house. The spaniel greets me. A cat upon the stairs. The quiet stillness of the house after half a day of disuse.

I locked the front door behind me and went into my study and sat down at my desk. The window looked out upon the lawn and the street. Thinking, better asylum than a movie theater. For one more month, at any rate.

Chapter 8

My study, next to the front door of the house. My chair, by the desk, swivels so that when I look up from the desk I can look out the window to the front lawn. The desk in my study, the most familiar place for my privacy, for secluding myself, anywhere in the world except the bed where I sleep. On my desk, a brown leather blotter, a tray with papers, class notes, notes for the article I was working on. The pile of papers of the manuscript of the book that I have been working on for seven years. A box with addresses on cards. A pile of books. Desk lamp with a shade. Stapler, a bowl with stamps, paper clips, coins, rubber bands. A paperweight shaped like an owl. Pens, pencils, a pair of scissors. A magnifying glass. Drawer open at left containing a box of typing paper. Pictures of Cynthia and the children, Harold and Elaine, temporarily knocked over by the overflow pile of papers in the tray. I remembered my promise to be all moved out by the end of the month, because the Benjamins—but that was another question and I forgot. I brought a coffee cup from the kitchen to my desk, and I sat down and leaned back in the chair with it. A stained coffee cup and spoon remained on the desk where I had left them from yesterday. He asked what I was going to do now, was I just going to sit there and lean back in my chair and loaf and let the time pass, and I said I thought maybe I would try to get some work done, try to get back to normal as quickly as possible. He said, Is that possible, and I said, Everything depends on my getting back to normal, my survival itself depends upon it, as if nothing had ever happened this morning. Then he said, How is it possible? and I said, It will have to be, why can't it be? and he said, What is normal? How do you know it is normal if a thing like this morning is so out of keeping with it?

Then he told me it wouldn't work. I began to tremble. Why not? I said. He said, You're doomed. No one will believe you. Why won't they believe me, I said. They won't believe it is possible, he said, they will be absolutely unable to square what you did this morning with what you are, what you always have been. They'll have to square it, I said. It happened and that makes it your problem, to make it square with everything else.

He said, This morning in the woods, you picked up a rock and bashed an old woman on the back of the head so hard you crushed the skull and certainly killed her. This makes you a criminal, a killer, a murderer. It does not square, it cannot be reconciled by any means whatever with what you have always purported to be—not with any of the kinds you have always claimed to be.

He told me, When Ralph Burr was a child he was always gentle and shy. He did not fight with the other boys but tried always to be reasonable and be a peacemaker, and he was respected for this by his friends, admired and listened to because he spoke such good sense about the disputes that arose. And he was a good boy, always, not in an offensive and priggish manner, not in such a way as to enable him to sneer and look down upon others, but because he genuinely and honestly yearned to be good, to do things that made him feel good about himself and would please his parents and his friends too if they could be pleased. When he was sixteen he escorted his old half-blind grandmother on the Pullman train all the way to the town in Vermont where she was to spend the summer with friends. Though he was not a leader and did not stand out among his peers, older people, teachers and grandparents, aunts and uncles, and friends of his parents, liked him and trusted him, called him sensitive and intelligent and sometimes even a sweet boy. And when he went to college he majored in English because he liked fiction and poetry (because, someone once said, he liked reading about the ways things looked and felt to people rather than about the way things actually were) and after the graduation and after the war he went on with his career, which was respectable and modest, exactly what his grandparents and parents could most easily approve: he earned first an A.B., then an M.A., and then a Ph.D., and he became first an instructor, then an assistant professor, then an associate professor, and finally, not long ago, a full professor. His name appeared now and then in small print in bibliographical lists; he was slightly known among students of romanticism; he was a suitably dull teacher, admired chiefly by graduate students and the better undergraduates who recognized the soundness of his scholarship and the extent of his knowledge within his field. (He made no claims to knowing anything about any other field.) He was known for being scholarly, rational, judicious, sensible. He served on committees, always quietly, and he always cast his vote with the majority.

So how, he asked, do you expect me to reconcile the bloody attack upon an unknown old woman in the park, this violent eruption of volcanic impulse, with the scholarly life of the mind of timid, reasonable Ralph Burr, who teaches literature courses to college undergraduates and graduate students?

He explained to me that the problem would not be in making them believe in the crime—you always make people believe in a crime, he said, for no crime, unfortunately, is beyond the scope of human imagination once you observe that it has been committed: this crime in the woods was done—all you need to say is that it was done and you did it, and they will believe you. The problem is to make them believe that you, Ralph Burr, are still the same person you were thought to be before the crime became known. The timid, gentle, scholarly professor, living his life of the mind.

Not so timid after all, I guess, hey? It's not exactly timid to pick up a rock and bring it down bash on someone's head—a forthright and assertive, let us say aggressive, act—so the timidity must have been some kind of a screen, some kind of a game you were playing, he said, with the ultimate aim of bringing people into range so you could go bang bash upon their heads, is that it? Even more so the sentimental gentleness, now more than ever disclosed as hypocritical distraction from the hard reality of your soul: pat the cat, play with the dog, to conceal the violent motion of your blood stream. As for the scholarliness, now of course the whole world will know what it means, this meticulous digging into old papers and books, leavings of another age, now dead, as if to live where life no longer is, all in the most orderly manner, this meticulous arranging of dead details, of counters in orders alphabetical or chronological or otherwise schematic—files and systems, cabinets full of the fragmented remains of what used to be life: scholarship like an enormous engineering job, a great trestle skirting a mountain canyon. They will take it as proof you were living on the brink of violence, chaos, destruction: road and railroad building in the Swiss Alps. And the life of the mind. Which we have always advertised to students and defended from philistines, from demagogues, from populist newspapers, as the best life, the most human life, the most evolutionary advanced life, the only life that is fully life. But they will say that this your life of the mind was a life of only half a mind, and they will look back at you and remember all those closed things that you had so contemptuously blocked off, they will note your failures at home, your failure to save your wife and children, your detachment from students, your habit of withdrawing from the society of others, your guardedness and reserve, and they will chatter vindictively as if vindicated about the other half of your mind that you had supposedly ignored, buried in a cage like a wild animal growing and growing and growing until suddenly it had to burst the bars and break loose. And that, they will say, is that for your life of the mind.

He said, You can lose your tenure for this.

The black-and-white cat jumped up on my desk and sat down on a pile of notes. (Blake? Wordsworth?) Began washing her face with her paw. Old maid cat, fixed like all the animals in this house. Good friend of mine for several years, dating back, with connections with Cynthia, with Elaine, Harold, even Mother and Father. I patted her head with my left hand. Then, remembering, I turned and patted her with my right hand, instead, the hand that had picked up the rock full of fossils. I patted the head of my old black-and-white cat with the hand that had smashed down the rock full of fossils, and she purred.

Then he asked me—just as he used to ask me long ago, and as he had asked me this morning—could you do it? Is it possible? Could you pick up the rock, or in this case the paperweight, and bring it down on the cat's head as hard as you struck with the rock this morning? Kill the kitty? I exclaimed. Why should I do that? Felt the muscles tighten in my hand with the thought—if not strike, strangle—and my control over them strengthen as I patted the cat still more deliberately, lovingly, poor kitty, oh no, how could I think of such a, oh poor old trusting big old good old kitty, stretching its head up to accentuate the voluptuousness of being stroked, flipping its ears against my fingers. Well, save the kitty then, he said—only think how much less drastic it would have been, if instead of what you did, you had thought of. But suppose I had, I said, how could I have faced myself, the horror, the shock to find myself having done such a thing? How could I have borne such knowledge of myself?

Perhaps you have always borne it, he said. Ask him—are there analogies? Are there comparable cases to help me judge how it would look to people? Is there record anywhere in the history of this world of a professor of English who bashed an old woman in the woods with a rock? Is there a professor of English anywhere in history who has committed a murder of any kind? A professor of any kind? Not the stereotypes of fiction, not the sinister villains of detective stories, selected for the very incongruity of their images (Professor Moriarty?)—but real professors in real historical fact? Or deans? Or doctors? He remembers a murdering doctor or two, yes. Vague dim recollections of crimes of passion and plotting, sensational trials of years gone by, quickly forgotten. But literary people, living the life of the mind? He remembers the trouble of Mary Lamb. They were sympathetic about that, weren't they? Madness —that is what they shall call it. That is how they shall get their hands around it, this jelly blob of chaos, to attach a name to it and form a judgment on it. That will be the charitable, compassionate view—if you can make them buy it.

So then I told him—told *them,* all of them—about my history of madness, which I remembered now after years of forgetting, the fears that haunted my mind so tangibly during the ripening years of my youth, and so censoriously forgotten since then. Told him how it was at some age of adolescent boyhood, maybe thirteen, maybe fifteen, how amid all the diary jottings of routine and success, crowded in among the wishful memories of happy childhood and beautiful vacation world, woven like a dark thread soon to disappear in the brighter tangle of groping successes and failures of staggering growth—I had this constant dark fear that I might not make it, that I would be cast off or cast myself off, quite by accident, and left to die. This was, I remember, while I was going to school, while I was passing and getting sometimes good sometimes mediocre grades in courses like geometry and chemistry and English, while I went out in the afternoons to play baseball with friends and practiced pitching, sometimes mastering and sometimes failing to master my fast ball and my curve, while I went on vacations to the beach and learned to swim awkwardly and took my father and mother out in a rented sailboat, sailed in a rudimentary manner, while I discussed careers with Berthold and couldn't make up my mind, and listened to music and felt torn apart by it and worried about what I liked and what happened when things I liked suddenly seemed to lose their power and became almost like nausea, and worried about the mixture of nausea and attraction in so many things, like pieces of music known too well and sometimes thoughts of girls I knew, while I hesitated to make dates with girls and sometimes did and kept close track of everything that happened, worrying about what I should expect and what was expected of me . . . While all this was going on, in memories of clear skies over a beach, white sand on the beach, and a summer cabin with splintery unfinished beams, and lying in bed by a screen with mosquitoes on the outside buzzing against the screen looking for an opening, and my hand under the sheet down in the opening of my pajamas doing stealthy work while I conjured up images of lovely girls and wondered how many years I would have to wait . . . While all this, which was the standard stock and stuffing of ordinary remembrance of those times (so many years ago), recoverable at will, there was also just as vivid but not so well remembered this black other fear, fear of the other side, that I wouldn't make it.

Explain it. Life was an intricate succession of branching roads and for every minor as well as major success or achievement there was a contrary road in the opposite direction that you might have slipped into, most of which went over a cliff. Quite apart from the routine and ordinary chances of everyday, such as the question of whether you would pass this or that examination or this or that course or whether you would get through high school or whether you would get a date with Ann Foley, there was the much bigger question of whether you would survive at all. Nor was this merely a question of escaping the hazards that everyone acknowledges, that we all talk about with our fingers crossed—accidents with the car, death in war, house burning down, dread diseases, not to mention such mishaps we are all subject to such as going blind or deaf or being disfigured or maimed. The blacker fear was one that nobody else I knew seemed to admit or to share—the fear that through some folly of my own I would banish myself from the society of people, or lose my freedom or lose my substance. Through some stupidity of mine, or some incompetence, or some panic, or greed, or cowardice, or impulse, I was acutely sensitive to every new instance that came to my attention, in the streets or through reading, of the multitudes of disasters that had struck people—panhandlers, drug addicts, prisoners—and every such disaster looked like a trap waiting for me. It seemed like an obstacle course, I thought my chances to escape disaster of some sort were no better than even, no better than fifty-fifty—indeed there was a time during those years (even while things on the surface appeared to be going smoothly with constantly expanding horizons) when it seemed to me impossible that I should get through life without putting in time, probably a lot of time, in a prison cell, for who knows what sort of reasons? Inevitable, I thought, because who knew what powers or desires or failings or illnesses lay yet concealed behind the as yet unopened doors of my inner mind? I mean—tell them—I for sure didn't know. You forget, when you grow older and you have pretty well discovered what you are likely for, you forget those adolescent years when it was a real question, like whether you would run in battle, or would you betray a friend under pressure, would you crack up in a crisis, would you connive, would you break important rules for some end if you knew you weren't being watched, would you do even worse things—along with all those other questions of what *could* you do or what were you incapable of, too weak for—and for none of those questions did you have any answers, and you had simply nothing to do but wait to find out.

So it was that I thought it extremely likely that at some time in the future under some paralysis of will, I would find myself unemployed and unemployable, begging small change for a bite to eat from strangers on a big city sidewalk. I saw myself picked up and thrown in jail in small towns on charges of vagrancy. I got hooked on drugs (you never can be too careful—beware, they reach out and grab you with their hooks when you aren't looking, when you are going around corners), and had to hold up jewelry stores in order to support my habit. That was why I was in jail, trouble compounded when I panicked and killed the jeweler one time when he tried to resist.

How hard it would be (I thought in those days) to ward off the insistent claims of disaster—especially when they sit within you, right in your own blood, inhabiting your mind, waiting for the moment when you relax guard, let the sentry doze for half a second, during which . . .

When I was thirteen or fourteen or fifteen (tell them this) I used to be afraid that I would kill my father or mother. My beloved father, my dear sweet mother. Not from hate, not from anger, not from any discernible motive of hostility or antagonism, but in simplest cool, killing. Correct that, too, as I lay in bed on cool summer nights in the cabin in the mountains while they lay in bed in their own room across the hall, and I clutched and held myself to the bed in so tight a grip it ached, in order to withstand the force that was trying to make me get up and kill them in their bed. Correct the coolness—not coldness of feeling either, that I feared would kill them, but my fear itself: fearing that I would kill them by the very force of that fear itself. As if the fear of doing it could make me do it. As if the mere observation that a thing so terrible was possible—it could be done—were enough to make me fear the doing, and once my mind had fixed on the fear, then the fear itself became the motive, as if I were doomed to do whatever I was afraid of doing. No doubt I feared this particular disaster because I thought it was the worst thing that could happen to me and the only question concerned the decision as to what was worst.

In that cabin in the mountains, when we had all gone to bed early and there was still light in the sky, I felt this fear. I heard them sleeping in the next room, through the thin summer-vacation walls, and I felt the fear tugging at me to get me to rise, to tiptoe to their door, to slip in, to leap and strangle before resistance could begin. I felt the temptation to put my foot out of my bed, to step on the floor, just to see if I could take this first step, and I fought against taking it, because I feared that if I allowed myself to take even that one little step, just in experiment, then nothing would prevent me from taking all the rest. And the worst of it was that the whole project was an experiment—fantasy answer to the fantasy question, *could you do it?*—with the great fear that the answer might be *yes*.

Felt it that summer also on the mountain itself, when we were climbing, my father and I, and he was happy to take his son up this same mountain that he had climbed as a young man years before, and I was happy to be so taken, to be honored like this, and we sat on a rock near the top and talked about many things, and we seemed very close. In spite of which, when we climbed a little higher, and I stood behind him and saw him standing close to the edge of a cliff, looking out at the mountains across the valley and naming them for me, I felt this same fear of the terrible: how easy it would be now to make a quick rush, to send him down a thousand feet by a light push—though I loved my father and felt closer to him than I ever had before and supposed his death to be the worst loss I could possibly imagine. Oh if I were to do such a thing then I would follow him over, myself, I told myself, for what could life be thereafter except to complete the destruction?

Other times, too: in the New York City subway platform with a train approaching and I became aware of the enormous consequences of a light but decisive push, and I backed away, back almost to the wall with the gum machines, to avoid the temptation. In those days moments of violence suggested themselves often: as I helped my father mend the back steps and I stood with the hammer in my hands while he bent down to take measurements; as we stepped into the rented sailboat from the rowboat in the summer at the beach; as I backed the car out of the garage at home while he waited by the garden. Always it was a question of fixing a grip on my muscles so that they would do only the mechanical things, the right and proper programmed things, and not those other things that my fear told me were just as easy, requiring no more exertion, no more effort. If I could drive a nail with that hammer, could I not also drive something else, and how were the muscles of my hand to know the difference except by the severity of the orders that I gave them?

Tell how I imagined then the authorities questioning me—for of course once such a deed was done, I would not dream of concealing it. If I had killed my father or mother (it would have to be both because I could not face the reproach of the one I had not killed), of course I would surrender at once to the punitive agents, of course I would tell them (through my tears) what I had done, of course I would offer no excuses, no alibis, avoiding such easy way-outs as saying "I blacked out," (which I had seen once some murderer offer as his excuse)—no, I did not black out, but at the same time, I would insist, I did not want to do it, I felt no hatred, no resentment, no anger, no motive, I could not help it, it was something inside me compelling me against my will, and your job is to take me and shut me up and put me on bread and water, blind me if you like, let me speak to no one or be spoken to by none, keep me in an isolated cell for the rest of my days.

In those days that fear was so strong, when it came over me, that I did not see how it could fail to be fulfilled, and I considered myself a doomed damned soul at the age of thirteen, even while everybody was saying what a nice sweet gentle intelligent sensitive boy I was growing up to be. How guilty I felt that they should think me so, and how I tried to encourage it! And then gradually, almost without my realizing it, my fear began to sink and get buried beneath the crystallizations of adulthood: I forgot the crimes and the violent cutting off from the world of men that I had so dreaded, and I actually began to believe that I really was the nice sweet gentle intelligent sensitive young man they said I was.

Imagined disasters became on the one hand less and less drastic and on the other less and less personal. In place of strangling them in bed, I feared that our carelessness would get Cynthia pregnant. In place of pushing him over the cliff, I felt a terror lest I should be paralyzed and unable to speak during my doctoral oral examination. Fear that I would stop doing work, that I would become lazy, start spending evenings watching television instead of studying or doing the research and preparations that my career demanded. Fear that I would forget to pay the mortgage and lose the house. Fear that I would accidentally say something insulting to Elias or something cruel to Cynthia, my wife—something worse than she could finally bear. And instead of personal torture and blinding and incarceration in a stony cell, my disasters, now less personal, came from the clouds, from enemy missiles and nuclear weapons, or from the pollution of hydrocarbons or sulfides, or oxygen starvation because all the little oxygen-making creatures in the surface of the sea have been poisoned by mercury and oil spills.

I thought my fear of pure violence in myself was merely a function of my not yet knowing who I was. I thought that becoming a professor of English and all that goes with that—husband, father, houseowner, all of it—had given the decisive answer to that question and the fear had vanished forthwith.

Only occasionally nowadays was I reminded of it, most rarely, if I happened to notice some unchecked opportunity for the exercise of pure violent power. Usually it was only a reminder of what I once had felt: "in those days I would have been afraid of an opportunity like this." So it was, for instance, two weeks ago, when I was walking through Burnet Woods, going up the steps in the woods and met, coming down, that extremely small and frail old woman. I knew her slightly—we had met before—we recognized each other, but this did not prevent her from showing fear in her eyes as she passed me on the steps. Perhaps it was her fear that reminded me—made me think of my old fears, not with fear now but curiosity—and I recognized the isolateness of our meeting and how easy it would be. I nodded to her and we passed, and I noticed a rock on the ground near by, and I watched her as she went down the steps, and I was annoyed with her for being afraid of me. And then two or three days later we met again at the same place, at the same time. And even though we had passed successfully the other time, and surely by now she had been able to remember who I was, still she showed the same fear as we passed, even more obvious, it seemed to me, than it had been before, and as I watched her going down the steps after we passed, I felt quite angry with her for being afraid of me. And in days following we passed on two other mornings before our meeting this morning, so we both knew that there was a routine or a habit that tended to bring us together at that time, and I was reminded every time of my childish fear of such opportunities, and she showed her fear of me each time, to make me more and more angry with her (the insult, the disregard of my role, my credentials, the slot I fill in the structure of this world)—until this morning when for the first time she seemed to show no fear.

So that obviously—tell him—my fears were justified, that was a real force in me that was threatening, with real power, and it was always there, remaining there, a wild animal, even when I had civilized myself to the point of blandness, waiting for a chance or an invitation, striking out quickly, suddenly, when no one was looking. The difference between now and then, those days of adolescent terror, was that I was determined now to outlive it, if I could, without succumbing to the indignity of panic. Especially as I had not destroyed anyone close to me as I had always originally feared. So I asked myself, why should I let one insane moment in the woods destroy my life?

It means that now I wait here, wait for the wake to clear, and I have and shall always have within me in the future a deep secret—knowledge of a major fact unknown to any other person. Trusting to my cultivated belief that the natural world remains always a natural world, that forces of retribution and nemesis are literary traditions and products of man's imagination but no necessary part of natural law, that if no one saw me when I killed the old woman, and I committed no stupid mistake to give myself away, then no one now or ever hereafter can see into me into my secret. Waiting to find out if that is possible. If I can keep that secret all my life. To see if it is true that we are all equal in the woods of the world. Does retribution pursue the fox that kills a squirrel? The unwatched life of the woods, the only ultimate record the fossil track in stone, which tells you, perhaps, some of those who lived here once, but never never tells you what happened to them. So I shall wait, trusting to my humanist faith that I am unwatched by any save myself, unwatched like a wild animal in the woods, like a weasel or a fox. And if it shocks me so much to realize what I have done, making me suppose

I am thereby at last actually the outcast I used to fear I would become, let me apply my intelligence and ask myself why I should be such. If they don't catch me—to put it in the bluntest possible way—why should I consider myself outcast? Why might I not go on living amongst us as before, like the rest of us? Why not? If I were an outcast, merely because my shock and my images of order say I am, then who else may not also be, living among us without saying a word?

Wait, wait, for a little time to pass. Not to let it blow over, exactly, for I don't suppose you can say that murders blow over—but the pressure on the mind can soften, memory can fade, time can pass. Just let this afternoon, this evening get by.

I saw Cynthia's face looking at me, and I asked: Did you ever imagine when you died, that you were leaving such things behind? Did you know the trouble I was coming to? Looked at her face but she only stared at me in her usual way, big-eyed wondering, always a little afraid. So I sat at my desk that afternoon, watching out the window the empty street, except when the children went by after school, and after a while the paper boy went by and flung the rolled up afternoon paper at my front door step. It bounced off and came to rest in the middle of the path, halfway to the street.

When he was out of sight, I went out to get the paper. He went out for it surreptitiously, guiltily, as if afraid to be seen, darting out to get it, darting back quickly to the house—even though I knew perfectly well that the act of going to bring in my own newspaper could not be construed other than innocently, even by the most suspicious of onlookers or readers.

Interesting how quickly you can scan a whole page and pages when you are looking for some specific urgent thing. I saw in an instant that there was no news about my crime—which could only mean that they had not yet discovered the body by the time the paper went to press. It was disappointing, and then I went back to the late bulletin item in small but heavy black print, two paragraphs at the bottom of the front page.

MAN FOUND DEAD
IN BURNET WOODS

The body of an elderly man was
found close to a nature trail in
school children on a nature walk
Burnet Woods park this morning by
from Clifton School. He appeared
to have been killed by a blow on
the head only minutes before the
body was found, about 9:50 A.M.
Police theorized that robbery was
The victim was tentatively
73, of 963 Terrace Ave. An empty
identified as Andrew Kirschner,
wallet was found close to the
longed to the victim. The kil-
body. The wallet apparently be-
ling took place close to the spot
where a woman was murdered by
the strangler five years ago.
the motive

He tried to remember. He remembered the clock when he came into McMicken Hall. It was then 9:48 A.M. So that he must have passed by the place where the elderly man was killed at about 9:38, either before or after or within minutes of the time the murder had taken place. Filled him with fright. Might have been himself. Then he checked his hip pocket to make sure his wallet was still there. Yes. He tried to remember. A man named Andrew Kirschner, 73, of 963 Terrace Avenue. He tried to remember. And then he remembered, yes, as he started to climb the steps up through the woods, puffing, he looked up and saw starting down at the top a small figure, an old man in a shabby black overcoat coming down in slow small steps, two steps and a half step down, two steps and a half step down, while Burr slowly climbed, thir-ty-four, thir-ty-five, thir-ty-six, thir-ty-seven, remembering his fears coming back to him.

Part Two

Chapter 1

Naturally, when the protagonist of a novel has fallen out of character to commit an inexplicable crime of violence, he will have moments of fright afterwards. Partly it was the lines in the paper:

> An empty
> identified as Andrew Kirschner,
> wallet was found close to the
> longed to the victim. The kil-
> body. The wallet apparently be-
> ling took place close to the spot

Deciphering, the protagonist came up with the coded message: "An empty wallet . . . apparently belonging to the victim." Which was a great relief to somebody, if you could believe it. But why should it be coded, why should you have to decipher it? The hero told his narrator to suspect a trap there: only a guilty reader would take the trouble to decipher it. An innocent or ordinary reader would simply accept the incoherence as normal everyday life. But the protagonist of a novel would be obliged by literary tradition to decode the lines, thereby giving himself away by falling into the trap. If he then said that it was an *empty* wallet belonging to the *victim* he would prove himself to have decoded the message and thereby confirmed his guilt.

Whereby Ralph Burr came to the quick conclusion that the safe way was to assume that the opposite was true: "a wallet full of driver's license and credit cards, apparently belonging to the murderer, was found close to the body." But by God, if it were that clear, they should have caught him already—why hadn't they already come to get him? Quick, Burr reached for his wallet, only then remembering that he had just checked it a moment before. This time however, he took it into his hand to look at it, to make sure that it was indeed his wallet. And now at last, he realized, there was the question of his driver's license and all his credit cards to be checked out. Asked me reproachfully: Why didn't you remind me of this before? Why did you let me go through the day so bland and smug, never thinking to check what identification I had left behind? He opened his wallet and set them out on his desk, item by item, the contents: three ones, a five, and a ten. (Remembering, yes, I used my wallet to get into the movies, and used it again for lunch.) Two crumpled yellow deposit slips from the bank. An old receipt for American Express Traveler's Cheques dating from last summer. A crumpled slip of added prices from a grocery receipt. Then the cards: a general identification card:

RALPH H. BURR
3447 Byrd Avenue
. . .

In case of accident, please notify:
CYNTHIA BURR, same address
Or
ARTHUR BURR
Clinton, Vermont

Out of date. Then his faculty identification card (. . . is a fulltime member of the *Faculty* of the University of . . .), and his Operator's Driver's License, his Blue Cross/ Blue Shield card (Hospital Care Corporation, Ohio Medical Indemnity, Inc.), his membership card in the Association of American University Professors, his Public Library card, his automobile insurance card, and then the charge cards: Union 76,

Texaco, Mobil, Sohio, and of course, Master Charge. Jesus, he said to the narrator, with all that identification, how come they haven't caught me yet?

So I explained that what he had to worry about was not the identification he had now but what he had left behind at the scene of the crime. Did he still have in his wallet all the cards and other data that he had when he started out this morning? How can I remember that? he asked. Well, said the narrator, do you carry any other credit cards besides these? Burr couldn't remember. He didn't think he did, but of course he never could be sure which of his cards were supposed to have duplicates and which did not. I asked him how it could have got out of his wallet in any case, since the wallet itself remained inside his pocket. Advised him that the safety of the wallet was a pretty sure sign of the safety of its contents. Agreed that it was a pretty stupid thing to commit a murder while you are carrying so much identification, but he seemed to have gotten away with it and no need to panic now, for Christ sakes. Reminded him how swiftly and confidently he had checked his security at the time, after having dumped the body in the leaves, clearly remembering the almost automatic checking of his belongings by a swift pat of his hand, checking his wallet on his hip (yes), his glasses in his shirt pocket (yes), his keys in his pants' pocket (yes). Everything was where it belonged and he resumed his puffing way up the steps (for-ty-one, for-ty-two, for-ty-three), with perfect certainty, undoubted conviction that he had left nothing behind and if he could get to the top of the steps unobserved he would get away free. Told him now, if you had such confidence then, there must have been a reason, you must have checked soundly and efficiently, and you knew what you were doing.

Still, the protagonist would be only temporarily relieved, as his mind began to sail off into a great new arc of panic on the question of his confidence so stupid as not even to look around in the leaves to see if he had dropped anything—as if he had a charm protecting him. Panic soaring like a gull now as he tried to remember everything he had with him at the time, and realized that the only way to be safe was to take two inventories: an inventory of everything he was carrying when he set out from the house this morning, to be compared with an inventory of everything he had with him now. For whose wallet was it, he asked, if it wasn't mine? They found a wallet, the paper says so. "Probably belonging to the victim"—but how do I know, unless I can prove it wasn't mine? My old one, that I replaced last December? Did I really take it out of my suit? Or was it rather something else, some other object that I might have been carrying, mistaken by the police (deliberately to catch the decipherers of code?) for a wallet? No no, irrational, says the narrator. Even so, said Burr, you need two inventories, one before and one after.

And began at once on the easier of the two, the inventory of everything he had with him now. Went to his coat and emptied the pockets: his gloves, a pair of theater-ticket stubs, a crumpled pack of cigarettes with three cigarettes left. A brown university envelope, interoffice mail, folded in half with his name on it. This one gave him a shock: suppose they found it? Asked, could they track him down from theater-ticket stubs? Guessed that was not likely. What about the receipt for a restaurant bill, that he also found in his pocket? Also shreds of other more ancient tickets and receipts, transparent plastic wrappings of gone cigarette packs, the shredded remains of an actual cigarette, flakes of tobacco, tiny balls of paper—pockets full of guilt.

Forcefully the narrator tried to seize his mind, insisting that anything he found now, in his coat, his suit, his house, was not left behind to incriminate him. And there was no conceivable earthly way for him to find the things that would incriminate him, and no possible way for him to make this morning's inventory now in the late afternoon. And still failed to soothe him for more than a moment, as Burr now suddenly thought of the incriminating shoeprints he must have left behind. Shoeprints, bootprints, surely no one ever committed a murder in the woods without leaving prints behind in the mud? Remember, was there mud? With a desperate gesture, Burr raised his foot and took off first one then the other shoe. Looked at the soles for signs of mud. The soles smooth and hard. The heels were what he had to fear, they made a print. No mud, though. No relief, either, stupid, remembering what these shoes had done since they had stepped in the mud by the body, if there was any mud—shoes that had climbed the steps and walked across the meadow, wiping off any mud they might have gathered on the grass, or if not on the grass then on the slick tile floors of the university buildings, or on the steps of the bus or the carpet of the movie theater or the sidewalks of downtown. Long time and many surfaces to remove any mud that might have clung to his shoes to tell him that he had stepped in the mud and left his print indelible and final where the old woman/-man lay dead. And there is nothing you can do about it now, said the narrator. Except throw them out on the chance, said Burr. And he held them in his hand, his good shoes, wondering for a moment if the risk were bad enough to justify throwing them out—and held back, as if reasonable again, saying let's wait a little before doing such a drastic thing. Besides, if you throw them out they'll look in your garbage cans and find out that you tried to throw them out.

If not mud, blood. This was even worse, a new sailing curve of terror as he recalled suddenly how insouciantly he had disregarded the danger of being spattered by blood when he struck and afterwards when he dragged him/her into the bushes. Remembering, of course that was why he had dragged him with such indignity by the feet, so as not to risk touching the bloody mess. And no doubt that had left a trail of blood in the dust from the steps into the bower of leaves. But how could he have been so sure that he had not been touched somewhere on his clothing by blood, that he had not carried it in full view of all strangers and friends during his wanderings of this day, the classic betrayal of the murderer by literary tradition? So he checked again, spent a half hour examining his shoes, his coat, his suit, his shirt for some sign of blood, and found himself, extraordinarily yet apparently, truly clean.

But there was still the problem of the old woman/old man mixup, which he tried once again to solve, to find the trick or the trap in it. Why did they say, why did the newspaper insist so that it was an old woman who had been murdered when he knew perfectly well, could remember perfectly clearly, that it was an old man? Why did they insist that it was a very small little old woman with a round face, with thin white curly hair with little white ringlets on top, when he remembered with absolute concrete vividness and clarity that it was an old man, dressed all in dark gray, very short, hunched forward, bareheaded with short white hair, a broad hawklike mouth and little eyes looking up at him suspiciously and full of hate? Remembered his shabby trousers, his plain black shoes, his gray socks, as he picked up his feet to drag him into the woods. Remembered the indentation in the head, the staining of the hair, the muddy brown-and-red mess all through the back of his head by the time he got him into the leaves? What was the matter with them, couldn't they read sexes, couldn't they tell an old man from an old woman?

Obviously, said Burr to the narrator, this is their trickiest trick of all. They want to catch me up. They print it wrong because they expect me to be outraged by the mistake. They want me to come in and say, How come you said an old woman was killed when it was really an old man? And then they will say, but Professor Burr, how do you happen to *know* it was really an old man? And that way they'll have me, you see? said Burr. So obviously the thing to do is to pay no attention, pretend you didn't notice, pretend you don't know any better. If they say it was an old woman, pretend it really was an old woman, and that way they'll know you couldn't possibly have done it.

Just then I began to feel it again, for the second day in a row. I had gone back to my desk, and sat there, still unable to work, leaning forward a little, and I felt it, that same unmistakable harshness in my chest. Second day in a row, fifth or sixth time in the last two months, and no longer had track of how many times all together since the first one more than two years ago. Started with that familiar harshness that began to deepen then and become a clutch on my breathing—not hard yet, just a little persistent, what would not simply go away by sitting up straight and taking a few deep breaths. I sat up straight and took deep breaths but the feeling of being out of breath increased and deepened, a progression unmoved by any of the natural things I did to alleviate it. Then, just like yesterday in the office, I felt as parched and starving for breath as if I had been running twenty laps around a track, gasping and reaching and wracked all through my lungs yet unable to attain relief. Turning into pain, too, pain in my chest and spreading up into my throat and after a while leftward through my shoulder into my arm.

The familiar literary and classic symptoms for the heart. I knew them before and I knew them now, though no doctor had ever been able to pin them down. Tell the narrator how it frightened me as long as it grew, though the repetitions of the phenomena and the usual innocuous doctor's explanations had snubbed down my fears somewhat. Still, it adds to your sense of doom while it continues to advance. And I wondered if this was to be my doom after all.

I stood up. I went and leaned against the wall trying to make my body as straight as I could. I had learned from the first time not to lie down, for that made it if not worse at least more alarming. I saw the crest coming, I felt the crest passing, I recognized the first delicate signs that the flood that was making me gasp was beginning to subside. With this a great relief in the mind, and then the symptoms began to fade, the pain disappeared, my breath caught up, and I felt normal again—or even better than normal in that first surge of normal joy in my veins.

The doctor called it a cardiospasm, since there wasn't anything else to call it. I had had several cardiograms after the other times and always the tracing was normal, giving me no clue as to what was wrong. So the doctor called it a cardiospasm, suggesting that a bubble of gas had been pressing on the cardiac nerve, slowing down the heart and giving me a scare, but nothing to worry about. Since Natalie Fleet drove me to the doctor after yesterday's spasm and I had another negative cardiogram, I figured there was no point in going to the doctor again today. Nothing to worry about. Tell the narrator I believed it, but I didn't really believe it. Of course there was something to worry about. Of course I was doomed. A fire inside myself or a rock full of fossils bounding down a rocky slope in the woods. Occurred to me, they would never go after a man who was having a heart attack.

The narrator told him to pull himself together. The only way was to be fatalistic. If he had left any clues behind, any credit cards or theater tickets, shoeprints or cardiogram tracings, trust to it, soon they would come and get him, and nothing he could do would prevent it. If he had not left anything, no one would suspect him if he went about his business in the ordinary way. Allowing that if you are not doomed one way you are probably doomed in the other way, and there's always some kind of doom waiting for you somewhere, said the omniscient all-wise commentating narrator, the only reasonable course for someone named Burr is to go about his business in the ordinary way.

What this meant right now was to go out to the restaurant for dinner.

After dinner it would be nice to get his mind off things by going to a movie, but since he had already done that today, I decided to spend the evening at home and see if I could loosen up enough for a little scholarly work.

Chapter 2

The narrator said that each hour that passed uncaught was another step to safety. So that when Burr returned to his house after supper and found it still unguarded by policemen, he felt proportionately more secure than when he had returned to the house from downtown this afternoon. Let time pass quickly, he almost said, except for the other thing, that reminder of doom that he had felt this afternoon again to make it two days in a row, that medically harmless (they say) whisper from passing time to tell you that each hour that passes is an hour less to go. Let time go slowly, he almost said—only not yet, not quite yet, let me get past this and *then* go slowly.

I decided to sit on the front porch for a while after getting home. In the slowly fading light, I brought the wicker chair out to the little porch by the front door and sat in it. Courageously, for though the front of the house was shaded by a maple tree, the porch was visible to the houses next door and the houses across the street, and sitting on the porch, *he* was visible, and in his present situation he knew that it took courage to allow himself to be seen, especially on the porch of his own house where it would be so easy to identify him on sight: That must be Ralph Burr, sitting on the porch, since that's his house. I leaned back in the wicker chair and smoked a cigarette, dropping the ashes on the floor (dusty—no one does much cleaning around here since I have been living alone). Watched my neighbor Schultz three lawns away to the right washing his car in the dimming twilight. Saw three kids further down the street tossing a softball and failing to catch it, running to chase it under parked cars along the curb. Heard a power mower droning away behind me in the next block. Listened for birds, the cardinal singing loud and clearly in the tree in front, the chirring loud insistent whistle of a carolina wren, the tufted titmouse in the back yard with its loud dog-calling whistle. Listened for the baroque melody of the wood thrush, which for me was always the main theme of spring finally coming in after much preparation, but it was still too early in the season for that. And meanwhile the dimming light, the streetlights going on. And always the noise of the cars and trucks on the big city thoroughfares a few blocks away in all directions.

Regret selling the house to the Benjamins? No time for regret in our present crisis. The damn telephone. Alien sound of inner cellular life, breaking weakly but nervous and insistent out into the evening air where it mingles with the profound sounds of birds and traffic and machinery and games. It took Burr a moment to realize that it was his own phone ringing, heard outdoors unfamiliarly through his living room window. Startled him then as sharply as if it were an alarm clock, and he felt—yes—the momentary arrest of his susceptible heart. Don't answer it, said the narrator. But if my time has come? The narrator changed his mind. You can't avoid it. Be cool.

Italicize telephone voices, twisted and cranky. Low. *Ralph? Is that you Rayalph?* Yes. (Relief? Would a police officer call you Rayalph? Ah yes —in the instant of silence it takes to comprehend, mind hears the just-heard sound replaying—*Is that you Rayalph?*—and recognizes this time the unmistakable timbre of someone known to you, and as the sound begins to replay yet once more the face begins to fill in around the voice, bushy nostrils, cigar smoke, God damn—) *This is Paul Grummon.* (No need to tell me now, bushy nostrils and eyebrows too, cigar smoke, dimple smile in coarse gray cheeks) Hi. *Hower you Ralph?* Okay I guess. *Yabusy?* (At certain times of the year there is alarm in almost every rustle in the leaves. At this moment Burr thought he heard in the dimpled friendly voice of his friend his catastrophes multiplied yet another turn with friendship turned forever bad and a possible challenge to a duel.) Busy? Oh—no more than normal I guess. I mean (speech) I'm always busy but I'm adaptable too. (AAUP.) What's on your mind? *Been talking to Arthur Hoffman, wondered if he and I could come over and see you for a little this evening?* (Would the police conceivably make their inquiries through the mediation of two stuffy moderately senior members of the university's department of English? Of course not.) Why, I guess so, if you want to. (Pause to think about it. May I ask. . . ? Yes, try it.) May I ask. . . ?

So they said they would be over soon. Just wanted to talk a little about this question of the forthcoming chairmanship, wanted advice, or opinion, or information, or something. So am I still a candidate? wondered Professor Ralph Hathorne Burr. Stayed indoors to clean up the living room a little, piling the newspapers from the last two weeks into one great stack and taking it out to the kitchen, books back into bookcases, pick up the student papers scattered about, coffee cups back to the kitchen. I even got out the vacuum cleaner, but no time to use it when the doorbell chimed. Went to answer it, and Burr was still not convinced it was not the police.

Well, but it wasn't Grummon and Hoffman either—not yet. Ask the narrator, must we mention every detail? Obviously not, but you could mention this one because it reflects (does it?) state of mind. I had forgotten to turn on the front porch light and by now it was dark outside, but even so I could see it was not the portly stately forms of my departmental colleagues but instead a smallish shape in dark clothes recognizable as a girl, recognizable as a girl with glasses and long brown hair wearing a striped shirt and jeans, recognizable as the former girlfriend of my son, whose name was Natalie Fleet. Standing there smiling with a book in her hand, because it was she who had helped you to the doctor yesterday when you had that spasm in the office and this was (obviously) the book she had promised to get you, full of information about heart conditions and how to avoid a coronary. "Hi," she said. "Going by and thought I'd drop this over. Hower you?"

Fine—so she came in and sat down in a chair in the living room. "I was just remembering this thing about my uncle," said Natalie Fleet, "who had this heart attack when he was forty-seven and now he's fifty-eight years old in perfect health and he goes jogging, you know, running, jog jog jog, five miles through town, home from work every day. And there was also Lyndon Johnson—"

Tell her fine, thank you, and also remind her what I told her yesterday (putting it with as much niceness and humor as possible in the tone of voice): "Very encouraging—only of course you know I haven't had a heart attack even once. According to all the doctors it has nothing to do with a heart attack." Just then the doorbell rings again. She gets up, eyebrows raised, question on her face. "Yes," tell her, "I'm expecting Mr. Grummon and Mr. Hoffman." Her mouth forms a silent "O!" as if there were some matter of delicacy involved—confirming the narrator, who was much alarmed. I went to the door and this time it was Grummon and Hoffman, two portly alternatives, one short (Grummon) one tall (Hoffman), and there was also a third man with them, a very thin man, our blond medievalist with the sad eyes and the crew cut, Mr. Gomulski, whom I don't know very well. As they came in, shaking hands and greeting and full of explanations, I was full of this fright and embarrassment from the narrator, wondering how I could explain the presence of Miss Fleet (known to everybody, after all, as Natalie— known also as the special assistant of Grummon's most special enemy, Frank Stone) in my living room. Tell them she used to be Harold's girl-friend and used to come around the house often in those days, before she started to work in the office—but where was Harold now, where had he gone? Thinking instead, well maybe she will think of an explanation, and all the time wondering at the same time why the narrator was so alarmed—what was there to explain? Why shouldn't she be here? Might it not even be useful (said the narrator now) to distract Grummon from another scent, that is, if he had caught any whiff to arouse his suspicions?

Only when I brought my colleagues into the living room, Natalie Fleet was gone. Why such an enormous feeling of relief (ask the narrator) as if I had escaped from some real danger? Excuse me a moment. Went out to the kitchen. She was standing there, looking at the kitchen sink. Her striped shirt of cross bands red white blue and purple, her long straight brown hair with the soft bangs, the gold-rimmed glasses, her low slung brown corduroy flaring pants with a gold chain belt (so I was wrong about those blue jeans in the shadow), and she smiled as if there were some secrecy to be preserved: "Think I'd better run along if you're going to be talking to *colleagues*," she said. Pointing to the back door: "Can I go out this way?" Yes sure, but try to ask her, why this look of complicity or guilt, this secret ducking out the back as if there were something wrong about being here? Only I couldn't focus the question into speakable words. Made a couple of helpless shrug-shoulder gestures with the hands. Somehow they called her attention to the stack of foul and crusted dishes in the sink and the still higher stack on the table next to the sink. She broke into a grin: "My, you've got a pileup here. Hey, why don't I stop in and do them for you on my way back?" Oh no no no, don't think of it, that's not necessary. "Sure," she said. "It's not too late, I'll just slip in the back door, do 'em up for you. Don't mind." Shrug and deprecate. She emphasizes: "If it's not too late, I mean." Turn on the back porch light for her as she goes out.

When I came back into the room Grummon and Hoffman were having a literary argument. Grummon was saying, "I just been reading this goddamn French novel in which there was a murder but you can't tell whether there was really a murder committed or not, and you have this protagonist who seems to have done it but you can't tell whether he really did it or not, and in fact you can't tell what is real and what is imaginary or in fact you can't tell whether there is any difference between the real and the imaginary in that novel at all." Gomulski shook his head as if it were a shame and went chuck chuck with his tongue. Then Hoffman said, "Well maybe that's his point, that you really can't tell the difference between what's imaginary and what's real." "Bull shit," said Grummon. "I can tell the difference. I can tell the difference between this room that I'm standing in and some room I might happen to remember or dream up in my mind, I can tell the difference with the greatest of ease unless I'm a raging idiot or psychotic—so what's this novelist trying to tell me?" Then Hoffman said, "Okay, maybe if you can't tell the difference in a novel, maybe you shouldn't worry about it. Maybe that means the difference isn't important. Maybe that means you should read the novel in some other way." "What way?" said Grummon, "seems to me if a novel doesn't want you to make a difference between what's real and what's imaginary in it, like other novels, it ought to give some indication as to how you should read it instead. It ought to make itself self-explanatory if it's going to do a thing like that." To this Hoffman nodded. "I agree," he said. Then they noticed that I had come back into the room and they remembered what they had come for.

Now in the living room these four members of the Department of English, just below the most senior level, sat down to discuss the chairmanship of the department. The three who came to the house were a delegation representing themselves, all in their forties, as follows:

PAUL J. GRUMMON, Ph.D., Professor of English (American novel)

ARTHUR HOFFMAN, Ph.D., Associate Professor of English (seventeenth-century poetry)

JOSEPH GOMULSKI, Ph.D., Assistant Professor of English (Medieval literature)—and they had come to consult with me, as follows:

RALPH H. BURR, Ph.D., Professor of English (Romantic movement)—as to who was the best candidate, Kail, Stone, or Burr himself? According to the narrator, what they said was less interesting than a summary of it would be, and the whole conversation, which went on for two hours, could very easily be boiled down. Yes, it could be boiled down to almost any residue that you choose. What they wanted, mainly—tell this to the narrator, pass it on perhaps to Cynthia? No. Nor Laura—who?—was to find out what kind of a chairman (the correct word is head, however, for we have been using the word *chairman* loosely in deference to democratic principles that are voluntarily respected rather than official) Burr would make, on the small outside chance that he should be selected.

Why Burr? Tell him, for it was Grummon's idea in the first place, some months ago, that among the available full professors on the staff, Burr would be the most plausible compromise candidate between the camps of Kail and Stone. Tell how it came up first last fall, when it began, it became so obvious that the young people who wanted Kail and the old guard who wanted Stone could never be reconciled with each other's candidates, and at that time Grummon first proposed the name of Burr, since (tell her) of all the others Burr seemed to get along best (though not close) with both groups and nobody had any particular objection to him. Don't tell your secret knowledge (which you have no admissible explanation for knowing) that what Grummon really wants is to become the compromise candidate himself, but that knowing his own lack of popularity with the middle echelon, he has picked Burr to support. And so it came to pass (a year ago—amid memories of the still-tragic and still-unaccustomed loneliness of the house, emptied of all that had once been its life, while on certain private undisclosable hours this remembering Burr considered the consolations offered by a faculty wife whose name happened to be Laura Grummon, wondering if this might be the answer to his new way of life, while otherwise at nights he acquired the habit of weeping in his bed in the loneliness of the house —amid such memories is the memory of how much he craved the honor and the power and the glory of the slightly special distinction and enlarged authority that Grummon was advertising him for, until it came to pass) that the search committee chose to resolve the irreconcilable rivalries by looking for a candidate to bring in from "outside," meaning someone from some other university to introduce and set over us all. Which was the end for sure of Burr's brief enough hopes (Well, God knows I never supposed I was a chairman type, anyway) until it all came up again two weeks ago when the outside candidate they thought they flew away through, unavailable after all. Raising once again the possibility of a new effort to find the chairman inside, with hope once again for Ralph Hathorne Burr—if he really wants that kind of hope.

If he wants that kind of job, this talking to people and making requests of the deans and answering complaints and firing people and being blamed for every unhappiness, and no notable evidence of a talent for any of these things. Don't mention to anyone the dialogue overheard yesterday on the steps of McMicken, two voices coming down the steps, not quite recognizable—hide it in parentheses, set it down, put it in small print so that no one will find it:

(*First man:* Well I can think of one other guy they'd be damn stupid to pick. *Second man:* You mean Burr?

First man: They damn well better not.
Second man: Not a chance, not a chance.

The above conversation between two unidentified probable instructors, unidentifiable because the observer did not want to be caught observing and so went through the door and down the hall before they could come into view, took place around 3:47 P.M. yesterday, shortly before the spasm, which almost wiped it from memory, although it was remembered again last night when subject was alone with his animals in the house and again, possibly, this morning while shaving.)

So a visit from a delegation, even if they represent only themselves, to sound a man out, can—even if it be boiled down—restore somewhat the spirits of a man, even if he has his own doubts about his suitability. (Should he say, I wish you'd come to see me a day sooner? No, better not.)

What they wanted to know, boiled down, was what he considered to be his qualifications for the job (if any). They were interested (Hoffman) in what a less gentle critic might call the apparent death of his scholarly activities since the publication of his little book about a modern poet six years ago—the book that got him his promotion to full professor. Did this mean, was this to be interpreted as, well, I mean was this a sign that he was turning his energies, now at this stage in his career, to more administrative interests? (Are you working or aren't you? That was the gist. Is there any good reason why you can't work a little harder and more obviously, openly, publicly? Is there a chance here of our getting you into our grip, our grasp, our control? Should I answer: I am still working on my next book, approaching perfection—now in its sixth revision?)

Interested also (Grummon) if you'll pardon my indiscretion in bringing this up in the instability or stability now of his personal arrangements, now that it had been how long? How long has it been? Since what? Since, you know, since Cynthia? What he wanted to know was how long it had been since his wife's sudden death had shocked them all: year and a half ago November? Also how long since his children—? Also whether he felt reasonably well you know settled on a stable keel once again in calm waters renewed and able to take on the consuming interests and heavy burdens of such a job as this or whether in fact such

92

burdens might not indeed be just the thing to stabilize your life and give it direction and new meaning like an airplane which as you know, hah hah, flies better when it goes fast but simply falls crashes to the ground if it goes too slow. "Yes of course," I said. "Much better now I think. No, I don't think that would be any problem."

Well, said Gomulski, "I think what we'd really want to know is what your policies will be if you are made head."

"No," said Grummon, full professor contradicting assistant professor, "we don't want to know your policies. What we are trying to get an inkling of, what we are trying to feel out in you, if you'll pardon the expression, is simply how you feel about the job, how you feel about your colleagues, how it looks to you, how it *tastes* to you, whether you feel courageous or weak, whether you are a fighter or a buckler-underer, what your *style* will be. Policies don't matter, it's style that counts."

So I leaned back in my chair and explained to them what I expected my style to be.

Then, Hoffman: "What I really want to know is what your attitude will be toward young people. Will you be receptive to the ideas of students and young faculty? Will you continue to encourage student participation on department and college committees? Will you allow young faculty and students to develop changes in the curriculum or in the program for a major in English? Above all, do you intend to give the young faculty and the students a voice in the hiring and firing of department members?"

Grummon gasp: "Students in hiring and firing?"

So I leaned back in my chair, lit a cigarette, and as I then step-by-step formulated what my attitudes would be as regards young people, I explained these to my interviewers. They listened soberly, with anxious faces.

"The important thing," said Grummon, "is to stop Stone. The guy is vicious and I will not work for him. And of course Kail is out of the question." He looked at me. "It's in your interest to stop Stone," he said. "You are aware I assume that Stone was the only member of the committee who voted against your promotion when it came up six years ago?" I was not aware, and it brought Stone's face clearly into the focus of my imagination: Stone tight-lipped, staring at me severely, disapproving of me. "You are aware that Stone has a way of telling tales on people to get an advantage and will stop at nothing. You don't want to get into a position where he can blackmail you—"

"Oh, come now Paul," said Hoffman.

"All right," growled Grummon. "I merely wish to say that you can't trust Stone a moment out of your sight. And if you" (looking at Burr) "don't want to be yourself an alternative to Stone in running against Kail and our young anarchists, then you should please tell us right away so we can find somebody else."

Tell him this observation on the side—that when someone like Grummon (or specifically Grummon, short and portly, bushy nostrils and nervous dimple in round shiny cheeks) when such a Grummon warns you as he always does of the untrustworthy tendencies of a tight-lipped and severe, but seemingly straight individual like Stone, when he speaks, as he always does, of blackmailing tendencies and getting things on you, you begin to wonder if it is himself that he is describing. If he is the one who always thinks of putting the squeeze on people, of getting an edge on them, of saying one thing and intending another, and of relishing with cruelty the management of power over your best and nearest colleagues? This on the basis of a familiar principle in the literary tradition: that if you tend like Grummon to be constantly criticizing people then no doubt you will be most likely to pin on them your own most distinctive faults. You can tell a man by what he criticizes in others, the more critical the better.

So after a while I suggested coffee. Went out to the kitchen to wash out a few coffee cups taken from the pile of dishes that Natalie Fleet had said she was going to come back to, put water to boil on the stove, spooned a spoonful of freeze-dried coffee into each cup, and waited.

There was a meditative, reflective silence among them while they drank their coffee. Did Burr meditate and reflect or was he merely dreaming and composing fictions in his mind? Anticipating the moment when Laura Grummon should tell Paul the secret stories that had never happened—what was to stop her, when the time was right? And what then would he do? Change the subject. What would they all do if they made him chairman and then, after a few months, the news broke.

Narrator asks, which news you mean? The Laura Grummon news, the Burnet Woods news? Doesn't matter? What would they do when they found out such things about their prize candidate, so newly inaugurated into our confidence and trust. Tell him if they make Burr chairman it is a clean slate, wipes the record clean, everything new, they couldn't do anything to him then, not Paul Grummon, not even the police.

Leaning back in my chair with my coffee, I heard Burr beginning to talk—listened with astonishment, alarm growing in paralysis, as I took in gradually what he was saying. "I walk to work most mornings, to keep in shape. Did you know that? Good for my health, good for my spirits, especially on pleasant spring mornings like this morning. I walk my regular walk through Burnet Woods."

Pause.

"I always go through Burnet Woods. I went through Burnet Woods this morning."

Pause again. Grummon, Hoffman, Gomulski, sipping coffee, smoking cigars or cigarettes, listening still with indifference, if listening at all.

"Do you know Burnet Woods? You know the steps down to the playground from the road, down beside the stone slide? I usually go down that and then I go up the nature trail, up the long flight of steps through the woods to the bandstand at the top. I went that same way again this morning—as usual."

Pause, watch them. Gomulski starts to talk: "Yeah, well you know I sometimes walk to work too if it's not too cold, except the trouble it's all the way uphill and by the time I get to my office—"

I heard Burr interrupt him: "Seems there was a murder there this morning."

"Where?"

"Burnet Woods."

"Another one?"

"Another?" said Burr. "Have there been others there recently?"

"I don't know," said Gomulski. "I'm always hearing about murders this place and that place."

"Well there was one in Burnet Woods this morning. In the paper. It was right where I walked."

Grummon: "Kind of shake you up a bit, hey?"

"For all I know I walked right by it. Took place on the steps. Someone hit an old man on the head with a rock and dumped him in a pile of leaves."

"Yeh, I saw that," said Grummon. "A rock, was it?"

"A rock full of fossils," said Burr.

"Oh, that's an interesting detail, isn't it? My paper didn't have that."

"An old man, or maybe it was an old woman—"

"A man," said Grummon.

"One of these shabby, ancient, evil-looking old people that you see walking around the streets these days," said Burr.

All three of them looked at him rather strangely.

Grummon: "I think these shabby old people are very forlorn and pathetic."

"Oh yes I didn't mean—"

Hoffman: "You must feel you had a close shave. Hard not to feel it might have been you."

"Hm," said Burr. "Hadn't thought of it that way before." Trying to get hold of himself, regain control over what he was saying. Said: "Got me started being afraid that someone might think—" Stop!

Silence. Everyone looking at me to see what I was afraid someone might think. "Someone might think what?"

Finish your sentence: "That I knew something about it."

"Why? Did you see anything."

"Nothing to speak of." (Was that safe?) "Funny how guilt works."

"Paranoia," muttered Grummon. Observe again, how when someone like Grummon diagnoses paranoia in others, individuals, friends, wives, as well as institutions and nations, he is really diagnosing himself, for that is a general principle that will help you to cope with people like Paul Grummon. Meanwhile I heard Burr going on, trying to complete his explanation: "I mean like I really felt rather upset. Like someone might think I . . . well—"

Couldn't bring himself to say it, as if afraid that saying it would actually plant the suspicion in somebody's mind. But when someone else understands, then it's not so bad, like Hoffman, who completed the thought: "You begin to be afraid someone might think you had done it yourself?"

96

"Exactly!" said Burr, beaming. "That thought occurred to me and I guess I've been sort of nervy, jumpy, these days lately—I really have been, can't quite say why—anyway it upset me so much I knocked off before lunch today and went to a movie."

Explain to him the motivation for this speech that unfolded as the speech unfolded—to tell the truth wherever you can, to account for something like going to the movies in advance, so that no one can try to unsettle you by asking you all of a sudden unprepared—why did you go to the movies that afternoon? Only it didn't take into account the unmistakable look of astonishment, of widening eyes and staring, that appeared on all three faces as he spoke, and the embarrassment of silence following. "You upset rather easily," said Grummon, coldly.

"Oh no, not ordinarily. No I am sure not. It was only—today—and I am sure that the kinds of things a chairman has to cope with, I am quite impervious to and not likely to be bothered by the kind of thing that comes up. It was only today, I didn't get so much sleep last night."

Everyone wanted to change the subject, so we had a conversation about African artifacts. Grummon began looking at the walls and ceilings, the books and the pictures on the wall. Finally he said, "I thought you sold this place." I said, "I did. The Benjamins bought it." Hoffman made a sympathetic face: "You *sold* this beautiful old house?" I explained: Had to, with Cynthia and the children gone. Can't hang on to a big old place like this all by myself. Added: "Most of the furniture was inherited by Cynthia and I've agreed to ship it out to her brother on the West Coast."

"When are you moving?" asked Grummon. The puzzled look on his face.

"End of this month."

"Do you need any help?"

"I might need some when the time comes," I said. Then everyone immediately offered to do what they could to help me get moved. I thanked them, said I would call on them, said everything was under control.

"I must say," said Grummon as if with admiration, "You certainly couldn't tell, looking at this room, that you were going to move out of here in less than a month."

Before they left Grummon said they would keep me in mind as an alternative to Stone against Kail, but meanwhile they wanted to sound out other members of the department. In any case, as I well knew, the decision-making and nominating power remained not with them but with the search committee and ultimately with the dean. And there was nothing I could do now but wait.

Chapter 3

I took the coffee cups out to the kitchen and looked at the stack of dirty dishes Natalie Fleet had said she might come back and do. Our meeting had lasted about an hour. The dishes stacked up represented a week of breakfasts and some light suppers. I wanted to do them now, for the first time in many days, except that Natalie Fleet had offered to and I ought to wait and give her the chance. I considered her disappointment if she came back and found them already done—as if I wanted to deny her excuse to come back. Excuse . . . ? Now he asked me why she needed an excuse and warned me against my natural tendency to overinterpret. Realizing that my doing the dishes would not keep her from coming back, if she came, because she couldn't know I was doing them until after she had come, like lots of other things she couldn't know. He said he doubted that she would really come back anyway. He told me that when a girl sees a mighty stack of dirty dishes like that, she may feel sorry for the man who has to get rid of them and have a generous impulse, but once she leaves the house and gets back to her friends, she is more likely to forget and excuse herself saying, it's his problem not hers and he's always managed before, hasn't he?

This reminded him of all the work he had to do to clear out of the house by the end of the month. A little more than three weeks left. Start packing boxes soon (first he would have to find a moving company and get boxes). Get Cynthia's brother's furniture together, find a mover for that, too. Then he remembered that he had not yet found an apartment for himself to move into. It was time to get started on these tasks, in which case he ought to begin by getting rid of this week's stack of dishes in the sink. He figured the only reason not to do the dishes now was in case Natalie Fleet didn't come back this evening, he could speak to her in the office tomorrow, using the dishes as the basis for his reproach: When are you going to come and clean up my dishes? Impossible.

It didn't make any difference now in any case, he said, pointing out that I had already begun to do the dishes, without decision, scraping, water in the dishpan, hot suds, apron, soapy hands. According to the narrator it was something to do, activity to keep the mind from abrading too harshly against the facts of existence. To keep the narrator busy— or in this case to keep him silent (make the narrator wash the dishes, and you'll get some peace) so that he would not keep asking what it meant, that moment of embarrassment and shock just before his visitors left. "You upset rather easily," said Grummon, coldly said the narrator. Because they had at that moment caught the birth like an acorn of suspicion, wide-eyed with the incredible possibility that their colleague and choice candidate for department head had recently committed a murder, violent and arbitrary, to be designated in the newspapers as a "senseless slaying." "You upset rather easily," said Grummon, said the narrator coldly. Not because they suspected him of a crime because no possible extremity of mere conversation could bring them to such an extremity of suspicion concerning their mild and malleable and controllable candidate for department head said the narrator coldly, but because he admitted to such easy upsetting, and what was to prevent him from capsizing under the pressures of such a job?

At that moment, said the narrator portentously, though no one yet mentioned it in words, Ralph Burr was dropped unanimously out of the running, by all his former supporters for the job.

(Since by his own account he went to the movie before lunch, would anyone think to ask how he knew about the murder before the afternoon paper came out? Only rely, said the narrator, on the normal failure of close attention where one's interest has not been provoked, but have an explanation if someone should think of it. Retrospective transfer, say—

100

you already were agitated about something, and later when you read the item in the paper—?)

Doing dishes, deliberate thought control, to keep your mind off unspeakable things. Activate the narrator to keep your mind off unspeakable things. Thinking—this is the narrator speaking—of dishes, of the imminent return of the girl Natalie Fleet to help with the dishes, so as to keep your mind off unspeakable things. What to tell her when she comes to do the dishes, to keep her mind off unspeakable things.

To avoid unspeakable things, he suggested (hands slippery in soapy dishwater) another question: take that other moment of alarm that occurred this evening when Grummon and his friends arrived at the door and almost met Natalie Fleet in your living room. And the relief that followed when she ducked out of sight. What about that? As if Natalie Fleet were to disclose your crime. As if in a case like this a secret of any kind, no matter how innocent, took on the guilty hue of the great secret, and even Natalie Fleet in your house were tinged with your crime and revealed it by her presence.

How unreasonable! says Natalie. *What have I to do with your crime when I don't even know what it is? Didn't even know that you had committed one.* Ask her then, he says, to explain it herself: Why did you duck out of sight when Grummon and the others arrived? *Why,* says Natalie, *to save you embarrassment and irritation. So people won't start asking questions about what is going on between Professor Burr and Miss Fleet before you want them to, or so you won't have Professor Grummon saying to you, "So you have started fooling around with the office staff, I see" with obvious disapproval, or if that is unlikely so you don't have him worrying about your getting trapped by spies from the enemy camp on account of I am Professor Stone's special assistant.* No, he says, tell her that's not good enough, point out that Paul Grummon probably would not give a damn to find her here, it wouldn't matter to him. Then he says here is a much more likely reason why you were so alarmed and then so relieved. For suppose Grummon had been able to go home and report to his *wife* that he had met Natalie Fleet here? Consider that: Paul Grummon goes home and says (ever so accidentally and casually or ever so deliberately and slyly, whichever interpretation you want to put on his hound dog scent-pursuing qualities): *Guess who was visiting at Burr's house tonight? Natalie Fleet.* Adding perhaps, if Laura says nothing: *I wonder what that means.* And maybe if she still maintains silence: *Maybe old Rayalph is coming out of his shell at last.* As I heard these postulated words, notice this sudden feeling of having had a narrow escape. No wonder you felt so relieved.

Better explain it to Natalie Fleet, he advises me, since she looks puzzled: *What does Mrs. Grummon have to do with your alarm?* she asks, somewhat irked. *What's it to her?* No reason, I'll tell her, annoyed in turn. Burr backs off at this mention of Laura Grummon: no reason, no connection, he would say. Pay no attention. Still perhaps the narrator remains uneasy, detecting a motive in Burr's feeling of relief, a connection, a possible story—something at any rate not quite right. Which Natalie, of course, will pursue. *What is it?* demands Natalie, conjuring her own image then of Laura Grummon driving up to Burr's house on an afternoon (Tuesday perhaps? suggests the cooperating narrator, when Grummon is tied up all afternoon with his seminar in the library?) parking in the driveway at the side of the house, coming in the kitchen door (same door as Natalie left by this evening, notes narrator) conjuring Laura Grummon tall and graceful, younger than her husband (actually, she lets you know, she is Grummon's second wife, but that was years ago): long black hair, loose and free over her shoulders, heavy eye makeup, wearing a canary-yellow dress. She sees her now, reminiscent of tennis-playing days long ago, of days at the beach, of golf and sailing, days still visible in the look of her now (though we did not know her then, said the narrator, and Natalie was only a child—what we knew were others, who are now gone, what you are remembering in particular is a long-ago Cynthia, long-ago young in sailing and the beach), though that hair (Natalie will notice) does not have quite the natural smoothness it would have had then, and the face, the eyes show anxiety gathered over a passage of years, and the knowledge that Laura Grummon was/is a great beauty is best confirmed in soft and dim lights. Still, watch Natalie conjure her into the kitchen, into this empty house with all the animals, and as she does so, show Natalie herself the house. Follow her upstairs into the bedroom. Watch the sunshine through the thin bedroom curtains while this conjured Laura Grummon smiles uneasily, slightly preoccupied, as she turns her back to you in her canary-yellow dress and asks you to unzip her down the back.

So that's it, Natalie will say, observing her own conclusion. *Professor Burr and Professor Grummon's wife. A little scandal.* Watching her drape the canary-yellow dress carefully over the back of a chair and stand in her bra and panties, hands at her back to undo her bra. *How long has this been going on?* Burr sees, look at her imagination taking off into the past, conjuring Laura's dropping panties back deeper and deeper into the first darknesses of his Cynthia-shock, dropping them into his blackest early mourning, until finally she goes even before that, asking, *Before Cynthia—? Was this going on before Cynthia—? Was this why Cynthia—?* Catch her then, Burr tells narrator, bring her back to the flat gray truth. While Natalie conjures imaginings let Burr stiffly and firmly stick to fact: no Laura-bra or panty ever fell in his empty house (full of animals). Ask narrator to correct her, the simple truth, how doggily loyal and faithful a person Burr has always been, both while Cynthia lived and after she died. Announce the dull fact, his intrinsic fidelity, inborn, and the stern and gloomy celibacy, never questioned, of all time since her death. Meanwhile Natalie conjures as if she had not heard, *while Laura Grummon takes off first the bra then the stockings then the panties,* conjuring *Laura standing there trying boldly to display herself, body as frank as speech on a weekday afternoon* while Burr denies, his mind closed to all youthful folly, the parts killed in him by that permanent age accelerating shock, admitting exception only perhaps in darkest night hours in time of insomnia, or times of haste and work when unmonitored thoughts may (it is true) sometimes slip by the mind unnoticed, *conjuring the still healthy color of her flesh, the large liquid breasts with the pale pink nipples, the dark hair in the crotch, though her eyes always a little anxious.*

The narrator says we owe Natalie an explanation *Laura Grummon's eyes still anxious as she* something better than Burr's simple flat denials to justify her conjuring *eyes still anxious as she lolls,* to pull it all together. The narrator would like to dig back, shuffle into the records of those hateful days, better not to look at, better left alone, thrown-out days like days in a garbage can, those days of shock after Cynthia, with Harold gone too and Elaine on the verge. To explain her conjurings to Natalie, though Burr resists. The narrator will recall helpful neighbors and colleagues. Helpful Grummonses, helpful Stones, inviting him to dinner. The inner gullet of feeling was all eaten away, but there was dinner (narrator will tell Natalie) and Mrs. Grummon—Laura Grummon, who had always made him feel a little embarrassed, as if expecting something from him—saying to him *eyes still anxious as she lolls* "If we can help you in any way" *back on the bed and stretches up her arms to him* "If there is any way in particular that I can help" *So Natalie will suppose Laura and Ralph together on the bed, formerly Ralph and Cynthia's, without clothes, without last names, entangling limbs, murmuring like the young* in the Grummon living room in those eroded days, while Grummon sat in his deep armchair smoking his cigar and drawling conspiratorially *poising himself over her body, sheltering her, lowering himself down* about Stone and his conspiracies, trying to line up a faction *upon her, finding his way into her, genitally, just as he always faithfully used to find his way into* while Grummon's wife drew him away from that conversation into the kitchen to give him more sympathy and advice, reminding him that all was not over, that we must look for *Cynthia, burying deep* new vistas in life, revitalization *warm close contained* rehabilitation without guilt and meanwhile remember *private familiar ancient* "Any kind of help I can give, don't be afraid to speak" *yet not Cynthia* "I mean what I say" *someone else (conjured).*

To simplify and make it most plain to Natalie *while she understands and supposes Laura in his bed putting her bare arms around his bare back while he looked at her, Laura, thinking feeling wishing Cynthia but recognizing himself in the depth of new not-Cynthia Laura, and he began to go and she with him* the narrator must show how far Laura went, Laura's initiative, her attempt. Perhaps Natalie won't believe it *Back and forth, deep in and back he goes* with Cynthia scarcely *x* months dead (how many? *x?*), in the kitchen at a party, how Laura in a long red print dress, flowing to the floor, took Burr aside and in words most direct and explicit (in accordance with her principles) virtually offered herself to Burr. Reasons therapeutic. (Virtually) *Faster and faster with a rising surge, probe* But it would be more important and still harder for her to believe, says narrator, what a time it took Burr to penetrate Laura Grummon's directness and explicitness to grasp what she *rising surge under the close-pressed bone* explicitly meant and harder still to believe what he did with it when he did grasp it. How she took him into a corner of the kitchen at this party (her flowing long red dress, like one of the young ones dressed in the costume of another century in the fields—also heavy delineating eye-makeup, indefinite age) to ask again the question she had already several times asked quite publicly: "Are you getting everything you need?" Standing close enough to make him uncomfortable, how to behave, *surge rising approaching a crest* reminding Burr of some reputation that he was vaguely aware Laura Grummon possessed (and narrator too must be vague about it), of rumors mostly forgotten from forgotten sources, about attentions she paid, kindnesses rendered more than was regular, interests shown to flatter younger faculty members (though Burr would scarcely, could not possibly count as one of these)—he could not remember, really, what sort of a reputation it was. Only this sense again that she was always expecting something from him —he never knew just what. He had always supposed that what she expected from him was a display of wit (or, failing that, wisdom), and it always stunned him witless *cresting until it broke on the shore with shuddering and golden spray and then withdrawing, backing away, slow sinking, with arms, face concealed in breasts,* and yet once more she repeated: "Are all your needs taken care of?" and his feeling that he didn't understand what she meant.

So that's it, crows Natalie again, still not understanding, believing what her own imagination is likely to make up, though Burr shakes his head and continues to deny. *Let me take you,* let Burr say to Natalie, *through this empty house, full of animals. Left over from the days of family, which still he occupies in silence and images, while two dogs chase a cat up the stairs.* She said, "What about your material needs?" *We have downstairs four rooms—also a small front porch with space for two wicker chairs—a living room cluttered* "Your *physical* needs?" she said. Tell Natalie that to the narrator this was clearly a sexual suggestion, but Burr feeling his wit challenged could not believe this and it wasn't for him to say so in any case, so instead he was puzzled and said: "Am I getting enough to eat?" "Well, yes," she said. "And your other physical needs?" she went on. *Cat baskets in the corner, a dining room with newspapers piled upon the table, a study crowded with books and a messy desk, and this very kitchen with this pile of dishes here. Upstairs a bathroom and three bedrooms. The big one in front is the master bedroom with two front windows looking out to the shading maple tree, and the big double bed where Cynthia and I used to sleep and now I sleep alone. And there is Harold's room next to the stairs (not forgetting the share in Harold's memory to which you have a rightful claim) with his childhood books and remnants, his high school track trophies, his pictures of ball players—in case he comes back. (Say: When gentle Harold out of college dropped the world to see, what letters forgot he to write? Where be he? A postcard from Hong Kong last December. Works he in the merchant service?) Across the hall Elaine's room with its horse and dog books* "What other physical needs?" asked Burr.

Coming ever closer, moment by moment—narrator tells Natalie—to the point where a decision would have to be made. She said, "Don't you have any other physical needs?" What do you have in mind? said Burr. Then Laura: "What about your x-ial needs?" What? said Burr. "Your actual needs. Ass ay ax." Eh? "Are you meeting your sectional needs?" Sects? said Burr. "Sects, yes, exactly," said Laura. Oh, said Burr. "Ess ee ecks. Are you satisfying your sectsual needs?" Oh, said Burr again, believing he understood at last.

"Oh," exclaimed Burr. "My *sectsual* needs! I see what you mean! Am I satisfying my sectsual needs?"

and her posters and color photographs of John, Ringo, Paul, and George, and Simon and Garfunkel and Janis Joplin and and her large brown eyes smiling at him, almost laughing now, though still and always a little anxious, and still obviously expecting something from him, and she said, "Well?" *and Jimi Hendrix, all left behind at home while Elaine settled* and Burr stood slightly liquored and baffled, still not sure what was expected of him in moments like this *with a group of others on a farm out West, writing an occasional note and expecting* which made her laugh and say, "Don't be afraid. You can confide in me" *a baby, whose father Burr has never dared ask about.* Then Burr realized *The baby should be born by now, but he has had no word. Meanwhile* what was expected from him now, he had to decide something, *meanwhile her room waits, inhabited by the cats who sleep comfortably two on a bed but sometimes fight when a third tries to join. There is a cat box (kitty litter) in the upstairs hall by the bathroom, and another in the entrance way to the cellar* thinking, If he said, Yes, she would ask him to explain how he was meeting them, and thereby expose him in a lie, and if he said, No, *The dogs can be turned loose in the pen that Harold and I built in the back two years ago (when we were still father and son), and then they come in to sleep in all the rooms* she would challenge him to do something about it (though Cynthia was but *x* months dead) and, very probably, would offer him herself for the purpose.

And never get another offer like that in your lifetime, says Natalie, *so naturally you* did naturally what was the natural Burr thing to do, says narrator, telling her how, when it finally came to the point, when Laura Grummon said, "You can confide in me," Burr stiffened, stretched, leaned back against the kitchen wall (against a rack of hanging kitchen forks and gravy spoons) and said, "I have no sectsual needs. You don't have to worry about me, I'm managing quite well, thank you."

Wow, she will say. *I bet that turned her off!* Tell her, So you see, he speaks the truth when he speaks of his enduring celibacy since Cynthia's death—at least in the gross and literal sense. Ask narrator, a little anxiously, will it put Natalie Fleet off too, that story? Will she be disappointed in the blasting of her conjurings?

She'll ask what Laura Grummon did then. *Did she get very angry?* No —tell how she backed away, a little startled, how the smile faded and the anxiety grew and then the smile returned, but a different smile now, a colder smile, on guard. Tell how quickly she dropped then the question of his sectsual needs, though it was a long time before the narrator might suspect her of anger on the point. And indeed for at least a season still, despite his rebuff, Laura Grummon continued generously to give him her advice and counsel and consolation, never mentioning again his physical needs nor whatever humiliation she might have suffered from his *what Natalie would call rudeness.* Tell Natalie how they talked, so much private and intimate. Tell her about the subtler more difficult questions that the novels used to deal with, the Henry James duties in your relations with Cynthia—explain to her the subtle and complicated terms (moral, psychological) of the Jamesian *conjuring Natalie too in a furry white bathrobe, sitting in* martyrdoms that mattered so much to *the living room in Cynthia's bathrobe talking of Cynthia* Cynthia *and the children. Looking at her conjured* high-civilized consideration for each other, *bright bare knee peeping out from her white bathrobe and the loosely closed V opening below her throat* competitions in goodness in the days *Natalie's Laura's Cynthia's long black long brown short blonde wavy hair* competitions in goodness in the days before her illness cut her down. And then one day she got tired of talking about Cynthia. She began to talk about herself, about lovers she had had, also of her problems with Grummon, of his affairs, though she thought he had stopped having affairs, since he had gotten involved in politics. Said that she and Grummon tolerated each other's affairs, it was part of their agreement, although Grummon tended to be vindictive and nasty toward her lovers.

Meanwhile, when he came back to his own house alone at night, as time passed and wounds seemed to heal, often Burr himself perhaps played conjuring tricks in the dark. Conjuring Laura Grummon back, conjuring her to his room in the sunshine, in a canary-yellow dress, unzipping her back, standing there in bra and panties, hands at her back to undo bra. Conjuring off the bra, the stockings, the panties, then the still-healthy color of the flesh, the large liquid breasts with the pale pink nipples, the dark hair in the crotch, though her eyes always a little anxious. Then he supposed her in bed putting her bare arms around his bare back while he looked at her, thinking Laura Laura Laura, and beginning to go with her, riding. But still it was an empty house, and yet again he would conjure, conjuring her now to ask once again that question she had actually asked him once, and this time conjuring up a different answer for himself.

Tell how, while he sat in her living room, drinking her beer, and listened to her talk with such equanimity about her understandings with Grummon, he conjured her and waited for her to ask him that question once again: *Are you still free of sectsual needs?* she would ask with a touch of kindly irony, and this time he would not miss the cue, this time he would leap— Only the narrator must admit that she never did bring up the question again, and since Burr was waiting for her to do it, it never did come up again. And as the original question receded into the past, moment by moment, though she had concealed any hurt reaction at the start, little by little and quite steadily, Laura Grummon became cooler and more distant. It became awkward. Not long after she got tired of talking about Cynthia, she got tired of talking about Grummon too. Then she got tired of talking about intimate and private things of any kind. And finally she stopped seeing him altogether.

Though he did not stop conjuring, he stopped conjuring her. It no longer seemed possible. He conjured instead all kinds of women, a dazzle of them, students graduate and undergraduate, young colleagues, secretaries, wives, mini-skirts, maxi-skirts, jeans, shorts, a great field of women like flowers to be cut and himself in the midst of it. He conjured himself a freedom such as had never existed in his life, and sometimes the conjuring seemed so real he almost exulted in it, though he could never make his exultation last. But Laura Grummon was no longer a part of it.

Narrator says it was just as if they had broken up with a bitter quarrel between them. Yet there had been no quarrel nor harsh words, nor any breakup or even discussion though he scarcely ever saw her anymore. Yet it was just as if they had been involved in an intense love affair, now shattered. He felt the cold and angry bitterness of the former mistress, and the rueful regret and shame of a secret in the past that he would like to obliterate, and the sense of evocative places and times, loaded with memory, with fragrance, with snare to catch a man and turn him inside out again, of places and times to be avoided, and even of the jealous husband who knew and was only biding his time. All the fear, the shame, the regret, as if the very thing he had so stiffly and primly refused had gone ahead and happened in spite of him. As if he had been conjured from a fiction into a reality.

Will Natalie understand that? Probably she will be more concerned about another question: she will still want to know why you refused Laura Grummon. What can the narrator say to that? Were there any answers, or was it simple fright? Say that it was simply she was the wrong woman. Made her approaches, kind and helpful, unusually honest, everything in her favor except that he kept wishing she might be some other woman? Not sufficiently attractive to make him yearn. Would that do? Natalie doubts, recalling how much you did yearn just a little later, when it was too late. And won't Natalie also ask how any affair could be as one-sided as we have made it out, anyway? Surely she wouldn't have made so bold, Natalie will say, unless you had given her signals of some kind?

Well then, say instead how dangerous it was to get involved with the wife of a colleague, especially when the colleague was Grummon. Dangerous, awkward. Suppose Grummon? And what future in such a connection?

But we are skimming too shallow, says the narrator, in our memory of the time. Forgetting the bereavement that still loomed like a mountain. And even if Burr was forward-looking then, even if he wanted to get out from under the shadow and begin a new life, probably he was still afraid, when it came to the point, that the new woman, the other, the not-Cynthia, would only remind him of Cynthia again and the future would drown in the past.

More likely he was not forward-looking at all then but still holding back: afraid to tangle with another woman because it still seemed like an infidelity to Cynthia. Or because he was still in that phase of a loss when you try to keep alive, as if still present, the image of the loss, and you fear every presence, such as a new-woman, a not-Cynthia, whose vividness might make the other fade.

Or else because he was still committed to a depth of concentration upon a certain period of time—in which next to himself Cynthia remains the chief occupant. Let the future come slowly, he would have said, trying to preserve his own life and the life-vessels of continuity between cruelly broken ages: not ready then for a new time, for a Laura. Because he had memories still in the tray, still being developed, and he had to wait for them.

Or else it was because he had recognized something coming in his own life. Felt its shadow in the first horror of Cynthia's end and recognized its importance to him. A shadow, a darkness coming. A day turning into lasting night. Himself merging into that night. Saw the necessary blankness, the openness and emptiness towards which he was moving, which could not allow anything, new-woman or not-Cynthia, to obstruct that course.

Or perhaps, says narrator somewhat scornfully (since Burr doesn't like or doesn't understand that last explanation), it was simply that he couldn't think how to behave in a moment like that, didn't know what might be expected of him. Didn't want to take the initiative offered to him or look like a fool. Saw himself confronted with the immediate demand that he play some kind of a part different from the parts he was accustomed to, and not wanting to play parts now he simply—refused.

And now you're afraid of her, says Natalie Fleet, *Are you afraid of me too?* Smiling. *You're afraid of women?*

No, Burr would deny it. Tell her that it is not Laura as woman that he fears but Laura as Grummon. Warn her about Laura Grummon, who is indeed, say, someone to be feared. Because she has such a pride *conjuring her into the back room behind the kitchen where she stands in her long loose-flowing red print dress and puts her fingers to the buttons on the front* such pride with such possibilities of revenge and malice. Warn of her vindictive malignity, never yet displayed in all its force, and the destructive power she has, once she decides to use it *revealing her clean breasts with nipples and then her dark belly and the navel and then* remember her own stories of her past lovers and how Grummon responded to them. Her revenge: to tell Grummon, to start new conspiracies in his mind, feeding his paranoia with slanted stories, enlarging the circle of his enemies and placing you among them. For surely you must know that Laura Grummon is as conspiratorial as her husband, and see what has happened to all her previous lovers, every one of whom she has learned to hate, see it in the contemptuous anecdotes she tells about them. Why should you be exempted from contemptuous anecdotes?

And why should Natalie only smile and say, *That's life,* as if it were of no account, when you tell her this? She will ask how could that woman possibly hurt you? How can she touch you? Tell her then, Good! Tell her we knew she would say that, and ask her to come quick, help us now.

111

Tell her we need her to help against unmentionable things. Then I saw that I had finished all the dishes in the kitchen, and I looked at the clock and realized that Natalie Fleet would not be back tonight. Surprising how disappointed I was.

Went upstairs to bed, thinking of unspeakable things.

Chapter 4

They put the murder of Andreas Kirschner on the second page of the morning paper in a small item. Unlike the big front page scandal murders or the assaults of the strangler or the attacks on middle class people inside their houses—as if they judged this to be the work of some routine criminal, some mugger who went too far ("Police theorized that the motive was robbery"). It took imagination, looking at that small item and thinking of it, visualizing it in the actual place where we had so often walked, to see it as anything else.

I decided this morning, by act of will to restore as much as possible the routine of normal life. To put out of mind by force the morbid efflorescences that had lately been crowding my thought. To go through a normal day in the normal way, to have breakfast, to go to work (glad that, as this was Wednesday, I did not have to teach a class today), to talk to people, read and study and plan lectures all as usual. To cut off firmly these mad imaginings, as I called them, that had grown up about this Kirschner murder in Burnet Woods, to put it as far away from me as possible, to put it as if I had never heard about it, had not read about it, as if it had never happened. It was for such reasons as these that I drove to work this morning instead of taking my usual walk through the park. Passing Burnet Woods in the car, I did notice two police cars parked on the drive within the park, and this did make me think of the murder, but I was able to turn my mind to the question of the department headship once again (wondering how long and how sincerely and energetically Grummon would continue to support me) and in that way I managed to keep my mind out of the worst of the sinkholes.

The day advanced in a normal fashion. I began by writing some letters of recommendations for students, some of whom were looking for jobs and others applying for graduate school. I tried to fit my recommendations to the individual students, praising some for intelligence, some for industry and hard work, some for reliability and scrupulousness and integrity, some for drive and energy, and some for their originality and the vitality of their imaginations. All of my recommendations were hedged by the proviso that you can never make a positive prediction about anybody, because people are always surprising you, the ones you expect to achieve something are always turning out to have unpredictable weaknesses, and the ones you did not think had anything, suddenly develop extraordinary gifts—but making all due allowances, I was willing to stake much of my predictive reliability on their possession of the particular qualities that I said they possessed.

I took the letters to the office to be typed, giving them to Natalie Fleet for the purpose. Told her then I was sorry she was interrupted in her visit last night, and she said she was sorry she had not been able to come back and do those dishes. Told her I did them myself, thank you. She asked if I had read the heart book yet, and I said, no. I wondered if I could invite her to come around again tonight, but I couldn't think of a pretext, so I let it go at that. Back to my office, where I began to study and get ready for tomorrow's classes.

At lunch I ate with Kessler, Kail, Elias, and Parker. We talked about the Kirschner murder, and again I mentioned how I had gone by the scene of the crime yesterday practically at the time it was committed. Laughter again at my narrow escape, how nearly I might have gotten mugged myself. It was Kail who mentioned that the old man had a son who was in the college. Surprised me—how could he have a college-age son when he was listed in the paper as seventy-three years old, but they all said it was perfectly possible, if he had a younger wife: he would not have had to be more than fifty-three when the boy was born. The son's name was Berthold Kirschner, said Kail. He was majoring in political science and was one of the more active of the young radicals.

114

The two policemen came to see us early in the afternoon. They wore brown business suits, neat and not elegant, young men of heavy build —one of them wore a Phi Beta Kappa key, and I thought at first that they were book salesmen making their seasonal tour of faculty offices. Burr knew they were policemen, though, the instant he saw them, perhaps even before he saw them.

Polite and deferential. The man with the black hair knocked timidly on the door jamb (my office always stands open), while the one who looks like a blond bully stood back looking at the ceiling and cracks in the wall, in the hall. "Excuse me sir," said Blackhair. "Are you Professor Ralph Burr?"

Yes I am.

"We're from the city police. May we disturb you for a few minutes?" Quick flash of something dirty-white palmed in the right hand of each of them, which claimed to be identification but which might have been a pornographic poem. Come in, sit down. What can I do for you?

Sitting down at Kessler's desk and in the student chair (Kessler not in), "Sorry to bother you, Professor, we thought you might be able to help us." Gave names: Freitag and Watson. "I don't know if you saw in the paper this morning about a homicide yesterday in Burnet Woods?" (Freitag.)

Yes I did see something about it.

"Looks like a mugging case: murder and robbery. An old man, killed on the steps—you know the steps?—going up to the bandstand from the playground."

Robbery?

"Presume so. They found his wallet next to the body, empty. Makes a strong presumption of robbery. Why else would anyone kill a feeble old man?"

Can't imagine.

"Some sex thing maybe, but this looks like a clear case of assault with intention to commit robbery." All this was Freitag. Now Watson interjects, with a confidential grimace: "Drugs, you know. They commit robbery and kill people in order to buy drugs."

It's a violent world.

"It sure is, right? You can say that again. It's a violent world. Now the reason we're here, okay? We just wanted to ask if you remember seeing anything that might help us."

(Suddenly threatening to sweat like a squeezed sponge: don't let them see that.) Why me?

Freitag moment of hesitation. "Um. Yes. Well—We were given to believe that you were in Burnet Woods yesterday morning, right? Walking to work, weren't you? Okay?"

How did you know that?

"It is true, isn't it? Right?"

Yes—I walked to work through Burnet Woods. I often do.

"Right. Well, did you see anything unusual? Okay?"

Can't say. No, I can't think of anything unusual.

"What way did you come through Burnet Woods? Right?" Well, as I remember, I came down the street to the pond, crossed by the nature museum and went through the playground and up the steps to the bandstand—"Up the steps?"—yes, I presume that was the site of the murder. And then I crossed to the shelterhouse and over the meadow and so up to the university campus. "About what time—do you know?" I think it was ten to ten when I arrived. About nine-thirty when I started out. So I must have gone up the steps around, oh, somewhere around quarter of ten, twenty to ten. "Nine forty-five." More or less. "Well, did you see anybody?"

I honestly can't remember very well. "Anybody coming out of the woods before you went in? Anybody in the playground?" Don't think so. "Nobody on the steps, right?" No. "When you came out at the top, did you see anybody there?" Can't remember. Yes, I think I saw a couple of students parking their car—a boy and a girl. (Freitag and Watson look at each other and nod.) "Yes, okay? Anyone else?" Not that I remember. Later, in the meadow, far off, a worker driving a yellow tractor. "Yes, right? We know about him. And you really don't remember seeing anyone else?" Trying to remember. It's hard to bring it all back. "Yes, I understand. You didn't see a tall colored guy, very thin, wearing a leather jacket?" Why no. Do you suspect—? "We have some reason to suspect it was a black guy did it." Really? (Freitag-Watson shows surprise at Burr's surprise.) "Usually is in this kind of case, you know." Oh.

"And I take it you didn't see anyone who could have been the victim himself?" An old man? "Yeh. Dark overcoat. Short." Can't say. Quite sure not. Yet—I did, yes, I think I did see an old woman. "An old woman?" Listen, you sure it was an old man and not an old woman that got killed? (Freitag-Watson look puzzled.) "An old man. Dark overcoat. Short. Did you see an old woman?" No, I'm wrong. That was the day before yesterday. An old woman I sometimes pass in Burnet Woods. "Was an old man who got killed." Yes I know. Didn't see him.

"Okay, well listen maybe you can help us this way. You went by about quarter of ten, right? Did you see any signs on the ground about half way up the steps? You know. Any scuffings on the dust or signs of a struggle or a body being dragged?"

"No," said Burr. "No signs. It didn't happen until after I'd gone by."

"You sure of that?"

"Of course, If I'd seen any dead bodies, you think I wouldn't have told you?"

"Yes sir, but this body was concealed. You might have walked right past it."

"No," said Burr. "It wasn't concealed that well. Lying there in those leaves—I couldn't have walked by without seeing it, if it had been there, I'm quite sure."

Freitag-Watson looking at him a while before speaking. "Those leaves?"

Burr anxious. "It was thrown in a pile of leaves, wasn't it? Wasn't that where the body was?"

"How did you know that?" said Freitag—alone again and very quiet in his voice, while Watson stared at his shoes in profound embarrassment.

Burr trying a desperate save. "Wasn't that in the paper? Or did I just imagine it?"

Freitag-Watson looking relieved. "The paper? Oh, maybe it was in the paper."

Silence while they all try to think of what to say next. Freitag-Watson, "Well, thank you, I guess that's all we have to ask you. If you think of anything else, you might let me know."

"Sorry I can't be of more help," said Burr. "Oh yes—can you tell me, how you knew I was in Burnet Woods yesterday?"

"Student saw you. Recognized you—the kid you saw parking in the circle. Said it was you coming up out of the woods when he parked."

"Who was he? I didn't recognize *him.*"

Freitag shrugged. "Said he had you in a course five years ago."

Burr laughed, somewhat. "I sure have a terrible time remembering students," he said, as if it were something to laugh about. Both policemen laughed too, harder than was necessary, thought Burr, to please him perhaps? And then they left.

Chapter 5

When they got back to the station house later that afternoon, Freitag and Watson sat down in the inner office to put together all the evidence they now had in order to arrive at some sort of a conclusion. They had the interviews with the two students who had parked at the top of the circle; the interview with the victim's son, the radical activist Berthold Kirschner; they had the interview with the man on the tractor; they had the interview with Professor Burr. They had a cast of a shoe print in the mud. Also some thread from an overcoat liner that had got caught in the victim's shoelaces. Also a torn movie ticket to the Esquire Theater, date unknown. Also a restaurant receipt from Frisch's Drive-In restaurant for a big boy platter. Also a symphony concert stub, for a concert two months ago, a seat in the balcony. They had four rocks containing fossils—one dominated by trilobites, one primarily shells, another containing long cone-like creatures, and the fourth containing a mixture of things. They had sent to the Symphony to see if there was any record of who occupied that seat that night; they had sent the overcoat thread to the crime lab; so too the fossil rocks, looking for evidence as to which of them had been the murder weapon and whether any of them contained fingerprints. Spread out on the table in front of them was a large plan of that portion of Burnet Woods, into which had been placed little pins with flags to show the positions of all known persons at a certain moment. They had a pin with a black flag to represent Mr. Kirschner, two pins with green and red flags for the students parking their car in the circle, a pin with a yellow flag for the man on the tractor, a pin with a gray flag for Professor Burr. On the sidelines, because they did not yet know where to put them, they had a pin with a brown flag for the tall young black boy who was their chief suspect, and a pin with a white flag for the little old lady whom the professor had implicated.

"If," said Watson, "I can build a time machine to cover the minutes between 9:29 A.M. and 9:56, moving these pins around according to their necessary movements for each minute during that interval, we ought to be able to discover the murder automatically."

"Work on it," said Freitag. He sat with his hand running over his chin and sometimes spreading out to shade his eyes. He was thinking very hard.

Finally he went to the Suspect Board on the wall. At the moment there was only one slab on the Suspect Board: on it was written in chalk, BLACK BOY. He said, "I guess we'd better get all the other possibilities up here too." He picked up a number of narrow black blocks to be stacked on the Board, and wrote a name in chalk on each one. He wrote NEWHOUSE on one—this was the male student—and CONNIE, the female student, on another; MORELLI (the mower) on another; OLD LADY on still another. "Should I make one for the Professor?" he asked. "Nah," said Watson, "It couldn't be him."

"Nevertheless," said Freitag with professional seriousness, "We are supposed to take every possibility into consideration. I grant you it is not really possible to suspect a full professor of English at the university of a brutal mugging murder in the park with motive robbery, but the fact that he was there at the time puts him, technically, under suspicion, and therefore I had better make out a board for him too and add it to the stack." With a flourish of chalk then he wrote BURR on another block. "Tell you what, though, Watson. I'll put it at the bottom of our list of suspects, where it will be least likely to cause offense should any unauthorized person come in here and ask us what we think we're doing."

When he was done the blocks with the suspects' names were stacked from top to bottom in this order:

BLACK BOY
MORELLI
OLD LADY
NEWHOUSE
CONNIE
BURR

"Why do you put Morelli above the old lady?" asked Watson.

"Strength," said Freitag. "According to the Professor, the old lady was very short and probably she was very frail. Morelli is a big strong man."

"Yet both Burr and the students agree that Morelli was sticking to his tractor, way over here at the other end of the park at the time. And we have no report of anybody seeing an empty tractor sitting around."

"Right," said Freitag. "Better change it around." He took out the MORELLI block and inserted it down next to the bottom between CONNIE and BURR.

Just then Berthold Kirschner burst into the room. "Pigs," he said. "I want to know what progress you are making in finding the murderer of my father. I demand that my father's death be avenged!" He was a young man with fiery long blond hair that swept in great sweeps around his pale girlish face.

"Yes sir," said Freitag. "Let me show you." He showed him the map with pins, and the Suspect Board, and explained Watson's plan of building a time machine. Then he went on: "As it stands right now our prime suspect is the black boy. The difficulty at present is that we have no way of identifying him as yet, nor have we been able so far to find any witness who saw him near the scene of the crime or anywhere in the park on that morning."

"You don't know who he was, and you have no evidence that he was there?" said Berthold. "Then why is he the prime suspect?"

"We know it was him," said Freitag, "because crimes of this kind are always committed by people who fit his description. In fact, that's how we got his description."

"What about the old lady?"

"She's a pretty good suspect too," said Freitag. "At least we know that she was there—we have the professor's word for that—the only problem being that we haven't yet been able to get her there at exactly the right moment. According to the professor she was there the day before, and we haven't yet been able to prove she was there at the time of the crime."

"The time machine might be able to take care of that," said Watson, "if we can find out who she was and when she left the house yesterday morning, if she left the house."

"The case against the black boy is stronger, though," said Freitag, "because of past precedent and probability, and also because he himself would have to be stronger. A question has been raised as to whether the old lady would have been strong enough."

"We could test her when and if we bring her into custody," said Watson. "I could work out a strength testing machine for hitting things with heavy rocks."

"Ah, pigshit!" exclaimed Berthold. "It wasn't no black boy. That's fuzzy pigshit pure and simple. This was a different kind of crime. This was an establishment crime—an intellectual crime. This wasn't no robbery crime, no common mugging, no striking out of the oppressed lower classes at the fetters that bind them—because my father didn't have no money to begin with. His wallet was empty when he set out on his walk."

"You sure?" said Freitag. "How do you know?"

"Because I borrowed his last bill just before he left the house. I said, 'How about some bread, Bud'—"

"Bud?"

"That's what we call each other. A term of affection used by members of the older generation to express equality. My father and I used it to reduce our sense of the enormous age difference between us."

"I see. Go on."

"Yes, I said, 'How about some bread, Bud,' and he said, 'How much?' and I said 'How much you got? I need it to get through my day at school,' and he opened his wallet and said, 'The only thing I got's a ten and here it is,' and I took it and saw into his wallet: Empty, not a damn thing else. So it couldn't have been for robbery they killed him."

Freitag got up and went over to the Suspect Board. Watson pondered and finally said: "But it could have been robbery and they didn't know his wallet was empty. Sometimes they kill them for an empty wallet, you know. And they found the wallet on the ground next to his body, so somebody must have been looking at his wallet as if they hoped it had money in it you know what I mean?"

Freitag (writing with chalk on another slab) intervened: "Nah, his wallet wasn't next to his body."

"Yeah it was hey, Freitag," said Watson.

"Nah it wasn't. I took it out of his pants when we found him, looking to see if it was there. Happened to drop it, and that cop whatsis picked it up. So that was just a rumor about his wallet being next to his body. Wouldn't have mattered if he had had money, but if his wallet had already been emptied that makes it a whole new ball game—maybe."

(Turning his back and concealing what he was doing from the others, Freitag wrote BERTHOLD on the slab, and then inserted it, with the lettering turned in, on the Suspect Board between BLACK BOY and OLD LADY. When he came back to the table you could see what looked like a blank slab in that place.)

While Freitag worked attaching an orange flag to another pin, Berthold in his orange jacket spoke. "An establishment crime, a weird strange intellectual crime. Motiveless, blank, arbitrary, wanton, random violence breaking through the hypocritical shield of society today. Don't look for the black boy who did it—he's got some motive, some reason, some *heart,* for Christ sake, some emotion to make sense out of the crimes he is driven to—whereas this crime, sheer blind violence with no motive against a victim just because he happens to be there, so blind I bet he could hardly even see his victim, didn't even know who he was—"

"How do you know that?" said Freitag.

"—because how else do you explain a stupid crime like that, when my father not only didn't have no money, my father is so senile he dresses so shabby anybody who can see is going to know he hasn't got no money or anything of value on him, so why kill him except because he is still a human being, more or less, the remnant of a human being? A crime so stupid you know it has to be subtle and intellectual and weird and strange, expressing the true ill of our society today. So stupid so subtle you have to look for the murderer where you least expect to find him, you look for him in the character who harbors and nourishes that true ill of our society today, growing it in himself like a biological culture— or any kind of a culture—you have to look for the murderer not in your normal middlingly violent black boy, but in the man who's most likely to keep his violence contained so that it festers and accumulates gases and pollution, the man in whom the emergence of violence is likely to be so great a shock, so grossly polluted by containment, that it will take the most arbitrary and irrational form and kill a poor senile old man simply because he happens to be there as a remnant of human. That— you filthy fascist pigs—is the kind of reasoning you must make if you want to solve this particular crime."

"What conclusion does your reasoning lead you to?" asked Freitag, gloomily.

"I suggest that you put BLACK BOY down at the bottom of the list and that you interrogate BURR some more."

"Burr!" exclaimed Freitag and Watson in unison. "Why Burr is a *full* professor in the Department of English. He is respected as one of the gentlest and mildest and most shy and timorous of men. They call him a gentleman, and you don't hear much of that nowadays, you long-hair, rotten, communist hippies. He is one of three candidates for the post of head of the department, chosen because he is a compromiser between factions, a peacemaker. He is a publishing scholar, or at least he used to be until he got his promotion and tenure, and his name has appeared in print and in footnotes. He has a former wife who committed suicide, but it was not his fault, and he is a father, with two grown children (dirty long-hair, rotten, communist hippies, unfortunately, who have left home). He is kind to animals, and takes care of three dogs and five cats in his large empty house, where he lives alone. Why should you suspect the Good Professor Burr?"

"Because, as I have already explained, this was an establishment crime, an aneurysm in the spiritual vessels of society, an outbreak of establishment sickness, and Professor Burr is the one figure that the establishment fascist pigs would be least likely to suspect. Which makes him—you see?—in truth the *most* likely to suspect. Besides which, according to your map, Professor Burr is the only pin except the victim himself who went anywhere near the scene of the crime. For you have the testimony of Newhouse and Connie who saw him actually emerging from the woods from the very steps where the murder took place. And look on your map, look where you put his pin, there on the steps right next to my father's pin: if those pins are right, you would think he met my father right there on the steps."

"I see what you mean," murmured Freitag-Watson. "We intend, of course, to reconsider all the evidence in the further course of our investigations, and we shall bear your suggestions very much in mind. Meanwhile, may we express our thanks for your contributions, and we shall let you know when we have come to a conclusion about this case. Good day, sir!"

"I have a gun duly and properly registered," said Berthold, "when you are ready for me to help you catch him."

"Yes sir, thank you."

Just audibly as he went out, "Fascist pigs," said Berthold routinely.

"Dirty communist hippy," muttered Freitag-Watson casually.

"Well, let us consider once again our evidence," said Freitag, sticking his pencil in his mouth. "According to Newhouse and Connie, Burr came out of the woods at 9:50 just when they were parking their car, and Morelli was mowing across the meadow. According to Burr, Newhouse and Connie were parking their car at 9:50 and Morelli was mowing across the meadow. According to Morelli, Burr crossed the meadow just after 9:50 and Newhouse and Connie crossed it a couple of minutes later. All our witnesses corroborate each other. Therefore they must all be telling the truth, and therefore it is difficult to see how any of them could be suspects."

"There was a discrepancy you wanted to check out," said Watson. "What was that, do you remember?"

"Oh yes, now what could that have been? Some discrepancy to check after we interviewed Professor Burr. What was it?"

"Leaves!" said Watson. "Something to do with leaves."

"Leaves, yes, leaves! Yes, I remember now. Just a routine check, to check the newspaper to see if it mentioned that Kirschner's body was dumped in a bunch of leaves in plain sight of the steps."

"Have you checked the papers on that?"

"No, didn't seem worthwhile. But now, after the doubts Berthold has raised, perhaps I should do so."

"What will you look for?"

"I shall look to make sure that the newspaper did in fact mention that Kirschner's body was dumped in a bunch of leaves in sight of the steps."

"But it *was* dumped that way."

"Of course it was. But I want to see if the paper mentions it."

"What if it does?"

"Nothing. But if it doesn't—then, you see?"

"What?"

"Then we ask, how did Burr happen to *know* that the body was dumped in a bunch of leaves. Then you see we'll have a real money question."

"Ahh, I see!" breathed Watson.

"Yes indeed. And if we take that discrepancy and add it to Berthold's theory, that gives us two pieces of evidence and then—I am very much afraid, much as I hate to do this—"

"What?"

"Why then, I guess we'd have to put Burr's name right up at the very top of the suspect list."

"What will we do then?"

"Then? Well I guess we'll have to interrogate some more. Try to shock him and break him down. Check out his shoeprints and the lining in his overcoat. Look for his fingerprints on the victim's clothes. Find the rock with the fossils in it and catch him trying to lie that it was another rock. I think we should also go back and interview his colleagues, people like Professor Grummon."

"Him?"

"Indeed yes, for don't you remember? Did not Professor Grummon say he could give us more information if we asked him? Should we not go back to interview him, to ask him if he did not have recent conversations with the suspect in which the suspect talked about walking through the woods on the morning of the murder and perhaps said other even more damaging things?"

"Ah yes, very good."

"Yes, and then—let the evidence accumulate, and then when the point is just ripe we come to the point—pop! We descend on him and catch him by surprise and terrorize him into a confession—that dirty liberal pseudo-intellectual!"

"Hate to do it, though, don't you?"

"God yes, it breaks your heart to see good men, upholders of the system, go down like ships striking icebergs."

The narrator should terminate this scene when Watson brings the papers for Freitag to go through. The same moment that Burr in the library is searching out once again the same papers for their items about the murder. To find out if—Desperate. The narrator—admitting and apologizing for this failure to stick to a first person narrative, as originally agreed. It turns out to be impossible to tell this story in the first person, from Burr's point of view alone—or at least impossible to tell it half so well or so clearly. If he doubts this, tell him to consider the difficulties that would have faced us if we had tried to present this most important scene of the two policemen while sticking strictly still to our own limited point of view.

Chapter 6

Meanwhile, Natalie Fleet. Kept reflecting an image of her, two images, three, many, proliferating, bouncing around in my mind, flickering like butterflies: Natalie Fleet in the office this morning when I gave her my letters to type, seated at her desk, her long brown hair, her pale sad young face, her gold-rimmed glasses, and when she stood up to take the letters from me her very short dress, beige or tan, mini-skirt flaring out high on her thighs (her clear and well-formed young thighs). And Natalie Fleet reliving last night when she came so spontaneously to my house with the heart book, standing in my living room in her red, white, and blue striped shirt and her brown corduroy jeans, bending over to stroke the yellow cat. And Natalie Fleet on Monday in her short purple office dress, driving my car for me while I sat beside her, watching as she manipulated my steering wheel, my turn signal, my gas and brake pedals —her bare knees and thighs with her short skirt. And Natalie Fleet looking at me in alarm, fright on my behalf as I gasped, and she said, "What's the matter?" All this with the continuing non-image of Natalie Fleet's failing to return while the evening grew late, while I did the dishes and the certainty of her coming back faded away into the opposite certainty. Now as the day advanced these images became more lively, more insistent. They were visions, and suddenly he said to me, You must pay some attention to this. What? I murmured. You were disappointed that she did not come back, he said. Yes, I admitted. You are even more

128

disappointed as you reflect upon it today, he said. So it seems, I said.

Maybe she'll come back tonight, he suggested. He rang the doorbell and I went to answer, this evening at home, and there stood, identical with last night, a smallish shape in dark clothes, a girl with glasses and long brown hair wearing a striped shirt and brown corduroy pants, recognizable again as Natalie Fleet. Ah hello, come in, you say. I thought since I couldn't stay last night I should come back tonight, she says. What do you do now? he asks. Invite her to sit down. Ask questions, get a conversation started. Find out what is on her mind that makes her so eager to come and see you in the evening.

That's the trouble, he says. You'll have to invent reasons for her to be so eager, but you'll have to invent the eagerness itself first. She won't come back tonight, because you have no obvious reason for her to do so. Why should she? Surprising enough that she came last night, but why should the surprise be doubled tonight?

Of course—and that was why I was disappointed. She won't come back, he said, unless—Unless what? Unless you make sure that she does. Is that possible? I asked. Action, he said. That is what action is for, to make things happen that would not otherwise happen. Perhaps you can steer the direction of events. I asked how. He considered. There is probably only one way short of violence, he said. No violence, I said—once again as always before I am a man of no violence, I abhor force and coercion and all destructive actions. Yes, he said. The only way is to ask her. Maybe she'll say no—but maybe she'll say yes. And you will have done what you could—you'll have had that satisfaction at least.

I asked him to tell me how to ask. Just ask, he said. Pick up the phone —No! Too formal. Go into her office—also too formal if not necessary. Recall that she will bring back letters to be signed sometime this after-noon, ask her then. When she comes to your office, sign the letters and say, 'Natalie—I hope you'll come back to see me at the house tonight.'

'What for?' she will ask—or if she does not ask it she will look it. Because she will need reasons, he said. Not enough simply to ask her, you must give her an explanation, an excuse, a pretext. Nothing elabo-rate, no tricks—simply tell her something close to the truth. Tell her you'd like to talk to her. 'Natalie, I hope you'll come back to the house tonight so that we can have a little talk.' The words have a quality of portentousness that alarms her. 'Talk about what?' she will ask. Or if she does not ask, she will expect to be told. If she comes to the house then, she will expect you to explain this very particular thing you wish to talk about, and she will find it strange if you are unable to say what it is. 'What did you want to talk about?' she will ask. Oh, nothing, really.

Try again, less formal, less definite: 'Natalie, I hope you'll come back to the house tonight so we can continue our talk of last night.' Really? And what were we talking about last night? She was going to do my dishes. 'Come back and do my dishes.' Quit your kidding—you can't ask a girl to the house to do dishes, especially since you did them last night yourself—there aren't any dishes to do.

But he says you don't have to assign a topic in advance if you want to have a conversation. A friendly chat, a pleasant unplanned talk— surely you can arrange for this. But still she looks at you strangely. For you are asking her to go out of her way, to walk at least three blocks, to give up part of her evening, and no matter how casual you make it, this will give it weight, make it purposeful. In the faculty and staff ladies room she will say to the young girl with white hair who works in Romance Languages, 'I wonder what he wants.' She will ask what the mystery is, and if you say it is nothing but a desire for a little talk, she will attach to that desire all the weight of her own evening that she has sacrificed. She will see you as pressing, possibly even as courting, cer- tainly as needful. Tell him no, avoid that. Avoid needing her, avoid courting her, avoid letting her so interpret it. Tell him it is not that kind of a connection.

Well, he says, how about her own pretext when she came to the house last night (Pretext? Did she need a pretext too?) The book about hearts —work that in your own turn, he suggests. 'Natalie, thank you for lending me that heart book. Why don't you come around to pick it up?' In the ladies' room, however, she complains bitterly. 'Can you imagine the nerve?' says she. 'After I went to all that trouble to take the heart book to his house, he asks me to come by and pick it up myself. When a girl loans a guy a book, since when does a gentleman make her come and take it back herself? The least he could have done—if it's too much trouble to take it to my apartment—is to bring it to me in the office. And he hasn't even read it yet. After I went to all that trouble!'

Well then, he suggests, you might instead find something interesting to show her. 'Natalie, I was disappointed last night when you did not come back, for I had intended to show you something that I am sure you would have been interested in. Why don't you come around again tonight, so that I can show it to you?' Very good, that one—tell him so—if he can also say just what particular thing he intended to show. His animals perhaps? The trophies of Harold (second place in a track meet, runner-up in a tennis tournament)? His records (a few, standard, much loved but without novelty, with a stereo set old and scratchy)? Pictures of his gone family? Guide books for easy travel in Europe? She says to the girls in the ladies' room: 'He invited me over to look at his objay dar. Or maybe his etchings—I don't know. Perhaps it was his stamp collection. Probably it was his animals, his dogs and cats. He wanted me to see his collection, whatever it was, and all the time he was rubbing his hands together like a spider grinning, heh! heh! heh! They do, don't they, spiders rub their hands together?' In the house she says, 'But Professor Burr, what made you think I would be interested in your scrapbooks? Why sir, you begin to make me think you didn't have anything to show at all—you got me here under false pretenses!'

Like a villain in a book. He says, Be natural. Invite her over for coffee, maybe a drink, as you would a friend. He asks, Isn't that what you want her for, for talk, for a friend. 'Natalie, since you couldn't stay last night, how about coming over tonight for a drink?' She tells it in the ladies' room: 'That may be what men do with their friends, and he may think I'm his friend, but I'm also a girl. If a gentleman invites a girl to his house for a drink—without coming to get her, without escorting her from her place to his through the dark dangerous streets at night, expecting her to find her own way over and back (even though I did just that last night)—it seems to me there are certain niceties a gentleman remembers. Seems to me if he wants to invite me for a drink, the least he could have done was treat me like a lady and take me out to dinner.'

Dinner! Warn him, stop him before it is too late. Shock, the audacity. Me, ask Natalie Fleet to dinner? Tell her, sorry, but we are talking about a man who hasn't had a date with a woman in twenty years. Not even (especially not) with Laura Grummon. In the ladies' room she laughs: Guess who came into the office just now to ask me for a date. You'd never guess, of all people, I nearly died! The young, white-haired girl from Romance Languages giggles. He says, Your false pride. What do you care about a couple of giggling girls in the secretarial department? The reason you haven't had a date was that you were married—but of course Natalie Fleet knows that you are not married now. He says, You have reverted to fourteen years old.

Not so, I said. Tell her the reason I am afraid to take her out to dinner. The reason is that I am afraid to go out. Afraid to be seen. Must stay out of sight for a few days. Not go out while the police are still trying to plot my flag on the map and switch me around on the suspect board.

He said, You are "out" right now. And tonight you shall go out to eat your dinner, whether you have a date or not. (But only near home, in the neighborhood, the hamburger house on Clifton Avenue, or the Chili Parlor. Not a display, as it would be if I went out with Natalie Fleet.) Irrational as usual, he said. You must learn to disregard your fears when you want to do things. I remembered one occasion—but never mind. I said, 'If Natalie Fleet really expects me to make a date with her and take her out to dinner, she has got to have it explained.' In the ladies' room, she said, smugly, 'I always knew he wanted me, desired my body, craved me sexually, but he always pretended not to until the night he asked me to dinner.'

Strenuously, severely, austerely. Explain how it cannot be, how mistaken she is. Remind her where we came from (I opened the front door —I had forgotten to turn on the front porch light, but even so I could recognize the smallish shape standing there in dark clothes as a girl with glasses and long hair wearing a striped shirt and jeans, Natalie Fleet smiling with a book in her hand), how she took identity in the beginning as Harold's girl friend, two years ago, picked up in a college class. Tell her how glad you were that Harold finally had a girl, and they were two children, and you were glad for his sake.

(Her mouth forms a silent "O!" as if there were some matter of delicacy involved, and when he comes back into the room with Grum-

132

mon and the others, Natalie Fleet was gone.) Tell her, then you were the *father*, going through the living room where they were sitting on your way to the study, while she looked up from the couch, snuggled next to Harold, and said, "Hello Mr. Burr." It was easier then to identify her as a member of the children's generation. Tell her how you regarded her, how pleased you were on Harold's behalf, that he had found himself a real and steady girl friend of his own, even though she did seem—so she seemed then—inconspicuous, studious, quiet, rather drab. Her constant uniform of those days, always the dark jeans and a plain dark shirt, sometimes with the lettering of some camp. Pleased on Harold's behalf, tell her, and a little contemptuous too that my shy like-me son had not found a more spectacular girl, one more fond of color and display. (Pointing to the back door: "Can I go out this way?" She looked at the dishes piled in the sink and began to grin. "Do 'em up for you," said Natalie Fleet.)

Explain to her how it is with a father and his children. She was then how old? Nineteen? Twenty? Mainly she was a child because Harold was a child and she was Harold's, and a father feels the same barriers of incest and age and distance around his children's friends that he feels around his children. There was a famous conversation with Harold one night—a conversation that he did not ask for, that Harold manipulated until it reached a point where he exclaimed of himself and Natalie: "How could we possibly be virgins?" Well, tell her, that was a revelation and in those days it seemed hard to believe, even though he knew that the children's generation nowadays was also the sex generation. And they were no less children for it, playing with grownup life. Perhaps they were even wiser than the grownup generation—Burr would not want to speak on this. Trying still to be pleased on Harold's behalf, although the distance and difference from himself seemed greater than ever.

Tell her how daughterly she was. (Then Monday she was standing in the doorway to his office looking at him with an expression of open alarm, fright, and she cried out, "Professor Burr, are you all right? Is something the matter?" He leaned against the desk with his arm and gulped for breath, and she stared, shocked.) She would greet me then like an old friend or like a daughter—"Hi, Mr. Burr!"—with a look as if I shared their secrets, as if indeed she knew what Harold had told me and thought it made a special bond between us. As if she assumed it cleared the air, glad because I did not make a fuss of disapproval or raise an awkwardness. Tell her she assumed too much, no doubt—I in my conservatism still raising the old anxious questions that my own youth had had to face—yet still pleased on Harold's behalf, as I watched the signs of their still deepening intimacy or else habit, that summer in those heavy days of Cynthia's depression that the doctor said we should regard as illness, days of the home we did not then know was dying, while Harold clung to Natalie Fleet and I could see that he was clinging, and I listened for him coming home late at night, imagining that I knew their lives and their intimacy, seeing this in her eyes when she came to the house and gave me a knowing glance when I met her at the door. Explain to her the contrast between Harold here and my own quivering and fearful innocence at that age. Explain to him the general difference between Harold Burr the young and Ralph Burr the father. (As he sat down, she used his phone to call the doctor, and while she waited, the phone at her shoulder, he noticed the purple dress she wore, very short like all the dresses she wore to the office, exposing most of her thighs. Her long brown hair still hung loose and free. Her gold-rimmed glasses looked different but he could not remember well enough to determine what the difference was. Her face had more vitality, more color than in the old days. No doubt she was touching it up a little.)

Then in the fall—now almost two years ago—when everything collapsed, she dropped out of the scene altogether. Tell her how in the midst of such crises you scarcely noticed her absence. There was the collapse of Harold, the rage of Harold, and then he left. What did he do about his quiet little girl friend when he left? Tell her you never knew, you still don't know. Was there a fight, a struggle, tears, laments, accusations? You never knew. Nor ever thought to ask—with Cynthia's tragedy culminating in November, leaving Burr with only his daughter Elaine and the animals. And even Elaine stuck it out only for the winter, and in the spring, a year ago, she too was gone.

About the same time that the forgotten Natalie Fleet suddenly reappeared with a job in the office, wearing a dress for the first time he could remember, and acting as if she were no longer the same Natalie Fleet. "Why hello, Mr. Burr," she said brightly, that first day when I walked into the office. "Did you know that I'm Mr. Stone's new assistant? I'm going to be working here from now on." (She drove up to the corner with my car and I got in, and then she drove me downtown to the doctor's office. Her short purple dress left her legs bare—her knees. My steering wheel my turn signal accelerator brake. She talked freely, chattery. She had to tilt her head up, nose up, in order to see properly where she was going. She was driving me to the doctor's office. When she got to the doctor's building she let me out. She said she would park the car and then come and join me in the doctor's office. She was doing everything for me. That was Monday.) Looking very different in these ensuing days from the way she used to look. Admit noticing the change— her clothes, the short dresses and skirts, the colors, the difference in the look of her face—as she graduated suddenly from children's generation to working-girl generation. Attracting attention for being pretty, sexy. With the young men in the department, students, graduate students, instructors, finding excuses to stand around the office, growing interest. She came to department parties. She was popular, they said. She had lots of dates, apparently. Lots of boy friends. There were rumors about her, about her boy friends. According to Harvey Kessler, discredited, she had what earlier generations would have called an easy reputation. (She waited in the doctor's waiting room while he gave me an electrocardiogram. She was sitting there in her purple dress reading a magazine when I came back. "Well," she said, "I certainly hope the doctor is right." She insisted on driving me home, even though by now I was all right again. She would not let me take her home but drove me in my car to my house, put the car in my garage, and then walked off by herself in the late afternoon to her own place, which she said was only a few blocks away. She said, "I walk by here every day." It did not occur to me to invite her into my house, not even for coffee.)

According to Harvey Kessler, discredited—(discredited, according to Natalie Fleet, changing history, driving him home from the doctor's office on Monday, when she happened to mention Harvey Kessler. "Professor Kessler doesn't like me," she said. "I've heard he tells stories about me." Burr noted without remark that she did not ask him if Harvey had told *him* any stories about her. "What sort of stories?" I asked. "Stories. Tales. Lies, I guess," she said. Lies? Why should he do that? I asked, annoyed because I don't like to hear about people I know telling lies and doing other bad things without explanation or provocation. "Because I wouldn't—well—" Wouldn't what? "Nothing," she said. "Never mind. He got mad. He's been mad ever since.") According to Harvey Kessler, discredited, the unmarried graduate students and instructors had discovered how easy she was. According to Harvey she took it for granted that if a young man had a date with her she would etcetera. Which made her a valuable asset to the department and adornment to the office in the eyes of the younger men. So said Harvey, who denied any interest himself, though what he said sounded like admiration and amused appreciation rather than malice and dislike and a desire for revenge.

Tell her this is one of those cases where you don't like to take sides, you never can be sure who has discredited whom, nor who most maliciously distorts, or simply reveals the facts—and cite that as yet another reason why you could not consider taking her out to dinner tonight or any other night: discrediting stories discredit everybody. Add it to the other reasons. And make these other reasons clear. You don't take her to dinner because, as her friends in the ladies' room already know, a dinner invitation turns into a courtship and a dance, turns him into a man and her a woman and raises questions like the one that Harvey, discredited or not, with malice or appreciation, had raised about her. Explain to her therefore most carefully why this question of the man and the woman, which you had never expected to come up between you and Miss Fleet, cannot possibly come up now.

Tell her because in the first place you have already a commitment to another woman that you need not identify as Laura Grummon in order for her to understand. Even if this was never quite real, still there has been no formal resolution and you cannot ignore it. And when it does end, as it surely soon will, tell her other reasons why you could not think of a Natalie Fleet as taking the place of a Laura Grummon. Mention a girl like Mickey Staley, with the soft blond hair, instructor of history.

Speak of Mickey Staley as ideal beauty seen from a distance. Tell of your plan to take Mickey Staley out to dinner when you finally get Laura Grummon's approval—a plan you have kept in mind for several months. Locate Mickey Staley, occupying a certain fixed position in the mind, a niche set at a distance, emblematic of that distance that must be traversed once you are free to traverse distances. (Narrator asks, Have you ever spoken to Mickey Staley? Natalie Fleet asks the question. Tell her that not having spoken to her yet, having seen her distantly in the dining room daily for part of a year without speech, is an advantage. It leaves all possibilities for discovery still open and the future unlimited by probabilities.)

If she needs so many reasons, add the considerations of military policy, show her Elias, or would it be Grummon? making a stuffy little huffy puffy speech about senior faculty members getting themselves involved too intimately with the office staff. (Will she ask, why on earth shouldn't they? Would Elias or Grummon really care? Would you have to resort to rules from the old army perhaps: officers shall not fraternize with enlisted men, with the old reasons, it breaks down discipline? Will she seize on this to ask, It's discipline that you want from me?) Or add the more likely Grummon objection, how by working for Stone she really belongs to the camp of the enemy—how do we know that she is not a baited trap? How do we know that it was not Stone himself who sent her to the house last night to spy?

But admit that all these objections are trivial against the one big all-covering one, which is that she is a child still with an electric blanket invisibly protecting her and grounding his lust. (Narrator says, taboo! Say boo to her: Boo boo taboo!) Make the necessary concessions. Admit on Monday in the car noticing how high on her thighs was the hem of her short purple dress, noticing the knees and the thighs. Admit also last night noticing how the horizontal stripes of her shirt made curved lines around the shapes of her separated breasts. Admit how much we have seen, her attraction exerting itself upon the young men who look at her in the department office—but always vicariously, just as in the old days when you were so pleased on Harold's behalf, in those days when she was still denying her own color and was still so unmistakably a child.

Now, tell her, you see why they consider her an asset to the office, even before knowing the quality of her work, you understand the magnetism that makes them speculate on her morals, principles, standards, and rules, if any, that makes a Harvey Kessler speak as he does about her, whether or not he speaks truth or slander. Admit you enjoy the excitement she raises in the young man's chest and groin, you enjoy the imagining of his pursuit of the adventure—while still kept off by that invisible yet inevitable distance, that insulation that prevents you from taking that excitement into yourself and making it your own.

No need to explain it to her in fact, for she should be the first to recognize it herself—the fact that as she was once Harold's girl friend and Burr was the *father*, so, though Harold is long gone and she herself is much changed, yet still for her he remains a father and she for him a child. Other girls her own age may not have this effect on him, but for her the wires of incest still protect: she is daughter, and employee, and youthful friend, but she cannot be his girl or his woman.

The narrator said, And you never knew this until just now? All along, never thinking to ask a question about Natalie Fleet until this afternoon —wonder, will this knowledge change things between you?

Thought held in suspension (where are we?) in the middle of the afternoon. I heard clicking steps approaching in the hall, which was now mostly empty. Natalie Fleet, he whispered, and then Natalie Fleet came around the corner, sure enough Natalie Fleet, in the beige dress (another short skirt—shortness of skirt was her style since she had moved out of the children's generation), holding papers (my letters), a friendly look on her face, look that arouses confidence. She stood near me in my desk chair as I read the letters over. She stood near, and the narrator said that if I were a young man in her own generation it would be a sign to touch her bottom and I would want to do so and I might even try by putting a hand first around her hips, or her thighs, say. As it was, I read the letters, reading first one and then the next and the next, while she stood by and handed them to me, and I hunched over and signed them all, all the while trying to remember what solution I had reached in the problem of how to get her to the house tonight.

The last letter signed. "No mistakes?" she said.

"No mistakes," I said. "Thank you." I gave her the signed letters and leaned back in my chair. She paused a moment. She said, "How are you feeling today?"

Oh—this was the heart thing Monday and the trip to the doctor, when she had come upon me in the office having my spasm and had taken charge, driving me in my car to the doctor and then home. "I'm all right now, I think," I said. Other things, unmentionable, had occurred to me.

"No recurrence?"

"No." Now the question of inviting her. Open mouth and start to speak, he said, though I could not remember even yet how we had decided to do it. Then I remembered that we had not decided anything. The problem had never been settled. We had decided not to ask her to come and talk, nor to return the heart book, nor to invite her to come and look at the collection (what collection?), and certainly not to invite her for dinner. We had decided that there was a taboo against sexual feeling and therefore any kind of sexual formality between us. The only way was to get her to come of her own volition without inviting her to come. I asked, How does one manage that? Meanwhile she turned to go. Her skirt flicked off her rump as she walked toward the door. The muscles in the backs of her thighs rippled lightly as she walked, such as a young man would notice or I if it were some other girl. Action, he said: Mouth open, tongue ready, form a word, form the vowel "eh," prepare to aspirate, "h"—not that word! "Natalie!" I cried. She kept on walking. Louder, he said. "Natalie!" She stopped and turned in the door: "Sir?"

God damn, now you are embarrassed! he said. *(Sir?)* I said (suggest it without asking), "I was disappointed when you didn't come back last night."

"Oh, I'm sorry," she said, animated, amusement, some concern.

"I had to do the dishes all by myself." (What are you doing? he demanded, warning me to smile my utmost, reduce everything to the most trivial level possible). "I'm sorry," she said, "I got tied up—so late —I completely forgot about those dishes." Look how childlike now she shows her concern for having somehow offended the Father-Boss-Professor Figure. Reassure. Laugh. "Don't worry about it! I was only disappointed because I didn't have a chance to—" (To *what?* he said. Tell her quick) "to talk with you last night, which I was looking forward to." Curious expression on her face. Leave it there? Let her draw her own conclusions?

But she'll never draw them right, he said. Not unless you tell her. Then he said, Dinner! It's the only way. No, I said. Must absolutely be avoided.

"I wonder if maybe tonight you might like to" (Go to dinner with me, he said) "come over to the house," I said. (Fool, what are you saying? he said. Rape, she said. Incest!)

See the look of sweet perplexity on her face as she repeats, trying to make sure she understands the questions: "You want me to—to your house?" (What she wants to know is why, he said. Even if there is no reason, she would like to have at least an ostensible reason, some agreed-upon excuse for the request. As for you, you have already committed incest with your question, you might as well regularize it for her and invite her to dinner.)

"Yes, this evening. My house so we can—" (Block. Talk? Talk about what? she will say. Give her incentives, he said.) "I'll give you some coffee. Or a drink" (That's better, he said) "yes, come over, and I'll get you a drink, if you'd like." Still she looked puzzled, and again he said *dinner!*, and this time it came through: "Let me take you out to dinner first."

He heard himself utter these words and he felt a profound shock with himself. But for her it was an instant change, as if suddenly all became clear. All her perplexity vanished, replaced by a broad happy smile. "Oh I'm so sorry," she said in well-rehearsed tones. "I'm tied up at dinner." Then the puzzlement begins to find its way back into her face, or perhaps it is more purely curiosity now, and she said, "But maybe later in the evening—"

"Yes, yes! Can you come around later? That would be nice."

She looked a moment, still puzzled, considering. He needed excuses yet and suddenly remembered one of the narrator's rejected suggestions: "I have something I'd like to show you."

"Oh really?" she said brightly, as if clarified again (even while he

140

rebuked me: How are you going to deliver on that? What are you going to say when she asks?).

"Okay!" she said, as if in sudden decision. "I'll come over. When?"

"Whenever you say," said Burr, feeling as if he had scored a great victory over something.

She seemed still rather sober, puzzled, unsure what to think of his peculiar invitation. She said, "Sometime after eight-thirty?"

"Good," I said. "That would be nice."

As she turned to go her expression changed, and I caught a glimpse of a look I was not meant to see, that broke across her face before she could turn completely away. It was the uncontrollable grin of a child who has just scored a triumph, possibly a naughty triumph, or has discovered a powerful secret perhaps but doesn't want to let you know about it. Just wait until she can tell her friends, goes this grin. Grin and giggle with the girls in the ladies' room.

She went clicking off down the hall. According to the narrator my first feeling of success was instantly clipped short by my glimpse of that childish grin, and my first reaction to that was a feeling of humiliation, embarrassment, as I thought of the giggling in the ladies' room. Followed directly by a sweep of anger. I said, Damn fool, I warned you. I said, Damn girl, you won't get away with that. Set you straight, I said to her. Correct your misunderstandings. Grinning as if there were no difference between you and a man of forty-five. I'm Harold's father, never forget that. Impervious, maker-of-taboo. Grinning as if I were just another sex-smitten instructor or graduate student or undergraduate. Correct these errors, I told him. She doesn't realize the taboo. Make sure she understands, I said. (Then Harvey reminded me that every date for her is an implicit agreement to etcetera. Ignore that, said Burr to the narrator. Deny it. Delete it. Keep it out of sight.)

Chapter 7

Remembering (through waning afternoon and hasty supper hour and early twilight evening of waiting for her to come back) two years ago when Harold would bring her to the house. Tell her how in those days I sometimes noticed them in the living room as I passed through on the way to the study, huddled together on the sofa reading the comics or going over some catalogue while the stereo played rock, the girl then as now with her long brown hair and glasses but less colorful, her jeans, her plain dark shirt with lettering from some camp. Remembering that in the ease of this afternoon's success, the ease with which I had managed to persuade her to come back to the house, alone, tonight. Narrator calls this a success, a victory, easier than I expected. Just ask her to come and she'll come, he says. Who needs pretexts?

Impure though, I have to tell him. Query again that evil grin that I was not meant to see but did see nevertheless. The grin concealed from me, which meant (according to intelligence) that she had scored a secret victory at Burr's expense. Query what this victory would be, and why it should be at Burr's expense. Victory because she had gotten herself invited back to the house, says narrator? Why object to that? At Burr's expense, intelligence reminds. Because Burr has lost something to her, which obviously she knows. Lost what? asks narrator. Suggest an answer: Self-respect, dignity, detachment. To the girls in the ladies' room: Guess who's the latest one to make a date with me? And without even asking me out—won't even take me out, invites me to his house? Because she thinks you want to be a lover and are too proud and stuffy to admit it, says intelligence, but she knows better, she thinks, designating you as a puffy, stuffy, old damn fool.

Narrator, who wants to keep things always moving, happening, says this can't be so bad since she did agree to come. A mild joke for her in the midst of a success she welcomes, which is a success for you too. Asks what could there possibly be to fear or avoid? Intelligence, however, notes the true significance of her ill-concealed grin, and warns. It means that she does not recognize the difference, does not understand that important discriminating restraint, what we have called the *taboo* that makes of Natalie Fleet a daughter to Professor Burr rather than whatever else. It means very simply that she does not realize that he is like a father to her. That whether or not she feels put off by his twenty-five-year seniority over her, she does not realize that he is put off by it. Means that she supposes, assumes, takes for granted, that he looks at her exactly as any other man would look at her, a younger man, that he wants to play the dating game like a man of twenty-to-twenty-five, that all men when they look at her think one thing, think: sex breasts body thighs short skirts wow. An assumption of power on her part that ignores all the authorized sources of power that he has acquired through the years, as father, as professor, as boss, as man of years—as if years made no difference to a man, as if a man of forty-five were as claylike and fawning and puppy-like, with a tongue hanging out as far as his penis, just as much a doll to play with as a man of twenty-to-twenty-five. No, said Burr, thinking he was much offended by her assumptions. Refuse to be food for her female vanity, he said. Tell her how trivial the problems and techniques of courtship look to a man of forty-five who has serious things on his mind. Tell her how little he cares for dates, for taking her out to dinner, for dressing up, for buying corsages and trinkets, for flattery in all its little forms, for dancing and night clubs and all the modern commercial American Mating Game. Tell her No, Burr is a professor with serious things on his mind, a man of forty-five years, no time to be trivial, nor ornamental, nor sexy.

Narrator is perplexed. Suddenly, he says, it is no longer clear why you want her to come tonight. No wonder it was so hard to give her a good reason to come, when you can't even remember yourself why you want her. Because a pleasant evening chat—said Burr. Chat about what? What is it we have to say to her? Because last night when she did not come back, we felt a sharp keen bite of disappointment, which kept biting all day today until we loosened it by asking her to come back. Disappointment about what? asks narrator.

He presents me a scene: Natalie Fleet comes to the door, wearing identical with last night the redwhiteblue striped shirt and the low slung brown corduroys. Comes in, sits down in living room, and you bring her a drink as promised. You sit down in one chair and she sits in the other. Take a breath. 'Well—' you say. 'What would you like to have a conversation about?' 'I don't know,' she says, 'I guess I'm not properly prepared.'

Burr to narrator: Because you always want to make things clear and connect events to clearly divined or defined forces and motives unmixed with the unknown, suppose you tell me. You say what it was I wanted when I invited Natalie Fleet back.

Narrator tries. Because of the disappointment—yes, start with that, by means of which you recognized the need she had suddenly uncovered in you. Because she came so completely unexpected, when you were expecting something else, many things else perhaps, all going in a certain terrible direction, and in the midst of that, suddenly she appeared promising by the very suddenness and unexpectedness and undirectedness and unboundedness of her appearance a future equally not to be specified. Because in the midst of narrowing inevitability (that I as narrator was drawing around you, would you say?) she appeared with the promise of indefinite possibility. Of which the most important thing was the indefiniteness—she came at a time when you most needed the feeling of not knowing what the possibilities might be. Conversation, who knows what direction it might go? Revelations, who knows of what or to what purpose?

So it was last night, says narrator, while you felt the doom ringing you in the distance like a forest fire all in a circle closing in, while your ignorant colleagues circled in much closer to test your weakness in your work, and all the while life was coming to a close—when suddenly she appeared at the door with a book for your heart, as if there was a new world somewhere after all—no wonder you were disappointed when she did not come back.

As soon as the narrator said this, Burr got very depressed. He had forgotten that he was doomed. But the moment he recognized Natalie Fleet as an alternative, he realized that he was doomed as he had not realized before—even if Freitag and Watson and Berthold were unable, as he still believed they would be unable—to pin a crime on him. Doom was there, nevertheless, doom was inside when not outside, doom was all around, thrown into dark prominence by the bright light of Natalie Fleet's impossible possibility.

Just ask then, says narrator, for a friendly evening chat to dazzle the doom away. I agreed, just make it a friendly evening chat, calm and soothing, I said, a consoling and comforting evening chat, a healing discussion. Narrator objects, as if this were not the same thing, not what he meant, but tell her, I say, all we want is a balm, a calming, all we want is desperate, all we want so desperately, so urgently, all we want so painfully, so insistently, is the help she can give, all the help she can possibly give, the great deep help she offered instantly without words last night at the moment she appeared so unexpectedly at the doorway with the heart book in her hand. Tell her, help!

Are you insane? she asks. What kind of help can I give? What kind can anybody give? She could help me move, I said. She could help me find an apartment, and she can find movers and help me pack and help me get Cynthia's brother's furniture ready to ship, as promised. She can help with all the work that has to be done in the next four weeks that I haven't even started and can't seem to move. (In the ladies' room, she says to the white-haired girl from Romance Languages: 'I'm a secretary, right? If a professor asks me to help him find an apartment, I don't have to do it, do I? If he asks me to become a furniture mover and lug his big things around and carry his piano on my back, I can tell him to go to hell, can't I? I mean, it's not part of my job when I signed up to be a secretary, is it?')

Narrator reminds her however of day before yesterday in the afternoon, how I recognized the sign first while I was bending over the lower drawer of the file cabinet in my office, filing student papers. Bent over, recognized the first mild burning sensation in my chest, and I straightened up in order to stretch it out, but the burning increased and I realized that my breath was getting short, I had to gulp for it, I began to gasp for it. All the time struggling with it and at the same time thinking how to describe it to the narrator so that he could tell about it, and I decided to postpone the student papers, I put their folders on my desk and went to the window where I stood keeping my body as straight and my lungs as distended as I could, groping for the air, trying to draw in deep for a chemistry to replenish my blood. Telling the narrator to mention the pain that was beginning, while as I gasped I looked out the window and noticed in the back of my mind the tree just outside, the cardinal hopping from one branch to another, the wild-haired students walking by on the sidewalk below.

Then because it was hard to bear I turned around and leaned straight-armed against the desk and bore down heavily on it, pushing hard and gasping, gasping, as I began to wonder in earnest if I was going to die. Just then I saw Natalie Fleet in the doorway, looking at me. I had not heard her approaching because I was breathing too hard. Purple dress with the very short skirt. Looking at me full of shock.

"Professor Burr, are you all right? Is something the matter?"

"Just a little—ah—seizure." Sat down and tried to lean back as far as I could.

"*Seizure!*"

"Nothing to worry about," I said.

Her concern. "Can I get you anything? Smelling salts?" I merely gasped. "You want to lie down." Very anxious. "Call the doctor?" Told her, no, it was beginning to ease up. Would be over in a minute. She waited and watched while the spasm faded away, and then it was gone. Then, when I felt recovered and normal again except a little shaky from the shock and the scare, I explained what it was and how it had always been diagnosed before.

She said. "You'd better go to the doctor anyway."

I said, Perhaps I should.

She said, "Would you like me to take you there?"

Not necessary, I said. She'd be glad to, though. "You'd better not drive yet. Better take it easy." She did everything, then. She called my doctor and arranged for me to come right down. I gave her the keys to my car and told her where it was, and she went out to get it. She was very helpful, says narrator, she was full of help. Natalie Fleet *is* help, says the narrator, and when she came so unexpectedly to the door last night, she raised the dazzling possibility of help in the midst of doom. No wonder you were disappointed. But how can I help? she asks. (To the girls in the ladies' room, she asks: What does he expect me to do?)

Narrator says: The real reason you want her to come is you want to make a confession.

Object to that. Terrified. Confess to Natalie Fleet?—ask this in such a way as to maximize the absurdity of the idea. Give myself away? Remind him that I expect to go free, I do not expect my crimes to be caught. If I confess to Natalie Fleet, what is to keep her from telling the police? Confess, to throw my guts into the flowing stream of human knowledge and life? Tell him he is ahead of time on that, Burr sees no reason to confess just yet, feels no compulsion to do so.

Narrator says to confess would make a better story. Burr angry, refuses to be trifled with, asserts his importance as a living human being. Narrator says to confess would bring together all parts of him including the wretched indigestible parts that he was trying to discard and would thus protect his importance as a human being against disintegrating forces. Burr frightened, afraid of what would happen if he confessed, still wants to get away with his crime and a minimum of embarrassment and distress if he can manage it.

Then the narrator says that if Burr does not intend to confess to Natalie Fleet he has lost his motive for inviting her to his house tonight. You'll have to improvise, says narrator, admit your lack of purpose, drift and let things happen. See what will happen.

Again he shows me a scene: Natalie Fleet comes to the door, wearing identical with last night the redwhiteblue striped shirt and the low-slung brown corduroys. Comes in, sits down in living room, and you bring her a drink as promised. You sit down in one chair and she sits in the other.

Take a breath. 'Well—' you say. 'What would you like to have a conversation about?' She hesitates: 'I guess I didn't really prepare my talk for this evening.'

You say, 'It doesn't matter. We can talk about Harold for a while.' Then she says, 'Let's not talk about Harold, let's talk about you.'

Now, says narrator, *you* say something. Burr says, 'What do you want to say about me?'

'How I have always really loved you,' she says says the narrator. No, change *loved* to *wanted:* 'How I have always wanted you,' says Natalie says narrator. 'All the time I was going with Harold I was really thinking about you, wishing to get at you through Harold, until now two years later here I sit in this same room alone with you, and this was the real reason why I came to the house last night—' says she says narrator, 'because I thought now you are alone perhaps now we could—' Narrator makes her stop so Burr can say something. 'Could what?' says Burr. She looks at him softly, smilingly, yearningly: 'Make love together?' phrased, says narrator, like a question, a request, a plea. 'You and me?' 'Take me to bed with you?'

Now, says narrator, I have given you your opportunity, make your confession.

'O I am sorry,' says Burr. 'So touched and moved by your grateful words, so moved and stirred and drawn, attracted, yes, reciprocate the feeling, yes very much, must confess toward you, but nevertheless must refuse your most kind offer. For you must understand the barrier that stands between us, that you are only a child and I am a father, I am Harold's father, and you are a secretary and I am a boss—that is a barrier too—and you work for Stone, you are a spy from the enemy's camp, I know you don't intend to be, but I have to consider it, it is part of the barrier that stands between us, and besides this I already have a woman who is looking out for my interests, named Laura Grummon, and if I get her approval, then my idea was to see if I could rouse up an interest in Miss Staley, you know Miss Staley, and so that constitutes another barrier between us. So you see that it is really a taboo, this barrier between us, and there are things about me, you don't even know about, to make the taboo into a real electric fence, and therefore you see, how grateful I am, how much I wish we could, how much I wish—' Narrator says maybe she starts to take off the striped shirt. What kind of an adjustment does Burr make now? He says, 'If maybe you can explain to me why it isn't really a barrier? Give me a good reason for disregarding the taboo?'

'I won't tell anybody,' says Natalie.

Narrator gasps a little. Then suggests we show the scene again, corrected. She sits in the living room chair with the drink that you have just brought her and says, 'I have a confession to make.' (Let *her* make the confession, says the narrator.) 'How I have really always wanted you—'

Now make your little speech about the taboo, says narrator. But Burr cannot speak. Taboo comes into mind and quietly drifts out again. Tell her no, says the narrator. Tell her, Thank you I am so sorry but no. No no a thousand times no. Still Burr stares, wondering.

Narrator asks sternly: What would you really say in such a case?

'I should have taken you to dinner,' says Burr.

Narrator smirks, giggles, laughs almost hysterically. In spite of which failures in gallantry and self-knowledge, she is coming to the house anyway tonight. Coming to your living room to have a drink with you. A new world of possibility opening up. If only you knew what it was.

Then he checked his rising expectations to speak in the severe tone of austere realism. In realism you would never refuse her offer, he says, which proves the death of the taboo. On the other hand, he continues, in realism she would never make such an offer. Does this, he asks, bring the taboo back to life? Will you confess? Or will you wait for her to do so?

And now the whole day was shaped into a great funnel of energy and motion and quiet thought all pointing toward that moment in the evening when, by her promise, Natalie Fleet will return to our house for a visit.

Chapter 8

I went home soon, quickly. Brought in the paper, read it. Went out for a quick early supper at the Chili Parlor. Came back to the house, tried to read a novel in the living room, while I waited for the promised visit of Natalie Fleet.

First person on the spot will never know exactly what Burr expected from that anticipated visit. The narrator with a little organizing detachment keeps trying. Suggest once that Burr, released from taboo, felt first beginnings of a new future, some new partnership to displace the sterile guardianship of Laura Grummon, after Cynthia. Or if not that (because time seemed so short), try the possibility of some explosive tearing loose of the veils of the present, see seduction and sex suddenly liberated under pressure of time, with this girl of indefinite potential who had often danced in his imagination. And yet observe too (narrator) that if Burr for the first time felt free to hope—in an electricity of excitement —that she was bringing him an orgy of herself, yet something still diverted his thought and what he foresaw instead was an orgy of talk, his talk, revealing, explaining, disclosing, unburdening, while the image of the girl divesting herself of clothes, the stimulated image of the girl, naked, putting herself around him, kept dissolving into an image of their voices, his voice and hers, an image of words dissolving all differences.

So might the narrator, but first person cannot say anything of what we anticipated that night except general opportunity, an opening up of possibility—but who knows what possibility it was—a possibility of life, of things happening, difference, change, all concentrated into the short time that was left. For that was the other thing first person kept forgetting and never understood, but the narrator in his detachment might perceive: namely, doom, our powerful (Burr's powerful) recognition that there was an end near at hand, that time was truncated, that one, two, three days and nights and no more remained before it ended, before nature blew up or Burr blew up or the university blew up or civilization blew up or life blew up—who knows? only the knowledge that life remained briefly to be lived now, tonight, or never, and that was why Natalie Fleet was coming.

Probably, said Burr, they will follow her and in that way they will learn where he is and be able to make the arrest. He objected that they already knew where he lived—he was no fugitive and there was no need to hunt him down with bait and a trap. Didn't matter, said Burr. They would need her to prove his guilt in any case, and that was why they would follow her. He didn't care. Now he resolved that he would make his confession to Natalie Fleet and only to Natalie Fleet—because she had dared, courage and kindness, to come when he asked, with the flimsiest of pretexts or no pretext at all. Therefore his confession to her, and the reward to her too, and his great joy of this one night with her before, following her, they come to take him away.

Doorbell. She stood in the open door, like last night dressed again in brown corduroy flaring pants and this time a flowing top in red and gold and blue with long flaring sleeves, smiling shyly as if not sure that she should be there. Come in. Sit down. Glad. She said, "I didn't know. You said you wanted to see me. You had something you wanted to show me?"

Embarrassed, now it sounded as if we had got her under false pretenses.

"Well, I don't know," we said. "There isn't much to see." Confession. "I guess I just wanted to talk."

Her expression puzzled. "Well—" she said. "What do you want to talk about?"

"Would you like some coffee?" we asked. Oh, thank you. "Instant coffee?" I don't mind. I never drink anything but instant.

After bringing her the coffee, we said, "I don't really have anything to show you—unless you want to see all the cats and dogs." She laughed. Looks like they're all here, in this room. "Or I could show you baby pictures of Harold." Grimace. Thanks, I think I can do without.

"Actually I feel I got you here under false pretenses—somewhat," we said. A right move. You could see her relax a little when you said it, begin to smile more easily. What do you mean, false pretenses? "I just wanted to have a talk with you," we said. "Nothing special, nothing important. If that seems wrong to you, you don't have to stay—"

"Why should it be wrong?" she said, gaily. "Why shouldn't we talk? I don't mind." She settled more relaxed in her chair and said: "I just figured you didn't have any very special reason, this afternoon."

Tell him good, it's working out fine. Then she said, "What do you want to talk about?" It puts us back where we were. What do we want to talk about? We didn't know. No idea. The uncomfortable tension of words wanting to emerge, but how can you let them emerge, how can you dig them out even with a shovel, if you don't know what they are? He said, it's at moments like this when many a man perhaps would translate his tension of words into something physical and begin to lay hands upon her. He asked, and is that maybe what you want to talk about? Answering, most certainly that's what you want to talk about— or do it without talk if that is possible. Time to make a move. Yet he said No, it's not time to make a move, and there are words to be spoken even if you don't know what those words are. And then once again he said what he had said a while before when Burr had not paid attention to him: You want to confess your crime. Like Raskolnikov and Sonia.

No, said Burr, I don't want to confess my crime.

You are about to confess it, he said, whether you want to or not.

I heard us saying, "Have you ever wondered what it would be like to be a character in a novel?"

She smiled—beautifully—leaned back in her chair, ran her hand back through her beautiful hair, and said: "I guess so. I used to think of myself as the heroine of some novel with lots of love affairs—but then I decided that real life is more interesting."

This was a cliché that annoyed us because it threatened to distract us from the point. We said, "Real life is more interesting, but it's not so clear. One thing that makes it more interesting is novels. And it includes novels."

"Even so," she said, "I'd rather have adventures than read about them."

"Oh sure," we said, "up to a point. There are some adventures you'd rather read about than have."

"Maybe so," she said.

"Of course so," we said, dogmatically. The narrator took our words, our speech, our little lecture that we were addressing to Natalie Fleet and included them in the novel called *The First Person in the Woods* so that the reader could profit from them too. We said, "With a novel you can learn what it feels like to have adventures that you'd never want to have in real life. With novels you can live all kinds of life without having to suffer for it."

"I guess it wouldn't be so nice to be the heroine of a novel if she has to suffer," said Natalie Fleet.

"Most of them do," we said. "The protagonists of most novels suffer at least for a while, not just the tragic heroes. Most of them suffer goddamn miserably, even the comic ones, even when the reader laughs at them and doesn't take them seriously. It's not much fun I can assure you that."

She said, "Sometimes I've thought a novel should be written about me as I am."

"Without suffering?"

"Without any *more* suffering," she said with a smile.

We smiled too. "Wouldn't really be very interesting, would it?" we said. "A novel about ordinary daily life? Would you care to read such a novel?"

"Not unless it's very well done, I guess," she admitted.

"A novel needs action," we said. "Even quiet novels of character, you look and see there's more action than you realized. Conflict, struggle, change, tension, the unexpected." Continuing, lecture: "The reason anyone might want to be the protagonist of a novel is that the novel will give you importance—or say it will find your importance and show it to

153

other people—readers—and make you known to them and make them feel about you, not necessarily friendly but anyway important. But in order to do this most novels put their characters through a meat grinder of misery and humiliation or frustration or disillusionment or suffering. So it might be a rather hard choice deciding whether you want to be protagonist of a novel or not."

"I don't think I'm likely to have such a choice," said Natalie Fleet. She was leaning back at ease, now, playing the game, twisting a long lock of hair around her finger, studying us with a curious part-amused expression on her face. Now she asked: "Why do you ask such questions, Professor Burr? You planning to put me into a novel?"

"Call me Ralph," we said.

"Yes sir. Are you writing a novel?"

"No no," we said. "I'm not talking about the problems of the writer. Just the novel he makes—just projecting, you know, into the situation of his characters."

She leaned forward, "But according to Professor Hoffman," she said. Playing the game of critical argument. Yes—? "According to Professor Hoffman, the characters only exist as projections of the writer's imagination. They don't have any other existence, so how can you talk about me becoming protagonist of a novel anyway? I mean—*whose* novel would I be protagonist of?"

"Except," said we (assisted by the narrator maybe, ordering and making our speech clearer and more coherent than it otherwise would have been?), "that the characters *do* exist elsewhere than in the writer's imagination. They exist in the novel, and the novel exists. They exist in the reader's imagination where they are perfectly real, because you have feelings about them, you care what happens to them. If you can imagine the world of a novel as you read about it, you can imagine the characters who live in it. And if you can do that, you can ask yourself the perfectly legitimate question of what it would be like to be the protagonist of some such novel with some such world."

"Yes sir," she said, smiling slightly (but not unkindly, says the narrator), at our possible pomposity.

Meanwhile we gathered forces together. Felt a certain trembling, like the tightening wires of a suspension bridge in a wind storm, as we realized the point we had come to and what I was about to do. Then I said: "You know about that murder yesterday morning in Burnet Woods?"

She wrinkled her nose. "Oh yes! Wasn't that terrible?"

I said, "I happened to walk through the park yesterday morning at a time very close to the time at which the old man was killed. I climbed the steps, the very steps, where he was killed and dumped, and I passed the very spot at a time very close, before or after, to the time at which he was killed. On my way up the steps I passed an old woman. So naturally it occurred to me, to think not only of the man who was killed —who might have been the old woman—but also the man who killed him. And from that grew the idea of being the protagonist of a novel about that murder, the murder committed by a protagonist who is in every other respect identical with me."

She said, still half-smiling: "Gruesome imagination! Why should you want to be the protagonist of that kind of a novel?"

"I don't. Never said I *wanted* to be the protagonist of any kind. But suppose I were—that's the point. This is the point—when the murder happened, then the idea occurred to me, that is the kind of protagonist I would be. Occurred to me, this is the beginning of a novel featuring me."

(As he spoke, Burr challenged the narrator: Why are you lying? Why the subterfuge? Why make a confession at all if you are not willing to admit the whole truth instead of this sniggling evasion?)

"A novel with you as a *murderer?*" she said, disbelieving. "A brutal senseless murder like that? I don't understand. Why should you think of yourself as that kind of a protagonist?"

(Because that's what we happen to be, said Burr, but) we said, "Don't know. Because it's so completely different from the actual me. So completely opposite to anything I might ever actually do. Yet somebody did it. Somebody bashed that old man over the head with a rock full of fossils—"

"Full of fossils?" she said.

"Right. A detail I happened to notice in the novel. Somebody bashed

155

him over the head with such a rock, and since somebody did it that proves somebody was capable of doing it. Some human being did it, therefore it is a humanly possible thing to do. Yet I never thought I would be able to do a thing like that, not even when I passed that old woman on the steps that same morning and thought about it. Yet, if it was a humanly possible thing to do, why should I suppose it was not possible for me? Maybe that's how I began to see myself as the murdering protagonist of such a novel. Must have something in common with the man who bashed the old man."

She merely looked at me, amused, puzzled, not believing, wondering.

Come closer, said Burr. Be more bold. After a nervous hesitation, I said, "What would you say if I told you that I actually did kill that old man in Burnet Woods yesterday morning?"

Natalie Fleet's expression did not change. See her tightening a little, though, tense, wondering what I was trying to prove. Finally (as noncommittal as possible) she said, "I wouldn't believe you."

"Of course," I said, as if relieved. "But what if I merely said, as I just did, that I cast myself as the protagonist of a novel in which I did such a crime?"

Natalie Fleet smiled gently: "I'd say you had a strange imagination and maybe you were deeply troubled by something that you couldn't clearly express."

I laughed at that. "Good, very good. You'd say I was trying to tell you something and was using the situation of the murderer—or should we say the fugitive? that is to say, the hunted, the quarry?—as a metaphor to tell you what I was otherwise unable to tell?"

She nodded, smiling still, expectant, wondering what Socrates had next.

"But suppose I were to say that I was using the metaphor of the novel to express the real truth which I was afraid to admit, namely, that I actually did kill that old man?"

Adamant smile: "I still wouldn't believe you."

"Why not?"

Hands out, gesture of impatience. "My God, you're not the kind to kill old men in the park!"

Laugh. "But still I have a strange imagination, you'd say. Guess so.

I can visualize it well. I see myself climbing up those steps—do you know them? Have you ever been there?—climbing up, step by step, puff puff, and looking up and seeing the old man coming down the steps, the old man silhouetted against the light shining through the trees at the top, and as I go up step by step, he comes down step by step, and we draw constantly closer. And sometimes lonely contact between two people in a lonely place has an alarming, unnerving effect, especially if you have plenty of time to see it coming, if you can count the steps as the stranger approaches, and maybe you become aware for a time of the absolute wildness of things behind the civilized screen, you become aware of himself and yourself as entities of absolute and brute life, unwatched, possessed of power and crushable by power. Perhaps first you think that he will attack you, that he is the wild one and the reason you are afraid, until it occurs to you that he is old and you are stronger than he. So then, perhaps, as I passed the old man I happened to see the back of his head, I happened to realize that since he had not attacked me it was in *my* power to attack, to crush the back of his head, and I happened to realize at the same time that nobody was watching and that maybe it actually and really was in my power to do this, as if I had never understood my life before—I don't know. Maybe it was some thought like that, or maybe some other kind of thought. It doesn't matter, only that I picked up the rock on the moment and bashed him in."

She said, "You sound like one of my boy friends. Always worried about violence and uncontrollable impulses. Sounds funny to hear you talking that way."

"Childish?"

"I didn't say that." She groped a little, then found it. "I just want you to know, I *do* understand your feeling of leashed violence, held always under stern control. I understand it, I know about it. You can count on that, it isn't necessary to impress me with it."

"Impress you?" All of us dismayed, embarrassed, humiliated by this. I said, "I wasn't trying to impress you. I mean I wasn't trying to boast of violence. I hate violence. I loathe it. I dread it. I deplore it." Try to clarify. "I was merely trying to say something about the difference between life in a novel and real life."

"A literary lecture," she said with irony.

Ignore the irony. "Not primarily," I said. "I talk about novels as a way of trying to explain to you what my situation really is—which feels very urgent and serious."

Sympathetic look, now, eager to help. "What is your situation?" she asked. "Try to tell me."

I said, "My situation is that I have become the protagonist of a novel about a murderer."

This time she winced with impatience—just a momentary lapse before she could replace that look with another, turning again to a smile, curious amused patient listening. I said, "I suppose the first problem is to figure out what kind of a novel it is."

"Well," she said, with amused malice, "with your training and experience you ought to be able to answer that question easily."

"I don't know. Let's see. Some novels, you know, are realistic. They simply present a picture, as accurate and exact as possible, of the way things are, though really that kind of novel is maybe not quite as common as you think, and mostly they are interesting only if they present things as they are that you didn't know were like that. Like, if I am a murderer in a realistic novel it would interest you because you never realized I was a murderer before."

Natalie Fleet now simply staring and listening.

"Or—" it is the professor who continues "—a novel, like a dream, may be concerned primarily with showing things the way we would like them to be, satisfying some wish on the writer's part, or on the reader's. Like if I became a murderer in this kind of a novel, it might be a metaphor for what I would like to be, and if you sympathize, because you would like to be like that too."

Natalie Fleet leaning back in her chair, paying close attention.

"On the other hand," said the professor, "a novel may display chiefly what we are afraid of. It may show things happening that we are afraid will happen or people acting as we are afraid we might act or as we do not want to act. Present images of horror and dread or contempt or absurdity or revulsion. Like if I become a murderer in this kind of novel, it might be a metaphor for what I abhor, what I dread, what I most want to keep myself from being."

Natalie Fleet now smiling a little.

"And yet again," he said, "a novel may show some vision that is neither realistic nor wishful nor dreadful but simply wondrous and strange, a vision of things that are different from what we think of as the world, different in some particulars or broadly, as if to show us what life is like by comparing it with something unlike. Like if I become a murderer in this kind of novel, it might be a metaphor for its opposite, it might make clear how *unlikely,* how *impossible* it really is for someone like me to be a murderer actually, and you too, and that way you get to know something more about what my life is actually like."

Natalie Fleet amused: "If you imagine yourself as protagonist of a novel do you also imagine yourself as reader of the novel? Not to mention writer?"

I said, "I suppose I imagine myself as being read. As being watched, judged, sympathized with, maybe condemned. Someone taking an interest in me. That's what it means to be the protagonist of a novel. In contrast to real life, maybe, living alone in this house, where maybe there is no one to take an interest in me anymore."

She smiled gently. "You have your animals." Ha-ha! Show bitterness. She more gently still, a little sorry maybe. "Lots of people take an interest in you. You have students, you have colleagues. You have people like me—"

Interrupt, continue with the lecture. "Consider what it means to say I am a murderer in a novel. Maybe the murder projects and enlarges or makes concrete some otherwise inexpressible reality in my situation. That's a simple easy sort of explanation. Projects some fear of mine, like I said, or some buried wish or maybe both a fear and a wish. Have fun figuring it out. Or maybe it embodies or projects, like I said, what is least likely, least possible in me, brings me into your focus by shining the light of brightest incredulity on me. Have you considered? Maybe my being protagonist of a novel is just one of my metaphors to give my life meaning in one or more of these ways. Or maybe—have you considered? —it's true."

"True?"

Tell her. "Maybe I *really* am the protagonist of a novel about a murderer."

"Pooh, what does that mean?" she said. "I'm not in any old novel."

"It means maybe I really am a murderer. Maybe it's just my evasive way of confessing that fact."

"Why should you want to confess such a ridiculous thing as that?"

It was clear: under no circumstances could Natalie Fleet be made to believe that Ralph Burr had actually killed an old man or any other kind of person in Burnet Woods yesterday morning or any other time in any other place.

"Look," I said. "Notice this interesting contrast. Consider the actual murder that took place yesterday morning in Burnet Woods. You think you don't know the murderer, and perhaps that is true, perhaps you don't, and you are free to suppose, if you wish, that I don't, either. But what do you think of that act and of that probably unknown person, that murderer who is known to you only through that act—which we do know was performed? You think of the act as vile in the extreme. It arouses your wrath, vengeful feelings perhaps, and the murderer you think of as vicious, villainous, less than human. You would like to beat him, perhaps, he makes you so angry—this, even though you know nothing of his victim. The real murder arouses either your fury or your contempt or your fear. And the real murderer is an outcast. If he lives among us, as he probably does, he does so only by virtue of the conceal-ment of his crime, so that in his heart he is an outcast and in the hearts of the rest of us—including you—he is an outcast, as will become plain enough if they ever catch him. So that if, like I said, I actually did kill that man on the steps, I have become an outcast, and my visits with you and other civilized people are like the visits of a spy, and my real nature is like that of a small wild animal in the woods being pursued by a hunting pack.

"But now consider the difference if the murder takes place in a novel. The difference if your murderer is a character in a novel. In a novel, the murder that in real life is a repulsive act that outcasts its maker, in a novel it becomes an expressive image that communicates, that con-nects your murderer to other people. If I become an outcast by killing the old man, I rejoin the human community by doing this within the pages of a novel. Then the very fact of being an outcast becomes an experience elevated to human importance, an experience to be shared, or observed, judged, felt, by a responding reader."

160

Natalie Fleet still smiles, the fixity on her face suggesting that somewhere during my speech her attention had begun to wander and now she is no longer listening and does not know what we have been talking about.

I said, "If I said I was the protagonist of a novel who has committed a murder of senseless violence and is suffering now from the outcasting effects of that, you would fill with sympathy, you would try to understand, still more you would try to help me, perhaps you'd even love me—" She moved a little on that.

"But," continuing, "if I tell you I actually killed the old man in a moment of senseless violence you'll only recoil from me in horror and disgust."

"Would I?" she said. "But not if I understood you. It would depend on why you did it."

"Simply that?" I asked.

"Well, I mean—I mean I don't understand. Why on earth should you want to kill a poor old man on the steps in Burnet Woods?"

"Damned if I know," I said. "I haven't the slightest idea, I guess."

"That's what I mean," said Natalie Fleet. "In that case, why should you do it?"

"Suppose I said that I did, though?"

"But if you don't even know why you'd do it, why should I believe you?"

Suddenly it seemed to me that I hadn't been able to tell her anything in my confession.

Chapter 9

Burr said: "Maybe it's because I murdered my wife."

"What?" she exclaimed.

"Nothing. I say, only, maybe I killed the old man to make up for allowing Cynthia to die, and also for Elaine, who has gone to live in a commune, and also Harold who has dropped out of college and I think got stuck on drugs and in any case is out of touch, sailing on a ship perhaps or lost in a city like Hong Kong. Maybe I killed the old man because of them, and because now I am living all alone in this old house which I have managed to sell, though I haven't found another place to live or made any move to move, and because I am forty-five years old and my life has gone down the drain."

Natalie Fleet now leaning forward in her chair full of concern and sympathy (again the brown corduroy flaring pants and the flowing top in red and gold and blue with long flaring sleeves), saying, "I didn't know you were so unhappy." Ah, pity!

"I've committed a crime and I am being hunted down," said Burr.

"You seem to be torturing yourself with pointless feelings of guilt," she said.

"Don't know about guilt," said Burr. "Fear maybe. Or fatality. I think they are pursuing me and I only have a day or so, not more than two or three, in which to live the life of a man."

Touch of mockery in her voice. "They're catching up with you?"

"As if I only had a day or so to live," said Burr. "I apologize. I know I sound paranoid or persecuted—"

She laughed. "Why don't you be the protagonist of some other kind of novel?"

"What kind of novel do you recommend?"

"Some comedy maybe," said Natalie Fleet, "In which the hero tries to make the girl by portraying himself as a terrible, vicious, guilty creature full of crime, when all the time the girl can plainly see he is gentle and lovable and sweet and timid as—"

Alert! said Burr, shoots of excitement in the blood like hoses under high pressure. Hero of a romantic novel, said I, she and we and sweet warm feelings, soothing comfort and the future. A pornographic novel, said the narrator, even more excited. Prelude to an orgy, a release of clothes, what you always wanted but did not realize until today. Meanwhile, pride and self-respect at stake, Burr complained about her words: "The hero tries to make the girl?"

Natalie Fleet smiling brightly at him, as if all ready, as if great doors had been opened and great rooms illuminated by her directness, while he still wallowed in the moat of self-respect. She said: "Wrong?" He wanted to leap and grab, but one of us at that moment took offense, and he said, "Is that how you regard me?"

Burr trying to explain to her the point of view of one who would feel offended by her suggestion. Because he had tried to confess to her the deepest things in his soul and had displayed to her his deepest need. Because he had actually told her about the murder he had committed, told her as openly as it was possible to do, a mortal crime, and he had done all this because of his need for her, he had honored her with his need because he thought she, and he had told her the shortness of his time, the desperateness of, and still in her merely sexual vanity (it must be) she had merely laughed and suggested it was all only because the hero was trying to make the girl by portraying himself as. Because she refused to see the novel he was in as a tragedy and tried to turn it into a comedy or even—alert, said the narrator—a pornographic novel. Then the narrator said, What more do you want? And Burr looked at her smiling so brightly at him, and he said, Let's be the protagonist of a pornographic novel. Always wanted to be in one.

Concern now shows on her face. "Did I hurt your feelings? I'm sorry. Just don't understand all this talk about murdering and about being in novels. I guess I haven't really had any training in criticism and literary theory."

Burr smiled. "That's okay," he said. "It doesn't matter." According to the narrator, now that he knew what he wanted to do it was all simplified. There she was, across the room from him, lit by the lamp, not far away, looking at him in a manner of greatest sympathy and highly developed interest, a little uneasy because of mysterious attempts at communication that had failed, but now she was clarifying (once again in fact) as a human creature eminently, profoundly, potently, electrically, sexual, shaped and suggested by her tight binding brown pants (flaring below) and her loose long drape-sleeved blouse, suggesting sexual contact, exerting pull on him, drawing on him physically, force of magnetic field entering him in the belly, the chest, the groin, warming him like an electronic oven, making him want, want, want. And he, doomed, knowing that it was only a matter of time, of a day or two, perhaps even less, before they with their Suspect Board and their map with pins, and Berthold armed with vengeance, would find him out—he, full of consciousness of his doom, recognized his last hours of free life, of life as himself, but now you are free, the narrator said, to take a role for this hour and to play it. Disregarding at last, said the narrator—(since you only have an hour, or a night), all other intervening roles. Disregarding whatever taboos might still hover in the vague novelistic air, concerning dead wives fading in the past and former girl friends of former sons. Disregarding the possibilities of sinister traps, of treason and blackmail, of spies sent by Stone to seek out your weaknesses. Disregarding even the possibility that she was sent here with specific instructions to seduce you—which is quite possible, considering how easy it was to get her to come, how she came here the first time of her own volition and the second time with hardly any urging, and how after all the scary talk of murder which she did not understand, still she could be so bold as to make the provocative suggestion that the hero was "trying to make" the girl. Tell the narrator, What of it? So what if it is a trap, if the lovely spy intends to seduce you to accomplish her ends, tell him, What does it matter, so long as she is lovely, if he only has an hour or a night or two or three days of freedom and life? At such a time, what the spy can give means far more to a Burr than what a spy might take. Thinking (telling the narrator) I have too many secrets in any case. But what secrets have I left, anyway, if a spy won't even believe them?

Therefore, said the narrator to Burr, all you need do is play the role that you have now acquired. Defined thus: Widower in his mid-forties, playing host in his empty house in the evening to a pretty girl of long acquaintance, and no known ties at present standing in the way of either one. Widower's object is to let the girl seduce him. Wait, and in a moment she will ask him about his sectsual needs. This time he will not fail. Now his role is to actualize her willingness, to get her to a bed a couch or the floor, to make her accept him in her arms, accept his readiness in her readiness. Her role is to accept, gracefully, so as to complete his harmonious adaptation to his role.

How do it, though? he asked. According to the narrator, there was no problem, virtually no risk, the girl was ready, probably she intended just this, all this, nothing but this, before she ever came to the house, she knew what coming to the house meant, and to make it perfectly clear she had made that remark about trying to make her, a remark which he was expected to pick up and turn to advantage. Forthright as Laura's sectsual needs: already the situation was repeating itself. But suppose, demanded Burr, she had made that remark for the opposite reason. Suppose it was meant as a warning. Suppose she had come to the house not to be seduced but simply because I, as a full professor, as a full-fledged senior Boss Figure, had asked her. What if the bane of her life was Boss Figures exercising *droit de seigneur* upon their secretaries?

I said, "Would you like some more coffee?" (Strictly neutral. Neither seducer nor boss—just my own simple unassuming nonrole-playing self.) She made a face, pretended to gag. "Gad, I'd never get to sleep," she said. So much for my instant coffee. "How about a drink?" I asked. She looked at me with a very nice, very pleasant, intelligent, open and friendly look (incompatible with plots and spying, roles and maneuvers, treachery and blackmail—tell them). "No, better not. Maybe some ginger ale. Some Coke perhaps, if you have some?" Coke, of course. Up, man, into the kitchen, open for the heroine a bottle of Coca Cola. Ply. She follows us into the kitchen, watches as we open the bottle, break ice cubes out of the tray from the freezer, drop them into a tall glass. Her look of amusement is pleasing (tell him, make sure he explains this clearly) because it seems to invite you always into her own amusement, assumes you are sharing her sense of fun, partaking of her pleasant and funny, bright and sunny, intelligent girl's vision of the world. When he was in a good mood, at least, Burr did not in the least mind partaking of that vision, and even when he was not, he liked to see it on the nice young face of an intelligent girl because it reminded him of intelligences he had known in the past, and of intelligent summer places by the seashore on intelligent sunny summer days when they used to go sailing and intelligent girls in white shorts tied up rowboats at the public landing.

She looked at the sink. "You really got rid of them, didn't you?" she said. She looked in his refrigerator, and opened cupboard doors, and looked in his shelves. Appraising, taking the measure of his domestic goods? She was intelligent and civilized and had natural curiosity. She went to the back door and peered out the window into the back yard. He said something. He said, "Remember the days when you used to come as Harold's friend?" She gave him a quick look, anxious, embarrassed, with a grimace which she quickly suppressed, and she merely nodded. Then she said, "This time I'm *your* friend—I hope." Intelligent civilized question in the last part: I hope? Meaning, I hope that is how you think of me, and not any longer as one of the children, belonging to Harold. Play the role and advance the case. Burr said, "I hope that's why you're here."

She turned her back to the back door and leaned against it, a graceful giving gesture, as if she were turning herself to him and giving herself to him. She was full of graceful gestures, moving around the kitchen with long steps, turning about, bending over things, and now leaning back against the back door, where she said—she didn't say. Opened her mouth as if to say and then stopped, checked, because (said the narrator) she doesn't yet know if she can trust you. Think, said the narrator, what it was she might have said, think how to encourage her to say it yet— and meanwhile as she stood there, leaning back against the door, Burr felt his role taking shape suddenly, swiftly, powerfully, the sense of possibility shaped almost into certainty, and then she opened her mouth again and said (intelligently, civilized, curious): "Why did you ask me to come?"

At once the narrator started to gabble—indeed it sounded as if now there were more than one narrator, at least two, talking rapidly and loudly and argumentatively—but before he could listen to them he had blurted almost automatically: "Because I wanted to confess."

"Confess what?"

"Confess—" the automatic impulse beginning to fade, the voices of the narrators becoming clearer—"that I was the murderer in a novel."

She made an intelligent funny face at that (because she doesn't understand and it makes her impatient, said the narrator), and then she said, "Why me?"

Now he heard the narrator clearly, the narrators: the pornographic narrator who said, This is your cue, a whole series of cues that she is setting up for you, while you systematically and stupidly turn them aside, one after the next. Just like Laura, she is giving you one opportunity after another to make a plea for her or a grab, and you miss it every time. (As he looked at her—and now she was walking over to the window sill to look at the empty flower pots, dry and dead, left from Cynthia's time, that nobody had yet bothered to throw out—he felt in his role such a strong sense of her physical reality and such confidence in her accessibility that it was difficult for him to contain himself, to remember his usual ways.) Meanwhile the other narrator said, You are in a world of treachery and deceit—or let us rather say, of misunderstanding and irony, where everything that is said might be understood to mean one thing but might equally well be taken to mean something else, and even when there isn't a trap you never can know that there isn't until afterwards. And what the pornographer calls cues (says this narrator) are in reality warnings or perhaps simply frightened inquiries, for you have given her good reason to be afraid and you must try your best to reassure her.

"Why me?" she said.

He gave a carefully considered answer as honest and open as possible: "Because I like you, and I'd like to know you better," he said. "I would like you to be my friend." She smiled a little embarrassed still, reached out a hand and actually patted him on the arm, and then she . . .

Let's consider that carefully considered answer says the narrator. Let's go over it. Why me? she asked. First he considered telling her, simply, Because you came by last night, full of pornographic possibilities, and it made me wonder, in view of what I have heard and thought of you before, what sort of meaning you might have in your mind. But then (considering later what he considered then, in the few flash seconds of careful consideration before he formed his carefully considered reply) he considered the evasiveness of this as well as the offensiveness (she would be annoyed at his attempt to make her look like the seducer), and he considered instead the most direct, honest, frank, and forthright answer that he could imagine: Why you? Because *I* want to capture *you*. Want to take you to bed. Want to screw, want to fuck you. You, Natalie Fleet, after almost two years of vicariousness, of imagining the lost happiness first of my son Harold and later of my professional rival Stone—you Natalie Fleet after two days ago at the doctor's office and last night when you first came to this house of your own volition, to see me and not my son or anyone else—clarifying my desire and my purpose: to take off clothes with you and make love with you, you you screw screw, tonight here now.

Then (later building up the considerations that flashed then half formed and incomplete, ellipses of extending meaning glimpsed in a moment to be caught at leisure later, but in the glimpse giving shape to the careful considerations in his answer) he considered how such an appeal would fail. Because even if she had come prepared for such a proposal, you don't do it that way. Girls expect to be wooed and courted —even when they know the outcome and have made up their minds to accept it—and even more when they have not. Birds have their mating dance, their flapping wings and spreading tail, flutter and hop. He remembered how it was thought to be in the old days: how a girl being seduced did not want it believed that she had submitted of her own free will. She had to be induced, slipped into it unknowingly until too late, overwhelmed by the compulsion of feeling and ritual—or so at least he always used to believe, which may partially explain, said the narrator, why he never—

But considerations advancing in those flashing seconds, now he considered how times had changed—or he had changed—or both—since those days of indirect seduction and delicacy and care of persuasion. Considered now the new honesty or frankness (or whatever it was) of these new times and this new generation which so believes in calling a fuck a fuck. Admiring the blunt and direct approach as the proper answer to hypocrisy which is the curse of all previous civilized generations. Therefore it would indeed have been proper to tell her at this point (Why me? she asked) what he wanted of her—except now for the consideration that though she was a member in good standing of this new and most direct generation, he was not. She would know he was not, and therefore she would not be prepared for such directness on his part. Furthermore, she would be offended by it, since although it was proper to her generation it was not to his, and would therefore strike her as unseemly, much the way the sound of young slang ("groovy") on the lips of older people strikes the young as offensive. Then he considered still further that not only the manner of such a direct approach would offend her, so also would the approach itself, whatever the manner. Because he was forty-five years old and tending to forget it, tending especially to forget what this would mean to her, because (considering) to her he was not a contemporary but an older man, and perhaps not even an older man but maybe even so far gone as an *old man*. And if he showed himself (former Father Figure and Boss Figure) to yearn after her, to wish to make love to her, perhaps to her he would appear only as the protagonist in a fantasy novel of impossible wishes—perhaps in the literature of her tradition she would find the make love of his wish translated into fuck, and the yearning old man become a lecherous old man and the lecherous old man not clearly distinguishable from a dirty old man. Because, he considered, the young resent it when the old try to share their joys, and they consider it dirty.

But then (flashing of considerations in flash of seconds) he considered that she would not be like that, she was more compassionate. Very likely she was quite familiar with the trend of his thought and desires, very likely in her own free and honest new way, she knew well what he wanted and very likely was disposed not unfavorably (after all, she had come to the house twice), perhaps she was even wondering why he had been so slow to take up the cues she might have (experimentally?) offered. If so—considering now—what he really should do is apologize. Explain his incredible awkwardness, his impossible uncertainty. Tell her how little he ever. That no one before Cynthia herself. Some two or three girls a little experimental necking, always fell short, never got beyond. Nothing to the point until Cynthia herself. Then twenty years of marriage and nothing else until. And even then, not. So there was only Cynthia herself in all this. And not even Laura Grummon. Proving therefore his exceptional domesticity and his impossible awkwardness, his incredible uncertainty. As an apology for why he could not simply say, more directly.

And then, considering why he could not say, even indirectly, not yet —why he must still, finally ("Why me?" she said) he gave his carefully considered answer: "Because I like you, and I'd like to know you better. I would like you to be my friend." Innocuous yet possible, right tone of emotion, to which she smiled a little embarrassed still, reached out a hand and actually patted him on the arm, and then she said: "I'd like to know you too."

She took her Coca-Cola into the living room, held it in her hand while she walked over to the bookcase and began to study the titles. He watched from near by, not too close, conscious of the space she filled and what she filled it with. Became aware of a slight perfume, not strong but distinct. After a while she sat down on the piano bench, and began to pick out some music (Bach) standing open on the bench. Then she played (not well) an easy piece by Chopin that she had by heart. Then a few phrases of childhood jazz. A scale. An arpeggio. He stood near and looked at her magnificent flaring blouse in red blue and gold, noticed the loose narrow opening in front with its implications, noticed the thin shape of her shoulders in the blouse and the distinct small pair of breasts loosely contoured by the front of the blouse, and he wanted very much to touch her—it seemed, said the narrator, like a very natural thing to do, as if he had done it often before, though he knew very well that he had not. Up from the piano bench with a laugh. Now he showed her family picture albums that he still kept: pictures of his own childhood, himself, his mother and father, his summer place, himself at four, at nine, at twelve, at seventeen; pictures of one or two girls he had known; many pictures of Cynthia, in the beginning and later; pictures of Harold and Elaine as babies, as small children; pictures of dogs and cats.

They stood side by side leaning over a table where the photograph album was spread out, leaning but not touching. The narrator said: We still need a breakthrough. We have developed a warm and friendly atmosphere. She has stayed here an hour and seems relaxed. But we have come to the end of the album and we still have not broken the wall between us—civility and respect and the sense of difference. He said, To break through the barrier, it will be necessary for you, Burr, to say or do something different. Explicit and courageous. Without that, nothing can happen. If you don't act, nothing will happen. Still, as they stood there, the narrator repeated those words, and Burr, admitting their truth, kept trying to think of such explicit moves as were in his power to make and kept rejecting everything he thought of (touch her, arm around shoulder? No. Say, You're beautiful. No. Say, Well here you are at last. No. Say, Did you ever wonder . . . ? No. Say, God, if only we could . . . No. Say, Would you like to go upstairs and see my bedroom? No. Say, Would you like to spend the night? No. Go to bed? No, no. Say, would you like me to kiss you . . . ? No no no.)

She stood up from the table with a little sigh. "Nice pictures," she said, politely. Glanced around the room, glanced at him. Did he look anxious? "You know," she said, "I've always been fascinated by this old house. Is it all right to look around a little?" He jumped eagerly. "Of course, of course," he said. "Let me show you." Apology: "It's a mess, of course." Start in the basement, what used to be the game room. He repeated his apology in every room: "Hasn't really been cleaned up since Cynthia died." The ground floor, showed her his study, his file cabinets. Upstairs. He pointed out Harold's bedroom (Natalie's interest—long minutes she spent looking at the trophies and pictures on his desk) and

Elaine's room, and then they went into his own bedroom (master bedroom) where she went and looked out the window. (We still need a breakthrough.) Then he showed her the upstairs back porch, and he led her up the circular tower staircase to the attic, dark and dusty. On the way down she said, "I don't see any signs of your getting ready to move." "I'll get to it soon," said Burr.

"Do you need any help?" she asked.

I need a breakthrough, he said to the narrator. Tell her to ask if I have any sectsual needs. He followed behind her down the stairs into the living room. She's going to leave now, said the narrator. No, cried Burr, not yet, too soon. He went back to the picture album on the table still standing open. He said, "Did you see these pictures of my parents?" She came over and stood beside him and looked at the pictures again. (Breakthrough.) "I remember Harold showing them to me," she said. "They have sweet and gentle faces." Yes. The brilliant red blue gold blouse was close beside him by his shoulder, he could see it sideways out of his eye, also (glancing) the side, the top of her head, soft brown hair close, near to him, easy reach to touch. Her glasses. (Breakthrough. We need words that will make the difference. Meanwhile the old man or woman was just coming even with him, down the steps while he was going up. Meanwhile they passed even, he turned, he saw the top of the head, white hair, of the old man or woman just passing, close, ready to touch.) Close enough for him to notice the light perfumy air that still surrounded her, also a silver ring on her finger as she turned the picture to look at it. Shape of bone of her shoulder so close it almost touched his sleeve. Shape also of bulge in her blouse, bulged from the shape inside that swelled it out. (If words fail? Or better than words? The old man or woman's head was still in reach as he passed on down to the next step, and suddenly there was this knowledge of what was possible, what was possible if you bend down and pick up a large rock full of fossils. Suddenly you could see the real possibility of doing something drastic to that poor old man or woman's head with this rock of fossils, and seeing the possibility, the next moment was the breakthrough, the reality of bringing the rock actually down upon the head as predicted by his knowledge of the possible. Similarly in a novel either of courtship or pornography, there are possibilities.) Instead of words, she seemed to be leaning towards him, and instead of words it seemed not merely possible it seemed inevitable, inescapable, and then (lifting the rock) he saw Burr raise his arm and (after a fraction second's hesitation in the air let it fall heavily, crashing, full strength) let it fall lightly, tentatively on her shoulder.

Watch this moment of crisis—what will the lady do now? (Her shoulder is light and bony.) What she does—I told you so, said the narrator—is lean back lightly, responsively, against you, her back against your chest, as natural as can be. And then after a moment turn around sharply, looking at you, a tentative smile, questioning, her gold-rimmed glasses, an intelligent questioning look. Smiling, and her lip quivering a little, as if she didn't quite know—Sudden scare, Burr released her, and she stood back a step. Now the smile faded into the question. She asked, "Is there anything you—want?" Her voice faltering.

"Yes, yes—" Burr tried. It sounded to him as if only one of his vocal cords was working. And that one was scratchy. He wanted to cough— he did cough, averting his head just in time not to cough in her face. It brought a little smile back to her face. She said, "What—do you— want?"

He opened his mouth but this time both vocal cords failed. She stared at him, glasses, eyes, half smile fixed, penetrating, wise, full of gentleness, curiosity, encouragement, waiting for him to tell her what it was he wanted. He could not make himself say it. Even the narrator could not force him to say it.

So that after another moment, she said it herself. He heard her, speaking softly and most tenderly: "Would you like me to take this off?"

He waited wondering what she was trying to say, then heard it very distinctly: "Would you . . . like me to?" Fill in the words, wait for them to come back from the loop they have taken into outer space—here they come: "like me to take this off?" This what? Her hands held—Catch them, catch her meaning: Not would you like me to take the laundry. Take you to the doctor. Give you an electrocardiogram. No, not that. Not, would you like me to dress the animals, nor address the animals. Not would you like me to buy you new clothes, nor would you like me to take off my pretenses. Nor strip you of yours. No, what she said was a simple honest natural generous suggestion: would you like me to do your dishes for you? No. Would you like me to listen to your confessions for you? No. Would you like me to would you would you would you like me to go to bed with no not yet would you like me to take this off? Her hands held the hem of her rich flaring blouse. This blouse.

"Ya-ya-yes-yes, I would," groped the revival of Burr's voice, sounding like rocks rumbling in the bottom of a river.

"You mean it?" Smiling, almost delighted now, but as if she still doubted him. "Do you mean it?"

"I mean it," said Burr.

She stepped up to him and said, "First kiss me?" Oh yes, certainly, of course, arms around, hold her, mouths open, tongues, skill of tongue, gentle kiss with the practiced gentleness of Natalie Fleet. Again she looked at him, holding him, leaning back head to look up at him, as if well aware of how much she was helping him, how much he needed her help. She said, "Should we go upstairs again?" Yes, yes, and he followed her as they went back up to the bedroom, where in the days of the house's life, Cynthia, and after its death, conjured shadows. Two cats were lying on the bed. Natalie Fleet went to the windows and pulled the shades.

Meanwhile the narrator heard him saying—and tried to stop him, but the words came out as if there were no will or decision in them at all —"Do you realize the difficulties in what we are doing?" (Natalie back turned going to the second window—corduroy pants from behind, the red gold and blue flaring shirt loose down to below her hips—) Natalie said: "What difficulties?" He heard Burr saying, "I'm forty-five years old," and, "I am the father of your former boy friend." (From behind he watched as with a quick motion she swept the colorful shirt up over her head and off. Her back was bare, she was not wearing a bra. She was looking down, hands at her belt buckle—) He heard Burr saying, "I'm not attractive as I used to be," and adding, "I'm pretty beat up and a mostly ruined sort of person." (With a swift motion she lowered the brown corduroys and stepped out of them, back still turned, and then lowered the small white pants and stepped out of them, with bare buttocks and then—) She turned to face him, bare except for her glasses, with small pink-tipped breasts and lovely brown hair that draped around her shoulders and went half down her back, and a small puff of brown hair in front, a more womanly figure, less slender and boyish than he feared. She came up to him, looking, not speaking, until she was almost to him, and then she said, "Why are you saying all those depressing things?"

He said, "Because I guess I can't understand why you want to do this for me."

She began to fiddle with his belt buckle, and said, "Don't you want me to?"

"Oh yes, very much, very much."

Working to open his pants, she said, "Can't I enjoy things like other people? It doesn't have to be a great big deal, does it?" Then Burr, "But why pick me? Not that I object, you understand, but why me?" And Natalie: "Why not? You're lonely and I like you. I always figured you liked me. So why not?" She said, "It doesn't mean I have to be all in love with you, does it?" He said, "You like me, do you?" She laughed and jumped onto the bed. He finished undressing and got onto the bed beside her. The cats jumped off the bed and ran out of the room.

She was an expert pornographer. Natalie Fleet lying back in his bed, her hair spread out on the pillow, holding him by the wand of pornography, which was all filled and stiffened, while she laughed softly and said soft things, spoke of being nice to him, spoke of being relaxed and enjoying things as they come, spoke of the secret enjoyments of her private life, spoke of skills in pleasure. Then in accordance with tradition Burr placed himself on top of her, and he touched her with his wand, entered into her, dark and sparkling, and probed slow and deep, this new incarnation of Cynthia's tradition, this youngest embodiment of all his imaginings and suppositions, of all that was outside the house brought into it, riding with her slow and cumulative until the golden bursting with its incestuous tinges and its dazzling picture of liberation from dead things.

She gave a shriek, and afterwards she stroked his head. She said, "I must say you don't seem like a forty-five-year-old widower to me." The

narrator suspected that in this matter of bed relations the twenty-two-
or twenty-three-year-old girl was treating him patronizingly, as if she
were the expert and he the novice. Like the protagonist of a pornographic novel, he kept wondering what the source of her expertise was.
He asked a few questions whose answers suggested an indefinite amount
of history that was not being revealed. She giggled. "Did you know one
time that year," she said, "you almost caught Harold and me in the act?
Did you ever realize that?"

No, Jesus Christ, Burr never realized that. When was it? he wanted
to know. She spoke of an evening when he and Cynthia had gone out
to the movies and she and Harold had occupied the living room in the
dark, how they were in the middle of it when the car drove up the
driveway, how they managed to stop and get their clothes on just in time
before he and Cynthia came into the house. . . . She said, "I always
figured you knew." She said, "Harold said you didn't, but I knew better.
I was right, wasn't I?" But the narrator warned: Don't tell her that
Harold lied to her ("How could we possibly be virgins?" he said)—
reminding him also that he had never known whether to believe Harold
himself, until now. Now she claimed more. "I also knew you wanted me
yourself," she said. What? Protest. "That was one thing I didn't tell
Harold, but I knew." He asked her how she knew, but she wouldn't tell.
"I never thought it would actually happen, though." He thought it was
not true, that she was deceiving herself, but he didn't know how to say
this, and he wondered what he might have done to give himself away.

She asked, "Do you like doing it with me?" Mm yes, said Burr, joyful.
"Do you like it as much as . . . you thought you would?" "Yes," he would
say—noticing and ignoring her sudden caution against a tactless com-
parison with Cynthia. At least that's what he guessed it was. The past
was settling down and now it seemed as if nothing could be quite as fine
as this ready and eagerly giving young girl. She was pleased with herself,
yet humble too. "I'm probably not very good at it," she said, "compared
to some people. But I don't care, as long as it's fun and we have a good
time." She said, "A guy told me once I was sexually unimaginative, but
I figure that's his problem. Merely means we're incompatible. I try to
be as uninhibited as I can. You like me all right, don't you?"

Oh, oh yes, said Burr. He didn't say how much else he wanted to tell her, as he realized now that he didn't want it to end, he would want it again with her, to keep doing it, to secure for himself the regular doing of it with her into the future, for as much future as he might happen to have. According to the narrator he was in no position to be jealous of her other lovers, whoever they were, but he could still need fiercely to protect his own newly won share of her. But no, said the narrator, checking him, you can't even ask for that, because there is no time, no future anyway. Ask for tomorrow night, maybe, or some other night, but no regularity, no formality—you'll only ruin it.

For a while they lay warm and quiet, close and resting, naked on the bed. Meanwhile the narrator ventured out of the first person, into her point of view, for an insight into why she had been so easy. It was, said the narrator, not at all as loose and casual and accidental as her words would suggest. True, she had her history, adventures that prepared her, but this was new and different. Why had she selected the forty-five-year-old man for such kindness, if not for special qualities that she had long ago seen and responded to in him? It was because she knew, through his shyness and the austerity of his manner and the distance of his position, she knew the warmth of his heart, the gentle kindness of his spirit. She had known first from Harold what kind of a father he was, and this had built up her great trust in him as a human being. Then, in the office, she became better aware of the sweep and bite of his intellect, as reflected especially in the memos and letters she had typed for him. And she had seen the secret muffled force and power of him as a man, she had seen it flashing in his eyes from time to time, lightened with his humor also flashing in his eyes, even when he did not speak—oh yes, she knew him far better than he had ever given her credit for. According to the narrator, Natalie Fleet really loved him, and the last three days had brought the flowering of this love—too late, now that everything was doomed and lost.

Later that night he took her home, and she promised to make another date with him as soon as possible.

Chapter 10

Let two days go by. Time for us to pull ourselves together from the shock of recent events, to resume with caution the pattern of normal times. We returned to the university the next day and taught our first class since the shock of Burnet Woods. We spent most of the rest of that day and the next in the library, in our study, with enough concentration to grade a set of student papers and prepare a lecture for the beginning of next week. We ate our meals quickly in little local restaurants and spent evenings quietly at home with the animals. There was no word from Grummon or the members of his committee nor from the official search committee nor from Elias or the dean. There was no word either from Laura Grummon, whom I had not seen or spoken to for several weeks.

Natalie Fleet was not free to come back to the house either of the next two nights (did not say why and allowed us to think it was not our privilege to ask) but she did come to our office in the morning for a few minutes talk. She also performed the notable service of finding us a moving company, calling on the telephone, arranging for a man from the company to come, probably on Saturday, to bring us boxes for the packing and to look at the belongings and make a preliminary estimate. This was the Lubbock Moving Company, and the man said he would come around to the house on Saturday morning.

Meanwhile in Freitag's office at the station house, Berthold Kirschner had taken over direction of the inquiry into the slaying of his father on Tuesday morning in Burnet Woods. This because it was recognized that he had more interest in the case than anyone else, since it was his father who had been killed, besides which he had the best, the most coherent, the most ingenious theory about the crime.

Now that we have seen him, says the narrator, we should describe what Berthold Kirschner looks like. In our original description we saw that he was a young man with fiery long blond hair that swept in great sweeps around his pale girlish face. Now that he has cut his hair however, we see that he has acquired a different appearance. He is a very large heavy-set young man, with thick muscular arms, a large fat bottom, a bullish neck, a heavy fat face, and a stubby crew cut. He is obviously very strong, and he looks in fact like a furniture mover. His mouth hangs open in a sullen pout and he has brutal angry eyes full of vengeance for the murder of his father.

Under Berthold's direction, the map with pins has fixed itself permanently on the minute of 9:48, Tuesday morning. Two pins stand side by side halfway up (or down, depending on your point of view) the steps in Burnet Woods. These are the pins with the black flag for Mr. Kirschner and the gray flag for Professor Burr. The pin with the yellow flag is far away across the meadow, and the students' pins of green and red are in the middle of the road entering the circle, representing them as still in their car, not yet parked. On the Suspect Board only two slabs still remain. At the top—all the way to the very top—Berthold has placed the board labeled BURR, indicating that the Professor is not merely the Number One suspect but is believed to be guilty beyond the shadow of a doubt. One other board remains on the Suspect Board, far below (separated by many empty boards). This is BLACK BOY; nobody knows yet who this is, but he remains on the Board just in case something goes wrong with the case against Burr.

The primary evidence in Berthold's analysis was that this was an intellectual crime, an existential crime, and Professor Burr was the only intellectual near the scene of the crime at the time. But this was backed up by considerable circumstantial evidence that had accumulated since Berthold came into the case. Most striking was the discovery of Burr's lie about the disposal of the body. You remember? He had mentioned how the body of the old man had been thrown in a pile of leaves, ill concealed from the path. How did he know that, they asked? By reading it in the paper, he had said. But they had examined every paper that mentioned the crime, and not one, neither the evening paper nor the morning paper nor the papers across the river or in the suburbs had mentioned that the body had been found anywhere except by the steps. Now, said Berthold, putting it all together, how could the professor possibly know that the body had been thrown in leaves, how could he possibly know that an attempt had been made to conceal it (even an unsuccessful one), unless he had seen it himself? And how could he have seen it if he denied that he had seen it? Only by lying, said Berthold —only a lie could explain the contradiction, and according to the rules, if the professor had lied on that point then you could assume he had lied on any other point you wished.

That was the crucial break in the case. Here Watson suggested that they go right in and arrest the professor, but Berthold said that they should wait a little while yet, and let more evidence accumulate, let him really damn himself. It happened on Wednesday afternoon, and during the next two days the case against Burr grew stronger.

For it was known now that he had mentioned the crime to Grummon and his companions, that same evening of the crime (Tuesday night). He had told them about going up the steps past the scene of the crime and admitted the guilty fear of being suspected of the murder. Why should he have such a fear unless? And then there is that significant agitation that he is known to have displayed for most of the rest of that day. How he canceled his class, how he went downtown, how he went to a movie in the middle of the day. And still the evidence adds up. Now it is known that on Wednesday night Natalie Fleet came to his house and stayed for many hours. She was observed in both the downstairs and upstairs windows, and at one point he was observed holding her in his arms. No question that he has begun an affair with Miss Fleet, which is in itself a matter for us to think about. What is most important though is that yesterday morning, after the beginning of this affair, Natalie Fleet called up the Lubbock Moving Company to ask them to come and make an estimate and bring packing boxes with them. It is evident from this that Burr intends to move, to escape—clear presumption of guilt. Fortunately it will be a while before the Lubbock Moving Company will be able to move him out of his house, and therefore despite this indication of intent to flee there is yet no need for haste while we accumulate more evidence.

And lest you doubt still, said Berthold at the blackboard (next to the Suspect Board), what do you make of the fact that a man who was known for his regular almost daily walks through Burnet Woods, has now, since the time of the murder, not once ventured into that park? Not once since Tuesday has he walked to work, taking his car instead. Why is he avoiding the steps where always before he loved to climb, listening to the morning birds of springtime, identifying their songs, spying them out as they flit among the bushes? Why has he not returned?

"Because he's guilty and afraid?" asked Freitag.

"Right," said Berthold. "Because he's guilty and—we know—afraid of the scene of the crime!"

Freitag to Watson behind the back of his hand: "That guy could make a pretty good cop now that he's no longer a dirty communist hippy."

"That's what I always say," said Watson. "If only these kids would cut their hair and get crewcuts we wouldn't have anything to worry about."

"Except pseudo-intellectual murderers like this Professor Burr."

"I never did like the looks of that mustache," said Watson.

On Saturday morning, Berthold came to inspect Burr's house. He arrived before Burr was up, and banged on the kitchen door. Stricken with fear, Burr's first thought was to tuck his head under the blankets and wait until Berthold went away. But he realized the pointlessness of trying to escape by that route. Clambering out of bed, he struggled to his feet, put on his bathrobe and slippers, padded down the stairs, while the cats and dogs, hungry, danced around him. Outside on the street he saw a large moving van: LUBBOCK MOVERS.

When he opened the back door, he recognized Berthold instantly, despite his disguise. He was disguised as a mover from the Lubbock Moving Company, and on his overalls he had a woven name in blue letters: *Buzzy*. But Burr was not fooled. He had not realized what a huge heavy man Berthold was in his overalls, with his square-shaped head and crewcut and bull neck and his heavy hanging pouting lips.

"Got a stack a boxes for you," he said. His eyes searched around the kitchen in the practiced manner of the professional sleuth. Under his arm was a stack of pieces of cardboard—the boxes all flattened out. "The small ones for books, the big for linen and miscellaneous items. Put em here?" Kitchen table. Meanwhile he kept turning his head all around looking at the ceiling, the walls, and the floor, searching for clues. He said, "Where's this furniture you want me to estimate?"

We explained: "I'll show you. I've really got two moving jobs to worry about. One batch of furniture is going to my brother-in-law on the coast. The rest goes with me."

Berthold's narrow eye. "And where are you moving to?"

"I haven't found a place yet."

He laughs. "Can't estimate that, then."

"It will be local," we say.

Eye opens, head nods, "Yah, okay. You call again when you've made up your mind where you're going."

Thinking his chances were better if he co-operated, Burr showed Berthold all through the house, going along perfectly with the masquerade, just as if he didn't suspect a thing. He showed him all the pieces that belonged to Cynthia's brother and distinguished them from the other things, that belonged to himself. At one point Berthold asked, "You going to get this stuff ready to go? You need somebody to pack it for you?" No thank you, said Burr. The dogs seemed to like Berthold. They kept coming up to him and sniffing his trousers, wagging their tails, going away and coming back again. "Hello there, fella," said Berthold to each one, again and again, the same words, "Hello there, fella," and it occurred to Burr that he was disguising his rage and fury very well. After a while he began to whistle, though, and the disguise began to crack a little. Burr recognized the song from many years ago. It was

182

called "Little Old Lady" (Little old lady/ Time for tea/ Dum dum dum/ dum dum dee/ You're just like that little old lady/ dum dum da dum dee). Burr thought it very unlikely that a hulking brute of a Lubbock furniture mover would be whistling "Little Old Lady" and thought that Berthold ought to realize this. Still he did not say anything. And as they went around the house, he watched Berthold's heavy-lidded but searching eyes, looking at everything, estimating and judging and picking up clues, making inferences quietly kept to himself, putting together all he needed to know about the nature of Burr's life. What is there in the house that will tell him about last Tuesday morning? he wondered. What will give me away? He couldn't see anything himself, but he knew that Berthold could tell the history of a shoe just by staring at it hard, and the only thing he could do was fatalistically to wait, let things take their natural course, don't help them along, but don't try to hinder them either.

"Okay, fella," said Berthold as he went out. "Call us when you've made up your mind. Better feed them cats now."

When he got back to the station house, Berthold said, "Okay boys, I got everything now. I saw the inside of his house and I saw everything in it, and now we know. Let's give him the weekend. Then we can close in on Monday morning, surround the house, and nab him."

That evening, Saturday night, Natalie Fleet came back. She came because he called her on the telephone and explicitly asked her to come. She came gently and full of concern, and when he asked her to spend the night, please stay the night, oh please don't leave me, she agreed. They lay in bed and made love and then they talked for a long time about childhood and about their lives and all the things that were lost, and they turned off the light and still they talked, and then they tried to sleep.

Then while he listened and realized that she had already fallen asleep in his bed, Burr touched her hair gently, and suddenly he realized this great desire not to surrender just yet, not to give up, not to get caught. He looked at this new girl who had spoken to him so sweetly, had done for him so tenderly, this kindhearted girl who liked him in such an honest uncomplicated way, and suddenly he realized that he wanted some of that life that he could live with her, that he wanted some of that future that he could put her into and live through—that she was good and he had need for good things like her.

Then—and according to the narrator this was really the first time it occurred to him—it occurred to him that he should escape before he was caught. It never would have occurred to him (narrator) if it had not been for Natalie Fleet. Now because he wanted some life with Natalie Fleet—even if maybe short—he wanted to escape. Take her with him of course. Quickly the idea took shape, turning into resolution and plan. To get away before Monday morning when—he knew—they would come under the direction of Berthold Kirschner to surround the house and take him prisoner. To leave tomorrow—Sunday—in the morning as soon as we can get started, that was the idea. To leave by car. To head north, to aim for Canada. Money? asked the narrator. Take his Master Charge, his other credit cards. Money can be sent after he arrives in Canada. Natalie Fleet can help. Take her with him. That was the most important part of the plan. He looked at her sleeping next to him, her thin bare little shoulder sticking up partly uncovered by the sheet. Tell her when she wakes up, don't wake her now, tell her in the morning when she wakes—tell, We are going to escape. Ask her to come with us: Please come, I need you to come, I have no reason to go except for you. Persuade her.

He went to sleep with his plan forming and re-forming, the words of announcement and persuasion replaying themselves in his mind. As he went to sleep the plan went into his dreams, the words went into his dreams, they played through his dreams like twisted strands of cord, they turned and knotted around each other, in images he tried to grasp and could not, images that tied themselves around his plan and his words, image-pictures of actual things, real things, that disappeared in a moment and when they were gone he could not remember what they had been, could not remember even that he had ever seen them—so how did he even know that he had seen images? It was a night full of waking. He felt bad when he woke up in the middle of the night, again and again, never sure whether he had been asleep or not, while the plan and resolution of his idea continued to reaffirm itself in his mind, and he was aware of a great uncomfortable feeling in his body, in his belly, in his stomach, a great bloated feeling, for a while a very heavy weight that seemed to be resting like a leaden block upon his solar plexus, and he pressed his fist against his solar plexus trying to shove the leaden block away—and as he shoved he kept preparing the words he was going to say to Natalie Fleet first thing in the morning when she woke: We are going to go. We are going to get in the car and drive away. We are going to leave everything, we are going to leave the house, and the chairmanship, and the moving, and the animals, and Laura Grummon and all other Grummons. Meanwhile his rebellious belly made him sweat (how hot the night was!), and he turned, twisted, tried to find a more comfortable position, and at times his body ached under the ribs and made him groan aloud. He thought of his heart and wondered if he was having another spasm, and he wondered how he could have one now, and why he should have one just when he had made up his mind to escape.

Then it was morning. The morning was very hot, the air humid through the open window, the wide lightly billowing white curtains, and still he sweated and felt very heavy, and still she slept, and once again he reviewed his plan to escape and the words that he was going to say to her as soon as she woke up. And why didn't she wake up? Impatience took hold of him now, even some irritation that she could sleep so soundly and not hear the shouting of his mind, and he looked at his watch and detested his own laziness and almost hated her for hers. Get up. He thought he should start by getting up himself. He remembered vaguely making some move to get up first—to go to the bathroom first, to get things started, to make a little noise that would help to wake her gently perhaps, so that he could then tell her his plan. Remembered vaguely, but he remembered also probably some feeling of a heavy weight that was sitting on him, like a great heavy man from the moving company perhaps sitting on him, like Berthold Kirschner in disguise sitting on him perhaps, although there was no one, he saw when he looked, only this very heavy feeling in his own limbs, this absolutely tyrannical refusal of his body to ease him in any way in his attempt to get out of bed.

185

No doubt he was still having dreams, half asleep, half awake, indistinguishable as it had been all night, except for the sudden clarity, the real truth of things, when I looked up at that moment and saw the two policemen standing there looking down at me. And beside them fully dressed in her short blue-and-red dress, which she had worn last night, was Natalie Fleet, looking anxiously at me—so I must have fallen back to sleep—and they seemed to be standing at some great height looking down at me, and I thought, so she turned me in after all.

The policemen were smiling as if they were good friends of mine— as if they expected me to be happy to see them. I wondered. Then I spoke: "So you caught up with me after all," I said. They laughed as if it were a good joke.

Part Three

Chapter 1

The two policemen in blue shirts with friendly faces. I was looking up at them as I lay on my back—embarrassed that they should find me in bed (on the floor, as a matter of fact) in my pajamas. (Underwear to tell the truth.) Discrepancies didn't matter. What mattered mainly was how glad I felt to see the policemen, as if their coming at last put an end to an intolerable situation. I said, "If you wait a moment I'll get dressed."

"Don't move," said the policeman, yet not in the brutal manner of the enforcer but in as kindly and considerate a way as you could possibly ask of these servants of the people. He was carrying two long sticks. Now he and his buddy unrolled the sticks, which were joined by a long rectangle of canvas and they laid them down on the floor beside me. Meanwhile Natalie in her short red and blue dress, anxious face, watched. I recognized the sticks as a stretcher and wondered why they wanted to carry me out. To help them I turned and moved as if to get on the stretcher. "Lie still," said the man. "We'll do it." Then he took me by my feet and the other under the shoulders and they lifted me and placed me on the stretcher, as if I did not have any strength in my body. Tell him how ridiculous it seemed, to be treated as so helpless, yet how natural and easy and pleasant to relax and let them move me in this way.

Just then one of the policeman picked up the floor lamp. "Must have knocked it over," he said. Who, me? Suddenly I remembered something. Remembered getting up. Gathering clothes, coming back to the bedroom from the bathroom. Remembered the lamp. With an inference that I must have collapsed somehow. The policemen bent down to lift up the stretcher with me on it. "Where are we going?" I asked. "Think we'll take you to Burnet Hospital—right, lady?" Natalie?

"I called the doctor," she said, "and we're to take you to Burnet Hospital. Everything is going to be all right, you don't have to worry about a thing."

Your heart! said the narrator, loud and clear and instantaneous. Adding, But you're all right now. The bad moment is past. (Better be past, said Burr—anxious.) I said, "Did I—" tried to think of the word for it. Asked the narrator. What is the word? Die, said the narrator. Did I die? No, that's the wrong word, for if I had died I would be dead. Did I— die temporarily? No. Sleep? No. *Almost* die? "You collapsed," said Natalie Fleet. Collapsed! Yes. Passed out. Stricken—struck. Fell.

Meanwhile the policemen who had not come to arrest me but instead to take me to the hospital, these policemen had lifted me up into the air and lightly I swung between them as they took me (lightly lightly) through the door and down the stair (floating floating) into the living room and out the front door, across the front lawn (sun on the face making nausea nausea), while neighbor children stood on the grass and silently watched, and put me into the back of the big red ambulance that waited there. Inside, cool and white.

"Natalie! Natalie! Where's Natalie?"

"I'm right here, right beside you." Oh the lovely voice, warm and low and soft, and her hand lightly soothing my arm.

"You coming with me? You must come. I need you."

"I'm coming with you. I won't leave you."

"I can't go to the hospital," said Burr. "I can't do this. I've got too many things to do!"

Natalie the lovely voice soothing: "Now just just relax, take it easy, don't worry about a thing. Everything everything will be taken care of."

Oh the peace of her voice and words.

He heard a touch of siren as they started off. One of the men sat on the bench facing him and held a little rubber mask with a hose that he tried to put over Burr's nose. Natalie sat beside him. Burr was thinking of all the reasons why he couldn't go to the hospital at this time—all his responsibilities—and he kept talking about them to the man who kept trying to put the little rubber oxygen mask over Burr's face. "Because Grummon, because the search committee, because they are trying to find a new head for the English department and they need to consult me, they need to consult all of us, but they need to consult me because they might want to turn to me as a compromise candidate if Kail or Stone—because how can I become serve as a candidate, as head, if you put me in the hospital?"

Oxygen. Natalie saying, "Don't worry about a thing."

"Because how can I afford to go to the hospital. What you don't realize is that my wife died a year and a half ago and my children have gone away, my daughter is living in a commune somewhere in the West and she is pregnant, you have to understand that, and my son has gone off traveling, leaving college, you'd probably call him a hippy although I don't approve of the term as such except when it designates—well anyway the last I heard from him is in Hong Kong and I don't know how to reply to him, I don't know what he is doing, whether he is on drugs, I hope not I certainly hope not, or whether he is simply traveling having adventures seeing the world, which would be a good thing, no doubt, if only he would let me know—maybe he is a sailor on a ship, I don't even know that—but in any case I don't know how I can *afford* to go to the hospital . . ."

"You have Blue Cross and Major Medical," said Natalie. "I've got your Blue Cross card."

"How did you find it?" asked Burr.

"In your desk, where you told me," she said. He had forgotten telling her that—even when she mentioned it, he did not as yet remember.

"But what about the animals?" he asked now. "My house has four dogs and seven cats living in it, and they need to be taken care of, they need to be fed, and the dogs need to be let out into the pen, even if you don't exercise them, and the kitty boxes need to be cleaned. What about them?"

"It's all right, we'll take care of them" said Natalie.

"And the moving!" he exclaimed suddenly. Explaining to the man who still quietly continued to try to place without forcing the oxygen mask on his face: "I've sold the house to the Benjamins, promised to be out of it by the end of the month. I'm supposed to ship all Cynthia's brother's furniture to the West Coast and I have to find an apartment for myself to live in—and I haven't even begun to look for one—and then I'll have to pack everything and get the movers to move everything —and I haven't done a thing, and how can I do anything if I have to go into the hospital now?"

"It's all right," said Natalie. "Don't you worry, we'll take care of it." *We?* Oh the ease and comfort of being soothed of your most terrible anxieties, relieved of your most frightening procrastinations—yet still the panic responsibility kept asking its questions, but suddenly it came to a point where he could not utter them—not in this group. Asking, What of Laura? How can I go into the hospital when Laura needs me? Someone must notify her, someone must relieve her, someone must keep her happy and content, someone must keep her mouth shut so she can't tell Grummon, someone must stop the inevitable blab, as I have struggled so hard for so long—trying to remember what secret it was that she held on him.

And then still more desperately Burr remembered his crime—his responsibility to his crime. Which he could not mention because of the policeman with the oxygen mask. They would be looking for him, he realized. Now they would not be able to find him. Could they come for him in the hospital? Shouldn't Berthold be notified where he was, what had happened to him? Tell the police— Then he remembered that his latest plan had been to escape. That escape was the last thing he could remember thinking of before— But how could he escape if he had to go to the hospital? Either way, if he wanted to help the police or if he wanted to escape—he could not afford to go to the hospital. Except for the kind man with the oxygen mask, and Natalie, who kept soothing him and telling him not to worry about anything, everything would be decided and done for him.

Yield, yield, he said. Let them carry you, let her carry you, now is a time for rest, for letting them take for a while the burdens and responsibilities and anxieties. But still he was anxious—now about Natalie Fleet herself. There she sat, beside him in the ambulance. Presumably she had called the ambulance, as she said she had called the doctor, and now she was promising to take care of everything—but what was it that would bind her, hold her to that? Ask the narrator, flatly, why should she? Why should she even go so far as this, to accompany us to the hospital—much less take on such burdens as she appeared to be promising? It would be different if she were our wife. Or even a mere motherly friend with as long-standing a connection as, let us say, Laura Grummon. But here she is, mistress for not more than three days, and suddenly plunged into such a business as this—why should she stay? Ask the narrator, won't she leave at the first opportunity she gets? Won't she duck out as fast as she can, once she gets us to the hospital, no doubt, and has notified someone else of what has happened? He heard Burr saying to her: "Don't leave me. Stay, stay by me, won't you please?" and Natalie softly almost like singing: "Don't worry, don't worry about a thing."

In the hospital there was a long wait in the emergency room, but it did not seem long. Something peculiar seemed to have happened to time at this point, where things went slowly and yet seemed neither slow nor uncomfortable. There was an emergency room doctor listening for a long time to his heart, bent over his chest. There was an electrocardiogram. There was Natalie reading a magazine. And Natalie sitting beside him where he lay on a high flat hospital bed, talking to him, he guessed, about things that had just happened as if they were long ago.

He became aware of a gap in memory somewhere in recent time and realized that he had already been working on it for some time, trying to find out where it was and what was missing. It went back to the moment when the policemen arrived and looked at him where he lay (on the floor, in his underwear)—the recognition that something was missing before that moment. He understood that he had passed out—the narrator had explained that to him back there in the room, the moment the policemen had mentioned knocking over the lamp. And at that moment (and not until that moment) he became aware of the gap in his memory. But at first he had not been able to see where it was.

The gap was blind, and he was blind looking at it. How had he come to be lying on the floor in his underwear? The question did not even occur to him until a few minutes ago, that is, sometime in the ambulance, was it? Or perhaps in the emergency room, or perhaps now in the room upstairs to which they had taken him—even the moment of formulation of the question itself seemed indefinite. How come he hadn't wondered about it while he was in the ambulance? But then he realized that maybe he had wondered about it then. He just did not know what he had wondered about and what he had not. The questions kept coming back at him as if they were fresh, as if they had never occurred to him before, and yet clearly, obviously, they had occurred to him before, and perhaps even they had been answered before.

Still he fingered at the gap in his memory, trying to remember. At the near end of the gap, the smiling policemen speaking of the lamp he had knocked down. At the far end a night blank, since the dark last night when he was riding his nakedness hard upon and in the nakedness of Natalie Fleet. By God, had he collapsed while making love to Natalie Fleet? But no, he remembered a difficult and painful hot night that followed, with discomfort in his belly. He remembered restlessness, turning over and over, and pushing his fist hard against his solar plexus. Okay, tell the narrator then, that must have been the beginnings of it, this heart thing, whatever it was (surely it was heart?) that had collapsed him. Remembered also some churning thought, some inquiry, some quest, that kept repeating itself all night long, spinning itself around in circles with knots in them, weaving in and out of dreams—some problem that he was trying to work out, something to do with the silent sleeping form of the girl (that would be Natalie Fleet) sleeping on the other side of the bed, but unable absolutely to remember what it was, what the thought was, what he was looking for. But it brought back to mind (had he thought of this before? had he already recalled this when he was in the ambulance and before and had merely forgotten it a second time, or had he truly not remembered it until now?) the morning, the sunlight in the window, the dragging heat weighing down some heavy resolve that he could no longer remember—remember only (but yes definitely remember this) the reluctant decision to get up, and the

194

depressed refusal of the body to obey until forced. Remember then the forcing of the body to get up (and Natalie Fleet still asleep! Yes, she was still asleep when he got up, though she was fully dressed in her red-and-blue dress looking down at him when the policemen came), and, plodding heavy, stepped into the bathroom, then either shaving or not shaving—Burr still could not remember—and back to the bedroom to get his clothes. Remember also the impatience in the idea of waking Natalie Fleet, the irritation that she had not waked of her own free will, irritation in the idea that he would be obliged to wake her, and remember also putting on his underwear at the foot of the bed while he looked at her. And then turning, and then—yes!—here it is, the quick warning of a faint, the quick liquefaction and dissolving of the room into a yellow and white speckled stream, with one quick sharp word, "Sit down!" There memory stopped. The far end of the gap. Burr was astonished how quick it was, he did not even have time to begin to carry out his decision to sit down, not even to turn to a chair, just the liquefaction and dissolving of all that was solid and then nothing—blank standing between that and the moment of the policemen come to get him.

The narrator told him, that was the moment of your death. He had died and managed to return, and all there was to know of it was the empty gap between two moments of life. He said it was not death, he had simply fainted and collapsed, simply lay unconscious on the floor for a few minutes—how many? Long enough for Natalie, violently awakened by the crash, to call the ambulance and the doctor and get dressed. But the narrator said it was as good as death—his preview of death, his glimpse from which he had been, fortuitously, rescued. And what did you see? Burr asked. Why, nothing. Quite absolutely nothing. That was the point, this moment of death so different from mere sleep in which there is always still the noise and machinery of a body and even a mind continuing to function. Whereas this was a gap not even black since there was nothing there to perceive blackness with, and not even a gap except as his living consciousness, revived and awakened, looks back and sees a gap between its shores.

The narrator kept commanding him to consider what would have happened if he had not revived, had not come back to life. Why, he would be dead. The condition of the gap, the nonperceiving even of the gap, would prevail now and now and forevermore. If Natalie Fleet had found him dead on the floor and called the undertaker instead of the ambulance, it would have been the same. The last thing, said the narrator, would have been that moment of liquefaction of the room, the room draining away, but it would not be remembered, because it took an effort and return of life for you to remember it as it was. And of course in fact, the narrator reminded him, in the gap, the gap made permanent, what will you remember of anything? Nothing of course—so that it will be not merely that life is over, it will be as if life had never been. Including, said the narrator, not only for you but for Natalie Fleet that the undertaker is called. Including the undertaker himself, not to mention the doctor and the hospital. And myself the narrator, of course, with all our readers—all as non-existent once again as they were to your consciousness before you were born. The narrator repeated that phrase: before you were born. It impressed him—the condition in the gap was the same as the condition before you were born as well as the condition after you died. And in that condition there was no condition. It will be, said the narrator, as if you never were. And since this will be true of us all, of Natalie and Cynthia and Grummon and Elias as well—not to mention Berthold and Kessler—it will be as if the world itself never was, as indeed it never was, before, before you came to know it.

Again and again that day in the hospital—and the next day too and for many ensuing days—the narrator kept working and reworking the incident, trying to make Burr see it more intensely, trying to dig things out of it, to find the extraordinary thing about it that kept seeming to elude us. Kept reminding Burr of that liquefaction of his room just at the moment of his death, how it all turned into spots and streaks, not only the billowing curtains on the open window, but the hot bed with its rumpled sheet, the body of the sleeping girl lying on it, and all the solid objects, the dark mahogany dresser that was supposed to be shipped by Lubbock Movers to Cynthia's brother on the coast, the chair, the rug, the wall, and the checkered wallpaper—all turned to liquid and seemed to drain away down a funnel into the empty gap and as it went it took everything else with it, the house, the trees, the buildings and roads and machines, the land, and also the people, and all the animals, both the animals in his house and the wild animals too, and the birds, the insects, the gardens and the wilderness and all the rest of the world, and finally the stars themselves, the sky and the universe, everything liquefied and drained away in an instant down through that funnel into the endless black that is the empty void of death. Death is a funnel, said the narrator, that sucks the universe into it—like one of those great black holes that the astronomers have calculated where all mass implodes to maximum or infinite density in zero volume, and everything intensely concentrated is reduced to nothing. And when you revived, continued the narrator, still and incessantly trying to push his lesson upon Burr, then you rebuilt the world on the struts of your consciousness—then at last as you looked at the solid three-dimensional world around you, the room, or the open sky outside the window, you felt the scaffolding upon which those three-dimensional sights were erected, the scaffolding put up by your own mind, your consciousness, you felt even some of the effort that is required of the mind to build itself a world.

And still all through the afternoon, as he lay on his hospital bed attached to a cardiac monitor, and Natalie Fleet came and went, visiting, the narrator kept fingering around the edge of the gap and elsewhere, sending out memory probes in search of the things he had forgotten, for it seemed to him as if he had forgotten almost everything, yet not knowing what they were he could not know, could not say what he had forgotten, both in the gap and outside. So constantly did his memory probe, looking for things whose loss could only be felt, or not even felt but only dimly intuited or guessed at, and he began to worry about his mind itself, about his capacity still to build a complete world on the struts of his consciousness, and later in the afternoon, when Natalie Fleet came back once again, he said:

"I wonder if I have suffered brain damage."

She laughed, "I doubt it," she said. "That's not likely."

"How long was I unconscious?"

"I don't know. Five minutes maybe."

"That's long enough to cause brain damage, isn't it?"

"Now, now," she said, "You haven't suffered brain damage, I'm sure."

Sometime during the afternoon while we talked, she told me how it had been with her that morning. How she had just waked up from hearing me moving about. How it seemed too early to get up, and she turned over, curled up, allowing herself to fall back toward sleep, when she heard this great crash—as if the bureau had fallen over. Or thinking the old house was beginning to collapse. Looked about, didn't see me. Then she sat up and saw Burr lying on the floor in his underwear. Out cold. Jumped out of bed. Instant memory of the trip to the doctor last Monday, of cardiospasm diagnosed as innocent. Instant thought of not so innocent, instant assumption that Burr had not merely passed out but had died. Leaned over him, his pale green face, mustache, and no sign of breath, felt his wrist, no pulse. Certain that he was dead.

At this point—now she told me laughing a bit ruefully—she must admit her mind turned quickly to the awkwardness (to say the least) of her own predicament. What would (blank) say? Well, let's not go into that. Confess that for a few minutes her main thought was how to get out of there without leaving traces that would implicate her. How she hurried to get dressed. And all the time thinking, with the assumption he was dead. And all the time someone telling her (who was that voice? she demanded. My God it was just like the voice of somebody else in my head). that she could not abandon him like that even if he was dead —that no awkwardness justified that. And at that moment suddenly Burr came back to life. A heavy intake of breath and then a moan and then a scream. (Scream? Did you say scream?) Yes, scream and scream and scream. Blood curdling, said Natalie, weird and wild. And then she knew that no awkwardness now could excuse her from her duty. Told how she turned and committed herself to do everything possible, putting a washrag on his forehead, speaking soothingly to calm him down (she succeeded quickly), going to the phone to call the doctor, who told her also to call the life squad and take him to Burnet Hospital. How she went back and kept soothing him explaining to him that he had collapsed but was all right now, how the ambulance was coming, how she had called the doctor, how she would take care of him—all of which was lost now in the gap. How he spoke of escaping from the police, of taking her with him, of his responsibility to his crime. She laughed. "You sure said some funny things," she said.

Dimly he remembered his crime and wondered vaguely if he had been exonerated. But his memory went probing around the gap again, now in search of the screaming that Natalie had mentioned. Yes, he thought he could hear it, dimly, remotely. He remembered it like a great rush of air—or scalding steam through pipes. And the pipes were like blood vessels in his brain, under high pressure of steam and ready to burst. He remembered the screaming of the steam in the boiler room and remembered vaguely failing to recognize that it was really the screaming of his voice—screaming for help.

So that was something, anyway, said the narrator—a slight encroachment into the area of the gap. If you keep probing, maybe you will find more. Meanwhile Natalie kept talking. "Do you think I should figure out some excuse to explain how I happened to come into your house on a Sunday morning and found you on the floor?" she asked. "Maybe I should just tell the truth and to hell what people say." Enough presence of mind (brain damage or not) for Burr to think: I don't want Laura Grummon to know about it. And I don't want Stone to know about it. And I don't want Harold to know about it. Or Harvey Kessler. And yet Natalie, I don't want Natalie to leave, I don't want anyone to take care of me but Natalie. He said: "You can say I called you up. I was feeling bad enough that I might have called you up anyhow." (Thinking, brain damage or no.) "I would call you up because it was you who took me to see the doctor last Monday, remember. So you can say I called you up because I felt sick and—scared. And then—(thinking)—when you came in you found me on the floor." She grinned. "You want me to tell that story?"

"If you wish," said Burr. "All right," she said. "Only this—if I found you on the floor, how did I get into the house?" Burr thinking. "Maybe you have a key." She laughed. "If I have a key what's the point of an excuse?" Burr still thinking. "Maybe I came down and let you in and *then* collapsed. No one needs to know in what room I collapsed."

She said, "Okay. Now tell me who you want me to notify."

Girders of mind composing a great dome with a whole world of people and things, of history and life, suspended within. The narrator kept making comments about the shortness of life, and how it keeps getting

199

shorter and shorter all the time. Remarking how small everything seems now, how rather fragile and delicate even big things that have always seemed so powerful, even great institutions, nations and wars and universities, presidents and chairmen and girls, doctors and policemen and ambulance drivers, as they swirl around in the outer rims of the funnel preparing to be sucked down through the center. Telling me to pay attention to the variable magnitude of life itself, how big the world can seem and how small, how great and imposing the presence of a person (anyone you name) and how small, how trivial, how ephemeral like a drop of water. As if the magnitude and stature of things depended on the power of your consciousness to blow up the balloon of its universe large or small, the size depending on how strong you feel.

The doctor came in. He was cheerful and jolly.

"Yes sir," he said. "Well you've had a mild coronary attack—not a bad one, not dangerous in itself, although in the first weeks after such an attack, of course, it is dangerous and it is necessary to follow a strict regime for a while. Let me explain. A coronary occlusion: this is the classic manifestation known commonly by the term *heart attack*. There are of course many kinds of heart disturbances and heart disease, valve malfunctionings, malformations, and other ailments, but the conventional heart attack is the coronary occlusion, which is what you have had. It tends to strike men in their forties and fifties. If you pass through this critical period without one then you are not likely to have one until old age, your late sixties or seventies. It is often extremely serious, of course, often it is instantly fatal. But yours as I have said is mild. This means that we can treat you and nurse you back to convalescence, and with proper care I think we can assure you a total recovery, and you will, within a few months, be able to do everything that you had been able to do before you were stricken. You may even consider yourself fortunate, for now you will perhaps take better care of yourself, and actually live to a riper old age than if you had not had this timely warning.

"Shall I explain to you what a coronary occlusion is? It is a stoppage of one of the arteries that feeds and nourishes the heart muscle itself. Caused by a clot formed in the narrowed passages of the artery, the passages narrowed by the presence in your blood of excess fats, in particular cholesterol and triglycerides. Why these fats stay in your bloodstream and clog the passages is something of a mystery. There is a distinct correlation between coronaries and cigarette smoking—you are a heavy smoker, of course. There is a correlation with being overweight, but this does not apply to you. Neither do you have high blood pressure, another high correlation. I do not think you overeat. Let me ask. Are you an anxious kind of person? Do you worry about time? About the press of business upon you, the imminence of deadlines?

"At any rate," said the doctor. "I can assure you that I expect a perfect recovery for you. You will be able to live as you wish, do all you want, exercise, have sex (quick glance at Natalie?), everything—except you should keep a close eye on your diet. But for a while you have to go through a special regime for coronary patients. We will keep you on the cardiac monitor for some days. You will have to stay in the hospital four weeks, if all goes well. You may not get up for any reason whatever for the next two weeks. Later we shall see what steps you may go through in returning to normal."

He turned to Natalie. "And you, young lady. Are you to take charge of him?"

She gulped like a child and shrugged with embarrassment. "I'll do what I can," she said.

Chapter 2

I asked Natalie: "What about the dogs and kitties? Who's going to take care of them."

"I'll manage them," she said. "I'll see they get fed."

"And letting the dogs run in the pen? And emptying the kitty boxes?"

"I'll take care of it," she said. "And then maybe some neighbor child can take over."

"How can I repay you?" I asked.

"I don't know," she said. "Don't worry about it, really."

She was the only one to visit him that first day, but she spent most of the day. The room had another patient in it, but the other patient could not talk. There were long times of silence and rest. On shelves up near the ceiling were the two cardiac monitors—one for the other man, one for himself—like two television screens with a moving green light tracing the shape of the heartbeat from left to right, a constantly changing jagged line.

The other patient was an old man with tubes attached, who seemed neither to hear nor see nor feel. He was in worse shape than Burr's father had been, except that Burr's father had died. The narrator reminded Burr of his father, five years ago. With his father it had been a short devastating illness, a swift-spreading cancer, cutting him down in the midst of his healthy old age, his middle seventies, slicing through his well-exercised health and wasting his well-conditioned body in a few weeks—shocking to his children, who traveled hundreds of miles from great distances to see him as he lay on his bed in the hospital with tubes attached to him. For several days—one morning he said (his voice wasted to shreds) in a tone of great astonishment: "I believe this is my death!" Two days later in the morning, as they watched, he quietly died.

With his mother, who died three years later, it was still more gradual. With her it was a series of strokes, the first shortly after his father died, beginning with paralysis of an arm, then the crippling of her speech, then deeper paralyses and crippling. Death put its foot on her lightly at first and then, step by step, moved into her, occupied her, took her personhood away. For a year she stared, sometimes smiled, with bland uncomprehending eyes. Ask the narrator—did she know she was dying? No, says the narrator, she could not know she was dying because she did not know that she was living, she did not know that she was still caught in the fix of a life that could be distinguished from the nonlife or nonconsciousness that surrounded it.

With Cynthia, on the other hand, lying dead in the bathtub in a shallow pool of water when he got up that cold November morning—tell the doctor, she never came to bed—with Cynthia (the doctor said you must regard it as an illness, for there was nothing you could do, said the doctor, her mind was made up quite decisively and a depression like that lasting over an extended period of time is an illness and there was nothing you could do except get her to a psychiatrist which you did, and even I could not really help her, it was like cancer growing in the mind no one knows unstoppable by any means we have at hand and you couldn't stop her and I couldn't stop her because a suicidal person like that lives all inside herself and none of us had more than the fleetest brief glimpses into the nightmare that she concealed within the inner lining of her quiet self-effacing manner and remember she did not tell you what she was crying about last night remember you asked her and tried to help and she wouldn't answer nor would she tell me and I insist you must not load yourself down with guilt or I shall have to do the same for a thing like this which can really only be regarded as the most unfortunate consequence almost like an accident of a mental and emotional break-down extremely difficult to diagnose and treat that can only be regarded as an illness about which we have very little knowledge as of this time said the doctor) with Cynthia it was foreseen and deliberately sought for, asked for, arranged for, desired, welcomed, planned perhaps for months or years, finally achieved after who knows how many failures of resolution?

With you, on the other hand, said the narrator—while Burr watched the green tracing of his heart as it continued to measure the intervals of his still advancing time—with you it was so swift and sudden that you did not even have time to know what was happening to you. For you the funnel suddenly opened and everything swept into it and away before you had time to sit down, and if that were your death you never would have known it—just as your mother's death was so slow that she never knew it either. (On the other hand, added the narrator, talking to himself, you are perfectly free to say, at any time you want, just as your father did, "this is my death." And you may also say that your father's consciousness of his death was short-lived and therefore not so much to be envied over your mother's lack of consciousness or your own.)

As they watched him, said the narrator, he quietly died. (They came for her too with a stretcher, two men in white. They covered her with sheets and strapped her on because she had stiffened in a bent position during the night. They carried her out the front door, across the lawn, covered.) In the afternoon they drove back to his father's house from the hospital. The narrator recalled how he looked at the landscape then —along the country road, the fields under a bright cover of snow, the hills beyond the fields with their trees brown and the snow appearing speckled through the trees. New England farmhouses, then the large white colonial houses of a New England village. Explain what we are doing here, said the narrator—in this classic setting from other times. My father—tell—was a liberal Protestant minister in a prosperous suburban church, who in old age, unable to retire, became a liberal Protestant minister in a rural New England church to a colony mainly of old people, retired from universities and businesses. Who called himself a man of words rather than a man of God, a persuader, a liberal but never very active, who kept himself informed about the problems of the cities, the ghettos, and the new movements of change and revolution, and sometimes interpreted them in sermons to his elderly congregation, but more often spoke both more personally and more poetically about the passage of time, the loss of the past, the approaching death of all of us (keeping the idea to herself, never daring to mention it). He still retained his old-fashioned belief in the values of the open country, in the idea that nature was a matter of woods and fields and wilderness and animals and good rural people, and he still worshipped the countryside where he lived despite the threatening encroachments of freeways and shopping centers, but he also believed that he and his parishioners were the last to enjoy such good things, and he would have felt guilty about it because of his reading about ghettos, except that he believed his knowledge that they would all die soon, being old, more or less excused him. He preached at many funerals during his last years there. And—narrator, tell—as we drove from the hospital after his own death back to his house with my mother (already partly paralyzed in her left arm), past the open fields covered with snow along roads with high ridges of plowed snow on the sides (barren maple tree, blasted by November on a frozen lawn), and in the sparkling sun of this bright cold day (gray cold November overcast) saw the winter birds in the branches, chickadees, nuthatches, juncos, and evening grosbeaks with their patches of yellow, and the countryside was full then of the memory of all the other times when he had driven through it with us along these same roads, (house full of the person, filling up the stairs, the rooms, voice), memories of his words connected with these places, these corners, these trees and fences, as we passed—the gentle countryside, open, rural, but not really wild anymore, its nature tamed, so that it was safe, no longer a menace or threat to humankind as it once had been—yet today it seemed nature had done its most powerful work there in the hospital room (medicine on the bathroom floor). . . . That was one part of it, says the narrator, this sense that these fields and hills that he loved had themselves had their hand in doing him in (there was an empty pill bottle on the floor beside the bathtub where she lay—also permission to the doctor for a confirming autopsy), and the other part was that this countryside had lost its soul now that he had been taken out of it (the blasted November maple tree over the frozen lawn as they carried her covered, dead, out the front door), since for me (Burr) it existed mostly through his eyes, since he had found it, shown it to me, lived in it (until now), loved it. Struts of his consciousness making a world around him, after which, as the narrator explained, it seemed as if it could only wither and shrivel and finally yield forever and wholly to the encroachments. (For a year and a half he lived alone in her house, which she left for the last time on a cold November morning, carried.) As if his father and the countryside he loved were not different but the same, a single identity incorporating also the people of the village to whom he preached and whose funerals he had spoken at. His father died, his mother soon after, and then it seemed the country, that is, the countryside, died with them. The past died. Burr's childhood and youth died. (She left a sad, intelligent little note, relieving him of blame.) His memory caught on places and people that no longer existed, his memory playing its games with fantasies, ghosts.

As he lay there that afternoon he tried going back into the past (stay away from the morning with the empty bed). Caught remembered moments and tried to lodge his mind now into his mind then to re-create the reality of a moment gone. He was at breakfast in the dining room on the upper deck of a steamboat, with broad high windows, and white lifeboats and net railings outside. Himself with father and mother, looking over the lifeboats to the dark houses and walls of the factory town where the steamboat had docked. Port on the way to a summer vacation. Broken memory, the next step was lost. Could not lodge himself in that mind anyway because that mind, his mind then, had no knowledge of his present mind scrutinizing it.

Instead the narrator supposed an hypothesis. Suppose you were the protagonist of a novel not of murder nor of academia nor of late century malaise but instead of your favorite science-fiction nightmare? What would you choose? Suppose, since our subject now is the lostness of the past, we make you a protagonist who is jolted back into the past by some cosmic accident. What would happen?

Let's not worry about the mechanism of the accident, said the narrator. A bolt of something faster than light, let us say, which we know from

the physicists is impossible, and therefore might carry you back in time
—penetrating you molecularly, let us say, like the rays of an x-ray,
carrying· you back not bodily perhaps but as a kind of photographic
image of yourself to be imprinted on some matter at the chosen time
in the past where you reassume your shape, a perfect copy, mind and
all, memory and all, of yourself.

What would you do? asks the narrator. Now, let's follow this. Let's
not put us back into remote ages as in the comic strips, neither prehis-
toric nor any celebrated era of the historical past, nor King Arthur's
Yankee-infested court. Take you back rather only to the recent past, the
times that you yourself dimly and romantically remember, the time of
your childhood, to give yourself the opportunity to see again and live
again with the mind of an adult those places through those days that
lie so large and still in the glass of memory. Where would you go?

Burr began putting together plans for revisiting—of landing in New
York, of going out to peek surreptitiously at his youngest childhood
home in the suburbs, of going to see that steamboat with its breakfast
memory, of attending performances and seeing games and gawking
again at the important public figures that at various ages and in various
fields he used to admire. But more important as his imagination began
to warm would be the interviews he would conduct with the people he
knew, with teachers, relatives, always being careful to disguise his identity, until it occurred to him to interview his parents themselves and
actually take a look at himself as a little boy crawling on the floor as he
talks to his mother. Who would then be young. Whom he could not
call "Mother." Could not explain that the little boy and himself were
one and the same.

Now the narrator wanted him to try again, pursue the logic of this
further—if he could go back, might he not go back a little earlier? Might
he not call on his mother while she was still unmarried, a young and
beautiful girl? Suddenly the narrator suggested: And what if you became
your own father? And then your father would be yourself, as you would
ultimately realize.

This was impossible for Burr to pursue in this form, because he knew
his father too well, the sense of difference was too great (he thought)

or at any rate there was too much circumstantial detail of his father's life known to him to make such a theory possible. But as protagonist, simplified, of an experience made essential, still the project might be pursued. If the protagonist's father were made one with his father, then of course he would not be so lovable as Burr's real father. Certainly they would not have liked each other so well, father looking at son and seeing himself there, and son would have reflected the aversion, felt it against him without knowing why. So Burr reasoned. Continuing, let us make it also that the father should die while the protagonist was still fairly young. Knowing who the child really was, he would have acted strangely at times toward the protagonist in ways that the latter would remember: he would have picked out certain things and insisted: You will remember this. He should have stressed his haunting consciousness of the flow of time and the endless loss of things. He would have the haunted look of a doomed man—for of course he knows what will happen to him, because he *remembers very precisely what will happen to him.* He knows his death is coming. He knows the date. He remembers the awed feeling of the child at the funeral, but remembers too the not very loving, not very friendly feeling that such a child must have had toward him. He remembers (because, repeats the narrator, he will have been that child himself) the child's memory of such a father as cold and strange and remote, austere, not very pleasant. The child's belief at that age (say seven) that his father did not really like him, and the child reciprocating, afraid of his father and not liking him very much either. And the father remembering his own feeling as a child cannot help reciprocating: now he sees it is true, he does not like this child very much in fact. As he watches him he sees not the childish charm that adults generally see in the children closest to them, the children they love—here instead the protagonist sees in this child the motions he remembers, all that was concealed, all that he was childishly ashamed of, he sees the disposition to lie even when he does not remember the lie, he sees the cowering fears, ill-concealed, he sees the selfishness, he sees embodied all that enormous complex of outgrown childishness restored, and he hates the child for it with all the force of emotion that he had expended on the long and difficult and (he had always thought) successful process of

208

growing up. And so the child would have been right to suspect such a father of not liking him, and more right than he could realize in sensing that the reason was that his father knew him too well, and right in connecting his fear with his guilt, to which, when he became the father he could only add the shame that this should be so.

And what of the mother, asks the narrator, still pursuing and pursuing? What drove the protagonist to seek out the lovely young girl who, he already knew, was to become his own mother? What bitter jealousy would drive him to crash through the taboo in that manner—or was it primarily the effect simply of his freedom (in one sense) from time, that because of that freedom from time he could make his approaches without fear of being known, while her restored youth enabled him to strip away enough of the specific associations of motherhood to allow him to see her (deepest oldest attraction) transformed into the guise of a sexy young girl? But having won her, married her, fathered *himself* upon her, would he not then be jealous of the child for receiving all the motherly attentions that she once bestowed on him, just as, he remembered, the child was jealous of him for receiving all the other attentions, whose nature he did not understand?

Now suggests the narrator, let's tighten the screws a little more. Might we not expect that a protagonist who has such an extraordinary experience as all that (incredible, really) would seek to make it known, would write an account of it before his death, which he knew was coming at such and such a date? And if he wrote it, might he not involute time most completely by addressing it to his son—to be read, say, at a certain date in the future shortly before the young man is to have the accident that translates him back into the past? In which case, we have a situation in which our protagonist reads his document before he writes it: reads it when he is in, let us say, his twenties, this account of his history by his father, which then becomes the prophecy of all that is going to happen to him, predicting all for him at every stage of the way. So he has both foreknowledge and hind-knowledge. He has conversations in which he hears himself, almost despite himself, saying word for word the things his father's manuscript has recorded that he will say. Of course at first he will be disbelieving; he will try to break the spell by doing things contrary to what the document records, but he will find at every point that he cannot really do so, that in some way at every point he is trapped or tricks himself into doing what he has read because it is already history, even though he, in his immersion in a time that is always under the illusion of the present tense, feels at every point as if he has control over his actions.

Now how would it feel, asks the narrator, to be in that situation, to know at all important points what is going to happen to you, to know when you will die, to see in advance the absolute limits of your attainments, to know not merely who will die and who will not but all the darkening cloud that is going to settle over you gradually as death approaches—to know all this, you without distinction except for this extraordinary experience with time which you cannot really tell anybody about—will it not be dark and depressing? Will it not account readily for the damned, haunted look that the child-protagonist will remember on the father-protagonist's face? Will it not make you long for all the normal uncertainty, that feeling of risk that characterizes every moment of our normal lives in time—when it is impossible to see around the corner of any second into the future and possible at every moment for the sudden opening of the funnel to take away the struts and liquefy and drain away in one instant all the concrete world suspended thereon?

The narrator visualizes. Suppose the time-accident of your protagonist lands him in some faraway place across the world, say in the early 1920s or late 1910s. Lands him for instance in China. He knows he will get out of China because his father's document (which he has read but it is many years yet before it will be written) says that he will—sadistically perhaps (i.e., masochistically) not telling him how. So he has to work that out—how to get out, knowing only that he will succeed but that it will be painful and humiliating, this also because the sadistic masochism of the document tells him. What will he want to do, where will he want to go? Home? Back to the States? But remember, says the narrator, he has gone back to the time before his birth, and he has no home. All he has is a destiny, because he has read about it. His destiny is indeed to return to the States, a States he has never seen, and find the woman who is going to become his mother, and marry her—all this in due course of time—and this destiny is the only home he has. But before he does that, suggests the narrator, let his document allow him a few months of unspecified what we can only call *free time*. A few months between the time of his arrival from China in Hong Kong (yes) and his arrival in New York where he will begin to make his fortune through betting on baseball games and seek out the woman who is to become his mother. Let the document specify that those few months are to be regarded, both at the time and afterwards, as the best period of his whole doomed life—best exactly because they have not been specified, a period in which, thanks to his father's restraint at that moment, he did not know anything about what would happen except that he would survive and end up, undamaged, in New York.

Now the narrator asks, what would he do during that undescribed best period? Think. Would he go to the centers of the history of that time to get his little glimpses of the historical figures, the way a tourist goes to the great geographical landmarks of the lands he visits? To get his look at Wilson and Clemenceau and Lloyd George? To watch Babe Ruth play for the Yankees? To go to England and interview Joseph Conrad in his old age? Or James Joyce or T. S. Eliot in the big burst of their still-youthful careers? Doubt it, says the narrator—especially since we don't seem to be doing much of that with the landmark figures living in our own day. And these revived celebrities of the past—won't they be cardboard figures, somehow, as you look at them knowing what will become of them—knowing especially that your own knowledge that you might glean from an interview is going to get lost anyway, swallowed in your own proven obscurity?

In the midst of a destiny of that sort, says the narrator, would not your best period be that in which you live most simply with the least possible consciousness of time, which is elsewhere and all through the rest of your life such a curse? Might you not, when you get to Hong Kong, ship yourself aboard some rusty old Conradian freighter—call her the *Greenwich*—simply to travel aboard her wherever she goes, ports around the world and much open sea, for as long as your document allows?

What you wanted during that time on the boat, said the narrator, was to avoid history altogether—as much as the voices of men would allow you to avoid. Avoid the segmenting of time, the confinement of life and action within the boundaries of dates. The gulls that throng in a great screaming mob along the rough rocks of a breakwater as you depart the harbor, the gulls that soar and dip flocking and screaming over the surf around the beacon at the end and lightly sail out to your ship as you meet the heavier swell of the ocean, the gulls that wheel and circle over the fantail of the ship—those gulls and the terns and the other birds of the sea, the gannet and the albatross and the great auk, like the eskimo curlew and the great condor of the mountains and the whooping crane —along with the dolphins and the sperm whale and the great blue whale, and all the animals of the sea and the land too, these creatures know no history, no unique dated events, while all the generations cycle and merge into one.

Against the constant insane reiteration in his mind of the reminder that he was living before the time of his birth—said the narrator—the protagonist of this nightmare (or *you*) would steady himself by leaning against the rail of the ship alone in the late afternoon, watching the sea, how it swirled and dipped under the heavy riveted wall of the ship— how the blue and green swirled down in circles with circular upwellings of greenwhite foam, and how the waves a distance out spat their bubbles and licked their peaks and tossed them and broke them off into the air, and how a further distance out the sea was black and blue with a grainy straightness and how the sky flung up and away and out from you into miles and miles of distance piled with masses of fairweather clouds standing in the blue, clouds that were places, like the valleys and passes and peaks in a range of mountains, places lifted or elevated over the sea where all place was fluid, and how even the places among the clouds, the places that you on the ship seemed to be approaching or appeared to have passed, kept changing their shapes and deceiving you as to distance and direction and ultimate reality—all this which would be just the same in 1919 let us say as no doubt it was in 1971 and no doubt in Roman times and lunar times and all the times of life dying. And you would lean against the rail and soothe yourself with the sight of distant land when it came into view, blue mountains merging with the sky on a sunny day. And you would comfort yourself in the cold discomfort of afternoons of dark gray clouds scudding low, with the sea at war with itself all black and gray and fierce and white, and you in the comfort of a wet shiny black slicker, and water hosing into your face, and then cold. And the comfort of looking, seeing, touching, anything that could be seen or touched—anything at all—and you saw how the moisture gathered in rivulets on the white steel wall of the deckhouse, and you noticed little patches of rust around the rivets, and you smelled the wind whipping around the deck and you caught in your nostrils a brief warm strand of cooking—of vegetable soup—delivered to the wind from the ship's galley ahead mixed with the smell of paint and the ship's engines. These things should comfort you—said the narrator—and soothe you and give your mind, obsessed with time, a temporary anesthetic.

And if, said the narrator, he doesn't write to you because he is a fugitive from some crime committed in Hong Kong or somewhere else, perhaps some old ship like the *Greenwich* will allow him to escape. As for you—suddenly bearing down on Burr—you don't want to go back into any part of your past, no matter how much you may remember and long, because everything that happened before last week lies in a connected chain of steps leading to the middle step in Burnet Woods—and everything since then lies in a connected chain of steps leading away from that.

No! Burr argued, tried to refuse it. Something that happens in the woods—an excrescence, an accident, a by-product, a discarded moment of time. No real part of his life, he would insist, no part of the continuity, no part of himself.

As he dozed in his hospital bed that first afternoon, the air-conditioner reminded him of a ship, the sound of the sea.

Chapter 3

We lie in the hospital bed, mostly immobilized during the first few days. Lightly attached to our chest, on a greasy spot placed there by the nurse and held in place by a loose heavy strap, is the receptor and the wires leading to the cardiac monitor overhead. If we move more than a little it comes detached and sets off an alarm that brings nurses running. It happens to all of us on the heart floor from time to time, and among those who don't feel bad it makes a good subject for jokes. We lie in our beds, careful not to move too much. The nurses crank us up and down, our shoulders, our knees. We can read, we can write on bed tables spread across our knees, but we are not allowed to get up. We have urinals and bed pans, and it is necessary to ring the nurse for them, for everything. We have a bulb with a button on the end, which we press in order to get the nurse.

We are awakened early in the morning, but nobody minds because we are not going anywhere, and it is easy to turn your head and go back to sleep when you feel like it. A black man in a white uniform comes each morning to take blood out of your arm. This too is a matter for jokes. At first we do not enjoy it—indeed we never learn to enjoy it— but we discover that you can develop a desire to have your arm punctured for the removal of blood, or even become addicted to having blood taken. We have breakfast on a tray and lunch on a tray and dinner on a tray. The dietitian comes in the morning with a menu card and we make our choices for lunch and dinner. It turns out, however, that the choices have already been made for us—marked on the card by somebody else.

Sometime in the morning a nurse's aide comes to change our bed— a complicated skill which she must perform without dumping us out. Several times daily a nurse comes to take our temperature and our blood pressure. Some of the blood pressure nurses, though they are pleasant and friendly and pretty, seem very inexperienced, finding it difficult to pump up the mercury and get it to drop right, sometimes repeating it several times before getting it right. The nurses are skeptical about blood pressure, they tend not to believe in it. Occasionally someone comes to give us another electrocardiogram. And others take our pulse.

Each morning either a nurse's aide or a student nurse comes to give us a bath in bed—with a bowl of soapy water and a wash cloth which she works more or less timidly or aggressively over our face neck ears chest arms hands back legs and feet, handing the rag to us so that we may do the private places under the sheet for ourselves. And she also shaves us, using our shaving equipment, which Natalie has brought from the house, with the warm lather and the warm razor cleansing. Each evening another nurse's aide gives us a back rub with alcohol, rubbing and kneading and pushing from the shoulders down to the small of the back. They are tending to our body, and Burr's narrator said that he had forgotten since childhood how much a body he was and what an etiquette of rules and natural laws govern this body. Realizing that it was because of his body that he was here now and problems in his body— regardless of what *their* cause might be—that kept him immobile in bed. And when the variously pretty nurses and aides come and do intimate things to his body that ought to be embarrassing, they lose their intimacy and embarrassment because his body has become so important. His life having become his body, his body is no longer private, and this whole institution is dedicated to making it work. His body was a universe-making machine, said the narrator—watch out.

His silent, aged roommate was replaced the next day by another, younger man, who was brought in with oxygen tubes taped to his nose. After a day he revived and became talkative. This was his third heart attack—he spoke of them as a traveler might speak of trips to Europe, considering them both a matter of distinction and natural part of life. His name was Angus, and he got along well with the nurses.

People came to visit. The most constant visitor was Natalie Fleet, who came every day, sometimes twice a day, and usually stayed long. She came dressed in colorful short dresses, looking bright and curious, young and a little anxious with her glasses and her long straight hair. She brought him news, listened to his worries, gossiped, reported on the errands she did for him, told him about his animals that she was feeding and exercising, brought him gifts (cookies for himself and the nurses, paperback books, magazines) to make him more comfortable. One day Angus, who seemed to be feeling better, noticed her and watched her during her visit. "That your daughter?" he asked when Natalie had gone. Burr laughed and shook his head. "Your *wife?*" exclaimed Angus. Again Burr shook his head: "My wife is dead," he said. Angus turned grave. "Oh—I'm sorry," he said. He looked somber, tragic. "That's terrible, your wife is dead. How do you stand it?" He went on, "You marry again?" Burr shrugged his shoulders, not knowing. "Yes, you marry again. You marry *her.* She'll be a good wife for you. She'll outlive you. Wife should outlive you," said Angus. "What does it matter if she is younger and has a younger boy friend even? You need a wife to outlive you. All wives should outlive their husbands." The nurses assumed that she was his wife, and they liked her and complimented him on her.

Grummon visited. He appeared one evening in the door and slinked in, as if it were a guilty matter—odd for one so usually truculent and aggressive. Bushy-nosed, gloomy-faced, he came and sat down in the armchair and did not know what to say. How is the chairmanship business going? Burr asked. Grummon shakes his shoulders without interest. Then he says, "How old are you, Rayalph?" Well, forty-five, I believe. "And I am forty-three," says Grummon. "I smoke as much as you do. I worry more than you do. I am overweight, and my blood pressure is higher than it should be." He sits there, hands under chin, scowling, allowing the conclusion to formulate in Burr's mind without words, waiting even long enough for the conclusion to fade away and be forgotten in the free current of reverie, before he brings it back and doubles its strength by hammering it into words: "If it could happen to you, it will certainly happen to me." Conspiratorial machinations like department politics at work inside Grummon's body or in whatever metaphysical place his destiny was being controlled. After a while, he said, "I don't think it is likely that I will live to old age." He got up to go. At that moment he paused and scrutinized Burr with his narrow eyes. Suspicion? He said, "My wife sends you her regards." That's nice —my regards to her too. "She might come visit you herself, if she has time." Brief shudders of complicated fear—hoping at least she would not run into Natalie. And more than ever the problem, since it was now clear to the narrator that Burr's connection with Laura Grummon should be terminated if it was not already, the problem of how to keep her from blabbing to Grummon himself. Blabbing what? Anything, everything—who knows? The secret knowledge, unknown to him, of indefinite scope, that he knew she possessed.

Yet, still she didn't come—not for a while, anyway. There were other visits. Harvey Kessler came, never looked at him, spoke abstractly about student unrest on the campus, as if he had inside information. Elias visited and spoke with shocked accents about routine department business. Hoffman and Gomulski paid visits. So did his neighbor Mr. Shomberg. Also two or three students.

One afternoon while Natalie Fleet was visiting, after he had been in the hospital about a week, he looked up and saw Laura Grummon. He had not seen her for several weeks, and her sudden appearance—the familiar large brown eyes, the long black hair flowing freely over her shoulders, richly dressed, shocked his heart with such a sudden aggression that the narrator realized as if for the first time how afraid of her he was. She saw Natalie and startled: "Oh excuse me, I'll come back some other time." Natalie jumping up (looking like a child beside the other): "I'm just leaving." (Burr distressed, because Natalie had only just arrived and he thought they had things to talk about.) As she goes out, Natalie waves to him behind Laura's back, as if to say that she would wait out of sight and come back later.

So Laura sits down. She said, "Who was that?" *Burr:* That was Natalie Fleet. She's a secretary in the office. *Laura:* So that was Natalie

217

Fleet. So that's the famous lovely Natalie Fleet. (Dislike?) *Burr:* She's very nice. *Laura:* Oh, I'm sure she's just lovely. So you're doing business from your hospital bed? *Burr:* She's taking care of a few things for me. *Laura:* Is that so? (Inferences? Suspicions?) *Burr:* She's agreed to feed the animals. *Laura:* Oh my God, your animals! I forgot all about your animals. I suppose that's something I could have done for you, if I had remembered. *Burr* (smile a little): That's all right. We're managing quite well now. Thanks anyway.

She leans back, sighs, adapts to her chair. Smiles, as if releasing bygones. Heavy eye-makeup. She says: I came by to see how you are. *Burr:* I feel all right. *Laura:* And to say hello. *Burr:* Hello. *Laura:* And to see if there is anything I can do for you. *Burr:* Thank you.

She says: I haven't seen you in quite a while, but I want you to know. If there is anything I can do to help. *Burr:* I appreciate it. *Laura:* Anything you need. *Burr:* Very good of you. *Laura:* Anything you'd like me to do. *Burr:* Certainly very generous.

Suddenly she leans back and smiles—recognition of some kind: Just as I told you the other time, all you have to do is ask, and don't be afraid to ask. *Burr:* I certainly do appreciate it. (Some silence now while she thinks it over before speaking again.) Then she says, *Laura:* I won't ask you about your x-ial needs this time. *Burr:* My what? *Laura:* Your actual needs. *Burr:* No? *Laura:* I won't ask about them this time. *Burr:* Oh, you mean my— (pause) *Laura:* Yes. Those. *Burr:* Yes. Well. *Laura* (with a glance now at the green line bouncing in the monitor): I guess you really don't have any, this time. *Burr:* Any? *Laura* (as if it were important not to agitate the even jiggling of that green line, hesitating therefore before saying it): sexual needs. *Burr:* Oh yes, sectsual. *Laura:* I guess your body has enough else to think about just now to keep things going without stirring up that side of things. *Burr:* Well, it is pretty quiet here.

Suddenly Burr realizes that she is reminiscing in fields where he thought only he himself had grazed. She says: No doubt that was forward of me to ask you about that, the other time, you remember. *Burr:* Mm. *Laura* (constantly watching the monitor, as if warned by that bouncing green line of the thin thread of calm by which the movement of ticking

218

time hangs nowadays): You do remember, don't you? *Burr:* When you asked me— *Laura:* Yes, sir. I'm afraid I gave you quite a scare that time. *Burr:* Oh no, it wasn't that. *Laura:* You know, I was embarrassed after that. I was *really* embarrassed. *Burr:* I'm sorry. *Laura:* Oh it wasn't your fault. Sometimes I'm too outspoken. Sometimes I just don't *think*. *Burr:* Neither do I. *Laura:* I declare: I didn't realize until afterward, you must have thought I was trying to *seduce* you myself. Isn't that funny? *Burr* (almost says, Weren't you? But catches it back): Ha ha. *Laura:* No wonder you were so scared. *Burr:* I wasn't scared. *Laura:* But don't worry. This time I can't ask you such a question anyway. You have to devote all your energy to being calm and restful and building your strength back slowly. I suppose there are some things you'll never be able to do again. *Burr:* The doctor promises me a complete and total recovery.

In the long and quietly humming silence that follows, Burr asks the narrator to contemplate the disappointment that surrounds her effort to remove a long-cherished assumption from his past. Does she mean it? Is she lying? he asks. Is this her way to reconcile what must have been an intolerable memory? Narrator munches in noncommittal silence, doubting everything. What difference does it make, he asks, if she denies it now, whether she would have denied it then? Meanwhile, in her chair, Laura Grummon has her own thoughts. Finally they emerge in something: "Natalie Fleet," she says.

Burr: What? *Laura:* I was thinking about your Natalie Fleet. I wonder if she has ever had an affair with Paul. *Burr* (jolted): With Paul? *Your* Paul? *Laura:* Do you know? Is it possible? *Burr* (Natalie having an affair with *Grummon?* How does a Burr express in words his sense of the maximum incredulity, the maximum impossibility, the maximum absurdity): I doubt it. *Laura:* I doubt it too.

Well, why did you ask then? says Burr. *Laura:* I suppose one never knows everything, does one? No harm in inquiring. *Burr:* Whatever gave you such an idea? *Laura:* Don't get excited. That bouncy line. Is that you? *Burr:* That's me. *Laura:* It keeps staggering along, bump bump bump. It keeps moving all the time. Makes me nervous. *Burr:* Just so long as it doesn't stop. *Laura:* What should I do if it stops? *Burr:* Call a nurse. But what made you ask that question about Natalie Fleet? *Laura:* You like her? *Burr:* She's a very nice girl. Very helpful.

Laura: You like her well enough to be upset if she's sleeping with Stone? *Burr:* With Stone? Jesus, who told you that? *Laura:* You are upset. *Burr:* N-no. It's just hard to believe, that's all. Almost as hard to believe as the one about Natalie and Paul. *Laura:* Well, it's probably a libel. It just happens to be the rumor I heard about her. What made me call her famous when you identified her just now. *Burr:* I think it's a lie. Who told you that, for Christ sake? *Laura:* Oh, it's just Paul. You know how Paul is. Always jumping to conclusions. Always making the most out of anything. Personally, I can't imagine Stone sleeping with anyone, not even his wife. I can't even imagine him sleeping.

Silence again. She was gazing dreamily at his green line, in which Burr felt lightning that kept jolting, deflected into the ground, just missing him, with repeating shocks of lies that had never occurred to him: that someone might think Natalie Fleet was Stone's mistress. Why should anyone think that, even someone who is always jumping to conclusions, always making the most out of anything? Narrator advises him to reflect on the obscurities in her notion first that Natalie was having an affair with Paul and the second notion, supposedly derived from Paul himself, that Natalie was having an affair with Stone. Narrator tries to advise him that it is probably all lies and if it didn't matter before, it does not matter now. Don't let that jiggling line jiggle loops of jealousy. Admit knowing that Natalie has probably slept with a number of people before coming to you and maybe even since then. Burr has accepted this, a more or less necessary corollary to her willingness to sleep with him. Only he has preferred not to ask *with whom.* And when someone suggests *with Stone* or even *with Grummon,* tell the narrator, irrational as it is, it shocks the monitor like lightning.

Laura: I guess you don't intend to tell me if you have been having any affairs. Before you got sick, I mean. *Burr:* Don't know just what to say. *Laura:* Doesn't matter. I guess I can just imagine what I like. But have you heard about my affair with Harvey Kessler? *Burr:* What? No kidding?

Now see how Laura laughs, leaning back in her chair, stretching up her arms, even for a moment kicking her legs. "No kidding!" she says.

"Isn't it wonderful. Harvey Kessler. Now I can forgive you everything, since I have him." Forgive me? says Burr. What is there to forgive? Again she laughs and shakes away the question with her head. "You won't tell anyone, will you?" Of course not. "Because Paul doesn't know anything about it, and I really don't want him to hear in an offhand way. Not for my sake, but his own. And Harvey's. I don't want to jeopardize Harvey in any way." Now a touch of mockery? "Harvey really admires you. It's most impressive, sir, how he looks up to you." Embarrassment while she laughs, or giggles, again. "You know he's such a radical, so anti-the-establishment. I always wondered what it would be like to make love to a revolutionary." Now you know? says Burr. "Now I know." You going to tell me? says Burr. "What's to tell? When it comes to love, he's as big a baby as any other young guy in my life. I'm *helping* him." Help? inquires Burr. "He says I'm showing him a new life. Change. Revitalization. New vistas." Oh, says Burr. "He's really gentle," she says. Then she adds: "Rather soft." Looks up at the green line again. Adds, "Like you." Does the line jump? Insult intended? Or is it a sympathetically offered matter of fact that a strong mind will accept? The narrator advises Burr to let it pass: Laura Grummon's judgments must be read in context.

And yet more silence. Laura asked: "Is there anything else I can do for you? Any urgent problems?" *Burr:* I suppose I need help in moving out of my house. *Laura:* Moving! Good God. *Burr:* The Benjamins were expecting to move in by the end of the month, but I won't be out of the hospital yet. And I have no place to move to. *Laura:* You'll simply have to postpone your move. The Benjamins will simply have to wait. *Burr:* Somebody will have to persuade them to wait. *Laura:* Yes, you'll simply have to get somebody to speak to them. *Burr:* I wonder who I can get. *Laura:* Oh, you'll find somebody.

At the door as she was going out, Laura met Natalie Fleet again, coming back. "Well here she is again!" exclaimed Laura. Note the look she gave Burr before she went out, full of meaning, full of assumption. Burr's narrator guessed that they would never have such a talk again. Guessed right too, said Burr's narrator later. She never came back. Too busy.

Meanwhile Natalie Fleet said, "That was Mrs. Grummon, wasn't it?"

Burr nodded. He stared at her. Finally he said, "Did you ever have an affair with Professor Grummon?"

Natalie putting hand to mouth, shock turning to laughter: "Wha-at?"

"Well, how about Stone?"

"Stone?" Still incredulous. Sudden glance back to where Laura had gone. "Is that what *she* said?"

"She wondered," said Burr.

"Oh God!" She rested her chin in her hand. "Well, it's a lie!" she said. "Both of them. Where do these stories come from?"

"Damned if I know," said Burr, glad of the denial, the perfectly convincing denial. Only one thing bothered the narrator a little, which was the evidence in Natalie's response that she had heard of the Stone rumor before, that it came to her not entirely fresh and original. Not that he did not believe her, nor that he cared about Stone, but any rumor, even the vaguest or most insubstantial, was a blemish on the perfection of a story, it undercut confidence in its coherence, and distracted you with worry about where it came from.

That night when the lights in the room were turned off, and there was only some light from the hall under the crack of the door and the ever-continuing dance of the cardiac monitors visible in the mirror, while Burr rested his head against the pillow and waited for his motionlessness to put him to sleep, the narrator insomniac, as if to justify and vindicate himself, still insisted on dancing with the stories and insinuations and denials of Laura Grummon and Natalie Fleet and their affairs. Raising questions about all the kinds of truths that might (or might not) have lain behind the words, the rumors, the denials. Wondering especially about Natalie Fleet now—this evening—out there in the world, where it was still only eleven o'clock, whereas here it was past beddy-by time. Raising questions of trust and distrust. Did he trust Natalie Fleet? And if so, what did he trust her for, what did he trust her to do, or not to do? Did it matter, if he were to die? And did it matter to Cynthia, who was already dead?

He noticed that the narrator had casually drawn up a list, thus:

RALPH BURR, protagonist, cross references

222

See
>
> Cynthia Hamlin (Burr) *deceased*

See also
>
> Laura Grummon
> Natalie Fleet

Then the narrator looked up Natalie Fleet, thus:

NATALIE FLEET, protagonist, cross references
>
> See
>
>> Peter nameless
>> Roger x
>> Harold Burr
>> blond crewcut slob
>> chemistry major
>> architect
>> Lewis Howard
>> Bobby
>> Ralph Burr *deceased*

Then he looked up Laura Grummon, but the record was blurred, illegible mostly:

LAURA GRUMMON, protagonist, cross refer . . .
>
> See
>
>> my promiscuous period
>> Paul Grummon
>> Dean Nelson
>> Thomas Elder
>> George E——s
>>
>> . . .
>> Ral . . . urr . . . *ased*
>> Harvey Kessler

Then his eyes went back:

> See
>
>> Ralph Burr *deceased*

Just then a pretty nurse with large breasts opened the door and came in to wake him and give him some pills. As she cranked up his bed and held out the paper cup to him, the narrator tried to peek into her record. She had a name tag, MISS THOMAS. The narrator said he couldn't find her record. She must be the protagonist of something, said Burr. The narrator said it would be nice to set up a new cross reference with her—

See also Miss Thomas, *nurse*

—leaning over him in her white uniform, with large breasts, pretty embarrassed face, climbing up onto the bed to lie there beside him. But instead she said, "Thank you," and cranked the bed back down and went out, and it was as if Natalie Fleet had gone out, but Natalie Fleet would be back tomorrow, he trusted. That was where the important question of trust lay, whether Natalie Fleet would be back tomorrow, as she promised. The narrator burned the records, with the cross references, saying they did not matter. Neither did Ralph Burr *deceased* matter— what only mattered was remembering the comfort of touching the rail on the *Greenwich* and seeing the rivulets on the white steel wall of the deck-house and noticing the little patches of rust around the rivets and smelling the wind whipping around the deck with the paint smell and the cooking smell mixed in it. Only now instead it was the intimate presence of the pillow around his cheeks, the same pillow he had had around his cheeks in the earliest days when Mother sang to him, and through nights of childhood and nights of studenthood, and nights in the army and in the youth of his career, and in the life of his marriage, on the night of the birth of his son, and on the night of the death of his wife, and the lonely nights after that, and now in the hospital, always the same pillow returning to his cheek every night for the nights of his life, connecting all the parts of his life together, the earliest and the last. As he lay there and sank and sank his body turned numb until finally there was nothing but mind hanging like a globe in the air.

Chapter 4

Let me introduce you to Mrs. Kroll, the real estate agent, said the narrator. We have met, said Burr, trying to hide himself, to pull the sheet over his head, but prevented by the wires from his chest to the cardiac monitor. Mrs. Kroll, a very large woman—so sorry to hear about his illness, she came right over to see him as soon as she heard, hoping she wouldn't be tiring or upsetting. Full of shock, said Mrs. Kroll, and dismay at the unexpected turns that life can take, and who ever would have thought that a still-young man like Professor Burr would be hit by such a thing as that? Full of anxiety, she said, for his swift recovery, anxious also not to bring him worry or burdens, now of all times when it was so important that he be unburdened, and for that reason she hoped (hoped Mrs. Kroll) that he had arranged for somebody else to take charge of the whole difficult business of getting moved out of his house by the end of the month so that the Benjamins could move in? (Question phrased in the form of a statement, as if this would reduce the burden that a question might place upon his chest. Why if you say so, said the comedian, much relieved, I suppose I have arranged for somebody else to take charge of the whole difficult business.)

Oh my God, said Burr to the narrator, for he did not like to be reminded of the problem—remembering that he had first thought of it there in the ambulance with Natalie Fleet, who assured him not to worry about a thing. Telling the narrator now, that if that is what she said then, didn't that make her responsible? If he was not to worry about it, presumably someone else would, someone else would take care of it, just as everything else was being taken care of—and therefore might he not justly say to Mrs. Kroll (a very large woman, sitting in the chair by his bed and looking anxiously at him) that it was being taken care of as far as he was allowed to know? "I know it's a shame to bother you about matters like that at a time like this," said Mrs. Kroll, "but it does raise a problem for the Benjamins, who are obliged to move out of their apartment by the end of the month. Now you know, according to the contract—"

Mrs. Kroll is a smiling lady with white hair and bright red lips, but Burr has seen (in the course of his dealings with her) the preparations on her face for a look of displeasure, and he knows that if she is displeased her nose will lengthen and harden and she will begin to look like the national bird, the American eagle (almost extinct in reality but living on as symbol). In relation to the American eagle, at the moment Burr felt like a disabled rabbit. Tell him therefore that the main thing is to get through the present moment without dismemberment. If we die it won't matter. Therefore—where were we? ("Now you know, according to the contract—" said she. Interrupt.)

"Right, right, right," said Burr, rabbitlike, "tell them not to worry. Tell them not to worry about a thing. Everything will be taken care of. Everything is going according to plan."

Here Mrs. Kroll widened her eyes in surprise and what looked like genuine admiration. "Why really?" she said. "Isn't that remarkable, isn't that wonderful. Why, everything is to be taken care of? You don't know what a relief that is. I wonder how you manage it, your children gone and everything, how you manage it from your hospital bed. You must have some loyal friends, that's all I can say. Because I know you won't be out of the hospital by then and I presume you won't even be able to walk up and down stairs for another two weeks after you get out. So I was trying to think of how we could relieve you of the burden of moving and still do our duty for the Benjamins—I was thinking how we could probably persuade the Benjamins to delay their move if we could provide them with some place to stay for a short time until you are stronger—for example, the apartment that you plan to move into, maybe—or if we shared expenses for them to stay at a hotel for a time—"

"No no," said Burr (for the sake of consistency, though I began to wish he hadn't moved quite so fast at first, seeing that Mrs. Kroll did have alternatives up her sleeve—but he was stuck with his consistency) "it's all right. I'm sure my friends will get my stuff out by the time the Benjamins want to move in."

She left, satisfied and admiring. But Burr had a difficult time for the rest of the day. He could not keep his mind empty. The feeling of pursuit, things he was not supposed to think about. Now besides Berthold plotting his course on the chart in the police station there were the Benjamins flying in formation behind Mrs. Kroll, and if you got away from one you ran into the other. On the monitor the jolts of the green line almost seemed to make a noise as he felt himself running: click clickety clickety clickety, like the tracks under a high speed fleeing train or the pounding of his heels in the dirt.

That evening when Natalie Fleet came, he told her about Mrs. Kroll's visit. He said, "You told me not to worry about a thing, so what do I do about this? Here's a problem, people expecting to move into my house, and I here, unable to move out. How do I keep from worrying about that?"

The astonished, scared—call it appalled—expression on Natalie's face. OhmyGod, again. "What am I going to do?" I said. She stared, open-eyed, blank. Then I realized that she had no solution. It had never occurred to her—and when she had told me not to worry, she hadn't known what she was talking about.

Now for the first time it occurred to me (said the narrator, the narrator told me) that not merely was there a sense of doom, of things coming to an end, but it was better that way. There were insoluble problems back on earth. One of these insoluble problems was that of moving, all by ourself, out of the house we have lived in for fifteen accumulated years, of carrying all those years out alone upon our back. No solution. Therefore we discover at last (said the narrator) the real value of being in the hospital. It takes us away from the world of insoluble problems. The important thing is to stay in the hospital—not to go back to the shore. Die here, said the narrator.

Natalie in a very small voice: "But you will still be in the hospital by then. And even after you get out it may be months before you can carry and move things about." Yes my dear and that isn't all. Her voice now very soft, thin, high, alarmed. "And you couldn't move anyway because you haven't got a place to move to. You can't go apartment hunting from your hospital bed—" Certainly not, not when I am not allowed to go to the bathroom but have to use a bedpan and a urinal. If I were to die, on the other hand, then some lawyer could take charge and move his forces like an army into the house to take care of what would then be called an estate. By dying you can translate a mess into an estate. Now explain to her also the complications she doesn't know about. Say: "There is also all that furniture that I am supposed to send to my wife's brother, which has to be moved out before anything else can go, and therefore has to be done first. And only I know which furniture belongs to him and which belongs to me, and I can't identify it because I am not allowed out of the hospital" (nor out of bed not even to go to the bathroom). Then Natalie with a voice delicate like a trickling mountain stream: "You can't do it. How can you possibly do it?" Right my child, so you see how wrong it was to tell me not to worry, for what is there to do about such things except worry, and how can you avoid worry except by staying and staying and staying in the hospital until everything really does turn into an estate? Which is what you must have meant when you told me not to worry, which is good advice, if you are going to die, the very best advice you could possibly give to a dying man (but not a living one), which I did not understand when you gave me that advice in the ambulance, not until now getting the message, to let it come, to die peacefully.

Still thinner, her voice now like a faint high silver sliver of wind upon wires, she said: "Would you like me to take charge of all those things?"

When he heard this, suddenly, convulsively the narrator burst out: Oh Natalie, my dear sweet good generous lovely Natalie, don't leave him, don't desert him, don't abandon him now, for God's sake and the sake of all goodness—goodness' sake—help me pull him through this trying time. For what can I tell him motivates you? What can I say binds you to him, to allow him to feel complacent about you and your visits and your taking charge of things for him? What holds you? Is it some love that you have not bothered to find the word for? But what has he ever given you to deserve that, in your short time of knowing, your two friendly nights together, when before that he could have been nothing but Father Figure and Boss Figure perhaps and Professor Figure no doubt? A bit of impudent curiosity on your part? So why should he trust you or expect you to love him, even for the moment, even long enough to get us through the hospital? So help me protect him, Natalie, from your own awakening, keep busy with me so that you won't ask yourself the question, pretend to yourself for my sake so that we won't be left alone. Just please don't ask why you should take charge of all those things, take on the burdens of a wife—a wife with an invalid husband and other unspeakable handicaps. Don't ask. The narrator's jealousy (What does she do at night after her visit to me? Whom else does she see? For what guilt is she doing penance by this attention to me?) sank low in the face of the narrator's fear: Do anything you want with these nights, Natalie my Natalie, only don't abandon us. Come back and back and back. (Each time she left, the narrator warned: she might not come back. That might have been her last visit. But said Burr, she said I'll see you tomorrow—just like always. Warned the narrator: If she suddenly decides not to, she won't tell you, she'll just stop coming.)

Meanwhile her bethinned voice was beginning to recover its strength as we began to work out the problems together. "Then you'll trust me to find you a satisfactory place to live?" she said. Oh, Natalie darling, I trust you to everything! "If you don't like it, of course, you can move again soon," she said. "Just so long as I know what you can pay for rent and what your general requirements would be." Requirements are like clothes and luggage and furniture. They all come off in the hospital, you don't see them in the tracing of the green line, but while you live they are part of you still, the overweight of your personality. "And then if you can make me a list of your brother's furniture, and when I go to the house I can make a list of other things there and perhaps that way we can figure out just what to send him and we can send that by Lubbock

Movers (Berthold Kirschner?) and if we miss anything, why we'll just have to send it later. Right?"

Right!

"And as for your stuff, well I'll just put everything in boxes. If you don't mind I'll bring in some of my friends, you know—guys. Strong guys who can do anything. They'll help me. It won't be very orderly, I'm afraid. You'll probably have a hell of a time trying to find anything, but at least we can get you moved, and you can worry about that later when you are more recovered. Okay?"

Okay! Oh don't leave him, said the narrator. Don't give him up! Just then Burr said, Marry me. Tell the narrator to ask her to *marry* me. By God, if there ever were a wife—But here the narrator frowned and shook his head. You forget, he said. Doomed men do not marry.

Now began a busy time on shore (on earth, in the world outside), all cleanly and neatly reduced to packets of conversation, reports of progress and questions and plan-making, with Natalie on her visits in the evening. She went to work for him. Five strong young men, students and friends, she enlisted to perform the heavy work (How did she induce them? What means of persuasion and control? Was there some promise of reward? or were they, all five, her lovers? Or are people just naturally generous before they get started on their careers? It does not matter, insisted the narrator. It is none of your business), five young men who helped her locate and look over apartments in the neighborhood and, in Burr's house, helped her move furniture and reduce his belongings to boxes. Every night she reported to him in his hospital bed, describing what she had done, asking questions, making new plans. It made him feel very busy, simulating work, vicarious. As if she were reporting to him news about himself.

One day soon after, says the narrator, Burr's story intersected with history. Rather, it just failed to intersect, for history struck the university campus, but Burr wasn't there—he was in the hospital, out of it. It was the students, speaking for history, who struck the university and closed it down, while Burr on his hospital bed watched his wavy green line and listened to the gossip that the nurses and Natalie and his occasional other visitors brought. The narrator was full of regret that Burr should

230

have missed this opportunity to connect his story with the great stories of our time. He munched on the cookies that Natalie had brought and passed them out to the nurses and Angus his roommate.

According to the historian, it began with the national news that several students at another university had been shot and killed by the armed enforcers of law and order during a demonstration against the President's war policy. All over the country, said the historian, the reaction on college campuses was the same—shock, outrage, fear. On this campus there was an evening meeting of concerned students and faculty constituting what they called an *ad hoc* committee of the whole, voting to close down the university the next day. The next day there were meetings of student groups and faculty groups and the university senate (representatives of everybody). First they voted a day of mourning, climaxed by a silent march in which eight thousand students, faculty members, and others walked from the campus down the hill to the center of the city and back again. Then there were three days of what they called a "voluntary strike," in which classes could be held or dismissed as the professors and students wished, without penalties for those who cut or did not hold classes. During these days groups of students sat in the administration building, accompanied by faculty members who hoped to be a restraining influence. Then the directors closed the university altogether for a week, because they were afraid that the students would break into violence. Finally, just before the university was expected to reopen, it was closed for the rest of the term by vote of the university senate, alarmed by threats of uncontrollable disorder.

The narrator asked Burr: you are the protagonist—should we ask the historian to analyze the complex issues that have exploded into this student strike this spring while you lie immobilized, out of range, in your hospital bed? Burr said, It is outside my competence. The narrator said, You ought to have strong opinions and make a commitment in an important historical moment like this. Your isolation may be part of the trouble. Burr said, I have my own problems to worry about. The narrator agreed to that.

Meanwhile his visitors came and described to the narrator the kinds of things that were happening in the university. The classrooms were empty—no classes—but throngs of students gathered on the bridge all day listening to the speeches. When there were no speakers they played recordings of speeches—Eldridge Cleaver and others—on the loud-speaker. From time to time there were marches of students through the campus, shouting in unison, "Strike! Strike!" and "Shut it down!" Although it already was shut down as far as classes were concerned. According to Burr's visitors the student crowds were mostly good-natured except when someone said something hostile—then they showed irritation or anger, but though the speeches were sometimes inflammatory, the general mood was more joyful than angry, the surprised discovery of power, perhaps, and there was also a certain caution that could be detected even in their seizures of liberty. Constantly stirring through the crowd was a concern lest the potential violence break out and really do damage or ruin everything. At the same time there was a strong curiosity as to what the possibilities for damage actually might be. Suppose you damaged as much as you could, what would the world be like then? A test, to find out what actually held up the authority that leaned on them, and to experiment creatively with the substitutes that might be imagined in its place. No one was quite sure whether we were still in a demonstration or in the actual process of a revolution being born. Students, said the analyst, have suddenly been faced with questions never before imagined, such as whether a university might be got rid of altogether. Vanish like life on a puff of wind from history or like life down a funnel of dissolution. Several of Burr's visitors, without raising *that* question, kept asking how, after such emotions, the university could ever open peacefully again.

Elias himself, the outgoing chairman, came to visit Burr. He was angry about the strike and spent the half hour of his visit expressing himself. He was especially shocked by arguments that he said Harvey Kessler was using. For example: "Harvey says the young people today are prepared to turn to violence because they have discovered that no other methods will work. I ask you, how can a man whose function, whose job, whose career, is dedicated to the teaching of young people —teaching!—how can such a man in this country embrace such a doctrine? I ask you?" (Asking Burr, as if it were Burr, not Harvey, who

was guilty. Trying to be Harvey, Burr suggested that he was not justify-
ing it, that he was merely reporting what the students thought—at least
this is what I hope Harvey meant.) "Well, then why doesn't he get busy
and show those children their errors?" said Elias. "If he understands
them so well and finds so much to sympathize with, why doesn't he take
more responsibility for teaching them the mistake in such doctrine?"
(Maybe he does, suggested Burr, without knowing, but Elias was not
satisfied.) "I know, you know, doesn't Harvey know—this is no place for
violence or coercion or force? The academic world—of all places in the
world? Doesn't he know? The one place where violence is most alien,
most incongruous, most incompatible? The academic world, the university, the world of the mind, sanctuary of reason and controlled feeling
and the human spirit—doesn't he see that this is the very opposite to
the world of war and brutality and violence and force, here where
mankind studies how to do away with those blind brute things? To bring
the concept of violence or force into the university is to chop off the
head of humanity, to turn us all back into beasts or war fodder for some
demagogue." (Burr nodding his head, telling the narrator that of course,
he agreed, but wished Elias in his righteousness would not so seem to
confuse his wrath with rhetoric or the object of that wrath with his
listener. With this the narrator noticed the muffled shame and even fear
which Burr concealed while he listened and nodded his head to these
familiar truths that he had been brought up by. And diverting attention
from that inner commotion by leaping again to Harvey's defense: "I
agree with you, and I am sure Harvey does too. I'm quite sure," said
Burr, "he believes as you do, but in order to cope with the students you
have to know what they are saying, even if it is naïve and full of holes.")
   "Well I only hope what you say is true," said Elias (and Burr telling
the narrator, uneasily, I hope so too), and then more excerpts: "I call
this strike a form of coercion, a kind of violence. I do not intend to
concede the principle, therefore I do not intend to concede to the strike
in any way except when conspicuously forced. Let force be seen as force!
Therefore I went this morning to my class as usual. I walked through
the picket line outside the building and when the time came I went to
my classroom and I intended to meet, even if the mob came running

through the hallways to break us up. I intended to go on talking, even if they came into the room and tried to shout me down, even if they came in and asked the students to leave, even if half the students got up and walked out—I intended to go ahead with my lecture as announced in the course syllabus and to hold my class responsible for it, for the material on that lecture whether they came to class or not. I intended in this way to show, to prove, to force on them my absolute belief in the necessity of protecting the mind's life against all philistine and violent and irrational assaults—only when I got to the classroom there was no one there. Not a single student, not one who had the courage to break through the strike, or investigate the building to see if I was there. Not even to see. I suppose they thought I was honoring the strike like everybody else, but you would think at least the more intelligent students would question their assumptions and come and see for themselves. Now I suppose I'll have to excuse them all, and in so doing give the appearance of approving the strike."

From his bed, Burr could see through the window the sun shining on the brick wall of the other wing. Unable to get out of bed, wired to his monitor, Burr listened to news in the world outside. Students testing for power, trying the feel of power, new power to feel out the forces of old power—while Ralph Burr lay still, relaxed and easy but not allowed to exert strength because of trouble in the mechanism of his strength and life. Your strength is your life, said the narrator. Your life is very thin at the present moment, a wavy pulsing green line.

The strike began as a temporary gesture, was then extended, then made permanent for the semester. To make Burr worry about his job, he said, trying to look ahead to next fall. But he couldn't keep his mind on that—as if next fall was of no interest to him, as if the narrator had told him the book would be over by then. Meanwhile Harvey Kessler came to visit. He did not mention Laura Grummon, nor did he speak of Natalie Fleet, and in fact he had nothing to say. Meanwhile Natalie Fleet waited in the waiting room at the end of the floor when Kessler visited, just as she did when Laura Grummon visited and when Elias visited, each time pretending to be "just leaving" when they walked in. And no one mentioned to him how much (or perhaps how little) people might have noticed that when you went to visit Burr in the hospital Natalie Fleet was always there, just leaving. God, she must be leaving him all the time, you would think. I wonder if it means he is thinking of getting married again—or if she is just, as he says, doing a piece of work for him, taking care of the problems he has left behind ashore. Did you say ashore? said the narrator. Sailing off to sea like (perhaps) his son Harold—*if* that is really what Harold is doing. But no one has heard from Harold in months, and no one has been able to inform him that his father is hospitalized with a heart attack. As for Elaine, about to have a baby in her commune in the West—let me show you this Get Well Daddy card she sent.

Nothing to do in the hospital but relax and let things happen as they will. All news from outside seemed a little unreal—because it is fiction? said Burr. Because it all swirls around in the outer rim of that funnel of dying that we have visited, said the narrator. We have seen everything dissolve into that funnel and we shall not soon forget it, said the narrator, and it makes all life seem a little thinner than it used to, it shows you the liquid base beneath all solid objects, including (especially) people, so even a great turmoil like the student strike and recorded history itself seem at this moment to us wired to our monitor a little thin, an eddy in the swirling life around the funnel's rim.

And all news becomes a little ridiculous. All connections with the outside world seem tenuous, like the wires to the monitor, easily disconnected, and also a little ridiculous. One day after the strike was extended to the end of the term, Hoffman and Gomulski came with great embarrassment to inform Burr that the search committee had decided, because of Burr's illness, to withdraw him from contention for the headship. Very apologetic—but obviously necessary, they told him, for you will have to take care of yourself, convalescent, and it would not be good for either the department or you to impose such duties on you at such a time. Disconnecting, said the narrator. Bit by bit, wire by wire. The narrator had a feeling of doom. It was not wholly unpleasant, if you could take a restful view of it. Merely a sense that things were coming to an end. The narrator tried to stick to a restful feeling about things.

Each evening Natalie gave reports of progress with the five young men in handling the baggage of Burr's life. On the night that they closed the university for the rest of this year, she announced that they had found and engaged a satisfactory small apartment for him. Then the five young men helped her bring together the furniture which had been identified, pretty certainly, as Cynthia's brother's. And they put Burr's papers, his books, into boxes. They packed his clothes and his linens and his dishes and bric-a-brac. His records and his pictures and his children's drawings. They found homes for his animals—all but the black and white cat and the black spaniel, which he said he wanted to take into the apartment with him. They ordered the moving van and set the moving date. They did feats of strength, carried heavy loads. They were an army. In two weeks they did what Burr in more than a year had been unable to begin.

In the night after Natalie had left, Burr began to cry in the dark. Why are you crying, dear, my little one? asked Mother. Because they gave my animals away. And because we moved and I forgot to say good-bye to anyone. I forgot to say good-bye to the house. Because we moved and I did not know we were moving until it was too late. But now, said Mother, we are going to live in a nice new home, in a nice new town with nice new friends, a nice new life, and everything is going to be wonderful and new. But still Burr cried because they took away the old house and the animals and nothing could ever be as nice again, no matter how nice and new it might be.

The next afternoon Mr. and Mrs. Benjamin came to see him. They had heard about his illness and wanted to thank him for having his house cleared out so that they could move in. They were sympathetic and talked about the symptoms and causes of coronary attacks and they told him how they intended to use the various rooms in the house. They said he must be a very nice man indeed to have such nice friends do such nice things for him. He said he didn't know any of the five strong young men who were doing the heavy work, but the girl in charge was a very good friend. Mr. Benjamin smacked his lips. She must be, he said.

Before they left they brought in the Benjamin grandmother, who had been with them and had been waiting in the waiting room while they visited Burr. "Just peek in a moment Mummy and say hello to Mr. Burr," said Mr. Benjamin. The old lady peeked timidly around the corner of the door. She was a very short and very small old woman, her hair white and thinning, soft with ringlets on the top. She was carrying a magazine rolled up, and she wore a drab old brown dress. Burr remembered that he had seen her before—tried to remember, then did remember, the day in the lawyer's office when they had signed and closed the contract for the sale of the house.

True, but that isn't the memory that is giving you the shock, says the narrator. Some place else—you have also seen old Mrs. Benjamin somewhere else.

She waves her horny old fingers childlike, or like a witch beckoning children into the oven, her mouth open toothless smiling, talking in a voice childlike and toothless: "Hello mis-ter Boor, glad to see youse again, hope youse feeling better soon, mis-ter."

Somewhere else. Looking up at him, close to, her eyes frightened. Then he remembered. His eyes clamped shut and he felt constrictions of terror in his chest that were almost like pain.

"Goo-bye mis-ter Boor, come and see us in your old house any-time, any-time at all, mis-ter. Bye-bye."

Take this message to Berthold Whatzisname in the police station. Tell him how much I appreciate their leaving Professor Burr alone during his stay in the hospital. What an extraordinary piece of kindness that is, yet how natural and wise and humane, since of course he could not possibly escape, to let him have these few weeks not to worry about a thing, anything at all, so that the damaged arteries of his heart can have the necessary care and rest to enable them to heal—to leave him alone and at peace while everyone is so good to him, until he has recovered sufficiently for them to move in and make the necessary capture. Tell him how fully aware I am of the humanity in their. Express to him my gratitude in its full. Assure him of my. Let him know it makes me feel. And fills me with almost tears to realize how really good people can still be in their hearts even in a revolution at such a late date in life as.

Chapter 5

In the station house that night, Freitag and Watson stayed up all night with Berthold, making plans and wrangling. Berthold wanted to arrest him in the hospital tomorrow morning first thing: "He's been there three weeks, getting stronger every day. If we wait until they let him out, he'll get away. Now he's sold his house and no one knows where he'll be and we'll never catch him. But if we go in and catch him now, then we can set up a guard in his hospital room until they are through with him, and then we can bring him along to the jail."

But Freitag didn't like it. For a while he was not clear why. "If he'd only let us know he knew we were after him—if he'd only express gratitude for being left undisturbed in the hospital, then I'd be happy to postpone it a while longer. As it is—"

Puzzled, scratching his head. For a long time during that night he found himself arguing against Berthold without being able to produce any reasons. "It's because you're soft," said Berthold with contempt. "Because you're always feeling sorry for the meanest filthiest criminal types. Because he's a professor! Because he has had a heart attack, you think he's entitled to special consideration."

"But suppose I get a heart attack someday?" said Freitag. "Or you." He prodded Berthold's huge furniture-moving shape with his finger. That night Berthold was still wearing his mover's disguise with the name *Buzzy* sewn onto the pocket. It helped keep his mind on the job, the vengeance that he had sworn. "I don't get heart attacks," said Berthold. "I'm too easygoing and relaxed to get heart attacks."

Early in the morning (about the same time that Burr, after a sleepless uncomfortable night filled with self-nourishing fears, saw the first faint tinge of dawnlight beginning to restore the substance of the brick wall opposite the window, and seeing it listened and failed to hear and missed the dawn-breaking song of the robins, first singers in the trees around his house, which he knew now he would never hear again because he would never wake in the house again) Freitag caught suddenly the reason why they were not yet ready to move in and capture their victim, even though his guilt was by now certain. "Because of the motive!" exclaimed Freitag. "We haven't found his motive yet. We can't arrest him until we know the motive."

"Oh damn!" said Watson.

Berthold snorted. "Mistaken identity," he said.

"What?"

"A case of mistaken identity," he said. "That's your motive for the crime."

"How do you know that?" asked Freitag.

Berthold looked at him as if he could not believe a police official could be so ignorant. "*All* murder is a case of mistaken identity. Didn't you know that, for Christ sake?"

"Oh," said Freitag. But he was not easily intimidated by mere scorn. "Well," he said, "that still doesn't solve the problem. We still can't arrest him until we know who it was he thought he was murdering."

"It was my old man is what he murdered," said Berthold. "That's all you need to know. None of this crap about his motives, you don't need that. Not when it's a murder. My old man didn't know nothing about that guy's motives when he bashed his head with his rock. All you need to do is go in to that hospital and get him. Give them nurses a shock. Christ you're not going to let him get away hiding behind some nurse, are you?"

Prepare your story. Yes, I did strike the old man, though I did not intend or expect to kill him. I struck him with a stick. As I started up the steps I saw him coming down. As we approached I saw him looking at me, an evil-looking old man. He had a wide nasty grinning mouth that looked like a gash, a wound, and he had white stubble on his chin, and as we approached each other (I wanted to avoid him, I wanted to go by some other route because as soon as I saw him I knew he could only mean trouble, but there was no way to avoid him on these steps except by plunging into the bushes, which would have impressed him as cowardice and probably only increased the chances for trouble) he kept staring at me as if making up his mind what kind of mischief would be best. So when we came together he stood in front of me and blocked my path. Now he was of course short and frail and probably hungry for all I knew, yet I am not a strong or violent person myself, and even such a frailty as that when it blocks my path constitutes a kind of intimidation. I am by nature polite and considerate, whereas his way was confrontation, to dare me to make it a question of strength of force. I said, "What do you want?" He grinned or giggled and what he said was unclear. It may have been a request for money or it may have been a homosexual suggestion, but I could not tell, what I was most aware of was his foul alcoholic breath and his challenge to my courage. I said, "Get out of my way," words of such a directness as in the years of my career I am unaccustomed to use, especially to strangers, and I was aware that my voice sounded tremulous as I uttered them, quaking with the fear of my daring and all the humiliation he was heaping on me in spite of myself. He must have detected that for it made him laugh, but it also enraged him. "Get out of whose way?" he said. "Who's going to make me, Professor?" Now I do not know whether he actually knew that I was a professor or whether he simply called me that to indicate scorn for my supposed lack of virility and courage and action. But it made me a little angry in the midst of cowardice, and I tried to dart by him, around by the side. But he blocked my way, and then stepping back a step or two he picked up a large stick, a piece of broken branch that was lying there, and brandished it. "Ha ho!" he said. "Now you get out of my way. I think I'm gonna whup you, Professor, I think that's what I'm gonna do." Now I was truly afraid as he lifted the stick and prepared to strike, and I made a reach and grabbed for it. But you see he was not very strong, and when I grabbed it he let go and now the stick was in my hand brandished over him. He swung with his fist feebly at my groin, hoping to paralyze me. I dodged, and I still did not know how feeble he was, nor how strong I was, for when he tried to come at me, I struck him on the head with the stick, lightly I thought, not really intending to hit him but merely ward him off, but as I did so he fell, and after a moment I realized to my (inexpressible) horror that I had hit him, that I had hit him too hard, and he was dead. You can well imagine the terror and confusion that beset me then. I knew of course that I was morally innocent, that it was an accident in self-defense, but I did not know how the law would regard me, and in my terror and confusion I decided the simplest way was to drag him into the leaves and allow the question of who killed him to remain unresolved.

No, said Berthold, that's my old man you are criticizing there. My old man was a quiet kindly old man, a senile old man without a thought in his head. It won't do, that story, neither for me nor for you.

And somewhere still there was a gap in memory, a blank space between edges. He could tell by the echoes that sounded from around it, without being able to see where it was, or he knew it was there maybe only because of some most vague sense of its presence. But still he fingered at the gap trying to find it, trying to remember, for he knew now there was more than just the gap on the bedroom floor, there was another gap before that, or the same gap extended back, and he kept fingering for it trying to find it, where it was and what was in it.

Please try to remember, he said. He started up the steps—heavily, he remembered that. He looked up and saw the figure of an old man or woman at the top, coming down. Slowly, awkwardly, two small steps and a half step, then down, two small steps and a half step. With heaviness going up. The narrator looked up and must have seen something, for suddenly the narrator could not speak. Tried to speak but could only utter syllables, matching the steps: twen-ty-six, twen-ty-seven . . . Then the narrator went away. Burr's mind chilled, as if someone had left the door open. His memory fails. He cannot remember the steps between twenty-seven and thirty-seven. Then count: thir-ty-seven, thir-ty-eight, thir-ty-nine, foe-ar-ty. He was all alone, he had left the narrator far behind. When he came even with the old man or woman, the old man looked up at him with his empty eyes and he raised his hands in front of him. Burr remembers that and remembers also picking up the rock and striking the old man hard on the head. He must have struck him so hard that he fell down dead. Then the narrator came back. *Now you've done it,* said the narrator. *Why did I do it?* asked Burr. *Damned if I know,* said the narrator. *I wasn't there.* Again Burr asked, *Why did I do it?*

Try me, said the narrator. According to the narrator, once upon a time, one morning old Mrs. Benjamin, the grandmother, see her getting up in the morning, in the smelly apartment where she lived by herself. Because the Benjamins did not want her to live by herself any longer, because she was getting too old to take proper care of herself, so they bought Professor Burr's house so as to have space not only for themselves and their children but Grandmother too. But on that particular morning, old Mrs. Benjamin burned the bacon and she spilled grease on the table and wiped it up with a towel, and then she ate a stale roll and forgetting that she had not had her egg this morning she took her breadcrumbs and went out onto the back landing to feed the birds. But when she got outdoors she forgot to feed the birds and the beautiful morning sunlight made her think of the house her son had just bought, and she went down the back steps so as to go visit her new house. So she walked with little short steps out to the sidewalk, up the sidewalk in the bright morning sunlight (Burr remembered that bright morning sunlight) up to Clifton Avenue where the traffic was, the air here thickened by the exhaust of automobiles, buses, and trucks, walked down Clifton past the hospital (where someday perhaps soon she too would come to rest, tended by nurses, she thought), then waited for the light so as to cross the street, over to the park, Burnet Woods. In the park she climbed up the hill—too deaf to hear the songs of the birds, the cardinals, the robins, the catbirds and titmice—up to the circle with the bandstand at the top where the students were parking their cars to leave while they went to the university. And then old Mrs. Benjamin found the path at the top of the steps that went down through the woods, down to the playground below, and started down, without breaking the rhythm of her steps, taking two little steps and a shorter one for each step downward. Looking down and seeing the man coming up.

As she descends she pretends not to look at the man coming up. It makes her nervous, angry, it supports the angry mood she was in when she started, and everything makes her angry this morning, even the sunlight, as also the cars and buses and trucks, and the birds that she is too deaf to hear. The man makes her angry because she knows she will have to pass him on the steps, because he will expect her to be polite and step aside as he does. Is that the real reason? The man makes her angry because he will see her—since there is no one else in the woods, no one else on the steps, he will be obliged to look at her, and it makes her angry to think that anyone should look at her now when she does not choose to be looked at.

But as they approach each other in the middle of the steps, she notices his mustache and recognizes him. Still he will not look at her, still he gazes off into the bushes and the treetops as he climbs as if she did not exist, but she fixes her eyes on him with ferocity as they come closer, to force him to look and acknowledge her presence and concede to her grievances.

A step apart, she stopped. "Mis-ter," she said. "Mis-ter Wazzur-name!" He turned to her, saw the thin white hair, the fringe of thin white curls on top, saw how small she was, how easy to. He saw a rock on the ground and bent down to pick it up. It was full of fossils.

She looked at him full of hate. "Don't you threaten me, mis-ter," she said.

Before he picked up the rock, he must have said something, said the narrator. She backed up, and came down again. A step apart, she stopped. "Mis-ter. Mis-ter Wazzurname!"

He looked. According to the narrator, "I don't know you," said Burr. He saw a rock on the ground and bent down to pick it up. "Don't you— " she said.

He looked at her bleary bloodshot eyes. "I don't know you," he must have said. But according to the narrator, at that moment Burr backed away. Memory blank, he backed off the path and into the bushes and stood there. In a trance, according to the narrator. Let the narrator talk to Mrs. Benjamin while Burr stood in the bushes in a trance, looking at his shoes. What did you and Mrs. Benjamin talk about? asked Burr.

Talked about you, said the narrator. She wanted you to let her into the house. Annoyed to hear that you had left the house locked, demanded the key. When I tried to argue with her, said the narrator, she became more demanding. She said she had a right to go into the house any time she wanted to, the rights of the new owner. She said once a house is sold, is sold. Said she didn't care what dates were on the contrack between you and her son, she said don't try no contracks on me. She became abusive, said she was moving into a big house, what kind of a house are you moving into? Said there was a difference between people on the way up and people on the way down. Said people moving out of a big house, must be something wrong with 'em, wanted to know what was wrong with you. She said she was an old lady, but you was older because you was moving out of a big house, she was moving in. She said you was a failure, a washup, a hasbeen, finished, through. She asked what right has someone who is washed up has been finished through to keep the keys of the house from its rightful new owner. She said she didn't believe in old age, she only believed in people going up or down, and everything else was a lot of crap. She said what are you going to do Mis-ter Boor, if you got hippy dope addick kids and a suicide wife, because the only way you was going was down and that proves it? For a long moment I tried, said the narrator, to shake off her bad temper and geriatric hostility like fluff but after a long moment I couldn't shake anymore and, said the narrator, I got impatient and went away.

According to the narrator the minute he went away Burr came out of his trance like a wild man. Lost all rational control, went berserk, savage. Let out a roar. The narrator hurried back, but it was too late. Burr was standing there, dazed, holding a large rock full of fossils in his hand.

Was she dead? asks Burr. The narrator hesitates, unclear. No—as a matter of fact.

Chapter 6

No, according to the narrator, they said anyway it was an old man, not
an old woman. Now according to the narrator, once upon a time there
was this old man who must have lived with Paul and Laura Grummon,
a room of his own on the top floor of their expensive Tudor-style house
with its broad lawns. That would be the elder Grummon, with thin
white hair and eyes that are foggy. Fading eyesight, for five years he has
been unable to read. He sees shapes, light and shadow, enough to go for
walks. He is too proud to carry a white cane with a red tip, and he can
just barely pick out the shapes of approaching automobiles at familiar
street corners.

That is, the Grummons think he has been unable to read for five
years. He has, however, a very large magnifying glass, and has been able
to pick out the essential content of letters left in Laura Grummon's desk
drawer on afternoons when she has gone out—enough to equip him with
more knowledge than you might guess and to substantiate certain views
of his about the Grummons in particular and the human race in general.

On this particular morning the elder Grummon wants to get away
from people—they grate on his nerves, they make him cranky, or more
cranky than usual this morning—so he goes out of the house (this bright
sunlit morning at the beginning of May) without telling anyone and
takes a long walk: down Lafayette Avenue to Middleton, and then the
whole length of Middleton, past the rich houses, the bird sanctuary, the

open field behind the school, then the brick apartment buildings and the older houses until he gets to Ludlow Avenue, the shopping district, then past the grocery stores and drugstores and shoe stores, cleaners, stationers, news store, and fire station, to cross over Clifton into Burnet Woods. In Burnet Woods he climbs up to the circle with the bandstand and then he starts down the steps through the woods going to the playground below.

An old man in a black coat, a very short and small old man, carrying a bundle, hair white and thinning, bald in the center top. He starts down the steps without breaking his rhythm, taking two little steps and a shorter one for each step downward. Looking down through his foggy eyes, seeing at first only a mess of green and brown, but after a while he becomes aware of the shape of a man, a shadow, coming up the stairs, getting nearer. Unable to see clearly, he pretends not to look though actually he does not know whether he is looking or not until he is aware finally that the man is about to pass him. At this moment, a rush of anger goes through his body which he mistakes for fear, and a rush of fear that he mistakes for common sense. They are about to pass when the elder Grummon says, "Don't kill me, please."

"Kill you?" It stops Burr completely, on the step, while the old man looks up with his foggy eyes trying to find Burr's face. "Why should anyone want to kill you?"

"Because we're alone here," said the old Grummon. "Because there's no one to see you and make you stop." He said, "After all the help I tried to give you, and all you want is to kill me dead."

"I never saw you before in my life."

There was no humor in the old man's face, not even malicious humor. He meant what he said, with bitterness and anger and hate, all marked deep in the habit-lines of his face, emotions that had kept him going for a lifetime. According to the narrator it frightened Burr—"don't kill me" interchangeable with "don't let me kill you, if you can!" Burr stepped aside, off the path, putting distance between them, holding out his hand to gesture the man past. But the man did not move and then —memory blanks—Burr backed into the bushes, into a trance. Try this, said the narrator, according to the narrator trying to reason the old man out of his fears. What did he say? asks Burr. Said he was afraid to turn his back to you, says narrator—soon as he turns his back, conko! No thank you.

Tried to reason with him says narrator. But he waved a stick around saying he's just as violent as you, by damn. When I said you wouldn't attack because it would be *out of character*, he said he didn't believe in character—it was human to attack undefended strangers, and weren't you human? When I told him that you wouldn't attack because you were basically and intrinsically a good man—that you had tried all your life to preserve the values of humanity, to be good teacher, good father, good husband—good intentions, anyway, he said professors always think they are better than anybody else but they all got the same sewer slime and guts. He said professors dirtier than anybody else because they wrap it all up in little plastic containers and put it on the shelves. He said don't talk to me about professors, I live in a houseful of 'em, always knifing everybody in the back and putting the remains in plastic containers on the shelf. He said professors talk about wouldn't hurt a fly and run down raccoons and dogs in the road every day. Said never turn your back because slime and guts are full of knives and behind every book is a dead raccoon. Then he told me to make you pick up the rock so he could see the murder weapon in your hand. So at least you wouldn't conk him when his back was turned. Then he told me to go away because all I ever do is tell lies. I told him, said the narrator, that it was safer for him with me around, but he started to scream, so I walked off, went a little ways up the path.

According to the narrator, as soon as he went away, Burr went berserk and came roaring out of the bushes in violent amnesia, holding the rock full of fossils. "Old man!" he shouted. No doubt the old Grummon looked at him full of terror in his eyes. "Keep your distance," said the old man. "Old man," said Burr. "You insulted. There is no murder. There is no weapon. Get that through your thick skull!" Raising the rock high above the old man's head. "I . . . I," said the old man, "I—"

Was it conko? When the narrator got back, Burr was standing there with the rock in his hand. *Did I do it?* he asked. The narrator muses, quietly and thoughtfully. According to the narrator, it is hard to remem-

247

ber. Easier to remember on that particular morning (bright sunlight at the beginning of May) this old lady who lives in an apartment by herself off Clifton Avenue is preparing to go to probably an art show (contemporary, works by students and young faculty, experimental avant garde) in a private gallery in an old house close to the campus. She was probably Harvey Kessler's grandmother, who has been described as a remarkable old woman, although she might just as well have been somebody else's grandmother. She had a painting of her own which she had rolled up in a paper bag, which she had promised the director that she would bring to the show this morning.

Not caring for worldly ostentation, she wears her shabby old black coat that she has had for almost ten years. She goes out to Clifton Avenue and waits to cross at the light. Notices the morning traffic, the cars, the buses, the trucks, the thickening of the air at this point with the smell of automobile and truck exhausts—occurs to her that she likes that busy industrial smell, it reminds her of travel and expectations before a trip, even though she is now committed with dozens of signatures and checks to wiping it out. To save mankind. For old Mrs. Kessler (probably that is who she is) is deeply involved in many a struggle and nationwide campaign to improve life, to save from disaster.

She crosses with the light, over into Burnet Woods. She is very small and she can only take short steps, but the morning air, the sunlight, the birds all have a part in the geography of her well-being and the architecture of her pride this morning as she takes her rolled-up painting to the show of avant-garde art. Proud of walking, her tough feet. Would prefer to go barefoot, like the kids. Wishes she could be young again to enjoy all the wonderful new changes in living that the kids have introduced. Would like to grow her hair long and go around without shoes, without a bra. Would have liked the freedom to be as sexual as you please—or as indifferent if you prefer that. Would have liked the recognition of your right to differ, to quit school if you wish, to avoid programs, to come back again later. Would have liked this great new political conscience that the young people seemed to have, and finding that your own private wishes and idealisms are shared by hundreds of others organizing or simply grouping together without organization to share the common feeling.

She walked with short quick steps but with ease, without tiring—she was used to walking, used to marching, she had marched in the South for black registration and civil rights, she had marched downtown in this city to protest war policy, she had marched to Washington to protest the Pentagon and again to protest the continuing war, she had been to Chicago at the time of the riotous convention, she had been to the rock concert at Woodstock with her grandchildren, she had been everywhere on top of the moment, riding history into the future with the young people who would live in that future, people fifty years younger than she, though actually she was quite sure she was younger now than they were despite those fifty years—walked up to the circle with the bandstand, and then started down the steps through the woods going down to the playground.

Starts down the steps without breaking her rhythm, taking two little steps and a shorter one for each step downward. Looking down and seeing the man coming up. No hesitation, no reason to. As she continues on down the steps she notices that he avoids looking at her. He pretends not to see her; she sees his eyes looking in other directions, at the budding leaves, the branches, the bushes on both sides, making only the quickest most blink-like checks on her to keep track of her—checks that she notices, as she notices everything, proving that he is afraid of her. Which she knew from the first moment she saw him—which makes her chuckle.

As they approach each other, her plan forms—influenced perhaps by the fear she detects in him or perhaps sheer devilishness. She notices his mustache, realizes that he is a professor going to the university, perhaps she even recognizes him, knows him. She sees that he intends to pass her on the steps without looking at her, but just as they are about to draw even with each other she blocks his path. He looks up, frightened, and backs away. Falls into the bushes. In his fright he forgets everything, in a trance.

According to the narrator, old Mrs. Kessler, if that is who she was, had spotted that he was a conservative professor with an uneasy heart, and she merely wanted to shake him up a little. Explained it to the narrator, while Burr sat on the ground with his eyes rolling—explained how lazy and fearful he was in his career, devoted to the dead written words of the past. Easier to pass on heritages than to make up new things, she said. Placing her bets with the narrator that Burr had never made a genuine decision in his life, that he had always taken the easiest course, the one with the least risk, the one least likely to change anything. Because, she said, giving him a glance as he lay there in the unconsciousness of memory loss, eyes rolling, all his life he thinks he is living in a flood, floating on a board, afraid of any move that would dump him off the board into the sea, until he has built the board into a great big institutional ocean liner floating on a pond. The narrator liked her, she made him laugh. You should have heard, said the narrator, how contemptuously she spoke of the categories of your life, laughing with me over how easy it must be to describe you. How, whatever the situation, you could always tell: you were a husband, so you did what husbands do. A father, you did as fathers do. Now your wife is dead, you do as widowers do, and your children have run away from home, and you— You do as middle-aged professors do, and what members of the bourgeois middle class. That way you keep from falling off the board. Then she said about shaking you up a little, let's see if we can get him to use a little force. What does a highly civilized man who does what highly civilized men do, do when his path is blocked by a little old lady? The narrator said, I warned her be careful, but she told me to go away. Told her that would be dangerous, but she said she wanted to try you in your natural state, whatever that means, without me to give you ideas.

According to the narrator, he went up the path. "Don't you want to get to work?" said Mrs. Kessler to Burr. Burr came back onto the path from the bushes. Again she blocked his path and laughed—a little old lady. He was shaking with fear or with something else. He was shocked by the narrator's betrayal and abandonment and did not know what he was shaking with. The old lady said, "What are you going to do? We're all alone—nobody's watching." But *she* was watching. She was looking at his face. Suddenly Burr looked at her and the moment she caught the look in his eyes the laughter drained out of her like water through a funnel. Something else in its place—alarm, fear, horror, how could a mere Burr tell what it was? He saw the rock on the ground and the top of her head, the thin white hair with the soft ringlets of curls. Full of tension now, she maintains her position: "You don't dare pick it up." With this, Burr will indeed see a connection between the two objects. He will bend down to grasp it, the rock full of fossils in his hand, and gaze at her, aware of a dumb angry power in his hands that he never felt before. "Don't fall off the board," she whispers, trying to grin, and it is hard to tell who is shaking, old Mrs. Kessler or Burr himself.

Then she steps down, close to him, so that his nose almost leans over the top of her head, and he holds the rock in his hands. And just at that moment she looks up at him, with a sudden release on her face of pure horror, collapse of pretense, her mouth opening as if she were about to scream. "I," she says, "I—" And at such a moment, with his fury sidetracked by plain astonishment, he will hear the narrator running back, crying out, No no. And no doubt there will have been a moment when the possibility of destruction was very high—yet surely no degree of gossip and ridicule and no spell of invitation and no flaunting of fragile heads close to the weapons of destruction will be enough to make a professor of English break the ropes that hold him or forget his lifetime lesson in consequences and rule, his profoundly taught lesson that crimes in a society get caught and punished, and his ancient supposition that as a member of society he requires society's system of regularity. She moves a step away, a step down, then another step, and the possibility begins to recede—unless he were suddenly to run after her. She moves further down and turns back and says, "Shook you up a little didn't I?" The rock rests heavy in his hands and he turns and tosses it into the bushes.

Chapter 7

No, says the narrator, and besides, once again reminding him, it was not an old woman, it was an old man. There was this old Andreas K, now he remembered, who lived in a room by himself on the top floor of a house occupied by Berthold and his family. This old Andreas, whose voice had lost its masculine bite and had turned soft, feeble old man with teary eyes, who perhaps had almost forgotten whether he was an old man or an old woman—as if it did not matter anymore. He cried a lot because of the brutal ways of Berthold and his wife, crying softly, with shaking shoulders, while the tears ran down to the end of his nose and dropped off, but he seldom spoke because it was an effort to form a word with his mouth and tongue and difficult to concentrate enough breath to make a comprehensible sound.

Now on a bright sunlit May morning with birds, this old Andreas wanders out of his son's house with nothing much left in his mind but habit, wanders out to the sidewalk, wearing an old habitual shabby black coat that he has had for almost ten years. He carries a paper bag that years ago would have carried his lunch, but the days of carrying lunch to work are long ago as are the days of going to work, and he does not know what is in the paper bag—a rolled up newspaper which he will discover for himself when he gets to the park and sits down on a bench. Which he will read and forget while he reads.

He goes to Clifton Avenue and waits for the light. When it changes, he starts to cross over, taking slow short steps, step step step, which bring him halfway across when the light changes again, making the cars in the first row wait while he goes on, unaware of them, and by the time he has got across the light has changed back to red and the car on the inside lane has had two reds to wait for.

Now he goes up the slope into Burnet Woods, straight up the grassy slope, ignorant of the road which climbs S-ways up to the same point, coming to the bandstand and the circle where the students park their cars, and goes on into the woods where the steps go down to the playground below. Enters the woods, starts down the steps without breaking his rhythm, taking two little steps and a shorter one for each step downward, his mind full of green leaves and branches and tree trunks and bark. A large green spongy cushion in his mind between the inside and the outside, while his legs and feet work automatically, operating on their own as if without command from the cerebral centers—so that the inside of his mind looks out vaguely at the passing greenery with what little there is that remains of wonder, or some minimal surprise, or perhaps nothing but curiosity, or not even that, vaguely watching the scenery that passes and not even wondering how it got there. Looking down, seeing but not really noticing the shape of a man at the bottom of the steps coming up. Perhaps he does notice it—perhaps the vague memory of some ancient habit of causes and effects does stir a slight agitation in the placid green pool of his mind, a slight realization that if there is a man at the bottom of the steps that man will probably soon be here and might say something to stir up a noise.

Meanwhile, down below, just as Burr put his foot on the lowest step, he looked up, saw the old man at the top—and just at that moment he felt the familiar ominous presence inside himself. Again that thickening, that tightening of the breath—making his lungs feel like a web or a screen with every wire sentient, as if breathing set up electric currents in his lungs that made them visible like a map. Made him stop in alarm. Two days in a row—that was too much. Still, at this time, the doctors had not found anything harmful (while Natalie Fleet waited yesterday in the waiting room). And yet to Burr, feeling it growing again, and looking up at the steps that he would have to climb, and seeing the old man at the top just starting down—to Burr it was doom, and the doctors were ignorant.

He paused and took deep breaths—already believing that he would fall dead before he reached the top. Then someone later in the day—perhaps that old man himself—would find him and report his death to —to whom? To the public? Yet as he paused, taking deep breaths, he felt the alarm passing—quickly this time. In another moment he was normal again, able to resume. Reminder or warning—he did not know how to take these things—but this one was short, and he assumed he was all right for today and resumed his way up the steps. In the interval the old man coming down had descended four or five steps.

As he began to climb, he looked up and became intensely aware of the old man approaching, as if it were something to fear. He realized that the old man had seen him when he paused to catch his breath, and though he knew the old man's head was empty, yet he seemed to feel a connection, as if the old man knew what the spasm was, or even as if he had caused it. Afraid of the old man. As he goes up the steps—taking them slowly so as to avoid another spasm—he pretends not to look at him, but the old man does not have to pretend: the old man looks everywhere and sees nothing—or who can say how little or how much he sees, and how quickly it floats out of the range of his attention and disappears as if he had never seen it? But as he climbs Burr notices something familiar in the way the old man walks, reminding him of something. It repels him—something unpleasant, ugly. Something reminiscent and ugly about his shape, too. About a certain automatic gesture of the hands, too, a kind of scratching about the neck that conveys to Burr an idea of nervousness or embarrassment—yet in the old man it is devoid of consciousness, a shell of a gesture without content, a habit of old forgotten fears.

Was that it? asked the narrator.

Abruptly the narrator stopped. Run, he said, turn back. Here comes the most dangerous man you'll ever see in your life. Burr looked up, disbelieving. That old man? Ask the narrator what's the matter. But now the narrator said nothing. He looked up with glazing eyes at the vegetable old man coming down—rigid as if the sight had turned him to stone.

Speak! said Burr, but the narrator could not speak. His mouth opened and he uttered syllables: twen-ty-six, twen-ty-seven. . . . Burr's memory fails. His mind chilled. He cannot remember the steps between twenty-seven and thirty-seven. Then count: thir-ty-seven, thir-ty-eight, thir-ty-nine, foe-ar-ty. He was all alone, he had left the narrator far behind. When he came even with the old man, the old man looked up at him with his empty eyes and he raised his hands in front of him. Burr remembers that and remembers also picking up the rock and striking the old man hard on the head. He must have struck him so hard that he fell down dead. Then the narrator came back. Now you've done it, said the narrator. Why did I do it? asked Burr. Damned if I know said the narrator. I wasn't there. Why did I do it? asked Burr again.

Go back then. Something unpleasant, ugly. A certain automatic gesture of the hands, too, a kind of scratching about the neck that conveys to Burr an idea of nervousness or embarrassment—yet in the old man it is devoid of consciousness, a shell of a gesture without content, a habit of old forgotten fears.

A gesture of his own—now the narrator remembered, this time he recognized it—a gesture which he had trained himself to get rid of long ago because it confessed too much. What it confessed, the narrator did not remember and perhaps had never known—except in the general sense that the gesture to Burr had a confessional quality, it admitted weakness, it exposed fear like naked parts. The narrator was surprised to see this old man displaying it, this gesture that he had never seen on anyone but Burr, which had seemed so private and exclusive to Burr.

He did not like to see it on someone else—now he remembered—even a vegetating old man. It seemed to suggest that in his mindless way the old man harbored Burr's secrets, and in his mindless way might disclose them to the world. Or as if a person, looking at the old man and then at Burr, would know at once all that Burr had spent a lifetime with the narrator trying to keep him from knowing.

Was that it? asked the narrator. Or was it simply that his face looked to the narrator's imagination like Burr himself—that as we saw him coming down the steps to us, the narrator was suddenly convinced that this is how we ourselves would look in years to come (if we survive) when we have been reduced to vegetating, teary, and habit-formed old age?

Whatever it was, all of a sudden Burr discovered in his possession a full-grown and still-growing dislike for the old man. Outside of words—dislike, hatred, bursting into flame inside him, almost making him twitch: it required the narrator to tell him what it was. Required the narrator to tell him that he disliked the old man because of his mindlessness, because he loathed vegetable human beings, because he loathed idiots, because he loathed all forms of living death. Not enough, said Burr, in the flames of his hate (while still he climbed the steps close and closer to the man—twen-ty-nine, thay-are-ty). You loathe him because you recognize him, said the narrator, though never knowing until this minute that he existed—this old man that you blame for everything.

Now in a frenzy, putting forth words to take care of Burr's rage, the narrator enumerated—because you might as well put blame where it belongs and fix it on him once and for all, for all those things that have gone so wrong, for that dying interest and that loss of vitality, for the dying teaching, and the fading away of students, for the decaying house and the shriveling loneliness, for the accumulating animals, and the failure to take action, and for all those losses, the loss of Elaine, the loss of Harold, the loss of Cynthia. On that man's head, then, be the idiotic sloth of Burr's life, blame him for the habits of caution and timidity, for the fear of adventure, for the fear of decision and change, blame also for the backing away from children, for the standing by and timorous watching while she plunged on her obvious course toward—blame him, the idiot, for the bathtub, the naked body with the legs and arms curled up, the head turned to one side, mouth open as if in a cry.

In that ugly moment, said the narrator, you put on that man's poor old empty shell of a head a curse for every defeat and frustration and loss you ever suffered, you felt in that moment the weight of all your failures as if piled on top of each other, and that old man, simply because you conceived him as empty-headed, old, and dying, became the villain, as if you supposed him to be acting through you or whispering in your ear, or who knows what kind of crazy mechanism for blame your mind had concocted then?

While still you counted steps, thir-ty-seven, thir-ty-eight, thir-ty-nine, foe-are-ty, darting your glance off into the bushes to avoid him and the strength of your loathing. But then, just at the moment you came even with him, just then, said the narrator, you happened to glance at him just as he was looking at you—his bloodshot teary eyes in terror—and when he saw you looking at him he raised his hands, palms facing you, in front of his head as if to ward you off, as if you had already begun to attack. It was that, said the narrator, that sign of abject panic—the narrator tried to speak. Address the man, stop him. Mouth opened, words formed, words without shape, without sound. Stammer, the narrator tried, could not speak. Then the narrator also panicked. All words stopped, silence congealed them all in their panic like sticky goo. The narrator said, "G-g-g," and out of the man's open mouth came a vowel, twice: "I-I-" It took only an instant to make an explosion, all that imprisoned power breaking loose, causing you to reach for the rock full of fossils, lift it up (while still his feeble warding-off hands rose higher and his eyes swam tears), and crash it down on his hollow head, which made a dull sound, and then he fell.

Burr: And what did I think when I saw the old man lying there where I had bashed him with the rock? *Narrator:* You knew that he was dead. You said to yourself, there is no need to test whether he is alive or dead, no need to feel pulse or look in eyes, for he is obviously dead. *Burr:* And how did this knowledge affect me? *Narrator:* You were surprised. *Burr:* Why should I have been surprised? Didn't I know how hard I had struck? *Narrator:* On the contrary, it was the hardness of the blow which was how you knew you had killed him. *Burr:* Surprise then to realize what I had done? *Narrator:* Not yet. That could not come until later, after self-consciousness had returned. At this point you were surprised first by how quiet it was in the woods. You heard a cardinal singing in the distance. The next thing, you were surprised to realize that you were still alive. *Burr:* Why should that surprise me? Did I suppose I was killing myself instead of the old man? *Narrator:* Not exactly that, for in fact you were not thinking at all when you killed him. But when the old man's cowardice enraged you, with all the compressed force of a life's imagined crash, still it could not break free into a rock until you were able to damn the consequences. That power of despair, or that conviction that your life was finished—like the old man's—you needed that before you could find the strength to do what you did. So that at the moment when you struck, you did not care who might be looking, since you had already determined that your life was over, and when you struck that old man so hard on the head (as if he were the bodyguard to death himself) it was true you had almost forgotten to make any distinction between his head and your own. So that indeed it was a surprise after he fell and you saw that he was dead, to realize that it was quiet, that a cardinal was singing, that you were still alive. And then after a moment, to realize that no armed policeman had jumped out of the bushes to arrest you nor (looking up and down) that anyone had seen you. Only after that were you able to form a shocked definition of what you had done—*Burr:* Clarify "definition"? *Narrator:* A category and a name for the violent physical thing that you had just acted out—the name is murder. It stands in the human as well as the literary mind as the ultimate crime. It was thus that you were able, after a few minutes reflection, to categorize what you had done—at the same moment that it also occurred to you for the first time that you might actually get away with it (get away with murder) and resume your life in the normal way, if you could only get the body out of sight and yourself away from the spot before somebody saw you. *Burr:* And did I then decide to get away with murder? *Narrator:* You tried your damndest. As soon as you realized that you might escape, you abandoned your despair, your gloom, your rage, you were seized with the desire to get away and the fear of being caught, and suddenly nothing seemed as delicious as life and freedom.

Burr: So then what did I do? *Narrator:* Hastily as you could, you dragged the body by the feet (so as not to get blood on your clothes) off the path and dumped it in a pile of leaves, and returned to the steps and hurried upward. *Burr:* Did I run? *Narrator:* No, you were afraid to be seen running, and you were afraid also that if you ran you might get a heart attack. But you walked briskly, and there were several minutes of real fear that you might be observed and caught before you had completed your getaway. But you did get away. It required the ingenuity and imagination of a Berthold Kirschner to catch you—and how could you have foreseen that?

Burr: I did not foresee that? *Narrator:* Well, perhaps you did foresee something of the sort. *Burr:* I did not really think I could get away with it? *Narrator:* I suppose actually you did not. Even as you saw the possibility of escape and decided to try for it—even as you realized how unobserved you were in the woods, like a wild animal catching its prey, with no one over you, nothing looking down upon you to make a record, of acts performed in silence or darkness or privacy, that will go down into darkness and never be known except to the perpetrator and his victim—even as you persuaded yourself of this, you were aware of tradition alive within you, saying that your life was now irrevocably destroyed. Yes, that you would be caught, and if you were not, that you would suffer so much over it you wished you were. *Burr:* Why should I suffer if I weren't caught? *Narrator:* The fear that you would be. The realization that what you had done would ostracize you, subject you to hatred and contempt, identify you as a suitable object for scapegoating passions. Just like your own passions. *Burr:* I should suffer because of fear? *Narrator:* Fear and guilt. Or guilt is fear. Guilt in the ostracizing and the question you would never be able to resolve, "Do I deserve to suffer, do I deserve to be punished, and if I do, how can I excuse myself for wanting to go on living my normal life?"

Burr: Didn't I feel any remorse, any distress for the victim, or any of the decent things decent people are supposed to feel about crimes like this? *Narrator:* Perhaps because you were too egotistically worried about what kind of a person this crime showed you to be, depriving you of any spare compassion. Or because you were too worried about getting away or getting caught, making you forget your victim. And then also, compassion for a victim can only begin when you are able to break the association you have made between the victim and the parts of yourself that you wish to punish. *Burr:* You mean I continued to hate the old man?

Here the witness hesitated, startled with a realization. *Narrator:* Why no. Evidently your hatred—for the old man at any rate—died instantly, the moment you realized he was dead. Obviously, for look how long it has taken you to discover even your motive for killing him—as if you had quite forgotten what it was. As if once dead, he had ceased to be anything but the man you had killed. As in fact you realized when you looked at him in that moment after your mighty rage with the rock full of fossils—the next moment looking down at his dead frothy face and realized that the man you had killed was a stranger. Total stranger, never saw him before in your life. *Burr:* Did I feel sorry for him? *Narrator:* You'd like to, perhaps, so as to feel better about yourself. But maybe it was hard to feel sorry for someone you knew nothing about. And you were trying too hard to escape. *Burr:* Not even when he put his hands up? *Narrator:* Maybe that makes you feel sorry for him afterwards, pathetic weak poor old man who somehow detects that he is going to be killed, you ought to feel sorry for that. However, you have Berthold feeling so sorry for the old man it turns against you, and maybe that polarizes your feelings.

Burr: Why did I become the protagonist of a novel? *Narrator:* Maybe if you hadn't been the protagonist of a novel you wouldn't have been able to commit that crime. *Burr:* Why? *Narrator:* People like you are seldom able to perform crimes like that unless they go insane. In novels certain kinds of people do things a little more drastically than they do in real life. If you hadn't become protagonist of a novel, you probably wouldn't have been able to do anything about that man coming down the steps. You would have seen him and hated him and wished and thought, and no one would ever have known anything about it. *Burr:* But suppose I had managed to kill him even so? *Narrator:* Then you would have had to become the protagonist of a novel in order to live with yourself, because it was such a cruel and ugly thing otherwise. And you would have been all alone, dark or invisible. *Burr:* An outcast? *Narrator:* Yes. *Burr:* I would have had to die to express that. *Narrator:* Don't worry. You'll die too.

Sometime in the night, Burr woke up, aware of a conversation going on around Angus on the other side of the room. The curtain between his bed and Angus's was drawn, but there was light on the other side of the curtain, visible above and below it, on the ceiling and on the floor, and the voices of people talking quietly, though he could not distinguish their words. He heard a man's subdued laugh, quiet and brief, and he turned to face the other direction, where it was dark, and closed his eyes to allow sleep to return. He was aware of the soft cool mothering pillow against his cheek, as friendly as if it had been against his cheek all his life.

Then in the darkness he became aware of a shadow close to him, close to the bed. Opened his eyes again and became aware, in the darkness, of a person standing over him, close to the bed. Looked and saw, in the subdued light that escaped into his side of the room from over Angus's curtain, a man looking down at him. He thought it was a doctor, and he said, "What's the matter?"

The man mumbled something—"checking," maybe—and Burr heard the continuing muffled voices of conversation on Angus's side. He asked the man what was the matter with Angus. "What are they doing to him?" he said.

"They are questioning him," said the man.

"In the middle of the night?" said Burr.

"Have a question for you too," said the man.

"What is it?" said Burr.

"Did you actually kill that old man in Burnet Woods?"

The question burned in the calm still of the hospital night like a fuse. Burr said, "Why do you ask that?"

"Or was it merely an imagined adventure on your part?"

Burr said, "Does it make a big difference?"

"Don't you think so?" said the man. "It makes a big difference to the law."

"That's their problem," said Burr.

"It doesn't make a big difference to you?"

"Seems to me, if you want to know whether I killed the old man or only imagined it or saw somebody else do it, you have to find out for yourself."

"You mean, you refuse to say."

"I can't say. Anything I could say would be only a half-truth."

The man, sounding annoyed: "Are you trying to tell me there is no difference between actually killing that old man and imagining it? That's sophistry—you know better than that."

"Yes," said Burr. "But is there any difference between imagining it and doing it in a piece of fiction?"

The man thought about that. Finally he said: "That means you did it. You confess to the crime."

Burr, unsure: "Is that what it means?"

Just then someone pulled the curtain in front of his bed, closing him in with the man. The man bent towards him and he shrank. There was the sound of heavy things being quietly moved. "What's the matter?" asked Burr.

"They're taking him away."

"Angus? Where's he going?"

"He's dead."

"Dead? Why, he was fine a few hours ago."

"He's dead now," said the man.

"I was talking to him just a little while ago."

The man looked accusing. "He had a mind just like you," he said. "He looked out at the world just like you."

"I—I—I," said Burr.

"Him too," said the man.

"I didn't kill him," said Burr.

The man looked at him.

"Are you going to arrest me?" said Burr.

"Why should I?" asked the man.

"You're not a policeman?"

"I'm Doctor Hussman. Cardiology. Just wanted to check you out. You may go back to sleep now."

In the morning, Burr looked over at the other bed as if to check his memory. The other bed was empty. In the late afternoon they put another patient there.

Part Four

Chapter 1

After four weeks, we went home. After the initial attack, our recovery was routine; we went through the normal stages of early convalescence in the hospital, and then we were sent home. All was changed, however. Our home as we had known it no longer existed. The Benjamins had moved into the old house, all the animals except the spaniel and the black-and-white cat had been given away, all our things had been moved to the new, small bachelor's apartment that Natalie Fleet had found for us. I had never seen it.

She came to take me home, driving my car. She helped me at the hospital cashier's desk, and she wheeled me in the wheelchair out to the car. She had brought along Harvey Kessler to help. She drove me to the apartment on a Sunday afternoon. It was near where I had lived before, on a street a few blocks away, but I did not know the street well, it seemed strange to me, crowded with houses close together as she drove up and stopped before a building that I had never noticed before—a trim new brick building with a pale grass lawn and trees two feet high that looked as if they had just been planted. She steadied me by the arm as I walked into the building, and stood beside me as we went up in the elevator. Unlocked the door. "Here's your new home," she said brightly. We stepped in.

"Sorry it's in such a mess," she said.

There was a living room, a bedroom, and a small kitchen. The living room was moderately large when empty, but it was filled now with furniture and things from the house, making it seem crowded. There were boxes along the walls and in the middle of the floor. "I'm afraid you'll be a long time finding things among all these boxes," said Natalie. "We tried to keep a list, but we didn't really know what to do, how to sort you out." "Yes, yes," said Burr, mixed between gratitude for the overwhelmingly heavy task they had performed for him, and dismay at the confusion of his things. And the apartment seemed so cramped. It had aluminum sliding window frames. There was a small balcony in the front where she had placed a wicker chair, where no doubt he was expected to sit and look at the street below. There was an air-conditioning machine in the window, making a hum. The kitchen was modern —everything was plain and smooth-surfaced with sliding doors and buttons to push.

"Here's Mrs. Brack," said Natalie. Mrs. Brack was a large elderly woman with a heavy laugh. She came into the kitchen, wiping her hands on her apron, and she looked like a character in many old novels. "Mrs. Brack is going to come in everyday to cook meals and clean up," said Natalie, repeating for formality's sake what everyone knew, "for the next month or as long as you need her."

"And there's your bed, all made up—and your desk," said Natalie, in the bedroom. His typewriter on his desk, and pen and pencils neatly laid out. In the living room again: "I'm sorry we didn't get around to putting the books in the bookcases. This evening, if you're willing, Fred and Hank and I will unpack them. You can supervise. Then the place will look more comfortable. We'll also unpack the boxes with the dishes and things."

The spaniel was happy to see him, his happiness twisting him into crescents. The black-and-white cat sat on a pile of boxes full of books and looked about curiously, withholding judgment.

"Now you've been up long enough," said Natalie Fleet. "It's time to lie down. Mrs. Brack will give you lunch, after a while, and I'll be back this evening with Fred and Hank to finish your unpacking."

"You're not going to stay?" said Burr.

"I can't, I told you," said Natalie. Burr noticed Harvey Kessler looking at her with curiosity, but he had already decided not to care what Harvey or anyone else thought. It did not matter anymore, there was no reason to conceal anything, as far as he knew.

When they were gone he listened to Mrs. Brack working in the kitchen, humming the phrase of a broken song over and over, and he looked out his window to the yellow brick apartment house next door —windows with curtains, a cement walk down below between the two buildings, where garbage cans were stacked at the back and bicycles parked by the entrance. He went out front to look at the view from the balcony. The view was the street: opposite was a row of old two-family houses, large and close together. They had little lawn plots in the front with narrow flower beds. There were three or four big trees down the street.

He tried to feel glad not to have the big house to worry about anymore.

He told the narrator: What makes the day decent and bearable is knowing that Natalie Fleet will come back again this evening.

She came back that evening as promised, with her two strong young friends. Looking as she had looked the night of her first visit, with the low-slung brown corduroy pants and a loose and colorful red blouse. Bright and cheerful, giving orders to him and her helpers. Sit him down in the easy chair while she and the two young men opened boxes of books on the floor. As they took out the books they showed them to him and stuffed them into the bookcases without order—that is, in the order in which they came. "You can organize them later," said Natalie. "The first thing is to get them out." She talked a lot, so did the young men, there were many jokes, much conversation about books they happened to discover, especially books with funny titles. "Look at all these books," said Hank. "Have you read them all, Professor?" "Of course not," said Burr.

Titles: *A Guide to the Birds of Eastern North America* by Frank M. Chapman.

Dictionary of Classical Antiquities by Oskar Seyffert.

Literary History of the United States by Spiller, Thorp, Johnson, Canby.

267

The Wings of the Dove by Henry James.
Collected Poems by Robert Frost.

"I don't read books," said Fred. "I don't approve of them."

They worked unexpectedly fast and after a couple of hours they were finished and ready to leave. "Now," said Natalie, "doesn't it all look more like a home?"

"You're not leaving?" he said.

"I'm sorry," she said, "I promised Hank. But I'll come and see you tomorrow—would you like that?"

Tell her yes, he told the narrator. Plead with her, for I'm scared. Stay with me. "Yes," he said, "I wish you would."

They left together. Gratitude and jealousy, said the narrator. Is she going to bed with Hank tonight? Burr asked. Don't ask, said the narrator. You didn't think she was going to stay sexless all that time in the hospital, merely because of a couple of nights with you, did you? Because she had done so much to help, she was also obliged to save it for you? None of your business. Enough to worry whether she'll keep coming to see you. Will she go to bed with me when I have recovered? asked Burr. When? said the narrator.

He spent the first night in his new home, alone, lonely, and frightened. Emotions snuffled around the apartment, sniffling and growling, as his animals used to do. He watched the unfamiliar shapes of reflected light on his wall from outside, and listened to the traffic on Ludlow Avenue nearby. He asked the narrator: Suppose I have an attack while I'm alone here? The narrator said, You are not expected to have an attack. But the telephone is by your bed.

He slept and woke and slept again. Several times during the night he began to cry, like that old man (he remembered) whom he had met in the woods. He missed the nurses in the hospital. He missed Natalie Fleet. He missed the animals they had given away. He missed Elaine and Harold. He missed the beach, the camp in the woods. He missed his mother, his father. He missed his friends in the high school senior play. He missed Cynthia.

The next day Natalie Fleet came to visit, and she came to visit every day but she did not stay late during the evenings, nor could he persuade her to spend the night. Not yet, she would say—as if it were something to wait for, something yet to come. Now it seemed as if everything was waiting. The narrator said, Everything in the past is gone. Everything in the future is yet to come. Wait.

Wait for the return of health and strength so that he can (one) go back to work and (two) screw Natalie Fleet. Wait for the time to pass to heal the losses you have lost, the bereavements, the house gone, the old life. Wait for time to find a more attractive apartment. Wait for time to strengthen your tie to Natalie Fleet. Wait for—wait for the police to come. Wait for a new life. Wait for death.

He lay in bed in the morning, hearing voices outside, and as he lay he studied the lace tracery of the curtains in the window, the familiar curtains that Cynthia had bought, and that Natalie had now put up for him in his new bedroom. The tracery was like a map of roads—he moved his eyes around them as if traveling along an intricacy of roads, around curves and through intersections, little journeys that he would take venturing out from some point, some knot in the lace that he called home. But constantly his eyes would get lost, he would leap off his road and across a hundred other roads until he found his home, some other knot in the lace just like the first, a hundred miles away—for the pattern of roads and journeys was repeated dozens of times across the curtain and up and down, always with little variations. And always as he followed the tracery it was impossible to keep on the road, to follow the track, always there was the frustration of trying to make it work out, always he would get lost and find himself in a different place, and always there was the problem of trying to find a perfect pattern for his journey that never worked out. Yet he could not turn his eyes away, he could not take his mind off the tracery, he could not refuse to look, though he tried, he was caught by it like an animal in a cage.

Waiting for Mrs. Brack to come and get me breakfast, he told the narrator.

One afternoon at the police station Berthold Kirschner said to Freitag and Watson: "I think we have given that professor enough time for rest and rehabilitation. I think the time has come for us to go and bring him in."

On the Suspect Board, the board with the chalk name BURR was at the top above a stack of boards with no names at all. All the other names had been removed. There was an asterisk (*) beside the name, and on the wall beside the Suspect Board there was a chart labeled KEY, as follows:

Confessed, under arrest
@ Arrested, no confession
* Confirmed, not yet arrested
& Convicted

"Are you sure it's time?" asked Freitag. He looked at Watson. "How much time has he had?"

Watson pressed a button on a machine on his desk. It was called an Automatic Electric Diary and Calendar, and when he pressed the button the machine whirled until the slot on the front opened on a notation: Entered Hospital. Then he pressed a button labeled "Count" and another button labeled "Freedom Days" and another labeled "Suspect" and another labeled "Sanctuary Days"; and finally he said: "Well, he went into the hospital five and a half weeks ago on a Sunday and he was let out of the hospital precisely four weeks later. So he has been home now for a week and a half, or ten days."

"Enough," added Berthold, "so that he can walk around his place freely and can take his dog out for a walk in the morning and in the evening, and he has a girl who keeps visiting him—"

"Does she—?"

"According to our reports he has not yet actually tried to with her since his illness, because he is still afraid that he might have an attack in the middle of it, but he is getting more and more interested, and if we do not intervene pretty soon we are likely to have a complication on our hands."

"Yes," said Freitag, "we don't want that to happen."

"According to our reports," said Berthold, "he should be pretty easy to apprehend. He lives in this apartment (pointing on a large wall map of the streets in that part of the city) attended only by that woman whose name is Mrs. Brack, and who will be gone much of the afternoon, and then goes home after doing the dishes in the evening. The girl named Miss Fleet may come to visit him in the evening, but she is not expected to stay very late. If we post our men around the building to keep an eye on it, we may be able to find an opportune moment without too long a delay."

"Sounds like a good idea."

"All I need is your authorization to go in and get him."

"Yes. You have my authorization. You may go at your earliest opportunity. How many men do you need?"

"I think six would be sufficient," said Berthold. "An even half dozen, two police cars, and a paddy wagon."

"I'll write out an order for that," said Freitag.

Then Burr went out on the balcony to watch and wait for them. He sat in the wicker chair in the midafternoon sun—a hot day, he could feel the heat in the air touching the skin of his arms, closing a grip around the flesh of his hands. Sat there, rigid in his chair, unable to divert himself or relax, unable to read the book he had taken with him so as to feign casualness, but he was unable even to feign it, to go through the motions, unable even to pick up the book and pretend to look at it. Inside he heard Mrs. Brack with the vacuum cleaner. He wondered whether they would really wait until she had gone, and he wished she would hurry up and go. The idea that she would see him arrested like a common criminal, that she would then know of his crime, this motherly woman whom he had never heard of until ten days ago and of whom he still knew next to nothing—this idea was frightening, humiliating, much worse than the simple idea of being arrested itself. In fact, he said to the narrator, the only thing he was afraid of now was the shock that others would feel when they heard about it, the blow to the confidence of his students, the respect of his colleagues, the friendly assumptions of those who worked for him and those who knew him casually. And of course Natalie Fleet, who had never been able to understand the confession he had attempted to make. These were what frightened him, and he did not want to see their faces when Berthold and Freitag and Watson came for him—but he was not afraid (he told the narrator) of the arrest itself or of what would happen afterwards, for the only thing that could happen to him now would be the negation of things, and he thought he was prepared for that.

After a while Mrs. Brack went out, and he was glad, relieved, thinking now they could come for him without a commotion. Still he watched from the balcony—the cars that drove by (he realized a number of drivers were using this short residential street as a way of bypassing Ludlow Avenue). He saw people walking by: an old woman, children, a girl with a dog, a pair of nurses from the hospital, some long-haired students. He saw the United Parcel delivery wagon stop and deliver across the street. He saw the U.S. Mail truck go by. He saw the man whom he now recognized as his neighbor downstairs come into the building. After a while he saw Mrs. Brack returning. She came in and began to cook his dinner, while still he waited on the porch, watching the people, listening to the chirp of sparrows, the call of the cardinals from the large tree beyond a couple of houses down the block.

Mrs. Brack called him in to dinner. He ate with her, quietly; he did not feel like talking. He had discovered that he did not have anything to say to Mrs. Brack nor she to him. After dinner he went back out to the balcony, carrying his coffee with him, which he set down on a little table next to his wicker chair—while Mrs. Brack finished up the dishes. It was still daylight outside, but as he sat there the light began slowly to sink. He had noticed the lengthened shadows along the street as the sun sank, though he could not see the sunset from where he sat because of the angle of the building and the building next to it. Then the light lost its luster and everything took on a clear but pale look, and he knew the sun had set, though the sky was still clear and bright, and he noticed the glistening jet trail of a plane far above, and much closer, though still very tiny, the darting specks of some swallows, and then some night-hawks with their buzzing cries and barred wings, catching insects above the twilight chimneys. He remembered the nighthawk was cousin to the whippoorwill, the dark rhetorician of the night in the remote woods, counting off time second-by-second in the deep night, in his own deep childhood, with his father listening, suggesting that he count to see how many times he goes without taking a breath. With the realization now that he was unlikely ever to hear a whippoorwill or his father again.

The sky was dimming. Lights had been turned on in the house across the street. Also the street lights, and the automobiles had their head-lights on. Getting dark: He hadn't realized that they would wait until night to arrest him—a bit of discretion that touched his heart with a sense of their fundamental kindness. Indeed he had often thought with gratitude of the consideration and delicacy and even sympathy which the police had shown to him through the whole course of this investigation, which moved him (he told the narrator) deeply as a confirmation of his belief in the fundamental good-heartedness of mankind.

Natalie Fleet dropped in, as promised, and she came out to sit with him on the balcony. A lovely warm June evening after a day that had been too hot. They talked casually in the dark about his plans for the future (as if he actually had plans), and about the wonderful progress of his recovery thus far and his excellent prospects for total recovery soon, and what he would do then. They talked of travel and new courses and new studies and new enjoyments that he had not adequately made use of before (concert subscriptions, for example). That is, he pretended to talk casually about all these things, although in reality it was one of the most intently conscious conversations of his life, as he watched himself acting out a casual scene with Natalie Fleet, whom he loved, and he was glad of the dark because of the great sweeps of emotion that would come over him and distort his face even when he managed to keep them out of his voice. So acutely conscious he was that this was their last conversation together in the free world. (Interrupting the narrator: Whom I loved?)

Yes, loved, said the narrator. Burr at last, in this extremity, recognizing how greatly he needed this girl, how helpful and generous she had been, what enormities of gratitude he owed to her. As if she were the only liaison between himself and the real world outside. And as he observed her in this pretendingly casual talk, and as he observed her dimly in the darkness (her very short skirt that she was wearing tonight, and her thigh catching a glint of light from the street), and felt as if she were the only friend he had left, as if in her person were brought together all the remains of those who had once humanized the harsh mechanical world for him, in her person gathered his dead parents and grandparents, his dead wife, his dead children, his dead closest friends, (so that now the very life of that world depended upon her)—no one alive was closer to him or knew more about him than Natalie Fleet, no one alive had taken on more responsibility for him. And as he realized this (the narrator told him) and talked pretendingly about his imaginary plans, it occurred to him that if he could have had yet a real life ahead of him, it ought to have Natalie Fleet as the central vitalizing heart of it. That if he were not doomed, he ought to marry Natalie Fleet, marry her right away, without delay, before she might escape. But because he was doomed, because Berthold and Freitag and Watson were coming for him, because he had committed a crazy and terrible crime in a moment of animal blindness that he must now pay for with his life, he would never be able to marry her, nor have another conversation with her, no matter how casual, after this one tonight.

And then realizing this, his need turned egotistical (said the narrator) and considered what he could take from tonight alone that would do for tonight what marrying her would have done for his life if he had been able to live. And with this he felt stirring the first clear and pure and unfearful surge of lust since his attack, the first surge down below that was not immediately encountered by the whispering anxiety up above, 'but are you strong enough?' The light glinted off her exposed thigh as she sat there and laughed at something he had said, and this time when the anxiety began to ask, the narrator answered forcefully, It doesn't matter, for Christ sake. If this is the last chance in life, it hardly matters whether you can take it or not. Try—and at that moment, without waiting for more thought, Burr cried out: "Natalie, for God's sake, let's get well now. Come on, let's go to bed."

"Now?" The surprise in her voice told him of the surprise in her eyes which in the dark he could not see. "But are you well enough?"

"Well enough I can hardly stand it," he said. She laughed, and he heard the embarrassment in her voice, the awkwardness, as she tried to give him an explanation. She said: "I can't, tonight."

"Why not?"

"Why—because I told you I have to go in a few minutes. I promised —well, I promised someone. And besides" (suddenly, as if it just occurred to her) "I'm in the middle of my time. In a couple of days, maybe, then—we can talk about it."

"Oh!" said Burr. Admonished by his narrator not to question. Not to challenge her excuses nor ask her to explain, not even the identity of the person she had promised, not even the sex, which she had managed to avoid specifying. Admonishment to allow Natalie the full operation of her discretions—as if any attempt to get behind it, to dig anything up that she was burying or hiding, could only make things worse.

Briefly he asked—couldn't he tell her that he didn't expect to see her again, that this was truly their last evening together, in case it might make a difference? But the narrator asked how you would make her believe a doomsday prediction like that? And while Burr was pondering the question, Natalie Fleet got up to go. As she left she gave him a kiss (quick and light on the lips)—which made him realize that, for all her attentions and their closeness, she had not kissed him at any time during his illness—and then she was gone.

And now once again he settled rigidly in his wicker chair on his balcony to wait for the police. It grew late. He heard the sounds of the city a block away on Ludlow Avenue. He heard a police siren—a police car going by at high speed. Then another one. He became aware of a continuing sequence of sirens. The fire engines went by on a cross street down the block—he heard them and saw their flashing red lights. An ambulance went by with a flashing light and siren on Clifton Avenue at the other end of the block. Some of the sirens wailed the high pitched up and down stream. Others went wobbling, a series of quick sharp screams. Others sounded the harsh two-tone yodel that he had first noticed in European cities, that only recently had sounded here at home. Listening he became aware from the sirens, from the police cars that he could see going through the intersections, of city trouble in the night, and the narrator spoke to him of what happens then, of the muggings, of robberies, of other murders, as well as accidents, shootings in taverns, fights, and people suddenly falling dead. And then it grew quieter. The street was silent now, no car had driven by in more than fifteen minutes, and only occasional cars on Ludlow, a block away. Still he heard the sounds of industry in the distance: he heard the low roar of a crawling diesel freight locomotive in the railroad yards a mile away and he could hear the crashing of the freight cars as they were switched about. And still there was the continuing far away howl of sirens speaking of disaster, of crime and accident and illness and fire, in quarters of the city. And for a long time still, Burr wondered which of those wailing sirens was aimed at him, until suddenly the night seemed to take a breath. Suddenly the sounds stopped. The city went limp. The narrator whispered. And then, when after a moment the siren started up again, Burr knew that something had happened. The siren was not coming for him. He knew it clearly now. They were too busy. They had too many other things to do to worry about him.

Go to bed, said the narrator. They are not going to arrest you. You're free.

Burr felt his legs shaky as he went inside. They never suspected me in the first place, he remarked with wonder. No, said the narrator. They simply changed their minds.

In the station house Freitag said: "What's the use? Vengeance is mine, saith the Lord. Why torture him? He's suffered enough waiting for us. Let's let him go."

"Pigs!" cried out Berthold. "You get the guy almost in your mitts and then you let him go! What kind of cops is that?"

"It's our business not yours," said Freitag, reasserting his authority after a long lapse. "We appreciate and thank you for your advice."

Chapter 2

So, he said, they really do mean to let you get away with murder. And you can have your new life if you dare take it. No one knows, and no one needs ever know, if you control yourself enough to keep it to yourself. You come out of the woods looking as clean as a collie dog and nobody can guess what bestial things that dog did when he was wild.

Challenging: Can you do it? Can you go back into normal civilized life and keep it to yourself? Can you be a professor again? Pass on the heritage of civilization?

Suddenly Burr cried out joyously: I can marry Natalie Fleet!

That same, that very evening—she came to his place and had dinner with him, cooked and served by Mrs. Brack, whom she helped. During the meal it was hard for Burr to contain his ecstatic feelings, to keep from mentioning his wonderful liberation. After the meal he went with Natalie out to the balcony again, to be out of earshot of Mrs. Brack in the kitchen. It was still daylight—the sun was low but had not yet set. Now! said the narrator.

Backed by literary tradition, Burr made a speech. He said: "Natalie Fleet, now I am speaking very seriously. I want you to marry me. I am not joking. This is a very definite intention on my part, I want you to stay with me, live with me, and be my. I learned it all during my illness, how much I need you, how close you. You are the best person I. No one is dearer than. I can't give you a great, but I can give you some. I can give you a. We can move into another, when I am. We can travel together in. We can even raise, if you want. I have a good job, I am a respectable. I love you now as much as I. I ask you, I beg you, etcetera, to marry!"

Natalie Fleet, flush-cheeked, wonder-eyed, listening to his speech, twisting her hands together, curling her ankles. Then, after his speech she made a speech of her own. "Oh I can't tell you how nice—how moved I—How grateful. What a tremendous thing this is that you have —I'm so sorry!"

"Sorry?"

Natalie Fleet's continuation. "I wish—but I can't. The answer has to be. It's impossible. I appreciate so much, but I can't. I probably won't marry anybody—I mean I doubt that marriage, home, and family—all those things you—is what I. I suspect not, and I feel under no obligation to force myself. But even if I should—I mean, even if I didn't feel that way about, I'm quite sure I couldn't. Not that I don't realize what a fine successful person you. But you are almost twenty-five years older than. And you have been seriously, you may never be the same again. Forgive me if this sounds, but I have to think of such things, if I am to consider your. When I am forty, you'll. Sixty-seven years old! If I were to marry you, I doubt that I could be—I mean sex, I'm talking about sex—I mean you're a different generation, you're accustomed to. You expect a wife to be. But I'm different. A different time. It's not that you're not attractive, but I'm just not made for that kind—Well, I mean I'm just not prepared to be so exclusive, if you get what I. I mean, I like you very much, I feel very close, yes, very good, I like doing things for, mothering you, babying you—yes!—I love all that, but I doubt that I *love* you quite the way people like you expect when you talk, etcetera. I mean I know I. For instance, I have made no attempt to be—you know, sex, I mean —during your illness—"

"Oh!" said Burr.

"Well, I didn't think we had anything that required me to. I still don't. So, it's not exactly the kind of thing you make a marriage out of."

Like many a predecessor, Burr said, "But you could change your mind about."

And she replied, with a bright smile: "If I do, you'll know."

Like all their predecessors, they did not stop with these speeches. She did not expect to change her mind, and he urged her to keep her mind open. She wanted to remain his friend etcetera, and she said he could still be her lover when he recovered, if he didn't mind. As for tonight —well tonight again she was tied up—

And then, quietly, just as surely as he had recognized last night that the police were not coming he recognized the impossibility of marrying Natalie Fleet. For why should she marry him—a middle-aged man with a heart attack, and worse things on his conscience than she had ever dreamed about? For God's sake, man, said the narrator, how much do you expect people to do for you?

She left cheerfully, emotional and grateful, excited and flattered by the compliment he had paid her, but she left behind a dead weight of depression that seemed heavier than anything since the murder. Heavier because this time it was as if for keeps, not to be pushed aside or rolled off his back by any accident or change of mind. The narrator said, Soon you will have seen Natalie Fleet for the last time. Already it is changed, she will never be the same. And there is nothing else, nothing left. You will live alone and do your job and no one will know you. You will have committed a futile murder in the park and no one will care. Even the police will not care.

Allow a day of this to pass, a dark heavy torpor full of gloom, while Burr spends most of his time sitting in the wicker chair, staring and not seeing, uninterested in anything, not reading, not wanting to start anything that would get him involved, that would require a focus of attention. His attention wandered freely and loosely, refusing to be bound, among memories of dead things, caring only for memories of dead things.

A day of this, bringing us to the third evening from that on which he fully understood that the police were not coming for him. Even a narrator would have little to say about him at such a time as this, so inward turned is his mind, so much a vegetable does he seem to one like Mrs. Brack who serves him his dinner in a silence of resentment for his own lifeless silence. Until suddenly, after he has finished eating, something happens to waken him up, some change that brightens him a little, as if he had come to a resolution or agreement with himself.

"Don't stay, Mrs. Brack," he said. "I'll take care of the dishes myself."

"You really think you can do it?" she said.

"Of course of course. You run along now."

"Okay if you say so," she said in her aggrieved manner.

Look very closely now. After Mrs. Brack was gone, Burr watched from the balcony until she had turned the corner, and then he too went down in the elevator and out. Out into the street in the twilight, as if in a daze —a daze, however, not because of confusion but because so much was going on inside his mind at that moment that the outside world, the tangible reality of the street, seemed vague.

He was being led. Tell who it was that was leading him. Probably it was the narrator himself, who had decided what was needed to break through the prison of Burr's depression, and now dragged him out into the street with all the force of a compulsion that could not be resisted. Where are we going? Burr asked. To the police, answered the compulsion. Why? asked Burr. To see Freitag and Berthold and Watson. To give ourselves up, said the compulsion. But why should I do that, said Burr, if I don't have to? But you do have to, said the narrator. Why? said Burr. Because I insist on it, said the narrator. Because you've still got me with you and I require it.

Again, why, and the narrator replies: Because I can't let you get out of here believing you can get away with murder.

He went down the street, past lawns and houses, down Howell Avenue past Ormond and Whitfield and Sherlock and Gano to Morrison Avenue, over on Morrison to Ludlow and back up Ludlow, past large lawns and houses in suburban-Tudor style with conical evergreens and lawn sprinklers in the twilight, trying to focus on the idea of the police station, wherever that might be. Meanwhile he was asking: Why not? Is that any reason? Is there any real reason why it must end? Why I can't begin a new life now? He pointed to his assets: Here I am, ripe, mature, full of the power of experience. Still only forty-five years old, in the prime of my life (still only halfway to ninety). Now you can build me a real career, he said to the narrator. A new start, founded on the wreckage of the stupidities of my youth. Why not?

Because murder, said the narrator. Because you indulged yourself and put yourself in my hands and let me lead your life—your own damn fault. You can't get away with murder in my book, said the narrator. Crime of crimes, much too rich for the likes of you. Do you know what a murder is? Can you see it? Burr looked. I see a man bashing another man over the head, he said. You see him smashing a universe down a funnel, said the narrator. You see him playing games with the fuse box. Short the circuits of existence. You don't dare, no one dares.

The narrator crying: A sad, a tragic story. Why did you do it? Narrative tears, sobbing, weeping. Just then the professor, who had been silent or unidentified for a long time, began to speak. Tried to drown out the narrator's weeping by lecturing. Really a very commonplace crime, said the professor. Consider some of the varieties of kinds and motives for murder. You may do it in a rage of passion, of jealousy against a lover or an unfaithful spouse, of vengeance against an enemy, of frustration against someone who has some power over you. You may do it to silence a threat, a blackmailer, or to get rid of a rival to your throne. You may do it in a business way to get rid of rivals to your racket. You may do it with careful calculation, laying your trap with care to conceal all clues, or you may do it hysterically in a fight in a tavern. You may legalize it under some agreed premise of the common good, as when you use a gas chamber or electric chair or rope, or you band together with guns to kill other troops or drop your murder from an airplane or missile. Not all killing is murder, remember. Nature exists by taking life from one entity and passing it on to another.

He came back up through the local business center on Ludlow Avenue, back within a block of where he lived, past the First National Bank and the Anderson Funeral Home and Krogers Supermarket and Home Federal Savings and Loan, past an apartment house and the local branch of the Public Library, and Organic Foods, and the Hitching Post (fried chicken) and Clifton Hardware and The College (One Hour) Cleaners, and Ludlow Delicatessen and Steirs Pharmacy and Jack's Fish 'n' Chips and Shoe Repair and IGA Supermarket and Rich's Stationery and Lance's Gift Shop and Pete's News Store, looking for a police station which he could not find, although there was a fire station at the end, at the corner of Ludlow and Clifton, opposite the northwest corner of Burnet Woods.

Now as he walked slowly (because of his convalescing heart) and the evening began to darken outside the range of the lights, the narrator forgot his sorrow as he got into an argument with the professor concerning how horrible a crime is murder. The professor said that most murder was commonplace and natural and the only reason we punish it so hard is to keep others from coming along and murdering us, while still the narrator maintained that murder in the abstract was a terrible and mysterious and blasphemous probe into the black holes beyond the universe and the normal uncalloused reaction was a shuddering dread of the unspeakable. But the professor said, Nonsense. People like to commit murder, said the professor, it's a very enjoyable crime to contemplate, an attractive crime in the abstract. That's why it frightens you so much, he said, why you tighten such rules around it, why you frown and shock so—because you know it's so pleasant and you don't want to let it go to your head. With this the narrator, all sorrow forgotten, began to laugh, while the professor went on expanding into oratory, pointing out for proof how much you enjoy reading about murder and seeing it in movies and art and you try to deny in anger the joy of people who do it, and he spoke of how you are always killing things, making changes and putting old life into the past for the sake of new life and how murder is the mother of beauty.

Tell Burr, said the narrator—it will make him feel better. He sat down on the bench next to the fire station. Surprised, wondering if it was still possible to get away, if the argument had changed the narrator's mind on that point. (The professor said yes, but the narrator still said no.) The narrator whispered, Did you hear what he said? Maybe it was not blind rage alone that lifted that ancient rock above the old man's head. Maybe it was sweet pleasure. (Burr still denying: No! The narrator laughed, making a trial beginning of a narrative: Once upon a time there was a man who couldn't tell the difference between his anger, his fear, and his pleasure. All three emotions were equally angry, equally fearful, and equally pleasurable. They were all the same to him. He was likewise unable to tell the difference between his own thoughts and opinions and those of others, and he was beginning to feel fuzzy also about the boundaries between his experiences and those of others.)

I must confess, said Burr, looking around nervously. I must find the police station. Shortly—he said. He got up and started to walk around again, with no plan except to get out of the lights a little, away from people who might look at his face—while he tried to work out what his confession would be.

Which he began to whisper to himself, not knowing himself how the confession would come out. It began to come out thus: It was I (whispered Burr) who went walking to work on that bright Tuesday morning, into Burnet Woods, crossing the playground, listening for birds, entering on the steps that go through the woods to the circle with the bandstand at the top. It was I who looking up saw the old man turned into an old woman surrendering my life descending the steps and I when she said I did not know what to do and I did nothing and when she asked me I did not know how to answer and I said nothing and when she asked me why I couldn't take a vacation I didn't know how my life was my work a career in the making and I was on the fifth revision then and why she said and still I said if she is being irrational I can't answer her with rational words and therefore did not answer her at all and when she became morose I said the trouble is she has become morose and she became sullen and withdrawn and more and more silent and when I asked her whats-the-matter she would either say nothing is the matter or everything is the matter, all of life or none of life, and I said in that case what can I do I can do nothing because I can't do everything and she said nobody expects you, its me its only me its all me my problem not yours and when she said that yes I said its your problem not mine and when she said kill myself I was scared I said to myself things have got bad very bad, something's terribly wrong with my wife Cynthia I ought to do something about it what to do about it you should never ignore when there is a real personality change and when there is a threat, these are signs but when I asked Cynthia do you feel any better today she said yes a little better, I guess I decided well I guess things aren't quite as bad as I thought they were and let's let a little more time pass before doing anything not knowing what to do anyway because when

I asked Cynthia what do you think I should do she would say don't do anything it's not your problem it's my problem and I would say you want to kill yourself that's not your problem only that's my problem too and she said don't worry about it I won't kill myself I'm too happy healthy life-loving a person to do that until that bright Tuesday morning I woke up and she had not come to bed and I went into the bathroom, bent arms and legs in a tub full of water, head thrown back fixed in a cry open-glassed eyes Cynthia, God no pulse stiff arms wouldn't bend and Cynthia, I cried and a note on living room table

Darling, I am sorry. I can't help it, I'm so afraid of what's happening to me. I'm afraid I am going out of my mind, going insane. I'm afraid I shall do some terrible and violent thing, some awful crime. I have to stop myself. It's not your fault, don't blame yourself. C.

(Ask the narrator, What sort of violence was my poor Cynthia afraid she would do? Who knows, said the narrator. It lived in her mind, and her mind has died.)

Is that the confession you want to make? he asked. He looked about him like a man waking up. From this point you could still see the remains of the twilight in the sky on the horizon to the west, beyond the roofs of the hospital in the middle foreground, across Clifton Avenue. The bandstand was still visible in the dim remains of daylight, and the woods beyond were already in the black of night. How do I get to the police station from here? he asked. Go down through the woods and out of the park at the other end, and then you'll be on Jefferson Avenue, he replied. You should be able to find a policeman on Jefferson Avenue, a busy street.

Only two shadowy cars parked on the circle at this time of evening —the students who park here in the daytime while they go to classes at the university are now all out spending the evening somewhere. The two shadowy cars, he notices, have people in them. Lovers, probably: Natalie Fleet, maybe. Tries to remember: Did he say a proper good-bye to Natalie Fleet? (Did he say one to Cynthia? Did Cynthia say a proper good-bye to him?)

Do you have any pain? asked the doctor. Only a little, he replied. Yes, in fact, a moderately heavy pain here in my chest, the shortness of breath prolonging, extending itself, which began when I first started to climb up the grass from Clifton Avenue, up to the top here with the bandstand and the circle. The doctor said, You are not supposed to climb hills like that this early in your convalescence. Do you have any pain in your left arm? Yes in fact I do: the pain in my chest, it's like a dull heavy burning sensation, an extension of my gulping for breath my gasps for breath, and the burning is elevated into a pain, and as I was saying it extends upwards on the left side and out into the left arm—a very characteristic (diagnostic?) symptom. Well, breathe deeply, said the doctor, and walk slowly. Exert as little as possible, but you had better get out of here fast as you can, for there don't seem to be anybody here but lovers.

Breathing deeply in an effort to keep the growing pain in his lungs at bay and taking tiny steps so as to exert as little energy as possible, Burr enters the path into the woods from the bandstand and goes to the top of the steps that go down into the woods. Then without breaking the rhythm of either his breathing or his steps, he starts down the steps, taking two little steps and a shorter one for each step downward. His eyes become used to the darkness in the woods. Looking down, he becomes aware of someone on the steps below, nothing more than a shadow perhaps, yet it seemed to be rising, approaching him.

The sharp fear stiffens him like a shock and perhaps arrests for the moment the spreading pain in his chest, but he will not let it reveal itself. He dare not turn and run, and therefore the only thing for him to do is to continue—without breaking the rhythm of either his steps or his breathing—until something, whatever it is, imposes itself solidly upon him. On he goes, plodding downward, gulping at his air like a drowning fish, watching but pretending not to watch the ascending stranger, who now seems to take shape as a dark heavy man, puffing a little, also not looking at him. The woods are silent at this time of night—no, there is a small sound of buzzing of insects, and the traffic of the streets beyond the park comes loud to their ears, the racing of automobile engines, motorcycles, trucks, and the constant sirens of police cars, ambulances, and fire trucks in the night. Meanwhile he continues his descent, two little steps at each level and then another little one for the step down, and the two figures in the dark continue, pretending not to look at each other, making only the quickest most blinklike checks on each other, keeping track so that they know exactly where they stand in relation to each other.

Until they meet. Two steps apart, then one step apart. He looks up. The stranger is bigger than he, like a gorilla in the dark, yet when he looks up, he sees the inscription stitched on his pocket, faintly in the dark. Reads: *Buzzy.* Then he knows.

Stop. The pain is overwhelming now, contorts his body trying to ease it. He says "How did you know I would be here?" The man's reply is lost in the convulsing sound of someone's breath. (*Narrator:* Did he say, I've been keeping track of you? Can't say. The narrator couldn't hear.)

Burr said, "I'm glad you came."

It is as if the man shrugged his shoulders. Then he raises one arm quickly making a fist, above Burr's head, enormous strength lightly manipulated. Together Burr's hands both go up, palms out, to ward off the blow, and then the funnel opens and all the world is liquid.

Chapter 3

The narrator outlives the protagonist by a short margin of time. Long enough to report that in the morning, they found the body of Professor Ralph Burr lying halfway up the steps going through the woods in Burnet Woods—a site, the police noted, where murders had taken place before. Because of the evident wound on his head, it was at first assumed that Burr also was the victim of a murder, but as soon as his identity was revealed it was made known to the police that he had been recently hospitalized with a coronary attack. It was decided to do an autopsy.

By this means it was discovered that death was actually the result of another massive heart attack. But the skull was fractured too. No one was able to say whether the fracture was caused by an assault or merely by the step as he fell against it. No one therefore could say whether the heart attack was the result of the fright or shock of an encounter with a felon or the result of a purely natural process. Nor could anyone determine why Professor Burr had ventured into the park at such a time, in clear violation of his physician's instructions. No one could say, in other words, whether his death was a murder, a suicide, or a natural one.

Nor could the narrator live long enough to know what became of others in the novel. Who was finally chosen as new chairman of the department? What kind of a life, and with whom, did Natalie Fleet decide to lead? The narrator is sorry he does not know. All he can say in addition is that Natalie Fleet did attend Professor Burr's funeral and that she cried because he seemed so patient and gentle, in spite of his curious ideas, and she thought his death was premature and unfair.

73 74 75 76 77 10 9 8 7 6 5 4 3 2 1